"Hugely successful in its day, *Souls for Sale* furnishes a fascinating window on early Hollywood. One of many stories about would-be starlets seeking fame and fortune in the new industry, forced "to sell their souls and bodies," it takes on new resonance in the #MeToo era. The book's heroine is a small-town clergyman's daughter, "young and starved for life," who, finding herself pregnant and unmarried, ventures west to Los Angeles. There she meets members of the "movie colony," finds work as an extra, then like so many other movie-struck girls of her generation, soon aspires to be a star. Released at the height of the star scandals that rocked the early movie business, *Souls for Sale* sets the stage the industry's efforts to manage its reputation just a few years later by implementing a "morals clause" in studio contracts aimed at curtailing debauchery behind the scenes, as well as a strict Production Code that regulated depictions of sex and violence onscreen."

— Shelley Stamp, author of *Lois Weber in Early Hollywood*
and *Movie-Struck Girls*

"Encountering *Souls for Sale* now, it's hard not to think of the Coen Brothers and to imagine this send up of small-minded America in their capable hands. With shades of *Oh Brother, Where Art Thou?*, *Hail, Caeser!*, and *The Ballad of Buster Scruggs*, *Souls for Sale* feels like a kindred script waiting for an update in our time, where truth and lies have taken on new significance."

—Marsha Gordon, Professor of Film Studies,
North Carolina State University

"Brother of the famously reclusive Howard Hughes, Rupert Hughes was already an author of some renown when he published his early Hollywood novel *Souls for Sale* (1922), a book so successful that the mogul Samuel Goldwyn hired Hughes himself to write and direct a screen adaptation. *Souls for Sale* begins as a standard critique of the motion picture industry at the time. As if taking a bite from the fruit of California's plentiful orange groves, Mem discovers that her talent is a valuable commodity "for which the grateful public would pay with gratitude and fame and much money." *Souls for Sale* heralds the birth of the New Woman, while also providing an insider's take on "the birth of an immortal art," which is to say, cinema."

—Mark Eaton, author of *What Price Hollywood?*
*Modern American Writers and the Movies*

"A reverend's daughter corrupted, a stage mother gone wild, a film comedian with a fear of marriage and a preference for lying infant-like on a woman's bosom, these are just a few of the characters making their way through the wilds of 1920s Hollywood in Rupert Hughes's successful novel, now back in print thanks to LARB and Sarah Gleeson-White. Pulpy and weird, and with more than a little of naturalism's determinism—imagine if Dreiser's *Sister Carrie* made it to Hollywood—*Souls for Sale* documents many of the realities of the early film industry. As Hughes tracks his heroine Mem Steddon's rise from film extra to screen star, he peppers his novel with discussions of contracts, layoffs, actors' craft (including a starlets' "cry-off" competition), screen makeup and on-set accidents. The actress and her compatriots also fill their time gossiping about many industry notables and bits of now-infamous Hollywood history, the Fatty Arbuckle scandal to little Jackie Coogan's finances. But, title aside, *Souls* is no Hollywood Babylon."

—Katherine Fusco, author of
*Silent Film and U.S. Naturalist Literature*

# SOULS FOR SALE

# SOULS
## *for* SALE

RUPERT HUGHES

*Introduction by* Sarah Gleeson-White

This is a LARB Classics publication
Published by The Los Angeles Review of Books
6671 Sunset Blvd., Suite 1521, Los Angeles, CA 90028
www.larbbooks.org

Introduction copyright © 2020 by Sarah Gleeson-White

ISBN 978-1-940660-57-8

Library of Congress Control Number 2019955486

Designed by Tom Comitta

# INTRODUCTION

## Sarah Gleeson-White

Rupert Hughes's *Souls for Sale* (1922) opens with a scene familiar to anyone who has read a Hollywood novel. The Reverend
Doctor Steddon, father of Hughes's feisty young protagonist,
Remember (or Mem, as she is known) delivers a fiery sermon
excoriating Los Angeles, that "Nineveh" of the Far West:

> The Spanish Missionaries may have called it the City
> of Angels; but the moving pictures have changed its
> name to Los Diablos! For it is the central factory
> of Satan and his minions, the enemy of our homes,
> the corrupter of our young men and women — the
> school of crime. Unless it reforms — and soon! —
> surely, in God's good time, the ocean will rise and
> swallow it.

The Reverend Doctor's tirade contributes to what was then
an emerging genre of fiction about motion-picture making,
which had, since the mid-teens, offered up a series of critiques
— from the affectionately mocking to the more vitupera-
tive — of Hollywood: the place, the industry, and its community.
Nathanael West and F. Scott Fitzgerald would most famously come to characterize Hollywood as a dump, a terminus of
shattered dreams and of "the human spirit at a new low of

debasement."[1]

Nearly two decades earlier, Hughes offered a more balanced view. The brother of eccentric industrialist and motion-picture entrepreneur Howard Hughes, he was one of the most prolific and feted American authors of the early 20th century, producing plays, short stories, and novels, in addition to histories, biographies, and musicologies. He was also, according to an account of the day, "the first writer of national reputation to complete a thorough apprenticeship at a motion picture studio [...] in order to direct his own stories and put them on the screen just as he wanted them."[2] Particularly astute at identifying new professional opportunities, Hughes began selling short stories to motion-picture interests as early as 1907. According to his biographer, James O. Kemm, "nearly 50 silent and sound motion pictures carried his name as writer and/or director or were based upon his novels and stories."

It would appear inevitable, then, that Hughes would turn to narratives about the motion-picture industry. In 1914 he wrote a one-act play, "Celluloid Sara: A Moving Picture Mix-Up," described by a *New York Times* notice as "a satire on the movies."[3] The entire play takes place on a film set, and its cast includes an ambitious star-in-the-making (the Sara of the title), a director of the (fictional) IXL Film Co, and a cameraman. The Rupert Hughes papers at the University of Southern California contain an undated and unfinished 125-page prose narrative titled "Celluloid." Unfolding in a New York nickelodeon, it chronicles the transition from a cinema of attractions to narrative film. In the process, it describes screenings of Edwin S. Porter's *Life of an American Fireman* (Edison, 1903), one of the earliest narrative films, and the Vitagraph Company's *Raffles, the Amateur Cracksman* (1905), a very early example of page-to-screen adaptation. Hughes also published short stories — "The Great Cinematographic Robbery" (1910) and "In Soft Focus" (1926)

---

1 F. Scott Fitzgerald, "To Alice Richardson, July 29, 1940," in *The Letters of F. Scott Fitzgerald*, ed. Andrew Turnbull (New York: Scribner's, 1963), p. 603.

2 "Why Rupert Hughes' Films are Popular," 1924. Rupert Hughes Papers, Collection No. 0173, Special Collections, USC Libraries, University of Southern California.

3 "Plays that Hold," *The New York Times*, February 8, 1914. Rupert Hughes Papers.

— as well as many articles, such as "Camera and a Passion Enough, says Hughes" (1921), about motion pictures and the industry.

*Souls for Sale*, Hughes's only published Hollywood novel, appeared first in serialized form in *Red Book* magazine from September 1921 through June 1922, the year Harper & Brothers published it in book form. Hughes himself then wrote the scenario for and directed the successful 1923 screen adaptation for Goldwyn Pictures. Typical in some ways of what Shelley Stamp has termed, after William A. Wellman's 1937 eponymous film, a "star-is-born narrative," *Souls for Sale* tracks the misfortunes and eventual fortunes of a rather artless clergyman's daughter whose fall into sin — an unwanted pregnancy to a lover who is then conveniently killed off — prompts her flight westward from the dreary Midwestern small town to Hollywood and eventual stardom. In some ways, it is a rather lopsided novel. It does not arrive in Hollywood until a good halfway through the narrative, preferring until then to linger in Mem's hometown of Calverley, spend time on the train to Los Angeles, and stop at points in between, such as Yuma and Palm Springs. It also abandons several subplots along the way.

Still, *Souls for Sale* has perhaps a more sophisticated understanding of film and the film business than any other 1920s Hollywood novel, and is notable for its even-handed account of and well-informed insights into the silent-era motion-picture industry. Most striking is the novel's sustained defense of the industry in face of what a 1920 *Photoplay* column coined "cinemaphobia," an apparently "incurable disease" suffered by those who "detest films with an uncompromising, unreasoning, irrational, 'bitter-end' detestation." The columnist singles out *Smart Set* co-editor George Jean Nathan as an exemplary cinemaphobe. Nathan had recently charged motion pictures with

> reducing further the taste, the sense and the general culture of the American nation. Like a thundering flood of bilge and scum, the flapdoodle of the films has swept over the country ... And today the cinema, ranking the second largest industry in the

> States, proudly views the havoc it has wrought ...
> They have bought imaginative actors and converted
> them into face-makers and mechanical dolls. They
> have elected for their editors and writers the most
> obscure and talentless failures of journalism and the
> tawdry periodicals ... Gentlemen, you would buy a
> soul, or sell one, for a nickel.[4]

William Dean Howells appreciated the absurdity of much of
the criticism leveled at the new medium and its broader practices and cultures. In a 1912 "Editor's Easy Chair" column for
*Harper's Monthly Magazine*, Howells shares a rather droll anecdote concerning what many a cinemaphobe apparently considered an especial danger of film-going: the darkened theater. He
writes, "The darkness itself has been held a condition of inex-
pressible depravity and a means of allurement to evil by birds of
prey hovering in the standing-room and the foyers." To manage
such dangers, Howells continues, "The pictures are sometimes
shown in a theater lighted as broad as day, where not the silliest
young girl or the wickedest young fellow can plot fully unseen."
[5]Just how the audience was able to view the film under such ludicrous conditions remains unclear.

The theater was of course not the only site of moral depravity and temptation attached to motion pictures. The studio,
Hollywood, and Los Angeles itself were also frequently depict-
ed as enticements to "Satan and his minions," a conviction that
reached hysterical proportions by the time Hughes began to
compose *Souls for Sale*. What is now considered to be the first
motion-picture scandal broke in the summer of 1921. Popular comic actor Roscoe "Fatty" Arbuckle was charged with the
sexual assault and murder of fellow actor Virginia Rappe. The
widely reported trial revealed an unsavory side of the industry,
and although he was acquitted, Arbuckle's career was effective-

---

4  Nathan, George Jean. "The Hooligan at the Gates." The Smart Set: A
Magazine of Cleverness 61, no. 4 (1920): 131–37. http://modjourn.org/render.
php?id=1428356358774254&view=mjp_object

5  Howells, William Dean. "Editor's Easy Chair." Harper's Monthly Magazine
125 (1912): 634-37. https://babel.hathitrust.org/cgi/pt?id=mdp.39015056097119;v
iew=1up;seq=714

ly finished. *Souls for Sale* weighs in on the scandal, presenting Arbuckle as the hapless victim of "the pulpits and the editorial columns, the legislative halls and forums and the very street corners" that "roared with a demand for somebody's destruction."

Much early Hollywood fiction, like Edgar Rice Burroughs's *The Girl from Hollywood* (1922), Samuel Merwin's *Hattie of Hollywood* (1922), and Frances Marion's *Minnie Flynn* (1925), was likewise preoccupied with the industry's alleged wickedness. As the titles above indicate, young women appeared to be at particular risk, whether as victims of predators who operated in darkened theaters, as viewers especially susceptible to the questionable morality displayed on and off the screen, or, in the case of those harboring motion-picture ambitions, captives to the desires of lascivious (male) directors, casting agents, and actors. The industry was, the consensus seemed to be, no place for a lady.

Theodore Dreiser acknowledged as much in his three-part exposé, "Hollywood: Its Morals and Manners," which was serialized in *Shadowland* from November 1921 to February 1922. The first of these installments, "The Struggle on the Threshold of Moving Pictures," is particularly concerned with the predicament of those "fame-hungry" young women, according to Dreiser's designation, who were assumed to be "potentially, if not actually, of easy virtue." He writes, "By far the greater number of girls and women who essay this work know very well before hand [...] the character of the conditions to be met." The casting director is a particular menace for he is "not above selling opportunities to the needy [...] for a return of a pleasurable nature." Mem, in *Souls for Sale*, grasps such "character of the conditions to be met" early on. And so she turns "her most languishing eyes" upon the casting director Mr. Tirrey, "the St. Peter of the movie heaven, empowered to admit or to deny." However Tirrey, indifferent to Mem's advances, explains with a rather tasteless quip that his only concern is that "your character will photograph, and a girl can't last long who plays Pollyanna on the screen and polygamy outside."

In her trajectory from small-town nobody to motion-picture star, Mem to some extent does resembles one of Dreiser's "fame-hungry" young woman who from the mid-teens began to flock to Hollywood. The widely reported arrival of "thousands [...] of waiting stars, first and second heavy leads, vamps, beauties, bit part workers, extras, trick performers [...] to say nothing of raw and inexperienced beginners [...] who are still about and hoping and waiting for things to take a turn"[6] occurred as a result, Stamp explains, of

> significant changes in the film industry beginning in 1913, chiefly the expansion of film production and the resulting rationalization of filmmaking techniques, the centralization of motion-picture concerns around Los Angeles, and the growing cult of celebrity attached to movie stars.[7]

Fan magazines such as *Motion Picture Classic* and more mainstream publications such as *Collier's* and *The Ladies' Home Journal* also published reports of "filmmaking feats [and] news of the glamorous lives led by film personalities," as Stamp puts it. At the same time, these reports — and Dreiser's *Shadowland* exposé is exemplary here — frequently and rather cruelly condemned motion-picture hopefuls as "silly creatures caught under the sway of overwrought emotion," just as they assumed they were all women.[8]

In *Souls for Sale*, Hughes derides the cinemaphobia that informed so much journalism and so many Hollywood novels in the late teens and early twenties. When Mem asks her friend Leva Lemaire ("really Mrs. David Wilkinson") whether "the moving-picture people [are] very wicked," Leva responds with what we might consider the novel's central proposition: "I don't know a single motion-picture person above reproach. [...] But then, neither do I know a single person in any other walk of life who is above reproach."

6  Dreiser, "Hollywood: Its Morals and Manners: 1. The Struggle on the Threshold of Moving Pictures," *Shadowland* 5, no. 3 (November 1921): 61.

7 Shelley Stamp, "'It's a Long Way to Filmland': Starlets, Screen Hopefuls, and Extras in Early Hollywood," in *American Cinema's Transitional Era: Audiences, Institutions, Practices*, ed. Charlie Keil and Shelley Stamp (Berkeley: University of California Press, 2004), p. 332.

8 Stamp, p. 332.

Hughes doesn't just reject moral hysteria, he claims motion pictures have an important social function: they "open a new world" and "help mankind by educating and exercising its moods." Several years later, Hughes would ask, "What difference does it make whether you call moving pictures an art, an industry, an amusement, a merchandise? The main thing is that they fascinate almost everybody. Their first duty is make their own rules, to be moving pictures."[9] But in the early 1920s, if *Souls for Sale* is anything to go by, he was convinced of the new medium's status as high art, a rather unusual conclusion for a Hollywood novel to draw at this or any other time. Several characters as well as the narrator repeatedly draw analogies between motion pictures — particularly as represented in the work of Charlie Chaplin and D.W. Griffith — and classic artistic masterpieces. All that distinguishes motion pictures from such long-established forms as the drama or epic is "the real blood instead of nouns" that they provide. As the scenarist Hobbes explains to Mem, "We're presiding at the birth of an immortal art. Some of us don't know it. But posterity will know it."

The novel also discloses the genuine craft involved in film-making. There is, for example, a lengthy description of the shooting of a spectacular yet dangerous storm scene, the success of which is only a result of "the moving-picture geniuses [who] exhaust a vocabulary of mechanical effects." Elsewhere, the reader receives a lesson along with Mem in the fundamental unit of film: the shot. Leva explains, while on location in Palm Springs:

> they take everything first at a distance — long shots, they call them. They have three cameras here, but something always goes wrong, or looks as if it could be improved; so they make a lot of takes. Then they come closer and take medium shots to cut into the long shots. Then they take close-ups of the most dramatic moments. All these have to match — though

9 "Critics and the Motion Pictures — a Talk by Rupert Hughes at a Luncheon Given by Samuel Goldwyn in Keen's Chop House, Friday December 30, 1931," 5 typed pages. Box 7, Rupert Hughes Papers.

they usually don't — so that they can be assembled in the studio for the finished picture.

While descriptions of shoots, sets, and studios are not so unusual in Hollywood novels — there are comparable scenes in Harry Leon Wilson's *Merton of the Movies* (1922) and Nathanael West's *The Day of the Locust* (1939) — accounts of the complex technologies and syntax of film are relatively rare, especially in the kind of detail that *Souls for Sale* provides.

As noted, the Reverend Doctor Steddon might condemn the motion-picture studio as Satan's factory churning out what Nathan termed "mechanical dolls," but *Souls for Sale* inverts such Fordist motifs of mechanical reproduction (commonly deployed — to this day — to denigrate mass entertainment), suggesting studios are closer to "the factories of the working classes in their overalls and caps. The make-up boxes the [motion-picture] toilers carried were merely their tool kits." Hughes takes care to catalogue these "toilers" — "famous artists, extra folk, camera men, executives, cabinetmakers, electricians, chemists, scene painters, decorators, cowboys, [...] cooks, [and] waitresses" — even as he underscores the industry's financial precarity, long hours, and ever-present dangers (Mem is nearly sliced up by the wind propulsion machine while filming the aforementioned storm scene), as well as the emotional demands it places on actors.

According to one of Mem's love interests, Tom Holby, star of the Bermond Company (a fictionalized version of Goldwyn Pictures), "We're a bunch of hard workers and the women work as hard as the men. They're respected and given every opportunity for wealth and fame and freedom." And, in fact, it is the labor of women that appears to interest Hughes the most; in this sense, *Souls for Sale* forms a significant contribution to the recovery work that scholars such as Stamp and those involved in the digital Women Film Pioneers Project have begun to undertake. Hughes's novel confronts the stereotype of the silly "movie-struck girl" that, as Stamp argues, "served to obscure the multi-faceted nature of women's contributions to filmmaking in the teens, not just as lowly easily dispensable 'extras' but as directors, writers, influential performers, critics, and commentators."[10] To begin with, the novel acknowledges the roles women played behind the camera as make-up artists and on-set waitresses, and in "the laboratory projection room, correcting the films." Mem finds this latter work particularly "fascinating," as she scours the prints for "blemishes, scratches, dust specks, bad printing, bad tinting, bad assembly, bad any one of a score of things."

Pioneering director Alice Guy-Blaché perceptively noted all the way back in 1908 that "women's chances of making a living have been increased by the rise of the cinematograph machines," and this is an insight Hughes's novel keenly pursues. [11] To begin with, Mem's entry into motion pictures in many ways runs aslant of the kind of trajectory set out in typical "star-is-born narratives," whereby a young woman is lured to the industry with embellished tales of celebrity and on-screen romance. Although Calverley has two theaters, Mem has in fact never watched a film or read a fan magazine until her train journey westward. And she falls into her first role as an extra, in Palm Springs, quite by accident — not as a result of "fame-hunger." When she does finally decide to seek a career in the industry, it is because she wishes to secure some kind of income in order simply to live and to support her struggling parents back home. In other words, Mem's turn to motion pictures is largely rational and pragmatic. She identifies an opportunity for independence — and takes it.

Well ahead of its time, *Souls for Sale* acknowledges that women had "few other avenues open to them for profitable, independent, and rewarding professions."[12] Leva, a war widow left with three children to support, "preferred [extra work] to her previous experiences as a school-teacher and a trained nurse"; it not only pays more but also affords her vicarious experiences of different characters and different worlds. And of course, employment also provided young women like Mem an alternative to marriage. According to Mem, "the old-fashioned housewife," such as her mother (at least as she appears in the first half of the novel) only

---

10 Stamp, pp. 342-43.

11 Quoted in Lizzie Francke, *Script Girls: Women Screenwriters in Hollywood* (London : British Film Institute, 1994), p. 6.

12 Stamp, p. 342.

grew plump on the toil of her smart husband, and contributed little but an appetite and a number of new beaks for him to feed. She was glad that she would not be such a woman. She would find her own food and pay her own way. [...] She would be no man's chattel to make or mar.

And so she rejects the director Claymore's offer of marriage, determining to stay the course of her career. With financial independence came opportunities to live, as Stamp writes,

rather unconventional lives — outside of marriage, free from their families, economically self-sufficient, and creatively employed — lives that must have held tremendous appeal to those eager for models of behavior different from the Victorian standards by which their mothers had been raised.[13]

The novel depicts communities of women who live and work together in Hollywood, household configurations that revise or altogether sidestep the patriarchal nuclear family. Mem's household of working women is eventually overseen by Mrs. Steddon, whom they all call "mother," and has "no more thought of chaperonage as a crowd of bachelors."

And yet Hughes is far from naïve. Mem's assumption that casting directors operate according to an economy of sexual favors is one of the ways the novel acknowledges the vulnerable position of women in the industry. And in a complex and quite interesting way, *Souls for Sale* presents an equally — and unexpectedly — sympathetic account of women such as Mem who, appreciating that they have something in demand — desirability — opt to sell, rather than to give it away:

She was determined to act. She needed money. She must have money. It never occurred to her that a pretty woman is merchandise. She had given herself

13 Stamp, p. 342.

away once [to her hometown beau], and now she found there was a market ready and waiting, with cash and opportunity as the price. She had wares for this market. She could barter them for fame and future. Since she could, she would.

Remaining true to the harsh realities facing working women in the early decades of the 20th century, *Souls for Sale* presents motion-picture culture as a means by which women could enter modernity, for good or ill. For them, as for Mem, "the cage was opened."

Hughes's own vast and varied experiences of Hollywood clearly contributed to *Souls for Sale*'s in-depth and largely sympathetic take on the industry. When he sold rights to his first stories in 1907, the industry was undergoing:

transitions on several fronts: in production from a cottage industry to a vertically and horizontally integrated industry; in exhibition from the nickelodeon to the movie palace; in film lengths from shorts to features; in film aesthetics from a cinema of attractions to one of narrative coherence and closure; in reception from genres to stars; and in audiences from predominantly working class to middle class.[14]

Although none of those early stories were produced, these dealings reveal his prescient recognition of the turn literary culture would take. Hughes had greater success in the transposition to the screen of his longer narratives, beginning with his play, *Tess of the Storm Country* (in turn an adaptation of Grace Miller White's eponymous novel), which starred Mary Pickford, and followed shortly by two novels, *What Will People Say?* and *Old Folks at Home*. In 1916 he found an opportunity to write original

14     Jan-Christopher Horak, review of *American Cinema's Transitional Era: Audiences, Institutions, Practices*, ed. Charlie Keil and Shelly Stamp (Berkeley: University of California Press, 2004), in *Screening the Past* 18 (2005): http://www.screeningthepast.com/2014/12/american-cinemas-transitional-era-audiences-institutions-practices/

material for the screen; with his second wife, Adelaide Manola, he composed the story and scenario for a 40-part serial, *Gloria's Romance*. Hughes would also direct seven motion pictures for Goldwyn Pictures in the early twenties.

Hughes, along with several other bestselling authors of the period, such as Jack London and Rex Beach, early identified in the new medium opportunities for the broader circulation of fiction, and even, in some cases, as Hughes's narrator colorfully puts it, to "lift [...] authors out of their hells of oblivion." At the same time, film producers began to grasp the value of strategically aligning their interests with the significantly older and more esteemed realm of the literary. In 1919, Samuel Goldwyn invited Hughes to join his newly established Eminent Authors Inc., a stable of bestselling authors headed up by Beach. The June 7, 1919, issue of *Moving Picture World* announced its formation:

> Rex Beach and Samuel Goldwyn Organize Group of Famous Writers, Who Will Supervise Adaptation of Their Own Stories in Motion Picture Form. Rex Beach and Samuel Goldwyn have departed from precedent in the motion picture industry in obtaining six of the most popular novelists in America, under exclusive contract for a long term of years, to supervise the production of their own novels and stories in motion picture form.[15]

What was particularly novel about Goldwyn's initiative, according to Beach, quoted in that same column, was that:

> [w]hile all of the writers [...] have had some stories filmed, none of them has ever been seriously consulted regarding the method of screen treatment of their stories, nor have they been allowed that intimate co-operation and supervision which prevails in and is vital to the author.[16]

15 "Eminent Authors Pictures Formed," *The Moving Picture World.* June 7, 1919, p. 1469. https://archive.org/stream/mopicwor40chal/mopicwor40chal_djvu.txt

16    Ibid.

Like Hughes, Goldwyn had the foresight to understand that story and scenario would be the underpinnings of the feature film, which was only then emerging as a genre. As he would recall in his 1923 memoir, *Behind the Screen*, Goldwyn became convinced:

> that the public was tiring of the star and [...] the emphasis of production should be placed upon the story rather than upon the player. In the poverty of screen drama lay, so I felt, the weakness of our industry, and the one correction of this weakness [...] was a closer co-operation between the author and the picture-producer.[17]

And thus the formation of his Eminent Authors Inc., the original members of which included, in addition to Hughes and Beach, Gertrude Atherton, Mary Roberts Rinehart, Basil King, Gouverneur Morris, and Le Roy Scott.

According to their agreement, the Eminent Authors were "to come to Hollywood to write in direct co-operation with" Goldwyn Pictures. After his "cantankerous reaction to the scenario"[18] of his 1920 novel *The Cup of Fury*, Hughes moved from his home in New York City to Los Angeles for, as the narrator of *Souls for Sale* has it, "It is well for authors to keep in close touch with their plays and pictures in the making." Hughes's relocation was permanent, and he signed a contract with the Eminent Authors Inc. That contract specifically stipulated that adaptations of his fiction be made:

> in a first class manner, under the general supervision of persons constituting the Producer, from scenarios approved by the Author, and with such titles and sub-titles as may be approved by the Author; and to prominently state the name of the Author in connection with the main title of every of the said motion

---

17 Samuel Goldwyn, *Behind the Screen*. George H. Doran, 1923. 235

18 Rupert Hughes, "Early Days in the Movies," Part 2, *Saturday Evening Post*, April 13, 1935, 120.

pictures.[19]

Indeed, every adaptation made from his fiction was to include in its title screen the words "RUPERT HUGHES PICTURE," and all advertising materials developed to promote these adaptations were likewise to include his name. Hughes recalled the rather spectacular way in which Goldwyn deployed his Eminent Authors for marketing purposes: "Great twenty-four-sheet placards were speared on the billboards across the continent. On one side was a beautiful actor or actress, on the other an eminent author or authoress."[20]

Goldwyn's experiment was ultimately short-lived; the Eminent Authors, operating at considerable financial loss, disbanded in early 1921. The authors were allegedly unable to master — and were, according to Hughes, little interested in mastering — what Goldwyn termed "the motion-picture viewpoint. [...] This attitude brought many of the writers whom I had assembled into almost immediate conflict with our scenario department," he recalled.[21] That said, the experiment wasn't a total failure. "Among the writers whom the Goldwyn Company brought to Hollywood Rupert Hughes was notably successful" — a result, Goldwyn believed, of Hughes's

> prompt recognition of the gulf between those two channels of expression, literature and screen, and to his determination to master both the technicalities and spirit of the latter. In addition to this receptiveness of mind he has a capacity for work which I have never seen excelled. Many times I have known him to arrive in the studio early in the morning, direct all day, go home that evening to work on a scenario, and then, after perhaps a din-

19 Hughes' contract with Samuel Goldwyn, 17 May 1919. Rupert Hughes papers, Collection no. 0173, Special Collections, USC Libraries, University of Southern California.

20 Hughes, "Early Day in the Movies," *Saturday Evening Post* (April 6 and 13, 1935), p. 120.

21 Hughes, "At Home in Hollywood," typed 183-page ms., undated. Box 1, Folder 10, Rupert Hughes Papers.

ner or a dance, write several chapters of his new novel.[22]

Goldwyn's Eminent Authors Inc. is only one example of more formalized attempts by the studios to recruit literary authors to their cause, initiatives more broadly indicative of the increasingly complex, imbricated relationship of motion-picture and literary cultures. Famous Players-Lasky, for example, quickly signed up several British literary luminaries, including Arnold Bennett, Edward Knoblock, Sir Gilbert Parker, and Elinor Glyn.[23] It should not be surprising, then, that Hughes's Hollywood novel is at least as interested in literary matters as it is in filmmaking. Indeed, *Souls for Sale* provides a valuable account, and is itself an embodiment, of the ways in which print culture underpinned early motion pictures. One of the more obvious examples of this is page-to-screen adaptation, including the (stalled) adaptation of W. J. Locke's *Septimus* (1909) referenced in the novel, and Hughes's own well-received adaptation of *Souls for Sale*.

When *Souls for Sale* appeared on screen in 1923, the A. L. Burt Company simultaneously reissued Hughes's novel as a photoplay edition. Photoplay editions, which first appeared around 1913 with the publication of Harold MacGrath's *The Adventures of Kathlyn*, were reprints of bestselling novels, plays, or short-story cycles already successfully adapted to the screen, or novelizations of original film stories. What marked them as photoplay editions was the inclusion of some or all of the following: a cover image taken from the screen adaptation (usually an illustration rather than a motion-picture still), cast lists, and stills. The photoplay edition of *Souls for Sale*, which announces itself as such on its title page, has as its frontispiece a still of Mem (played by Eleanor Boardman, Goldwyn's "New Face of 1922") in Palm Springs, and features three other stills from the film in the text.

---

22 Samuel Goldwyn, *Behind the Screen* (New York: George H. Doran, 1923), p. 245.

23 Goldwyn, p. 236; "When you consider," writes Goldwyn, "that Gene Stratton-Porter and Zane Grey had both been signed up by other California producers and [...] ultimately Kathleen Norris, Rita Weiman, and Somerset Maugham joined the cohorts of the pen, you will see why Hollywood was temporarily transformed from a picture colony to a picture-book colony."

Hughes's novel also registers the role of print culture in motion pictures by referencing, sometimes at length, title cards, promotional materials such as posters and billboards, and fan magazines such as those Mem reads on the train. These fan magazines provided new opportunities for authors — like Dreiser, Katherine Anne Porter, and even e. e. cummings — who not only found they had something to say about motion pictures but were also attracted by the possibility of vastly expanding their audience. Hughes also mentions actual scenarists — "[D.W.] Griffith, Jeanie McPherson, John Emerson, Anita Loos" — as well as the Screen Writers Guild, which had formed in 1920. By 1922, writing for motion pictures had become, Hughes's narrator tells us, "the newest indoor sport [...] a popular vice that replaced the older custom of writing plays." Here the novel gestures to the "scenario fever" that arose in the early to mid-teens, largely in response to the 1911 *Kalem Co. v. Harper Bros.* decision, which penalized Kalem Company for copyright infringement in the screen adaptation of Lew Wallace's popular 1880 novel *Ben-Hur: A Tale of the Christ.* Consequently, as Steven Price reports, "Anxieties about copyright deterred the studios from adaptation and prompted them to concentrate on 'original' stories." And so they began to solicit story ideas from the public "via advertising, advice columns in trade journals, writing schools, story competitions and so on."[24] Goldwyn's efforts and those of other studios to establish stables of authors also contributed to this "fever."

From a *Los Angeles Times*' "page devoted to the gossip of the moving-picture studios," Mem learns of the "herds" of "unimportant" authors in addition to the likes of Maurice Maeterlinck, whom Goldwyn had brought out in 1920, now making their way to Hollywood. *Souls for Sale* also includes a famous anecdote about Goldwyn's unsuccessful attempt to entice George Bernard Shaw to write for film. And on a studio lot, Mem encounters the youthful cast of *The Adventures and Emotions of Edgar Pomeroy*, an original 12-part serial written by Booth Tarkington, celebrated author of *The Magnificent Ambersons*,

---

24 Steven Price, *A History of the Screenplay* (Basingstoke: Palgrave Macmillan, 2013), p. 54.

whose *Monsieur Beaucaire* was one of the first novels by a living writer to be adapted to the screen.

Hughes, another literary author-cum-screenwriter, arguably also smuggles himself into the novel in the guise of Doctor Bretherick. Bretherick, the Steddon family physician, had once written "stories for motion pictures" and, like Hughes, was "addicted to plotty stories." When Mem confides in the doctor about her pregnancy, he "improvise[s] for [her] future what a moving picture man would call a 'continuity,'" enabling her to flee Calverley without cluing the townsfolk in to her real motivations. And so

> the continuity began to move. At first it followed the doctor's manuscript with remarkable smoothness. [...] It carried the frightened waif of village disaster to cosmic heights, to unheard-of experiences wherein [her] degradation became her salvation; her practice of lies taught her eternal truths.

Here we have not only an *in nuce* synopsis of *Souls for Sale* but also an indication of Hughes's own assessment of the value of motion pictures — that is, their power to "help mankind by educating and exercising its moods."

"When you write a movie you do what no man ever did before this generation," announces Hollywood-bound stage diva, Miriam Yore, to a "famous unknown writer" on Mem's westward-bound train. "We are the pioneers, the Argonauts, the discoverers." In its insightful, sustained defense of the motion-picture industry of the early twenties, Hughes's novel raises questions that continue to animate film studies today, questions about the artistic status of motion pictures, their relationship to modernity, and their role in the emergence of the New Woman. Ultimately, no novel of Hollywood's early days provides a more sympathetic account of, in Hughes's own words, a period when "a new art and a great art [was] being born in sore travail."[25]

---

25  Hughes, "At Home in Hollywood."

# SOULS FOR SALE

# CHAPTER I

"LOS ANGELES!" the sneering preacher cried, as Jonah might have whinnied, "Nineveh!" and with equal scorn. "The Spanish missionaries may have called it the City of Angels; but the moving pictures have changed its name to Los Diablos! For it is the central factory of Satan and his minions, the enemy of our homes, the corrupter of our young men and women, the school of crime. Unless it reforms — and soon! — surely, in God's good time, the ocean will rise and swallow it!"

Though he was two thousand miles or more away, as far away, indeed, as the banks of the Mississippi are from the Californian shore, the Reverend Doctor Steddon was so convinced by his own prophetic ire that he would hardly have been surprised to read in the Monday morning's paper that a benevolent earthquake had taken his hint and shrugged the new Babylon off into the Pacific sea.

But of all follies, next to indicting nations, cursing cities is the vainest. And Los Angeles lived on, quite unaware that its crimes were being denounced in the far-off town of Calverly. The sun itself took two hours to make the trip, and though it was black night outside the little church in Calverly, it was just sunset in Los Angeles.

There was scarlet fire along the ocean of oceans, whose lazy waves stroked the coast with lake-like calm. Over the wide sprawled city was a smooth sky all of a banana yellow, save for a stain of red grapes at the hem where the sky went down behind the sea wall of the Santa Monica Mountains.

3

Among the multitudinous gardens, along the palm-plumed avenues, the twilight loafed. The day seemed to be entangled in the jewel-hung citruses, the fig trees, the papyrus clusters, the hedges foaming with a surf of Shasta daisies, the spendthrift waste of year long roses, and the smother of vines rolling up white walls in contrary cascades and spilling a froth of flowers along the roofs of many-colored tile.

To the north lay Hollywood, the particular Hades of the cinemaphobes, but curiously demure and innocent in the sunset.

From certain surfaces there and in Culver City the light was flashed back with heliographic brilliance from acres on acres of the glass walls and roofs of huge factories, strange workshops where the enslaved sun and the chained lightning wrote stories in photographs. Millions of miles of tiny pictures were taken at a rate of a thousand a minute. Tons of spooled romance went rolling all over the world, so that the girl and boy who embraced before one camera were later observed by coolies in Shantung, by the Bisharin of Egypt, and the sundry peoples of Somaliland, Chilkoot, Jedda, and Alexandropol—where not? Wherever the sun traveled and the moon reigned they could watch this reeled minstrelsy gleaming for the delight and indignation of mankind.

Even when the sun had left this capital of the new art, some of the studios would glow on with a man-made day of their own. But most of the factories were closing now, since the toilers had begun betimes in the morning and were scattering homeward for rest or study or mischief. Los Angeles, the huge Spinner, was finishing another day of its traffic in virtue, vice, laughter, love, and its other wares.

Even Doctor Steddon, if he could have seen the realm he objurgated, would have confessed that the devil had a certain grace as a gardener and that his minions were a handsome, happy throng. But Doctor Steddon had never seen Los Angeles and had never seen a moving picture. He knew that the world was going to wrack and ruin as usual and he laid the blame on the nearest novelty as usual.

His daughter had heard him lay the blame in previous years on other activities. She wished he wouldn't.

But then she had not escaped blame herself, and she was in a mortal dread now of a vast cloud of obloquy lowering above her and ominous with lightning.

As yet the congregation had found no grave fault with her except a certain overfervor in the hymns. Her voice had a too-manifest beauty, an almost operatic zeal, as it floated from the loft of the volunteer choir some of whom would never have been drafted if they had not volunteered.

Sundry longer faced members of the congregation felt that it was not quite respectable for a girl, particularly a clergyman's daughter, to put so much rapture into a church tune. But Youth, exultant in a very ferocity for life, harried the old hymn like an eaglet struggling upward with a tortoise.

The words were all about a "joy divine," but the elders kept a measure in arrears, hanging back with a funeral trudge to save the day from the young rebel.

That one voice, shining above the others, had especially tormented tonight the old parson, across whose silvered head it went floating from the choir loft just abaft the pulpit. For Doctor Steddon could not understand the seraphic innocence of his daughter's voice. Hearing was not believing. He had known the singer too long and too well to be quite sure of the purity of her piety. He loved her, but with a troubled love. He felt the vague disapproval of the congregation and agreed that there was a little immodesty in the poignancy of her ardor.

Doctor Steddon – with a D.D. from a seminary that was more liberal with its degrees than with its dogmas—had been impatient for the choir and the congregation to have done with their hymn and let him preach. He was almost ashudder with a rapture of his own, the rapture of denunciation, of hatred for the ways of the world, particularly the newest way of the world, the most recent pleasure of the town.

His daughter, glancing across the choir rail, passed the book she shared with Elwood Farnaby, the second tenor, looked down into her father's sparse gray poll, which was turned into a cowl by the central bald spot. She looked almost into his mind and knew his impatience. And she loved him with a troubled love.

Her father and mother had named her "Remember" after one of the Mayflower girls nearly three hundred years after. Her father often wished that she had been  more like those Puritan maidens. But that was because he did not know how like she was to them, how much they, too, had terrified their parents with their love of finery and romantic experiment. For it is only the styles, and not the souls, that change. There had been loves as dire then as now, and sermons as fierce and as futile as the one that Doctor Steddon was so zealous to repeat, with only the terms and not the spirit altered.

And many an ancient exquisite anguish that had fretted the young she-Pilgrims of 1621 renewed itself in the mellow heart of this Pilgrim of 1921. The fuel was fresh, but the fire was from everlasting to everlasting.

Fathers despaired of girls then as the fathers of now of the girls of now; and as the fathers of 2221 will despair of the girls of 2221, the young and the old men of then and of now and of heretofore being but rearrangements of primeval manhood waging in the eternal pattern the love-wars which know no truce.

There are chronicles enough to prove that the same quota of the "Remembers" and the "Praisegods" of Plymouth and the other colonies suffered the same bitter beatitudes and frantic bewilderments as Remember Steddon and Elwood

Farnaby endured when their elbows touched in the choir loft of this mid-Western village. Miss Steddon felt a sudden tremor in Farnaby's elbow; then it was gone from hers; she saw his thumb nail whiten as it gripped the hymn book hard. Some thing in the words he chanted seemed to stab him with a sense of guilt. He felt it a terrible thing for her to stand before that congregation and cry aloud words of ecstasy over her redemption from sin.

Their secret, unknown and unconfessed, was concealed by the very clamor of its publication. And it troubled Farnaby mightily to be gaining all the advantage of a lie by singing the truth.

Then the hymn was over, and everybody began to sit down solemnly, the whole congregation closing up like a jackknife of many blades.

Before the choir had emptied its lungs of the last long "Ah men!" and sunk out of sight behind the curtained railing, the old parson was clutching the edges of his pulpit as he announced his text. This was but a motto on the banner of a Saint George charging upon the dragon that despoiled his flock.

Tonight he charged the newest dragon, a vast, shapeless monster, the 20th century's peculiar monster: the moving picture. This was the latest child of Science, that odious Science that is always terrifying Faith with its inventions, its playing cards, its printing presses, novels, higher criticisms, evolutions, anaesthetics and archaeologies, musical instruments of new and seductive blare, roller skates, bicycles, automobiles, hair ribbons, hats, corsets, incomplete costumes, and all the other tricks for destroying souls. The worst of all, because the latest of all, was the moving picture!

Though Doctor Steddon had never seen a moving picture, he had read what other preachers had said about them, and every day or two he had to pass the advertisements stuck up along the billboards or in front of a gaudy theater that had previously been an almost preferable saloon.

He had gazed aghast at the appalling posters with their revolting blazon of the new word "Sex"; their insolent questions about "Your Wife," "Your Husband"; their frenzied scenes of embraces, wrestling matches, conventionalized rape, defiances, innumerable revolvers, daggers, train wrecks, automobile accidents, slaughters, plunging horses, Bacchic revels, bathing suits, gambling and drinking and smoking scenes, and everything and everybody desperately wicked or desperately good.

He forgot that anybody in town had ever gone wrong before. The normal supply of delinquencies appeared to have sprung up suddenly as a result of these posters.

So tonight he launched upon a Savonarolan denunciation. The stenographer who had tried to capture Savonarola's eloquence had to give up and write, "Here I could not go on for tears." There was no stenographer to record Doctor Steddon's thunderbolts. If there had been, it might have been startling to see how many of the same bolts he had hurled at other detestable activities that interested the townspeople and therefore alarmed their shepherds. As each new fashion or public toy had come into vogue he had gone at it hammer and tongs. He had never succeeded in doing more than scare off a few people who were scared to death, anyway. He had seen the crazes steal in like a tide rolling over him and his protests, then ebb away after he had ceased to fight. Yet still he fought, and always would do as he always had done. With equal stubbornness youth went about its ancient business and pastime: girls snickered in church and exchanged sly eyelids with ogling boys; women wore the latest fashion the town afforded; couples scouted and flirted during the very prayers, and practiced romance industriously on the way home. And tonight the chief result of Doctor Steddon's onslaught was the thought in the heart of his daughter and various others, "I should like to see Los Angeles."

When the choir was not singing openly and aboveboard, it was usually busily whispering. Even Elwood Farnaby had to lean over tonight and whisper important news to Remember. He was not permitted to call at her house or to beau her home after the service. Singing beside her in the house of God, that was different. He told her now what he had just learned, that the factory where he was employed would close down the following week. Elwood had worked his way up until he had been made a foreman a few months before. He was to have been promoted to superintendent soon.

His firm made the adding machine cleverly trade-marked as the Kalverly Kalkulator, or "K-K-K." But people had suddenly ceased to buy adding machines. The world's chief business was subtraction and cancellation. The last of the uncanceled orders for the K-K-K would be finished in a few days. Mr. Seipp, the bank president, would not advance the money for further production.

Even the contribution baskets that were passed up the aisles during the services felt the omen. Those who had flung in folded bills laid silver down quietly. Those who had tossed in silver dropped copper with stealth. Doctor Steddon could see the leanness of the baskets from his pulpit, and it meant further privation for him.

To his daughter the news that Elwood would have no job in a week and would know no place to look for one had more than a commercial interest. It was the alarum of fate.

She had loved Elwood since they were children, had loved him all the more for his rags and the squalor of his home. He was the son of the town's most eminent drunkard, old "Fall-down Farnaby," a man whose office had been any saloon he could stand up in. Then Prohibition arrived and he had lacked headquarters, but not potations. An ingenuity and an assiduity that would have made him a great explorer or a great inventor kept him supplied at a time when there was no legal liquor at all, and when what illegal liquor there was to be had was so expensive that even cheap moonshine whisky cost more than dated champagne had cost before.

Among the slipshod children of his doomed family Elwood had somehow managed to acquire ambition. He had struggled up through a youth of woe to a manhood of shackled promise. He had latterly supported his mother and a pack of brothers and sisters. He had even been able to afford to go to the war, had seen France and won the guerdon of a wound or two that made him glorious in Remember Steddon's eyes and a little more lovable than ever, not because he won praise for a hero's little while, but because his wounds added to the burdens that she longed to divide with him.

Her father, however, had been unable to tolerate the thought of his daughter marrying the son of the town sot. Doctor Steddon felt that he was proving his love, his loving wisdom toward his daughter, by forbidding her even to meet young Farnaby outside the choir loft. He was sure that her love would wear out.

He did not know his daughter. Who ever did?

The great danger about the whole business of saving other people's souls seems to be that life keeps mocking the noblest efforts with failure as it mocks the most high-minded playwrights. It is baffling to find that nothing is more effective in destroying certain souls than the attempt to save them. Such souls must be like caged birds that go mad with fear when the kindliest hand is thrust into the cage.

They dash themselves against the bars; and if they escape from the tenderest palm, they flash away to the wild woods.

Doctor Steddon was never more devoted than when he warned his girl to avoid young Farnaby. When she refused his advice he forbade her to see the boy. She felt that she obeyed a higher duty when she secretly disobeyed her father. She met the young man secretly whenever she could steal away.

Her mother had neither the courage to oppose this stealthy romance nor the courage to inform her husband of it. The two lovers made an unwilling accomplice of her, and she was assured that they would marry, the moment Elwood could afford to add her pretty lips to the mouths he was already feeding.

The factory had promoted him twice in its heyday of high prices, and the time had seemed near when they could afford to announce their approaching marriage.

And now the chance was gone.

And this meant to the girl far more than a mere deferment of bliss. She had been trained, indeed, to regard bliss as by no means a right of hers. She had rather got the idea that bliss was pretty sure to be indecent sin. Marriage had been preached to her as a lofty duty, a kind of higher ordeal. Her father would have abhorred the thought that even its rites gave any franchise to raptures unrestrained. Wedlock to him was a responsibility, not a release from pruderies, a solemnity, not a carnival.

And now she was to be denied even that somber, laborious suburb of Paradise.

# CHAPTER II

ELWOOD HAD EXPECTED that the bad news would shock her. But he could not understand the look of ghastly terror she gave him. He forgot it in his own bitter brooding and did not observe the deathly white that blanched her pallor.

Yet he had noted that she was paler of late and had added that worry to his backbreaking load of worries. The sunset crimson was gone from her cheeks and her cheeks were thinner than he had ever seen them before. She coughed incessantly, too, and kept putting her hand to her chest as if it hurt her there.

Her cough annoyed her father as he preached and made him forget some of his best points. But his sermon annoyed her, too.

He was putting himself on record with fatal hatred of sin, and she wished he wouldn't.

A smile twitched her lips and dwelt there at the mockery life was heaping upon his oratory. He was denouncing moving pictures as the source of all evil. Yet his daughter had never seen one. Yet again that had not saved her from...

A white-hot wave drove the wan calm from her cheek, and a scarlet war ensued in her veins.

She was the daughter of Eve and of Adam and of all of the Eves and Adams since sin began. But to hear her father talk, it might have been a moving-picture machine instead of the serpent that tempted Eve to knowledge and started the eternal parade of wickedness.

To hear her father talk, this little town of Calverly had been a pre-Satanic Eden before the Los Angelesian movies crawled in. Yet even this young woman could remember that he had preached almost this same sermon against a long series of other amusements. He had never found the town anything but a morass of wickedness.

She felt a mad impulse to rise and cry down at him across the brass rail:

"Papa, don't! For Heaven's sake, stop!"

For the sheer sake of true truth, she was tempted to protest against the folly of such a crusade. It was bad enough in a newspaper. It seemed peculiarly heinous that such bad logic and such reckless falsehood should be shouted from a pulpit.

But of course she made no sound except to cough.

The climax of her father's appeal was a jeremiad against the desecration of the Sabbath.

The town's two little picture houses had proved so much more popular than anything ever known before, that they had ventured to slip in performances on Sunday nights without interference from the indolent police.

The theater managers had claimed that, according to their creed, the true Sabbath did not fall on Sunday night, but on Saturday. Of course they did not close on Saturday night, either; but then, they said, they could find nothing in Moses against movies. This plea was resented as a heathenish impertinence by the orthodox.

Doctor Steddon called upon his congregation to make a stand against the "continental Sabbath" and to save the American home from the danger of the new invasion. To Doctor Steddon the American home was a glaring failure except when he used it as a contrast with foreign homes.

His daughter was so distraught by the sarcasm of reality that she felt it a sacred duty to rise and proclaim her secret to every gaping listener there. But, of course, she denied herself the relief of expression.

When her father completed his discourse with his tremendous thunder against Los Angeles, he sank into his tall chair. The choir rose for the final hymn. After that came the majestic benediction.

On the way home under the wasted magic of the rising moon,

Remember did not walk as usual between her father and mother with a hand on the arm of each. To-night she kept at her mother's left elbow and clung so tight to the fat, warm arm that her mother whispered:

"What's the matter, honey?"

"Nothing, mamma," she faltered. "I'm just a little tired, I guess."

Her father felt a bit lonely, insulated from his child by his wife; and he had the orator's afterthirst for a draught of praise. He mumbled:

"How was the sermon, Mem?" They called her Mem for short. "You haven't told me how you liked the sermon."

"Oh, it was fine," she said, "perfectly fine. It ought to do a lot of good, too." She added to herself, "But it won't." Then she fell to coughing so hard that her father and mother had to stop by a tree and wait for her to be able to go on.

The big old maple sheltered them like a vast umbrella for a moment. Then their eyes were blinded by a great fierce light.

An automobile came straight toward them and ran up over the curbstone before it was brought to a stop by a driver, who gasped: "Oh dear! What's the matter with this darn thing?"

It was Molly Seipp, daughter of the bank president, learning to run her father's car since he had to discharge the chauffeur. She had chosen Sunday night for practice in order to escape what little traffic troubled Calverly's streets.

Seeing that the Steddon family had taken refuge behind the bole of the tree, she hailed them with her usual impudence of self-raillery.

"Don't be afraid! I'm trying to learn to back this fool car. It's almost as big a fool as I am."

Then she set the clutch in reverse, and stepped on the accelerator with such vigor that the car shot backward like a premature rocket and nearly destroyed the twin baby carriage in which young Mrs. Clint Sparrow had taken her dual blessing to visit their grandmother.

But Mem was coughing too violently to be thrilled by the unusual drama, and her father was too deeply concerned in her distress to protest even against Molly Seipp's profanation of the holy evening. Besides, she went to the Episcopalian church and was doomed, anyway.

Doctor Steddon and his wife stared toward each other earnestly through the gloom and their hearts exchanged counsels without words or looks. The rest of the way home Doctor Steddon was not a preacher anxious about his daughter's soul, but a father afraid for her life. Her health of body was outside the parish of a doctor of divinity; that was the business of a doctor of reality.

"Tomorrow, Mem," he said, "I want you to go to see Doctor Bretherick the very first thing."

Mem shook her head and looked frightened. She was afraid of doctors just now; their information was occult. But her father insisted:

"If you don't promise, I'll go fetch him over myself tonight."

This seemed to alarm Mem, and she gasped:

"I promise. I promise! I don't want you to go out again. Good night, mamma. Good night, papa. That was a fine sermon tonight."

She did not linger for her usual tryst with Elwood, but hurried to her room, pausing on the stairs for a long bout with her cough. Her parents waited in an anguish of anxiety for her to finish it. Then they put out the lights and went up to bed.

Throughout the night they heard her coughing, a pitiful little noise like the barking of a sick coyote. They were on a rack of fear, but their fear was not hers. The cough to them was an ominous problem. To her it might promise a solution.

# CHAPTER III

NEXT MORNING MEM WENT about her household chores and said nothing of her promise. When she was reminded of it, she put off going until her mother threatened to go with her. Then she made haste to set out alone.

She walked around Doctor Bretherick's block two or three times until she saw that no one was waiting. She caught the doctor, indeed, just hurrying out to his buggy. She asked him to turn back and talk to her. And she made sure that the door to his consulting room was closed.

She told him that her parents were afraid her cold was more than a cold, and she coughed for him and endured his investigations and auscultations and the odd babyishness with which he laid his head on her breast and on her shoulder blades. He asked her many questions, and she grew so confused and apt in blushes that he asked her more. Suddenly he flung her a startled look, gasped, and stared into her eyes as if he would ransack her mind. In the mere shifting of his eyelid muscles she could read amazement, incredulity, conviction, anger, and finally pity.

All he said was, "My child!"

There could be no solemner conference than theirs. Doctor Bretherick had attended Mem's mother when the girl was born. He thought of her still as a child, and now she dazed him and frightened him by her mystic knowledges and her fierce demands that he should help her out of her plight or help her out of the world.

He refused to do either and demanded that she meet her fate with heroism. Somehow he woke a new courage in the panic of her soul, but she was convinced that her future must be one of degradation in obscurity.

She quoted him the old saw:

"It doesn't matter what a man does, but once a woman slips she is lost forever."

"Nonsense!" he cried, and added: "Damned and damnable nonsense! It isn't true and never was. The only ones who get lost are the ones who lose themselves. Don't run, Mem! Whatever you do, don't run! Be sorry, and sin no more. But don't run!

"The public is like a cat. It has the pounce instinct. It can only jump on the mouse that runs. Cats don't mean to be cruel to mice. They just can't help springing when the mouse tries to get away. By and by they smell blood, and then it's all over. Hold your head up and carry your cross. And let him that is without sin cast the first stone. You've heard your father say that often enough."

"My father!" she moaned. "Don't speak of my poor father. What will he say? What will the people think of him? He'd never dare face the congregation. I must run away and hide. I just must. Or kill myself. I've got no right to destroy my father. And my mother! She has had so much sorrow, and she's trusted me; and he's been so good, and he tried to take such care of me."

"Care! Who can take care of anybody else?" the doctor groaned, with a crooked smile. "There's just one person who can take care of you now: the man who... "

This woke a pride of another sort in her heart. She was of a type increasing swiftly in the world (one of the few things called "modern" that are really modern), the woman who asks no man to take upon himself the whole burden of her food, her clothes, her thought, her destiny, or even her misdeeds.

She lived in a generation where the girl plans to earn her living as the boy had always planned. She had come subtly to believe that a wife should no more be supported by her husband than a husband by his wife.

Her father loathed and dreaded what has always been called the modern woman. He denounced her in the pulpit and at home. For a time he had explained "the wickedness of these modern days" by the disgraceful discontent of certain women, comparing them with the simple, sweet, home-loving women of old-fashioned days, and carefully omitting reference to the cruel, lawless, extravagant, home-destroying women who were just as old-fashioned and just as numerous in the days when he was young, as he had known when he was young, but forgot as he got old.

But after the women of his congregation had all become voters in spite of themselves, and he could see no change in their appearance or their activities, he dropped that denunciation and took up the moving picture as the new toy of his anxiety.

Mem herself had felt no stirrings toward scholastic pursuits, or toward a professional career as a doctor, a lawyer, or even as a trained nurse. She wanted to earn money only for one reason: that she might ease the burden of her husband.

Calverly had offered little encouragement, however, for a womanly career. To take in washing, sewing, cook, wait on the table, wash dishes, and make beds for other families, to work in a store or one of the few factories, these had made up the entire choice.

Love married her heart to Farnaby. The conditions of American society rendered it impossible for them to live together openly, but quite possible for them to meet and spend long secret hours together. Deferment made their hearts sick and tormented their senses. Opportunity was incessant and opportunity is close kin to importunity. They had no diversions, no emotional escape valves of art, theater, dance, fiction, where vicarious romance would divert the strain on their souls. Their very horror of sin magnified its temptations, gave it an eternal flame, an archangelic importance.

For them it was not merely a dishonorable, disgusting proof of unchecked idealism; it was a defiance of God, a plunge like Lucifer's across the battlements of heaven into the deserved damnation of hell whence there was no return forever. Perhaps the very tremendousness of the abyss carried them over the precipice when their lonely souls might have evaded a fall that looked less epic.

At any rate, in spite of many wildly beautiful battles, and many, many victories over themselves and each other, they lost a few battles. And a few defeats were enough to annul many splendid victories. And now Mem was a hostage of shame without means of defense.

And it was her nature to blame herself for her state, and to defend her beloved enemy from any of the consequences of the war.

When Doctor Bretherick suggested marriage as an easy salvation, he revealed to her the peculiar heartlessness of her fate. Marriage meant to her that two people went to church in two carriages, drove away consecrated in one, and thenceforward lived in the same house. That familiar exploit had been the one grand plan of Elwood's soul and hers.

But Elwood lived in the crowded shack which his father still owned, for lack of anybody to buy it. The house was full of children, and progressively the youngest brother always slept with Elwood. It was hard enough for Elwood to keep the roof over their heads. It was not to be thought of that Remember should join that wretched crowd.

At the minister's house there was much neatness and peace, but no more room than at Elwood's. The progressively next-to-the-youngest sister usually slept with Mem. It was unthinkable that Elwood should join that crowded ark.

For Elwood to leave his family and take a new house with Mem would mean that he must abandon his mother and the other children to the mercy of Fall-down Farnaby's brutality and indifference. That was, to a dutiful youth like Elwood, unthinkable.

So many things were unthinkable with these young souls! But Nature does not think! Nature wants. Nature strives to get, and getting, devours, or not getting, starves or shifts her approach.

Mem might have figured out numberless ways of arranging a marriage with Elwood if she had been more intelligent or less confused. But she was not brilliant of mind, and she was subjected utterly to the coercion of discipline.

She was like a flower grown in a pot on a shelf. Lacking strength to break it and go free, she would stay small and pretty and obscure. If something happened to break the pot and fling her out on the open soil, she would make a desperate effort for life, and if the soil were fertile she might grow to amazing heights and beauties; if the soil were sterile, she would simply die. But she had nothing within her to fling her off the shelf.

So when Doctor Bretherick proposed marriage he proposed something unthinkable at present, and, now that Elwood's job was gone, unthinkable as far forward as the girl's easily-baffled mind could think.

Doctor Bretherick, who knew so much about Calverly people, did not happen to know that Mem and Elwood had been meeting secretly. So he did not take young Farnaby into consideration. He was a little surprised when Mem refused to tell him the name of the man. He admired her wretchedly when he saw her trying to protect the fellow even from reproof.

"He's no more to blame than I am, and I have no right to ruin his life."

When Doctor Bretherick called the man a scoundrel she grew fierce in his defense.

Doctor Bretherick wasted no time on the expression of virtuous horror. He was an almost total abstainer from the vice of blame. When he found people sick or delirious or going insane, he did not revile them for recklessness in catching cold or catching fever or taking in devils for tenants. He tried to restore them to comfort and the practice of life. Love was endemic, and good fortune was more frequent than good conduct. He felt no call to insult the victims of bad luck in love. His answer to Mem's greed for all the blame and all the punishment was a gentle reminder:

"It's not a question, my child, of your rights or his. It's a question of the rights of a certain future citizen."

Mem wept and beat her clenched hands upon her brow and on the doctor's desk. He let her fight it out, finding no consolation fit to offer. He studied her as he had studied many another wretch tossing on a bed of coals and crazed with pains of body and mind. He saw how beautiful she was, how thrilling and how thrilled with that fire which builds homes and burns them up, kindles romance and devastation.

He felt a little sympathy even for the unknown man, and imagined how helpless the wretch might have been to resist that incandescence in which Mem was as helpless as he, since the flame cannot become ice by any power of its own.

The doctor reached out and clenched hands with Mem in the fiercer throes of her regret, or laid a fatherly caress on her bowed head.

"He must have told you he loved you," he said.

"But he does love me, and I love him."

"Then why is he unwilling to marry you?"

"He's not! There's nothing on earth he wants more than that. But he can't, he can't!"

"Is he married to someone else?"

Mem's lifted face was like a mask of horror, dripping with tears but aghast at such infamy. In every depth of shame there is a lower pit from which the soul recoils and finds a saving pride in its own superior height.

The doctor fell back before such insulted innocence. He sought a hasty shield behind another question.

"Then what other obstacle can there be? This is a free country. You don't have to ask anybody's permission?"

Mem was so distraught that she gave the one true reason, sobbing in the gable of her arms.

"The Kalkulator factory closes next week and his position will be gone." "Young Farnaby, eh?" the doctor mused.

Mem lifted her head again, and her hands twitched as if to recapture the secret she had let slip. But it was too late; she had not even protected Elwood from exposure.

The doctor thought busily. The word "Farnaby" presented the complete picture of the family whose woes and poverty he had long known. He felt encouraged after a first discouragement.

"Elwood's a nice boy," he said. "He'll do what's right. I'll call him up right away. Duty is more than skin deep with him."

Even as he took up the prehensile telephone, Mem snatched it from his hand.

"He wants to do what's right, but his first duty is to his mother. He's supporting his whole family. They'll starve without his help. And what he's going to do when the factory closes I don't know. He can't marry me. And I won't marry him and drag him down."

"There's no dragging him down. You'll make a wonderful wife and anybody ought to be proud to have you. You'll be a great help in his career."

"But how can we live together?" she cried, frantically.

"Don't. The main thing's the ceremony. Just you step out and get married. People will say you're a couple of young fools. But that's all they will say, and they'll enjoy a bit of romance in this dead burg."

He evaded Mem's pleading hands and called the factory.

Mem's embarrassment was overwhelming before the prospect of meeting in the presence of a witness the fellow-victim of the tidal wave that had engulfed them both one Sabbath evening.

A fervor of religious zeal and music had exalted their emotions then and made their hearts easy prey to the moonlight that waylaid them as she slipped out to meet him after her father and mother had kissed her good night.

A wheedling, cooing breeze had stolen through the vine-wreathed grotto of the porch, and had whispered incantations over them. Their remorse had been fearful, but its very frenzy was a kind of madness that prepared their dizzied souls for further need of it. For remorse, like other bitter drugs, establishes a habit.

Mem writhed in a delirium of remorse now. Such poetry in the proem, such hideous prose in the epilogue! Such honey, then such poison!

She was wakened from her fierce reverie, however, by the doctor's voice:

"Elwood's out; he's gone to the bank for the firm. I left word for him to call me as soon as he comes in. I've been thinking up a little plan."

Like many another earnest soul, Doctor Bretherick was addicted to plotty stories. When he had wrestled in vain with some wolf of disease for some agonizing patient he would forsake the never-ending mystery serial of pain and death and take up some volume of so-called "trash."

Like nearly everybody else in the country, Doctor Bretherick had tried his hand at the newest indoor sport, the writing of stories for moving pictures, a popular vice that had largely replaced the older custom of writing plays. So now he improvised for Mem's future what a moving-picture man would call a "continuity."

"This afternoon, after the factory closes, you and Elwood can meet and drive over to Mosby. I know the town clerk over there. He owes me a bill. I'll telephone him to make out the licenses and have 'em all ready for you when you get there. He can marry you or get a judge to, or a parson. You'd prefer a preacher, I suppose. Well, I can arrange that, too. I'll vouch for you both, and he'll say the necessary words and give you a nice certificate, and then you can telephone your father from Mosby and ask for his blessing. He won't give it over the telephone, but he will the next day when you two will drive back like a couple of prodigals. Your father will see you coming from afar, and he'll run out and fall on your necks.

"You can ask forgiveness, and then you can explain about Elwood's job and how you'll have to live at home 'till he gets another. Heaven knows you earn your board and keep at home, and they'll be mighty glad to have you there. By and by Elwood will find a new job, and you'll get rich and live happily ever after."

Mem was almost smiling at the shabby heaven he threw on the screen of her imagination. It was so much better than anything she had hoped. Then her old enemy, the arch-realist, the sneering censor, Poverty, slashed at the dream.

"I don't believe Elwood could afford the money. He'd have to pay the livery stable for the horse and buggy, and there's the license fee, and the ring, and the preacher, and the hotel, and, Oh, I don't believe we could afford it."

"I'll lend you all that," the doctor insisted. "I'm one of those authors that has enough confidence in his story to back it himself. You go ahead and get happiness and quit grieving. And don't you dare to change my manuscript. I'm one of those pernickety authors that believe actresses should act and let the authors auth."

Mem was laughing through her tears when the telephone rang.

The doctor's welcoming "Hello!" broke through a many-wrinkled smile. It froze to a grimace. As Mem watched, hearing only a rattling, inarticulate noise as from a manikin inside the telephone, the doctor's pleated skin was slowly drawn into new folds until his face, from being a cartoon of old hilarity, became a withered mummy of dejection. He kept saying: "Yes....Yes...Yes!" and finally, "That's right, bring him here."

He set down the telephone as if it were a drained cup of hemlock.

"It wasn't Elwood," Mem said.

"No. Yes. Well, O God! what a bitter world this is!"

Mem caught eagerly at grief.

"Tell me! What's happened? What's happened to Elwood? He's hurt. He's killed."

And since she had seized the knife from his reluctant hand and driven it into her heart, he left it there and said:

"Yes."

# CHAPTER IV

THE DOCTOR HAD NOT told the exact truth. For once his lie was worse than the truth.

Young Farnaby was not dead, not yet. But from what he had been told the doctor was sure that death was decreed. As his mind, so habited to fatal news, struggled with this message, it seemed better to leave Mem in her despair than to raise her to a brief suspense.

He would make a fight for the young man's life, as always; he never gave up while there was any life to fight for. Then if by some strange good fortune he should redeem this youth from the grave, it would be a glorious privilege to restore him to his sweetheart. But if he should keep her hope alive, then lose the war, he must kill her twice.

It seemed as if he had struck her dead already. For her clenched hands let each other go, her arms fell outward like the wings of a shot bird, her head fell on her breast, and she was slipping to the floor when he caught her.

For the mercy of this swoon he was as nearly thankful as he could be for anything. He got her up in his arms, carried her to the door, opened it with much fumbling, and staggered up the stairs with her to the spare room, calling to his wife:

"Get her undressed and keep her in bed till I come back. Don't let her talk. Don't mind what she says. But keep her here till I tell you."

Then he hurried downstairs to meet the crowd running to his gate in pursuit of an automobile. He recognized it as the Seipp car. Its fenders were crumpled and stained, and men got out of it, removed with much trouble a long limp body, and moved up the walk.

When, a little later, Mem came suddenly back to the world, she found Mrs. Bretherick bending over her. She felt blankets about her and a pillow under her head. Her shoes and stockings, her hat and her dress, were gone, and she was in a strange room.

Getting accustomed to wallpaper and chairs and chromos was the first business, before her soul could begin to orient itself. Then she recalled everything and began to cry out:

"Elwood! Tell me about Elwood!"

"Hush, my dear!" was all Mrs. Bretherick would say. She said it very gently, but when Mem tried to leap from the bed the old woman was very strong and held her down, coercing her with iron hands and a maddening reiteration of: "Hush! Don't excite yourself. The doctor says you must stay here. Hush now, my dear."

Mem's rebellion was checked by the sound of a loud nasal voice coming up from below. Someone downstairs was explaining something.

"You see, it was thisaway, Doc. I was standin' in front of Parlin's candy store right next the bank there, when I heard some fellers laughin'. Somebody hollered: 'Climb a lamp-post, ever'body. Here comes Molly Seipp!' And I seen the big Seipp car comin' scootin' along. Molly said afterward she allowed to shift from second speed to neutral and put on the foot brake. But she got rattled by the crowd round the bank, and slipped into high and stepped on the gas, and the car come boomin' over the sidewalk and mowed right into the crowd. People jumped every which way, and one or two got knocked down, but poor Elwood here, he was just comin' out the bank, and Molly was twistin' the steerin' wheel so crazy he didn't know which side to jump. And the car knocked him right through the big plate-glass window, you know, and up against the steel bars just inside and well, the bars was all bent, at that. Poor Elwood hadn't a chance.

"Molly climbed out the car and fell over on the sidewalk, leavin' the wheels still goin' round. I stepped on the runnin' board and shut off the engine. Then I and some other fellers backed the car out, and whilst the others picked up Elwood and Molly, I seen the motor was still goin' good.

"So we put Elwood in the car and we brought him over to you. Molly's all right except for hysterics, like, but Elwood – is they any hope for him? Nice boy, too, hard workin', honest as the day. He had two bank books in his hand, one of 'em the firm's, the other 'n was his own little savin's account. He always managed to save somethin' out of nothin'. He helt on to the book, Jim says, till he could hardly git it out of his hand. And it's all cut up with glass and covered with red so'st you couldn't hardly tell how much he had in the bank. Nice boy, too. He made a hard fight to live. Didn't holler at 'tall, just kept grittin' his teeth and mumblin' somethin'. You couldn't make out what he said. Could you, Jim?"

Jim's answer was not audible.

Nor were Mem's protests audible.


She had been bred to expect little of life, to make no demands for luxury, and to surrender with a cheerful Thy-will-be-done what the Lord took away with perfect right, since He had given it. So now she made no fight, no outcry. She lay still, her head throbbing with the words of Laurence Hope in a song one of her girl-friends sang:

> Less than the dust beneath thy chariot wheel,
> Less than the rust that stains thy glorious sword,
> Less than the dust, less than the dust am I.

It was the doctor who made the fight silently but bitterly, fiercely and in vain.

The only noise was made by the Farnaby family when they arrived in a little mob. They came up the street, Mrs. Farnaby from her tub, her forearms covered with dried suds, her red hands snatching her apron hem to and fro. She and the girls wailed aloud, and in the room below Mem could hear the young brothers crying. But none of them wept so bitterly or so loudly as old Fall-down Farnaby, who came staggering up the steps and floundered about the room, freed by drunkenness of all re-straints upon his remorse and his fear. And nobody had better reason to reproach his lot than the poor old prey of the thirst fiends, doomed to roll up the hill of remorse in his own hell a heavy stone of repentance that always broke loose at the top and rolled down again, dragging him with it.

Mem was benumbed with her sorrow. It was a proper punishment upon her, she was sure; and she spread her arms out as on a crucifix, thinking of herself as one of the thieves justly nailed to the tree next to that tree where the Innocent One suffered.

Doctor Bretherick had paused in his desperate battle to listen for sounds from the room above. He had gone to the stairs to ask his wife how Mem was. He had been glad of the prostration of her grief, but he was not deceived as to its sincerity.

Mem was still calm when his business was done in the room below and he had turned the spoils of defeat over to his aide-de-camp, the undertaker. Doctor Bretherick entered the bed-room and sent his wife about her business while he dropped his exhausted body into a chair and spurred his exhausted mind to further effort.

He took one of Mem's cold hands in his and petted it and chafed it, shaking his head in wordless sympathy.

"At least he didn't suffer!" he lied.

Her woe, for lack of other expression, made use of the smiling muscles, as she said:

"That's not true. I heard."

"Well," the doctor sighed, "his sufferings are over, anyway. He was a good boy, and you're a good, brave girl. And now what are we to do for you?"

She spoke without excitement.

"There's only one thing for me. I can't live, of course. I was sorry I was so sick, and I was afraid of my cough; but now I see that God sent it to me as a blessing. Do you think it will carry me off soon?"

The doctor shook his head. This frightened her. She gasped:

"Then it must be I must do it myself. It's wicked, I suppose, but have you got anything that isn't too slow or disfiguring? I don't mind the pain, but I don't want to go to hell with an ugly face."

The doctor was so familiar with deaths that he was capable of an occasional irony that looked like flippancy to those who met them only rarely. He was bitterer than Mem could imagine when he sighed:

"No, that's right. It's the pretty faces that go to hell, according to my understanding of it. Heaven is for the homely and the unattractive. Poor things, they need some consolation."

"Don't joke, for mercy's sake, Doctor!" she pleaded. "I couldn't live without Elwood, I don't dare to. I've no right to."

He cowed her hysteria with a sharp rein:

"You've no right to your own life now. It belongs to your father and your mother and to the life that has already begun. Suicide would be worse than cowardice and selfishness in your case, my child. It would be murder."

He was cruelly kind to her, like a driver who flogs and stabs a sinking beast of burden out of the deep mire of death and up across the steep crags to the valley beyond.

Mem's very skin shivered and seemed to rise in welts under his goad. Her heart struggled back to its task. Fiercely as it ached, it beat with a fuller throb. Her soul brooded somberly, though:

"Well, if it's my duty to live, it's my duty to tell the truth. I'll tell it to everybody. Poor Elwood shan't go into his grave without people knowing how I loved him."

He let her frenzy of devotion carry her up and down the room until she dropped into a chair, exhausted.

Then he took up the whip again.

"My poor little child, I've got to be terrible mean to you for your own sake. You can't do what you want to do. You said yourself that it would kill your father if he knew; it would drive him from his pulpit. And your mother would be crushed too, you said. And as for poor Elwood, wouldn't it simply turn the village against his memory? Everybody thinks of him as a brave, clean young martyr as he was. But just imagine what would happen if they learned what we know.

"No, honey, you've got to fight it out alone. It's pitiful, but you're going to be glad some day when you look back on it from happiness."

"Happiness!" she groaned. The word was loathsome, despicable. The possibility of it belittled her grief.

The doctor withdrew it. "I don't mean happiness, but some big, high peak of goodness. Your life is going to be lifted up because of this, if you'll only meet it as you must."

"Tell me what to do. Don't make me think. I've got too much to think about what's dead and gone."

Then she sobbed and sobbed till her eyes were drained again of tears.

The doctor was as weary as she wearier, for he had her burden to carry as well as his own.

He sought a little respite, not for relief, but for clear thinking. It was hard to think when a broken heart bled and leaped before his eyes.

"What you are to do is this: While I try to figure out the best plan for the future, you go along on home and tell your father and mother that you were here when Elwood was brought here. No, just go home with me and I'll tell them. I'll tell them the shock has prostrated you and that you mustn't be spoken to about it. You must be kept quiet, and when you cry you mustn't be questioned, just let alone."

"Can't mamma hold me in her arms? " the girl whimpered.

"Yes, and you can tell her the whole story if you want to."

"No, no! I can't! I won't! But I must have her arms around me. I must have arms around me to hold my heart together."

# CHAPTER V

THE DOCTOR HELPED the little widowed mourner into his old buggy, and she kept her face uplifted, clear of tears, through the streets and along the walk at home.

She broke only when she heard the doctor's voice telling what the father and mother who received them on the porch of their little house had already heard from a passing gossip. They stared amazed when Mem darted up the stairs without speaking, and they heard her crying in her room.

The doctor checked their pursuit and gave them his orders as if they were unruly children. When he had gone the mother stole up to Mem's bedside and gathered her baby to her breast. It would have been almost sweet to weep there if only the truth could have been voiced.

By and by the old clergyman crept up the stairs and into the room and gave his clumsy sympathy. But when he spoke of God's will and of the all-wise, all-loving Providence, Mem had to bite her tongue to keep it from blasphemy, from the savage delight of confounding the preacher with truths he could never have suspected. He even went so far as to plead that he had done wisely in keeping Mem from seeing Elwood oftener; otherwise she might have wanted to marry him.

This threw the girl into hysterics. She laughed so fiendishly that her mother drove her father from the room, and finally slipped away herself, knowing that solitude is the best medicine for that brief madness.

Alone with her soul, Mem grew afraid of herself. She knew

that she could not keep the truth choked back in her rebellious heart forever.

All night long she coughed and wept, and, fearing that the household kept anxious vigil, felt one more remorse added to her pack.

Next morning her father and her mother besought the doctor to come to see her. But he answered:

"Send her to me."

When they told her, she realized that he was afraid to talk to her in her own home, and she found strength enough to rise from her bed and go to him.

When Mem paused in his door until an onset of crying had passed, he almost smiled. She looked at him like a doomed animal and murmured as she dropped into a chair:

"Don't you suppose this cough will solve my problem and put an end to me before... before..."

He shook his head as he closed the door and went to his desk chair: "Your cough will take a long time to cure or kill. But it may come in very handy. I've got it all thought out. You can't stay in this town now, I suppose. Most of the animals crawl away and hide at such a time; so suppose you just vanish. Let your cough carry you off to say, Arizona or California."

She was startled at this undreamed-of escape. He went on:

"I'll tell the necessary lies. That's a large part of my practice. And practice makes perfect. You will go to some strange town and pose as a widow.

"You will marry an imaginary man out there and let him die quietly. Then, if you ever want to come home here, you can come back as Mrs. Somebody-or-other."

This reminded her again that she had others to think of besides herself. Her dazed soul, still trying to creep 'round the deep well of death, busied itself with the fantastic make-believe of the doctor. But she protested:

"How could I go any place and pretend to be a widow when papa and mamma would send all their letters to me as Miss Steddon?"

The doctor was ready for her. He would order Mem to be sent to the Far West immediately and to live meagerly in the desert somewhere, because her father was poor, being a parson, and had loved her too unwisely well to teach her a trade.

Once she was safely started, Mem was to write home that she had met on the train some old flame of earlier years and —

Here his hostile audience interrupted him. Life was slow in Calverly, and Mem could hardly imagine such a swift succession of events as Doctor Bretherick was so glibly planning for her. At any other time, to hear of going to California, or anywhere, would have been an epochal adventure. But Paradise was no longer within her rights. She had earned Sheol or some dire penance so well that it was ridiculous to propose romance, and romance in the Eden of palm trees and orange flowers. She revolted, too, from the pretense of having had another lover before Elwood:

"But I never had any flames."

The author was impatient at finding Pegasus held down to this tame hitching post of a life. He said:

"You've been away somewhere, haven't you?"

"Not much nor far," she sighed. "I was in Carthage once at Aunt Mabel's."

"Well, you must have left a lot of broken hearts there."

She sighed again as she shook her head. She was sadly glad to confess that no broken hearts had marked her path:

"Aunt Mabel was sick and I had to nurse her. That's how I got to go. The only men I met brought in the groceries and the mail."

"But you've got to have another sweetheart, honey. Your folks don't know that you never met anybody in Carthage. So we'll make one up."

"But they'd ask Aunt Mabel, and she'd say there was no such man there."

"Then we'll make him a traveling man that you met. You went to church, didn't you?"

"Oh yes!"

"Well, then, one day he occupied the pew with you and sang out of your book and walked home with you, and er, um, you had forgotten all about him until he recalled himself to you on the train, and he was so respectful that you couldn't snub him. And by a strange coincidence he was getting off at wherever you're going to get off at."

Mem was at her apple-blossom time. She was frosted a little with grief, but still white and fragrant, frail and lovable, difficult to leave upon the bough. He saw the tremor on her lips, the little zephyrs of hopeless amorous yearning that lifted her bosom, the soft, lithe fingers that intertwined with one another for lack of stronger hands to clasp. He said:

"You've got to forget yourself and your sorrow and your truthfulness for the sake of your mother and father, because —"

"Just tell me what to do — not why, but what. You must save me and them. I want to die, but it would be too easy, too selfish, too cowardly. Give me something to live for and I'll do my best. Only don't argue, don't argue!"

"That's the way to talk," he said. "Take my prescriptions as I give them to you, and we'll save everybody from destruction. But if you won't let me tell you why, you must ask no questions. I order you to go West and to find an imaginary husband there. His name shall be, let me see, what shall we call him? Wait a minute."

He reached back to an overcrowded revolving bookcase and took out the first volume his hands encountered. It was a history of medicine, and he was fond of it because it was also a history of the vanity of human science in its eternal war with death and of the bitter hostility that greeted every benefactor.

He rejected Galen, Harvey, Jenner, and came finally upon the name of Doctor Woodville, who went to the defense of Jenner in the great war for vaccination and helped to make the hideous ravages of smallpox as rare now as they were common in his time. Bretherick liked this name of Woodville.

He had sent patients to Tucson, which he pronounced "Tuckson," and also to Yuma, which had a wild and romantic sound. At each of these towns he planned that Mem should remain a week or two in her own name. In her letters home she was to say much of this Mr. Woodville and his devotion.

Then, as Doctor Bretherick's excited mental spinnerets poured out the web, she was to write that Mr. Woodville was called farther West and could not bear to leave her, pleaded with her so earnestly to become his wife and go with him, that her heart had told her to accept him. She was to describe a hasty marriage and request that her letters thereafter be addressed to her as "Mrs. Woodville."

After a brief honeymoon she could eliminate Doctor Woodville in some way to be decided at leisure. It would be risky, he said, to let Mr. Woodville live too long.

Mem had no experience of the dramatic limbo; but she began to play the critic and point out the difficulties and the spots where the action would break down:

"Suppose I met somebody at Yuma or Tuckson who knew me and wrote home. Suppose some accident kept me there. What if I fell ill and couldn't get away? And money; if I married Mr. Woodville, my father would stop sending me any, and then I'd starve to death."

The doctor frowned. His fancy had carried him skippingly over the high spots of the landscape, and now she had tripped him and cast him headlong. But he would not give her up. He pointed out the attractive features of his scheme, the travel, the new landscapes, the new faces and souls, the glorious adventures, the possibility of meeting a real Mr. Woodville who would replace the homemade product.

While he tried to sell the merchandise of his fancy, Mem's own imagination was riotous. She was young, starved for life, for other horizons. Death and disgrace were more untimely than her heart realized in its grief. The very perils of the enterprise made it a little interesting. But chiefly she found it acceptable because it was odious and difficult and a sacrifice for others' sakes. And so, at last she consented to play the part as best she could.

Mem rose to go. She was in haste to begin her career. But she gasped and sank into her chair with a deathly dread. Her first audience must be her father and mother, and she was paralyzed with stage fright, sick, dizzy with confusion and the abrupt collapse of memory.

Doctor Bretherick put his arm about her, lifted her to his breast, and upheld her like a tower of strength, quoting the words Walt Whitman used to the wounded soldier: "Lean on me! By God, I will not let you die."

Mem was not stirred by the doctor's promises of happiness and life, but only by the persuasion that she would be really proving her love for her parents by deceiving them. Doctor Bretherick offered to take the brunt of her first clash with her desperate future.

"I'll go home with you again and fix it all up with your papa and mamma. They'll take it kind of hard, likely, losing you right away, and they'll worry over your health and your going away alone; but we've got to do the best we can for their sweet sakes. If you stayed here you'd break your own heart and theirs and die in the bargain. My way saves your life and their pride. All they'll suffer will be losing the sight of you; but that's part of the job of being a parent.

"And part of the job of being a doctor is giving people a lot of pain to save them from a lot more, and scaring them for their own good. So, come along, honey."

As they set out upon the short ride to the clergyman's home the doctor felt as if he were advancing to a duel with an ancient adversary. He did not believe in Doctor Steddon's creeds. They were cruel legends, in his opinion. He pictured preachers as men who slander the beauties of this world in order to glorify a false heaven of their own concoction; who would make this world a joyless, barren hell in order to save its citizens from an imaginary nightmare of ancient ignorance; who minimize the hideous cruelties of this life and salve its agonies with words. He could not understand or love the God they preached. He did not believe their God to be the true God. His heart was full of love and of aspiration and of mystic bafflements and longings, but he was utterly convinced that whatever God might be, He was not this man-made God who inspired Doctor Steddon with such hatred of His world and its ways.

He advanced to the contest, therefore, with a lust of conflict. He felt himself a kind of Sir Gawain with a lady on the pillion, riding into a dark forest to conquer the giant ogre who denied her her realm.

But when he reached the castle he found it a humble cottage; the ogre was an undernourished old parson afraid of this world and the next, but most afraid of his beloved daughter's health. And at the ogre's side on the drawbridge the ogress was a frightened mother wringing wrinkled hands with terror.

Seeing Mem returning with the doctor, they had come out on the porch in trembling anxiety. They were already so abased of hope, that when the doctor told them that Mem would be all right if she could get away to California right away, they felt as if he had lifted them from the dust. He was not so much taking their ewe lamb from them as saving her to them.

They were fawningly grateful to him, zealous for any sacrifice to benefit their child. The doctor despised himself for a contemptible slanderer because of the mere thoughts that had passed through his mind on his way to the duel.

As for Mem, she was crucified with remorse. If her parents had only been harsh with her or stingy with the money she would require, if they had only mentioned the difficulties or celebrated their sacrifice as a duty, she could have found some straw to cling to as she drowned in self-contempt. But their terror and their tenderness were all for her, and her love for them gushed like hot blood until it seemed an inconceivable treachery to conceal from them the truth.

It was well that Doctor Bretherick came with her and stood by to check her outcry, for her heart was fairly bursting with the centrifugal explosive power of a compressed secret.

Doctor Bretherick kept her under the ward of his stern eyes until he had frightened the parents just enough and reassured them just enough to make sure that they would let Mem go, and go alone.

He gained a little acrid stimulant from Doctor Steddon's dread of seeing his innocent daughter leave the shelter of her home and go out into the dangerous world. The doctor knew too well from a doctor's long experience how far the beautiful ideal of the home is from the actual usual household. He knew too well that many a home keeps in more dreadful evils than it keeps out. But he could not say these things. He had a home of his own and a family of his own, and he revered the dream and the ideal.

And so the continuity began to move. At first it followed the doctor's manuscript with remarkable smoothness. Then Life, the ruthless Philistine manager, took a hand in it and twisted and turned it until its author would never have recognized it.

It carried the frightened waif of village disaster to cosmic heights unimaginable, to unheard-of experiences wherein this familiar experience of hers served as a schooling and an inspiration. Her degradation became her salvation; her practice of lies taught her eternal truths.

Her father, when he learned of this, wished that she had died in her cradle. But millions of people blessed her where she walked and smiled.

And by a miracle unequaled in the chronicle of any previous generation she walked and smiled and carried balm and spikenard all about the world without wings, yet with unwearying feet. She appeared in a hundred places at once by a diabolic telepathy in a multiplication that made of one shy, frightened girl a shining multitude. And at times each of her was of an elfin tininess, at times of titanic size. But all of her was always of more than human sympathy and spoke a language that men of every nation understood.

# CHAPTER VI

THAT CLERGYMAN'S HOME was really a theater. If there had been a cameraman to follow the various members about, it would have been what the moving-picture people call a "location."

The Reverend Doctor Steddon abhorred theaters or moving pictures and all forms of dramatic fiction (except his own sermons), yet everybody in the house was playing a part with benevolent purposes, of course. But then, benevolence is one of the motives of nearly all acting, to divert someone from his own distresses by exploiting imaginary joys or sorrows.

Vicarious atonement and all forms of vicarious activity are the actuating spirit of the vast industry of honorable artistic pretense that has flourished since the world was. All the world's a stage, as somebody has said, and everybody is always acting. If certain people charge money for acting, that means no more than the fact that most preachers charge money for preaching, and doctors for doctoring.

The acting in the Steddon home was of the most amateurish quality. But then, the audience was as amateurish as the playing, and collaborated, as audiences must if plays are to prosper.

The girl's role was the most difficult imaginable. She had to repress a hideous secret, conceal a frantic remorse, rein in a wild grief, and conduct it as a gentle regret.

She hated herself and her enforced hypocrisy. Romance had sickened in her like a syrup that bribes the palate and fills the stomach with nausea. Her secret was a vomit, and no easier or pleasanter to control. Her soul was so ill of it that her very throat retched.

Nausea was part of her condition, too, and would have tormented her if she had been the formal widow of Elwood instead of what Brander Matthews once phrased as "the unwedded mother of his unborn child."

She had been trained from childhood to believe herself a sinner lost in Adam's fall, and to search her heart for things to repent. She believed in an actual hell, and her terrors of the infernal griddles were as vivid as those that poor little seven-year-old Marjorie Fleming wrote down in her babyish diary.

She had great native gifts of self-punishment, a habit older than Christianity and found in all nations. Did not the Greeks and Latins have a comedy, "The Self-tormentor"? Mem was worthy of its long title. She was *heauten timoroumena*. Nothing made her more eager to get her gone from her hometown than her fear that at almost any moment she would reach the end of her histrionism, fling off the mask, and tell the venomous truth.

It was not merely a question of having to lie or to evade discovery. Mem had to dramatize herself, to foresee situations, and to force herself to be another self, to mimic sincerity and simplicity.

She was in the trite situation, familiar in the theater and in the poems and stories about the theater, where the broken-hearted mummer must conceal from the audience a personal grief.

It would have been easier if Mem had merely to play the clown, for hilarity could be carried off hysterically. But her role was one of half-tones, grays, and mild regrets.

Many people knew that she was fond of Elwood. Many girls and boys called to see her or dragged her to the telephone to offer consolation and satisfy curiosity. To them she must express a proper sorrow as a cordial friend without letting them treat her as too deeply involved. This was bitter work and she felt it a treachery to her dead lover.

To her mother she must play the same character. Her mother may have guessed that the tragedy was deeper than the revelation, but the poor old soul had had so much gloom in her life that she did not demand more than she got.

Doctor Steddon lived in such clouds that he had almost forgotten his refusal to let Elwood call on Mem. He knew that she had been at the doctor's office when Elwood was brought there, and the shock of this explained what confusion he recognized in Mem's manner.

He was acting, too, but his acting was the constant show of cheerfulness. He went about smiling, laughing, talking of Mem's swift recovery in the golden West. He said that they would all be glad to get rid of her for a spell. But his heart was a black ache of despair and fear of that death which he spoke of in the pulpit as a mere doorway to eternal bliss. His smiling muscles rebelled when he was alone and he paced his study like a frightened child, beating his hands together and whispering to his Father to spare him this unbearable punishment.

A hurricane struck the little town of Calverly on the day of Elwood's funeral. When Mem expressed a wish to sing with the choir at the service over their late fellow-singer, both mother and father forbade her to think of it. Her mother cried, "A girl who's got to be shipped out West has got no right to go out in weather like this."

Mem felt it a crowning betrayal of Elwood to let him be carried out to a pauper's grave in such merciless rain. Her heart urged her to dash through the streets, burst into the church, and proclaim to the world how she adored the boy. But she had to protect her father and mother from such selfish self-sacrifice and such ruthless atonement.

So she stayed at home and stared through the streaming windows. She saw her poor old father set out to preach the funeral sermon.

He had that valor of the priests which leads them to risk death in order to defeat death; to endure all hardship lest the poorest soul go out of the world without a formal conge. Doctor Steddon clutched his old overcoat about him and plunged into rain that hatched the air in long, slanting lines. He had not reached the gate when his umbrella went upward into a black calyx. He leaned it against the fence and pushed on. Then his hat blew off and skirled from pool to pool. He ran after it, his hair aflutter, his bald spot spattering back the rain.

Miss Steddon was not missed at the church, for there was nobody there to miss her. The whole choir saved its voice by staying away. Only the Farnaby family went dripping up the aisle and back.

The hearse and two hacks moped past the window where Mem watched. On the boxes the drivers sat, the shabbiest men on earth at best, but now peculiarly sordid as they slumped in their wet overcoats, disgusted and dejected, their hats blown over their faces, their whips aggravating the misery, but not the speed, of the sodden nags that might have wished it their own funeral.

Mem had to leave the window. Her impulse was to run out and follow the miserable cortege, to tear wet flowers from the gardens and strew the road with them, to fill the grave with them and shelter Elwood from the pelting rain. It was a funeral like that in which Mozart's body was lost and, like his widow, Mem had to mourn at home.

It was her meek fear of being dramatic and conspicuous that saved her from the temptation to publish her concern. But she stumbled up to her room and let her grief have sway. She smothered her sobs as best she could in the old comforter of her bed, but the other children heard her and asked questions. Her mother kept them away from her and did not go near herself, feeling that this was one of the times when sympathy gives most comfort by absence.

When her eyes were faint with exhaustion and could squeeze no more tears, when her thorax could not jerk out another sob, her soul lay becalmed in utter inanition. Then she heard a hack drive up to the gate and heard her father's hurried rush for the porch.

The old man was chilled through by his graveside prayer, but forgetful of himself in the exaltation of his office, and all ababble of pity for his client.

Mem heard her mother scolding him out of his wet clothes into dry, but he kept up his chatter:

"It isn't always easy to find nice things to say at funerals, but there was everything fine to be said over that poor boy, a good, hard-working lad that slaved for his mother and went to church regular, and, why, I don't suppose he ever had an evil thought."

Mem sank into a chair by her window. The rain whipped the panes and the wind rattled them in the chipped putty that held them to the casement.

The last few days had kept her thoughts so busy that she had neglected her housewifery a little. She was shocked to see that a spider had spread a web from the shutter to the vine.

The gale had torn the web to shreds and was threatening to rip it loose. The spider, sopping and pearled with rain, was having a desperate battle to keep from being swept away. He clung and caught new holds as a sailor clutches the shrouds in a tempest.

The girl felt a kinship with the poor beastie. Her soul and her body were like spider and web, and a great storm menaced them both. Her flesh seemed but a frail network that spasms of sobbing or of coughing threatened to tear to pieces.

Her soul was a loathsome arachnid spinning traps for flies, and storms of remorse and grief threatened to dislodge it and send it down the wind of eternity. But still her body clung to life and her soul to her body.

She began to long to be shut of the town, however, and the dull playhouse where she enacted over and over the same dull drama to the same dull audience.

Her father and mother drove her almost mad by their devoted gentleness. Hitherto they had both been strict, and a little tiresome with moral lessons and rebukes, making goodness a dull staple suspiciously over-advertised, and creating rebellion by discipline.

But after the doctor's first visit they heaped almost intolerable coals of fire upon her head with their devoted faith in her. If they had any doubts of her future it was only of the wicked people outside the fold who would attack and beguile their ewe lamb. They never suspected her of even the capacity for sin, though she felt that it was she who had seduced her sacred lover, and not he her.

At times her parents treated her with that unquestioning approval we grant only to the newly dead, and the unmerited homage was harder to endure than unearned blame, since it had a belittling influence where the other would have aroused self-esteem.

She was no longer at home at home. She had to draw on a mask the moment she came in. When she went to the doctor's office she encountered truth and the frank facing of it; she could be herself, a normal young animal who had done a natural thing, unluckily, and had lost none of her rights to life, wealth, or the pursuit of happiness. When she stepped off the Bretherick porch she was a very allegory of defiant youth; when she stepped on to her own porch she became immediately a Magdalen bowed with a shame she dared not even ask forgiveness for.

It was particularly hard to act a part all day long, and every day, since she had never been an actress before. If her audience of two had had more familiarity with the art, she might not have succeeded in duping both so completely. But they never dreamed of the truth. Deceiving them was so easy that she despised herself. Especially she loathed herself for taking their paltry savings. They had foreseen the cruel days that lie ahead of superannuated preachers, and had somehow managed to put away a little hoard against the inevitable famine, though this meant that even their prosperity was always just this side of pauperdom.

But they lavished their tiny wealth upon their scapegrace daughter and never imagined that the real cause for her spend-thrift voyage was to save herself and them from the catastrophe of a public scandal.

Money is always the most emotional of human concerns, though it is the least celebrated in romance.

Again and again Mem revolted at the outrage of robbing her own parents of their one shield against old age. She went again and again to Doctor Bretherick and demanded that he release her from her promises not to tell the truth and not to kill herself. But he compelled her to his will, and she was too glad for a will to replace her own panic to resist him. For a necessary stimulant, he prophesied that somehow in that land of gold she was seeking she would find such wealth that she could repay her parents their loan — with usury, with wealth, perhaps. Who knew?

"In these times," he said, "it's the girls who are running away from home to find their fortunes. And lots of 'em are finding 'em.

"Your dear old fool of a father is always preaching about the good old days when women were respected and respectable, when parents were revered and took care of their children. As my boy says, where does he get that stuff?

"He knows better! Why does he have to lie about it so piously? Why don't they use some plain horse sense, some truth with a little t in the pulpit once in a while and not so much Truth with a capital T?

"In the good old days the best parents used to whip their children nearly to death; the poor ones bound them out as apprentices into child slavery, chained 'em to factories for fourteen hours a day. They had no child-labor laws, no societies for prevention of cruelty to children, no children's court, no Boy Scouts or Girl Scouts, and the wickedness was frightful. And as for the grown-up girls, most of them had no education and no chance for ambition. If they went wrong they could go to a convent, or slink around the back streets, or go out and walk the streets at night. The drunkenness and debauchery and disease were hideous. Even the Sabbath-breaking and skepticism were universal. But still they call 'em the good old days.

"And they dare to praise them above these glorious days when women are for the first time free. And men were never free, either, 'till now; for men had the responsibility of women's souls on their own. And my God! What a burden it was and how they boggled it!

"This is really the year One. Now at last a girl like you can look life in the face, and if she makes a mistake she can make her life worthwhile and not fall into the mewling, puling, parasite and disease germ of the good old-fashioned woman. You ought to thank God for letting you live now, and you've got to show Him how much you prize the golden opportunity. It's just sun-up; this is the dawn of the day when man and woman are equal and children have a clean sky overhead.

"I was reading the other day a list a mile long of self-made women who had begun poor and finished rich. Some of 'em made their wealth out of candy and some of 'em in Wall Street;

some of 'em in all sorts of arts, paintings, novels, plays, music, acting. You might go into the movies, for instance, and make more money than Coal Oil Johnny.

"It's scandalous what some of those little tykes are earning. I tell you, Mem, if you've got any spunk you'll make yourself a millionairess. All this suffering is education. All this acting you're doing may show you the way to glory. Go West, young woman, and go up in the world!"

"I've never been anywhere or seen anything. I've never even seen a movie," said Mem.

"Well, as the feller said who was asked if he could play the violin, he didn't know, he'd never tried. When you get a safe distance from any danger of giving your pa apoplexy, sneak into a movie and see if you see anything you can't do. Looks like to me you might cut quite a swath there. Prob'ly you'd have to learn to ride a horse, throw a lassoo, and dance; but fallin' off trains and bein' spilled off cliffs in automobiles oughtn't to take much talent. And it can't be very risky, since I see the same young ladies runnin' the same gantlets and comin' up smilin' in the next picture. There's a serial at the Palace once a week that shows one wide-eyed lassie who is absolutely bullet-proof. They can't drown that girl, burn her, freeze her, or poison her. She laughs at gravity, bounces off roofs and cliffs and bobs up serenely from below. Her throat simply can't be throttled; she can take care of herself anywheres. Why, I've seen her overpower nearly a hundred bandits so far, and she looks fresher than ever. If I was you I'd take a whack at it."

"Do they have movies in Tuckson?"

"I think likely. I hear they've got 'em on both Poles, North and South."

Mem imbibed mysterious tonics at the doctor's office, and always came away buoyed up with the feeling that her tragedy was unimportant, commonplace, and sure to have a happy finish.

But the moment she reached home she entered a demesne where everything was solemn, where jokes were never heard, except pathetic old witticisms more important in intention than in amusement.

They began to irritate her, to wear her raw and exacerbate her tenderest feelings. She was beginning to be ruined by the very influences that should have sweetened her soul.

And at last, one day, quite unexpectedly, when she was under no apparent tension at all, when her father had gone to visit a sick parishioner and her mother was quietly at work upon Mem's traveling clothes, the girl reached the end of her resources.

Perhaps it was a noble revolt against interminable deceit. Perhaps it was a selfish impulse to fling off a little of her back-breaking burden of silence. Perhaps it was a mad desire to make someone else a partner in her lies. Perhaps it was the unendurable hum of her mother s sewing machine.

Whatever it was that moved her, she rose quietly, put down her needlework, went into Mrs. Steddon's room, closed the door, took her mother's hands from the cloth they were guiding, and said, in a quiet tone:

"Mamma, I want to tell you something. I'd rather break your heart than deceive you any longer."

"Why, honey! What's the matter? Why, Mem dear, what on earth is it? Sit down and tell your mother, of course. You can't break this tough old heart of mine. What is it, baby?"

She whispered it so softly that her breath was hardly syllabled. Her mother caught less the words than the hiss and rustle of her awe and the wild language of her trapped eyes:

"Mamma, I-I'm going to have, to have a baby."

The shock was its own ether. Mrs. Steddon whispered back, cowering:

"You? You! My baby! You? A baby?"

Mem nodded and nodded 'till her knees were on the floor and her brow in her mother's lap. Old hands came gropingly about her cheeks. She felt the drip, drip of tears falling into her hair, each tear a separate pearl from a crown of pride.

Then the shivering hands at her cheeks lifted her face and she stared up, as much amazed as her mother, in whose downward stare there was no horror or reproach, only compassion and infinite fear. And her mother fumbled at the dreadful question:

"But who, who..."

"Elwood."

The hands upholding her head dropped limp. The eyes above her were dry, blank, and ghastly: the mind behind them baffled beyond effort. Then they grew human again with a sudden throb of tears upon tears. And her mother groaned with double pity.

"Poor baby! Poor Mem! Poor little thing!"

Grandmothers acquire a witchlike knowledge of life. They know the things that may not be published. They see the cruel wickednesses of the world overwhelming their own beloved ones, and an awful wisdom is theirs. They know something of the mockery of punishment and they are usually derided by the less experienced for their lax ideas of the miserable bungling called justice.

Mem's confession was an annunciation of grandmother-hood to Mrs. Steddon. She was so stunned that she expressed no horror at the abyss of horror yawning before her feet. Two instincts prevailed while her reason was in a stupor: love of her husband, love of her child.

The decision was easy, and she made no difficulty of the gross deceits involved. Her husband must be protected in his illusions and protected from the necessity of wreaking his high moral principles on his own child. His child must be protected from the merciless world and the immediate wrath of the village.

She said little; she caressed much. She confirmed Doctor Bretherick's prescription and joined the conspiracy, administering secret comfort to the girl and to the father.

The nearer the day of Mem's departure, the slower dragged the hours between. But at last she was standing on the back platform of a train bound for the vast Southwest. She was throwing tear-sprent kisses to her father and mother as they blurred into the distance.

They watched the train dwindling like a telescope drawn into itself, as so many parents have watched so many trains and ships and carriages vanish into space with the beloved of their hearts and bodies.

They turned back to their lives as if they had closed a door upon themselves.

But Mem, as she returned to her place in the car, felt as if a portcullis had lifted. Before her was All-Outdoors.

# CHAPTER VII

THE WHEELS RAN WITH a rollicking lilt beneath the girl's body, throbbing likewise with a zest of velocity. Through her head an old tune ran that she had often sung with the homecoming crowds on church picnics:

> I saw the boat go 'round the ben',
> The deck was filled with traveling men.
> Good-by, my lover, goodbye!"

She was on a train going 'round bend after bend, and the train was filled with traveling men. Some of them, as they zigzagged along the aisles, swept her face and her form with glances like swift, lingering hands that hated to let her go. This was a startling sensation, a new kind of nakedness for her inexperienced soul.

The eyes of the women flung along the aisle also widened and tarried as they recognized in her something she had not yet found out: that she was very, very pretty, attractive, compulsive. She was like a magnet that had never met iron filings before, had never learned the mystery and could not understand it, as we think we understand what is merely familiar.

She was plainly dressed and had never been adorned. Only her neatness kept her from shabbiness. But she had beauty and appeal, the appeal of a ripe peach grown in somebody's orchard but thrust out over a wayside fence to tempt the passer-by. Some of the men who saw her did not care for peaches, or had had their fill of them, and regarded her with indifference. But others looked hungry, or at least betrayed an academic approval.

Such of the women as had no instinct of jealousy were gladdened by her prettiness and her youth, and felt that she brightened the roadside and sweetened the air. Others saw in her a rival, a danger; and suspicion narrowed their lids. They consoled themselves with the thought that she was wicked and worthless, an opinion which they could not know she shared with them.

On the train Mem had planned to do a bit of thinking. But after the first exultance of escape and the thrill of speed she relapsed into despondency and fear, fear of everything and everybody. She had still to act, but she was a strolling player now with an ever-changing audience. And this gave her a new kind of stage fright. The only familiar companion was remorse. She could not run away from that. Running away was a new subject for remorse.

She thought of herself as a convict, escaped breathless from a deserved punishment, to a wilderness of uncertainties, as a trusty who has betrayed the confidence of a kindly warden and rewarded confidence with deceit.

She had expected to find on the journey leisure for contrition and the remolding of her soul. But the world would not let her alone. Everything was new to her. Everything was a crowded film of novelty.

She knew the minimum of the outside sphere possible to a girl who had had any education at all.

She had never been on a sleeping car before.

She had read no novels except such sweetened water as the Sunday-school library afforded. She had seen no magazines at home except the church publications; and her girlfriends happened to be infrequent readers of fiction.

Calverly had no bookstore and the newsstands did little trade in the periodicals that are credited with the ruin of the young when the critics have time enough to spare from the theater and moving picture and the dance.

She had never been to a theater or a moving picture. She had never danced even a square dance, not so much as a Dan Tucker, a Virginia reel, or a minuet in costume.

She had never ridden a bicycle or a horse, and had never been in any automobile except some old bone-shaker that drowned conversation in its own rattle.

She had never gambled, or been profane or even slangy or disrespectful to her parents. She had never seen a cocktail.

She had never worn a low-necked, high-skirted dress. She had never seen a bathing suit or had one on. Girls did not swim in the river at Calverly. In fact, she had escaped all the things that moralists point to as the reasons why girls go wrong. Yet she had, as the saying is, gone wrong utterly, indubitably.

Yet no fast young men had led her astray, or so much as tried to lead her astray. She had never made the acquaintance of a fast young man. Her betrothed lover was slow and honorable and religious, everything a young man ought to be. But, unfortunately for her, one of the things a young man ought to be, must be if he is a man, is passionate; otherwise he can never be a husband or a father; and a woman cannot be a good wife and mother if she lacks those fires which burn when they escape and which no power has ever kept from occasional untimely escape.

And so, on a Sabbath evening the solemn young man to whom she was affianced had been somehow impelled, by seeing through the window her parents kissing her goodnight, to want to add his kiss to theirs. On the porch that frowned out the heathen moon he had held her hand a little more straightly than was his wont. He had drawn her to him and moved toward her. There seemed to be volition in neither of them; they just floated together with a mysterious bewilderment.

She had looked up in questioning surprise at the hot strength of his handclasp. He had looked down at her in questioning surprise at the unusual beauty of her shadow-blotted face. Not seeing her at all, she was somehow more beautiful than ever, since imagination had free sweep. And who can give laws to imagination?

Their lips had moved together by the same amazing attraction. The hasty brushing of her mouth with his had been like the drawing of a match along a kindling surface, and he had been impelled to return for another kiss, a longer kiss, the strangest kiss that either had ever known. And then a strange, a terrifying, irresistible mood had imbued them both. His arms were suddenly like fierce serpents about her, ruthless with constriction. Her arms were serpents suddenly.

They seemed to feel a necessity for becoming one; their hearts were turned to a sweet, shivering, poisonous jelly. Their blinded eyes were clenched to shut out the world and shut in the heaven that lifted them as on the little wings of cherubim.

Mem closed her eyes in a sudden return of memory like a re-experience. She almost swooned with a terror of remembrance, and her repentance seemed to flee, contemptible and ridiculous, as her reason had fled from that first visit of romance.

She was astounded at herself. She felt a hypocrite even to herself. She was not really sorry! She could never trust herself to learn. In spite of all that had proved the folly and the evil of her mistake, she wondered if it would not always recur to her as somehow a divine madness wiser far than any earthly reason.

Her brain was scorched with a furious thought whipping through it like a laughing flame. A mocking Lilith seemed to be laughing at her holier self. A new being inside her soul was rejoicing that she had given herself in all ecstasy to Elwood before he died. Even if he were damned for it, it seemed well that he should not have left this earth and this flesh without knowing its Paradise.

There was neither marrying nor giving in marriage where he had gone, and their reunion would have been a bodiless greeting of ghosts if this sweet world had not overwhelmed them and their worldly frames with its supreme rapture.

Elwood had never known anything but poverty, hard work, poor food, none of the silk and satin, none of the revelry and the wine and the splendor of the world. He had known nothing rich but her love.

He had been caught at his self-denial, putting a little of his earnings into the pitiful savings he had achieved. He had been struck as with a great shell and shattered like the splintered glass that filled his poor, crushed body. He had died fighting against any outcry of protest or of pain. He had died muttering something that nobody knew but she felt that he was stammering her name with his all-obliterated lips.

And her body was one music, her members chanted a triumphant song, because his body had known the symphonic music of her love.

Then the rhapsody died away. The Lilith vanished from her mood, and the little gray Puritan named Remember came back to the profaned shrine of her soul, aghast, incredulous, revolted. Romance had turned to a gargoyle of grotesque and obscene ugliness. She could not believe herself or trust her own profoundest faiths again.

She was afraid and felt herself condemned to destruction. She was a scapegoat going out into the wilderness, but capable of sudden frenzies of pride in her burden of sin, incapable of shaking it off, afraid of being lonely without it.

She returned slowly from the blind voyage of her soul into the invisible and wondered what had passed before her eyes in the long interim. She was learning to know herself and in herself to know humanity. Her ignorance had been abysmal. To those who can believe ignorance beautiful, it had been ideal. There was peace of a sort in those sheltered canyons, but now she was climbing the mountains, the crags. She would see strange snows, strange flowers, exquisite deserts, smothering Edens.

The clanking uproar of the entrance into Kansas City filled her ears and drove away the music of the fiends. Factories, warehouses, freight trains, roundhouses, warning bells at street crossings where watchmen stood with flags before long bars, all the usual noisy bustle of approach to a large town assailed her. The train seemed to hurry, though it went more slowly. It was the plenitude of objects of interest that gave it the illusion of speed, as it is in the passage of a life.

Mem had never seen a great city, and this metropolis had a tremendous majesty in her eyes.

Some of the passengers from Eastern points were getting off and she was fascinated to see how the porter whisk-broomed their coats and hats and palmed their tips with an almost dancing rhythm. One of the portly women passengers, whose voice had out clicked the wheels, asked the porter how long the train would stop, and when the diplomat said, "Eight minutes, miss," she made a loud declaration of her intention to stretch her legs.

Others made ready for a breath of air. And so did Mem, who was spying and eavesdropping on everybody, picking up what hints she could to disguise her ignorance of travel and appear as a complete railroader.

The passengers choked the straight corridor along the row of compartments, and Mem took her place in the line. One of the doors opened and framed a tall and powerful young man with a peculiarly wistful face. His eyes brushed Mem and he lifted his hat as he asked her pardon for squeezing past her.

He knocked at another steel door and called through, "Oh, Robina, better come out for a bit of exercise."

While he waited, some of the passengers were twisting their necks to watch him, and nudging and whispering to one another. When the door opened and Robina stepped out there was such a sensation and such a boorish staring that Mem turned to look.

A young woman of an almost dazzling beauty came out, smiling and bareheaded. She noted the yokelry in the corridor, and her smile died. She stepped back into her state room, and when she reappeared, she wore a large drooping hat and a thick black veil.

"I envy you the privilege of the veil," the young man said. Mem could not hear her answer, for the passengers began to move out, and she was carried forward with them to the steps and the station platform into a morass of handbags and red-capped negro porters. She escaped the tangle and found a clear space for her promenade.

It gave her extraordinary exhilaration to be in a strange city. It was Cathay to her.

Mem walked up and down the platform as if her feet were winged. There was a delightful frightfulness about wondering what she would do if the engine started suddenly. She would like to run and swing aboard like a professional train-man. When she saw that the engine had unlinked itself and departed into the distance beyond the cave of the station, she felt safe enough to explore all the way up to the baggage car.

The baggage men and mail crew looked at her with that new way these foreigners had of looking at her, and she turned back.

The other passengers trudging up and down stared at her — the men especially — all except the tall young fellow with the veiled lady. The rest were a funny lot, bareheaded or in traveling caps. She noted how they followed the tall young man and commented on his partner. But she could not catch their words.

Some of the strollers bought things to eat from boys who carried baskets of oranges, chocolate, chewing gum, and cigars. Mem felt a longing to buy something for the sheer sport of buying. But she had no money for extravagances.

Still, when she saw a newsman with a cargo of magazines, she could not resist the appeal. She would charge it off to education. She went so far as to buy two magazines devoted to the moving pictures. She had the curiosity of Blue Beard's final wife concerning that forbidden closet.

As she was picking out the exact change from the small money in her purse, one of the magazines slipped from under her elbow and fell to the ground.

She turned and stooped to recover it. Her hand touched a hand that had just anticipated hers. She looked up quickly and her head knocked off the hat of the man who had tried to save her the trouble of picking up her magazine. Their noses were so close together that he seemed to have only one Cyclopean eye.

Each thinking that the other had the priority, both stood up with a nervous laugh. She saw that the gallant was the tall youth who had crushed past her in the corridor.

His face vanished from her sight as he bent again to pick up her magazine and his hat. Then his face came up again like a sun dawning across her horizon; his eyes beat upon her like long beams. There was a kind of pathos in them, but also a great brightness, which, like the sun, he poured upon millions alike. But Mem did not know this. She felt warmed and healed, and she bloomed a trifle as a rose does when the sun gilds it. Meanwhile, with great calm and as much of a bow as he could make without a sense of intrusion, the young man solemnly offered Mem his own hat and laid her magazine on his head.

Then both of them laughed as he corrected the automatic mistake of his muscles. He blushed hotly, for he was not used to such blunders.

Mem found an amazing magnetism in his smile and in his eyes. She did not know that that sad smile of his was making a millionaire of him. He was selling it by the foot, thousands of feet of it. His smile was broad enough to circumscribe the world and his eyes had enough sorrow for all the audiences.

He did not take advantage of the opportunity for further conversation, but bowed again and turned back to the waiting Robina, leaving Mem in a kind of abrupt shadow, as if the sun had gone under a cloud. Robina was evidently not used to being kept waiting. She had had little practice. She resented the slight with such quick wrath that Mem could hear her protesting sarcasm, a rather disappointing rebuke:

"Don't hurry on my account, Tom." So his name was Tom! All that grandeur and grace, and only Tom for a title!

Robina's voice was not magnetic. But then, she was not selling her voice.

Mem was in such a flutter that she dropped her purse, the coins popping about like cranberries. Robina saw the catastrophe, but she had seen women drop things on purpose when men were near, and she held Tom's arm so that he could neither see the disaster nor lend his aid again.

As Mem knelt and plucked up a penny here, a quarter there, two young girls assailed Robina's prisoner with shameless idolatry. She paused, kneeling, and listened. One of them rattled on:

"Oh, Mr. Holby, we knew you the minute we laid eyes on you. You're our fave-rite of all the screen stars, and, Oh dear! if we only had our autograft albums with us. You got no photografts with you, have you?"

The other girl broke in jealously: "O, course he hasn't. What you think he is, a freak in a muzhum? But couldn't you, wouldn't you send us one apiece? I'll give you the address if you'll lemme a pensul."

Tom was indomitably polite, and, besides, it was bad business to snub an admirer. He was actually about to write their addresses in his notebook, when the conductor's long far call, "All aboard!" gave Robina an excuse to drag him away from the worshipers.

One of the girls groaned, "He got away, darn it!"

The other, in an epilepsy of agitation, wailed: "Say, looky! That lady under the veil is Robina Teele! Gee! and we didn't recognize her!"

Thus the Greeks were also stricken with a panic of reverence when the gods came down to earth.

But Mem did not know or worship these gods. She had only a vague impression of what was going on as she snatched at the last of her available coins and ran to the train. The porter had already put up his little box step.

The loss of any petty sum meant a privation, but her regret was swallowed in her vivid realization of what it would have meant to be left there in that town.

She was panting hard with fright when she sank into her place, and the train was emerging from the retreating walls of the city before she felt calm enough to examine her magazines.

On the cover of one of them was a huge head of Robina Teele, all eyes and curls and an incredibly luscious mouth. Remember had never heard of her or seen her pictures, because her films were great "feature specials," too expensive for the villages.

In the body of the magazine was a long article about her, and another about Tom Holby.

This was not so amazing a coincidence as it seemed to Mem, for both Robina Teele and Tom Holby had press agents who would have been chagrined if any motion-picture periodical had appeared without some blazon of their employers.

Mem stared longest at the various pictures of Tom Holby. She found him in all manner of costumes and athletic achievements, and she read the rhapsody on him first.

Having never seen a moving picture of anybody, she had never seen his. She had never seen a still picture of him, either, because he was not as yet important enough to be starred, and only such greedy pantheists as the young girls on the platform were as yet aware of him.

Mem was dumfounded to realize how ignorant she was. Here were people so important that people stared at them and begged for their pictures, while magazines published glowing tributes to them. And she had never heard of them!

Now that she saw him in print, her heart fairly simmered

with the thrill of her encounter with him. It was as if she had knocked the hat off King David as he bent to pick up her harp for her. She forgot for a long while that she was a respectable widow of a very poor sort, for it came to her in an avalanche of shame that she was neither respectable nor a widow.

But she was a fugitive now from her past and from such thoughts, and she caught up the magazines with a desperate eagerness, as if they were cups of nepenthe.

# CHAPTER VIII

DOCTOR STEDDON WOULD HAVE  sent up a new kind of prayer if he could have seen his daughter guzzling at the profane literature that had fallen into her hands.

The first of the magazines was devoted to articles about the famous film stars and their families, philosophies, and fads. Men and women, some of whose faces had stared at her from the billboards of Calverly, were presented here in mufti. Here was a dare-devil cowboy seated on the porch of a gorgeous home, with a delicious baby in his arms. Here were beautiful leading men smoking pipes and reading books or cuddling dogs. Here were women of all types, many of them evidently wealthy and all of them intensely domestic.

It was surprising how many of the prettiest of them were dandling babies. Womanlike, Mem cooed and gurgled at the fat babies. One of them sent a wonderful sweet pang through her heart. For the first time she felt a welcome and a love for the mysterious visitor whose secret couriers had caused her such a frenzy of terror.

For the first time her soul yearned within her, and her curiosity to see what her child would look like and be like overcame every other feeling. She had hoped to die. Now she wanted to live to solve this mystery story in nine installments. She felt for the first time pride in her amazing power.

She read every word of the first magazine, including the advertisements. Then a white-aproned waiter marched through the car, crying: "Fir scall flunch in dinin caw. Firs scall flunch dine caw."

The trek to the dining car was another new experience. The prices were terrifying, but the new dishes were educational. She chose the cheapest, but they were spiced with the sauce of novelty. She had never eaten at sixty miles an hour. It was strange to start to lift your fork and have it reach your mouth a hundred feet away. You might lift your spoon from your teacup in one county and have it reach your lips in another. There was much landscape between the cup and the lip. The view outside her dining room at home had never changed except from winter to summer. But here the world went racing past.

The man opposite her was unpleasantly interested in her thoughts. He lacked both the beauty and the homage of Mr. Tom Holby. Her animation, the restlessness of her eyes, her cheeks swimming with color, misled him into thinking she was trying to strike up a flirtation. He had no appetite for a flirtation even with so pretty a thing, but if she wished it, it was his duty to play the game.

Mem could not understand the Samaritan gallantry of this. She hated him and stared at the scooting scenery. Then she found that she was still staring at the man since he was reflected on the window. Then she stared at her food.

She lingered longer than was necessary in the hope that Mr. Holby and Miss Teele would visit the diner, but they did not appear.

She returned to her car and took up the second magazine. This was also devoted to the screen people, but it was more ambitious artistically. Some of the pictures were in colors, or laid on tinted backgrounds, and many of them were so audacious that Mem felt it hardly proper for her to look at them in the miscellaneous company of the sleeping car. Of course it was her duty to throw the accursed thing away; but then, she thought with profound sorrow, she was not doing her duty much nowadays.

Being an abandoned creature, anyway, she abandoned herself to this amazing repository of intimacies. Being a preacher's daughter, she also told herself that if she threw it away it might fall into the hands of people it would do more harm to.

Here were women of opulent beauty in tremendous hats, with Niagaral plumes, in skirts voluminous enough to conceal a family. There were others with almost nothing on at all. Some of these had a perfection of figure of which they submitted all the evidence. Some of them rejoiced in postures as extravagant as their costumes were parsimonious. Some of them had clutched a few furs or silks about them just barely in time, and looked so startled and so shy that Mem wondered why they had permitted the pictures to be published at all. She had not yet learned how much a baby stare conceals. She had not learned that she herself, for all her experience, looked at the world with a baby stare.

There were a few portraits of men even more garbless, foreign dancers and Americans in barbaric decorations. There was an article about a Cubist painter whose mad paintings made Mem's head ache. There was an article about a titled Englishman of fame who was going to write moving pictures.

There was a bevy of contestants for a beauty prize, the winner to be given a position in a movie studio. These girls came from all over the country; they hailed from villages, small towns, and the obscurer regions of big cities. They were labeled as "Miss X, stenographer; Miss Z, shopgirl; Miss Y, home girl"; and so on.

They had tricked themselves out in makeshift splendor, posed themselves in mimicry of famous stars, their hair down, their eyes up, their hands and feet draped in what they thought artistic poses. Some of them were very pretty and all of them ambitious to sway the world and garner wealth.

Wearied a little by the hubbub of beauty and its advertisement, Mem put the two magazines aside. They seemed to be hot with curious flames that strangely did not shrivel the paper. The people who were celebrated there by name and face and figure must, if there were any truth in her father's faith, be lost souls, damned to blister in their unshriveling skins forever. But how little they must know of their destinies! Or, if they knew, how little they cared! How sleek and passionate and glad they were, and how richly clothed! Richly unclothed, some of them; for the least attired had on the most jewels.

Mem glanced down at her own shabby skirt, and realized for the first time what a little Puritan she was: her knees so modestly drawn together, her elbows clamped in, her hands embracing each other like Babes in the Wood, her meek head bowed a little, her eyes generally lowered except for some brief dart upward as if she stood atiptoe for a moment.

Suddenly she was aware of her flesh in a way almost unknown before. From her earliest infancy the first duty imposed upon her had been modesty. She had always been pulling down her skirts and up her bodice, keeping herself inconspicuous. Even her loud laughter brought down the candle snuffer of reproof.

As far back into her babyhood as she could recollect, her mother had bathed her with averted gaze and kept the towels about her. Later, when she had attained the dignity of being too big to be seen and washed by her own mother, she had been instructed to keep herself concealed even from her own eyes. She had been warned that God was everywhere; His sleepless eyes were not even turned away in a bathroom. She had asked her mother once:

"Why does God go round peeking at people and doing things you tell me are not nice? Isn't God a good gentleman?"

Her mother had been properly shocked and answered innocence with horror. Mem had never even wondered for a moment if God had not been slightly misrepresented. It had never occurred to her that perhaps his poor, half-witted worshipers were endowing him with their own weak intellects, slandering him with their stupid reverence, and enforcing their own silly prejudices upon souls far wiser, though lacking the fearlessness of bigotry.

As a result of her reproved curiosities, Mem hardly knew herself. Her father had never maintained the earlier Christian doctrine that to bathe at all was a heathen abomination, a pollution of the soul under the guise of cleansing the loathsome flesh. Yet bathing in the Steddon home had been a rite of sanitation, not of luxury; a godly scrubbing, not a loitering in the perfumed depths of porcelain tubs. God had made perfume, but he wanted it left in the flowers to die and stink with them. And perfume was expensive as well as wicked. Mem had been able to afford only the least costly of sins, the sin that the poorest can pay for.

As she sat staring into the window, the landscape leaping past the double glass with its own glimmer of lights, she tried to fancy herself like one of those twisted girls who admitted the public to a bathroom acquaintance. She tried to imagine herself with most of her clothes in her headdress, and all her limbs exploited for the inspection of strangers, and her body contorted to show how limber it was and how smoothly round. Her fancy could not make the distance.

Yet she read in one of these magazines a statement that one of those peculiar women, this very Robina Teele, indeed was being paid more dollars for one week's publicity than her father was paid for four years of saving souls. The press agent may have squandered a cipher or shifted the decimal point a little, but Mem could not know that, and she was convinced that the world was all wrong somewhere. Plainly. No wonder people said it was going to perdition. She wondered what such women could be like at heart and at home.

As she glanced through the pages of answers to correspondents — and how countless the questioners seemed to be! — her eye caught this paragraph:

MAME L. — Yes, dearie, she will send you a photograph if you will send her 25 cents. Sorry to break your heart, but he is married. Tom Holby isn't, though, so far as I know. How much he gets is his own secret and the income-tax collector's, but it was stated that he lately refused an offer of a thousand a week to desert the company that made him what he yam today. Such loyalty deserves a posy.

Mem closed the magazine with a gasp. That young man refused a thousand a week! and her father had never had more than five hundred a year. And her father saved souls from hell, while men like Holby led them there in droves and would follow in God's good time.

She did not feel any impulse to rush to Tom Holby and warn him to flee from his doom. She simply hated him for selling his soul to the devil at such a price. She did not even admire him for cheating the devil. She just hated him and the cat-eyed Robina and all this Babylonian horde of scarlet women.

And then she heard a voice across her shoulder, a voice of

peculiar and unpleasant softness. She had read somewhere of a velvet voice. This one was of plush.

She felt uneasy before she turned her head and almost bumped noses with the woman who spoke. At this close range her resemblance to a doll was astounding; the eyes were vast and glassy, the nose a pug, the mouth full and thick with paint, the face smeared white and red, the hair kinky yellow, as if it were made of hobby-horses tails.

The voice of imitation velvet repeated: "What I was sayin was: few've finished th that magazine, j mind fi borried it off you? I ain't sor that nummba yet."

Mem hardly knew how to answer that face and that dialect. She handed the magazine up over the back of the seat with a smile of shy generosity.

The animated doll remained leaning across the seat. She must be kneeling on the other side. As she skimmed the magazine rapidly the way she ran her eyes up each page reminded Mem somehow of a cat licking one of its paws.

As the girl skimmed picture and text, she talked without looking at Mem:

"You're on the way to Sanglus, I s'pose."

"To where?"

"Lussanglus chief suburb of Hollywood. Nearly everybody in this strain is bound furl Sanglus."

"Just where is that?"

"My Gawd! Is there anybody on earth who don't know that dump? Or maybe you call it Loss Anjuleez. No two people pernounce it alike."

"Oh, I beg your pardon, I didn't catch the name at first. No, I'm only going as far as Tuckson."

"Too-son, eh. You're not on the screen, I guess."

"No-o, no, I'm not."

"It's the life! leastways it was. So many amachoors bein drord into it now, though, it ain't what it was. It's the money gets 'em all. Who joo s pose is on this strain?"

"I can't imagine."

The strange creature disappeared and came round to sit down opposite Mem.

"Joo mind if I set in with you awhile? You're alone, ain't you? Or is your husban up smokin, the way mine always is? As I says to Cyril only the yother day, If you'd a gave as much attention to your rart as you have to your tubbacca, you'd have John D. workin' for you! I says. Better to smoke here than hereafter, he says. He's awful speedy with the subtitles, that boy. I don't smoke, m'self. Not that I got any prejudices against it. But I think it takes away from a woman's charm. Don't you? No offense intended. Maybe you smoke, yourself."

Mem wagged her head in a daze. She would have been horrified to be suspected of tobacco, and yet since this blatant piece of ignorant artifice had objections to it, her inclination grew perverse.

The magazine engaged the visitor's attention a moment, and Mem studied her as if she were something in a zoo. There was aggressive impudence in the very way she sat her chin high; her nostrils aflare; her head flaunted now and then to shake away her curls as a mare tosses her mane aside; her shoulders thrown back; her bosom uplifted; her elbows agog, one hand set with fingers dispread on an emphatic hip; legs all over the place, and the skirt so short that one knee, bared by its rolled-down stocking, was manifest.

Mem was almost petrified to observe that the kneecap was powdered and rouged!

Yet she could not help noting also that it was exquisitely modeled, and the calves as delicately lathed as a Chippendale spindle. There was refinement in all the creature's outlines, yet hopeless spiritual coarseness. The conflict jarred on Mem, who had taken as little thought of aesthetic mysteries as any pretty girl could, and live as long as she had lived.

Abruptly the perfectly modeled minx shattered Mem's calm with the first curse she had ever heard a woman use.

"Well, I'm damned! Would ja see what they done to me!"

She whirled herself round and plounced down at Mem's side in a cyclone of perfumery. She pointed to the open page where there was a picture that had slapped Mem in the face. A young man clad in a leopard's pelt and nothing else danced while he held aloft like a cane the horizontal figure of a girl similarly revealed and concealed. She was flung backward, broken at the waist, a mass of hair flowing down from her reverted head; and she was pitifully beautiful. The name under the picture was Viva d'Artoise.

"That's me, Veva Dartoys — stage name, o course. They used that old pitcher of me with my first husban! The nerve of 'em! I ought to soo 'em for slander. It's three years old. Them leopard skins is all out of style. They done that to me just to save makin' a noo cut. Gawd! I hope Cyril don't see it. He's so sensatuv. I'll show you one of my latest."

And while Mem's soul was joggled as if the train had left the rails to run along the ties, the girl had left her and returned, carrying a sheaf of photographs, which she displayed with a frankness that shattered Mem's calm.

In some of them she was as fragile and poetical as if she had capered off the side of a Greek vase by Douris himself. In others her beauty was petulant and deprecatory, shy and inexpressibly pure. Again she was an acrobat reckless of consequences. There were pictures of her husband and herself, her husband looking as much like a young Greek god as possible, holding her in the air as high as possible. And each permitted the other to be seen in public like that!

Mem was so shaken that she could find nothing at all to say. She regained speech only when Mademoiselle d'Artoise brought out some scenes taken on the steps of her home, a charming little Spanish bungalow, with her husband mowing the lawn and her ancient mother smiling from the porch. In all these pictures Mademoiselle Viva held a baby, an adorable chubby thing that restored Mem to civilization as she understood it.

The mother explained: "I hadda leave him for a dash to N York. I and m 'usband hadda play a coupla dancers at a swell reception for the movies, o course. And they hadda shoot us on Fith Avenyeh to get local color."

"They shot you for local color! Where?"

"On Fith Avenyeh. We been shot all over the place. We used to be in vawdvul, but we drifted into doin spectaculars for the movies in the big perductions. It's the life! Hadn't you ever thought of takin a shy at it?"

Mem shook her head. Mademoiselle Viva smiled. Come on in; the water's fine. With your face and figger, there's nothin' to it."

Mem shuddered. Her figure was her own for only a little while longer. The Eden of the movies was not for her.

Viva was willing to gossip as long as anyone was willing to listen. She admitted this herself with the frank helplessness of a garrulous soul.

"Cyril's always savin I never stop. I'm what he hears talkin' when he falls asleep, and the first thing he hears in the mornin' is me talkin'. Sometimes he says, Are you talkin' again or yet?"

But Mem was an insatiable audience. Her information was a Sahara and no amount of rain could be too much.

All afternoon Viva chattered, giving Mem a liberal education in one of the countless phases of moving-picture life, a foreign world, another planet where everything was unlike anything she had ever imagined, where the very laws of social gravity were reversed. She was getting an altogether twisted idea of it all. Her guide was as trustworthy as a Peruvian Indian trying to describe the heroic wonders of the lost city of Machu Picchu. Mem's knowledge of Italy was gained from a banana and fruit peddler in Calverly. Her introduction to Movia was like that of one who enters Stamboul by railroad through the back yards of Constantinople. What she heard gave her no curiosity to see more, and an assurance that her dear old father had made a good guess at Los Angeles.

# CHAPTER IX

VIVA WAS STILL TALKING when the waiter came through again with his proclamation: "Fir scall fr dinner n dine caw! Fir scall fr din dine caw!"

There was a scurry among the passengers and Mem was eager to go, but Viva could not break off the story she was telling. Suddenly she stopped, stared, seized Mem's arm, and whispered, "Pipe what's comin'!"

Mem piped a dramatic woman of singularly noble face and figure and somewhat grandiose carriage. Following her was an elegant gentleman of a certain exoticism, a bit peevish over the bad manners the train displayed in tossing him to and fro.

"Joo know who that is?" Viva whispered, and did not stay for an answer. "That dame is the great Miriam Yore. She's been the grand slam at the Mettapolitan Op'ra for years. And the flossy guy with her is that big English author, What's-his-name. You know, he wrote, oh, all them books.

"They're bound for Movieland, too. Everybody's makin' that way. The comptition is somethin' fierce."

Her voice died as the two drifted down the aisle, pausing to talk in snatches, between dashes for the next leaning post.

As the train swung the great Miriam half across Mem's seat the author was saying: "Everybody tells me that Los Angeles is absolutely —"

Then they were gone, reawakening in Mem her desire to learn just what this fabulous city could be absolutely.

The return of Viva's husband released her to her own thoughts for the rest of the evening. Viva introduced the partner of her fate and her dances, and hurried away to the women's room to "worsh up for the eats."

Her husband said a few amiable nothings to Mem, but she was afraid to look at him. He, Cyril (ne Julius), was ordinary enough in speech and appearance, but Mem could only see him as the panther-pelted satyr who took the public absolutely into his confidence and swung his half-stripped wife aloft for all the world to see.

After dinner Mem found her way to the observation car and sat on the platform awhile, watching the dark world of her past fleeing backward to the horizon and vanishing thence into the stars.

But her interests were no longer backward. She wanted to look ahead. She rose from the contemplation of night and re-entered the car.

Noting that the writing desk was not in use, she was reminded of her task. She sat down and began a letter home. Her heart, weary with the day's excursions, melted again toward her mother and father. She wrote them a prattle of childish enthusiasm about the journey. She did not mention Viva or the others. She was afraid they would frighten her parents as much as they had frightened her, and not so agreeably.

She had finished her letter and was sealing it when she suddenly remembered Doctor Bretherick's prescription. She was to take a lover on the first day! The very name of the figment of Bretherick's mania had been crowded out of her mind by these curious, unbelievable people who actually moved and breathed. After a little groping, she recalled Woodbury, then Woodhouse, then Woodville. She took up the painful composition of a postscript with all the agony of an author trying to recall and to originate at the same time.

She had mentioned nobody that she had met. Now she must describe the important man that she would never meet. He was an imaginary, and therefore a quite perfect, character. She finally wrote:

Oh, I forgot! Who do you suppose I ran into on the train? You'd never guess in a million years. You know when I went to Carthage to take care of Aunt Mabel? Well, do you remember me telling you about the awfully nice man I met at church? Mr. Woodville was his name. Remember? Well, would you believe it, he is on this train! Isn't it a small world! He has been most kind and polite. I met him in church, as you remember, and somehow I feel much safer not being alone. I'm sure you'll be glad. He's very religious, but awfully nice I mean, so, of course, awfully nice. Goodnight again you darlings!

Being told that they recollected Mr. Woodville, her parents obligingly remembered him. Mrs. Steddon had been warned of this fiction and collaborated in it. Doctor Steddon was one of those who believe almost anything they read, especially when they hope for its truth. And there was nothing he hoped for so much as that his child should meet a good man and love him and be loved by him. That is the parental ideal, and Mem could have sent him no other message that could have so comforted him. He awaited the second installment of her romance with all the impatience of a country man watching for the stagecoach that brought along Charles Dickens's serials piecemeal.

He knew nothing of the wiles of story makers and did not suspect the trap his child was laying for him. Her name should have been Sapphira.

# CHAPTER X

AFTER SHE HAD FINISHED her letter and sealed it, Mem paused, wondering what to do with it.

She was in an agony of reluctance to send such a pack of lies to her mother and father. She recalled the Biblical warning against doing evil that good might come of it. But she dared not face the evil that would certainly come if the truth were told.

As she sat irresolute, beating the envelope against the tip of her fingers, she saw Miss Miriam Yore come into the observation car and pass on out to the platform. She was followed by the famous unknown author. They were both talking as before, and the motion of the car threw them this way and that without checking their prattle.

Mem was hungry to hear how great people talked, to watch them behaving. She had never seen any before.

She saw the porter of the observation car grinning in front of her foggily. He spoke twice before she heard back what he had said.

"Want me to mail yo letta, lady, at next stop?"

She nodded and gave it to him with a warm, "Thank you." He would have much preferred a cold quarter.

Mem saw that the platform was not crowded. So she drifted out with labored casualness and sat down, pretending to study the scenery and to be quite deaf. Practice was making her a zealous actress, if not a good one.

The author was just offering Miriam Yore a cigarette.

"Thanks, old thing, I don't dare. I've smoked myself blue in the face today. I've got to fill my lungs with fresh air while the porter makes up my drawing-room, or I won't sleep.

"As I was saying, I think you're quite wrong about the moving pictures. Of course, most of those that have been done are abominable, but that's because they were done for the wrong people by the wrong people.

"Have you seen me as Hypatia? There was a picture! Poetry, passion, splendor, drama. In that scene where the Christian fanatics drove the wonderful Hypatia to the altar and stripped her naked and tore her to pieces it was tremendous, you know; really! There was something there that only the camera could give. You didn't see me in that?"

She was a genuine "Have-you-seen-me?" — just what the French call a "m'as-tu-vu?"

"No, I must confess. I go so seldom. In England I saw mainly the cowboy pictures. I met some of the men of the 101 Ranch when they were on the other side."

Mem noted that he said "rahnch."

It must be glorious to say it naturally.

He went on: "I love the cowboy things; nursery instincts still surviving, I fancy. But the big spectacles such as you speak of, they leave me cold. They have all the faults of grand opera and no music. I can stand the silent drama, but not the silent opera."

"But what right have you to criticize if you haven't seen?"

"Oh, but my d'yah Miriam, if they had been worth seeing I'd have been drawn to them."

"Rot, my dear! utter damned rot, and you know it. You are the type of literary buzzard who is never drawn to anything except what is dead or is done in a dead style according to dead rules. You live in a time when a new art is being created before your eyes, and instead of leaping into it you are afraid, you hang back, like a child afraid of the ocean. You put in a toe and run shrieking; you go back, and a little wave rushes up to the seat of your little panties, and chills you; you feel the sand giving way, and scream for nursie to come drag you out.

"Why don't you plunge in and learn to swim; face the breakers; if you can't rise over them, dive under them. What are you afraid of? If the moving-picture people are as stupid as you think they are, how easily they can be conquered by as great a mind as you think you are."

The author squirmed. "Oh, I say, my dear Miriam, aren't you laying it on a bit strong? Aren't I on the train, going out to study your ocean? I want to swim. I'm going to try. Really!"

"That's better. It's a far better thing than you've ever done. You'll see. You've written good novels, stories, plays, essays, poems, all sorts of things; but men have done those for thousands of years. When you write a movie you do what no man ever did before this generation. And look at me. I've played plays, I've sung light operas and grand operas, and danced a little, but, good Lord! women have done those things for ages. In the moving picture I'm doing something that no woman before my generation ever did.

"We are the pioneers, the Argonauts, the discoverers. We shall be classics as sure as ever classics were. It's glorious!"

The author was a trifle jealous of such fine writing from a singer and an actress. He tried to put her in her place:

"I see what you're driving at. In fact, I've written much the same thing and said it to interviewers, who got it all wrong, of course, interferers, I call them. But what good did it do me? I was merely accused of trying to whitewash myself for going after big money. Of course I want the big money. I insist on it, or I should if they refused it. Which they don't. Quite the contrary. But what I mean to say, is:

"If I go in for moving pictures I shall not try to do any of your grandiose things. They're all right in their place, but I think there's more art in the smaller forms. I want to do something smart, satirical, the high-comedy thing. The pictures seem to me to need the aristocratic touch more than anything else."

Miss Yore yawned. "Beware of the aristocratic touch, my dear. It means boredom most of the time. I know no end of aristocrats who are interesting, but that's because they are soldiers or statesmen, big-game hunters, adventurers. But your deadly drawing-rooms, keep those off the screen or you'll bankrupt your backers."

The author yawned. "Speaking of bankrupting your backers, old dear, I hear that you are doing your best to accomplish that. I was told by a man who claimed to know, that you are getting ten thousand a week. Is it true?"

Miriam rose and smacked his cheek lightly. "Are you jealous?"

"Yes, I am, rather. They're only giving me 25 thousand for my new piece. They said they couldn't pay me more because you stars were such, well, the word they used was hogs. It's a shame to pauperize me to fatten you."

"Fatten? Don't use the hideous word! If you knew the agonies I go through to keep my flesh down. All this money and all this glory, and I'm hungry all the time."

She paused by the brass rail and gazed about the dark levels that seemed rather to revolve slowly about the train than to be left behind. And she sighed:

"Strange place this little old world! I was born on a prairie like this in a small town like the one we just rattled through. I was a poor daughter of poor parents. Dad kept a drug store — a chemist's shop, as you'd say. And now, well, I've sung before kings and queens; I've had princes make love to me more or less pitifully; I've had diamonds from dukes. I was engaged to a duke once, you may have read or heard that idiotic story that I can't kill about the two children I had by the Duke of... Why, I never was alone with the man! But, anyway, I've had those scandals and splendors, and now I'm going back at a salary that, Why, I could buy out most of the dukes I've met! And I get it all for pretending to suffer imaginary woes in imaginary situations.

"And you, you were the son of a rusty little Oxford don, and you're complaining because you get only five thousand pounds for the moving-picture rights of a silly fairy story you spin in a few months. It's a drunken old world and we ought to be ashamed of ourselves for stealing its money."

"But I have to give the British government 53 per cent of all I get," he wailed.

"The U. S. income tax murders me, too," she sighed.

She slipped through the door like her own La Tosca. The author laughed a dreary "Good night!" stood a moment finishing his cigarette and studying out of the corner of his eye the mute, meek auditor whom they had perhaps forgotten; perhaps had been playing to all the time.

He wondered if Mem knew who he was. She had not heard his name, and would not have recognized it if she had.

He felt like talking a lot about himself to somebody. But he was Englishly shy of broaching conversations; he was himself a tight little isle with a gift for spreading his power around the world and making people think that his loneliness and timorousness and lack of *savoir vivre* were reserve.

The unknown and unknowing Mem was afraid that he was going to speak to her. But he did not dare. He flicked his cigarette overboard majestically and made a good exit. Then he crept away to his lonely drawing room and shuddered at the prospect of entering the new world with its new people, a world of bounders, as he had been told.

He left Mem dizzy with what she had overheard. The contrast between Viva and Miriam Yore was complete. The moving-picture planet was plainly one of enormous size and variety.

But the wickedest thing about it in her eyes was the money it squandered.

The richest banker in Calverly was a pauper compared with the woman who had just left the platform. And all she did was to stand up and have her picture taken. Mem had never heard of Hypatia, and she did not believe that any such thing had happened as Miriam Yore described. She did not know that the moving picture had been taken from a historical novel written by a clergyman. Neither did the clergyman, probably, as he had been dead for a quarter of a century before the pictures were taught to move.

All that Mem knew of the Rev. Charles Kingsley's works was *The Water Babies* and a poem from which her father was always quoting, "Be good, sweet maid, and let who will be clever."

Mem was not clever, and everybody knew it. Yet she had not been good, and only two people knew it.

Not having been good, she just had to be clever.

# CHAPTER XI

GROWN SUDDENLY AFRAID of the night-shrouded plains and the loneliness of the deserted platform, Mem returned to the lights. Through car after car she pushed, seeking her own. She had not kept count of its number. Each car was now a narrow alley of curtains.

She was lost on a madly racing comet made up of bedrooms and corridors where men in their underclothes climbed ladders or sat on the edges of their beds, yawning and undressing. Tousled heads leered at her from upper berths or from cubbyholes. She had to squeeze past men and women in bathrobes straggling down the halls.

She was frightened. She had never believed such scenes possible. She was panic-stricken at being unable to find her own hiding place. Her porter was not to be found. At last she met Viva coming out of a washroom, dressed as if someone had yelled "Fire." Mem felt positively fond of her; a friend in need is a friend indeed.

Viva wore a gaudy kimono and kept it close about her with a modesty surprising in view of her photographs. Mem had not learned that artists of Viva's field are no less prudish in private for being so shameless in public. There's safety in numbers.

Mem greeted Viva with enthusiasm: "Oh, I'm so glad to see you! This must be my car, then."

"Yes, dear-ree," said Viva. "Was you lost? Your number's number sev'm, just this side of mine. Too bad you didn't take a section. Some big hick got on board whilst you was away, and he's asleep up in your attic now."

This was disconcerting indeed. The tenant of Mem's sky parlor had left a pair of his shoes in front of her berth, and his clothes were visible hanging on a coat hook.

There was no escape for the girl. She had to clamber into her pigeonhole and make the best of it. She had the curious feeling that she had crawled under a strange man's bed to spend the night.

Though no sane burglar would ever have wasted time on a village minister's house, Mem had always looked under her bed for one before she kneeled down to say her prayers. She hoped the man overhead would not take the same precautions.

And how was she to kneel down and say her prayers in that aisle? In the berth she could not even kneel up. This was the first night of her life that she ever omitted that genuflection. She had to pray lying down, and she asked the Lord to forgive her this one more sin.

She had asked so much forgiveness of late! She wanted to pray also that her letter should deceive and comfort her father. But she dared not ask prosperity for a lie. She dared not ask prosperity for the series of lies she was going to tell. Yet her thoughts and plans must be known "Up There." Yet again, if they were known. But it was growing complicated and she turned her thoughts to other things.

Getting out of her clothes and into her nightgown was an experiment in contortion. She was afraid to fall asleep, but there was a drugging monotony in the muffled click-clickety of the wheels and she soon knew peace and a much-needed oblivion.

All night long the train was speeding through Kansas, and the next morning was still in Kansas.

Getting dressed was another appalling experience for the girl, and she peeked through her curtains to see what the proper costume was for the sprint to the washroom. Viva was not there to help her, for Viva slept late and her section was a curtained cabin for hours after the rest of the car was made up.

The scenery was flat as a pancake, but there was no monotony in it for Mem. Towns and farms and farms and towns, windmills and tree clusters and barns and pigstys, were all wonderland to her. And dear, brave people were making their homes there.

Setting her watch back an hour just before entering the romantic state of Oklahoma was in itself an exciting experience. The names of the stations were literature, poetry: Arkalon, Liberal, Guyman, Texhoma, Dalhart, Middle-water, Bravo, Naravisa, Tucumcari, Los Tanos, Tularosa, Alamogordo, Turquoise, Grogrando, El Paso.

She lunched in Kansas, crossed Oklahoma in two hours, entered Texas, dined in New Mexico, and breakfasted again in Texas, went right back into New Mexico, and lunched in Arizona.

And what an encyclopaedia of scenery she studied! The endless flats of Kansas, with its broad lazy rivers slouching along their flat beds; the long famine of trees in bald levels, and then the sudden arrival in a morbid, fantastic realm where God had lost his temper or his patience or something and flung everything awry, desert and vast nightmares of rock! As if the landscape had been designed by one of those mad cubists she had read about the day before.

But everywhere there were evidences of human pluck; tireless ants fighting the Titans for control; weak men who turn chaos to order and tame the wild regions to dominion.

The scenery was such a book of adventure that Mem needed no other diversion. She was grateful for the fact that Viva had one of her sick headaches and did little talking. The heat and dust kept the great Miriam in her drawing-room, and Robina, too. She saw Tom Holby in the dining car but he did not speak to her, of course, because she did not speak to him. But she studied him slyly when he was not looking, and she wondered what could make him worth so much money. She had not learned that merchandise is worth just what it will bring in the market, whether the merchandise be ships or shoes or sealing wax, souls or smiles or tears.

She felt for this handsome youth the contempt that women feel at times for handsome men. She felt a personal grudge against him because he lived and prospered and won multitudinous loves, while her lover lay dead in oblivion. She abominated him for gaining so much wealth for doing nothing useful. She knew too little of life as yet to realize that beauty and foolish amusement are among the most useful contributions to existence and are not overpaid.

There may be some doubt as to the actual benefits and the actual efficiency of most human activities and inventions, including the countless medicines, religions, political expedients, mechanisms of transportation, and other elaborate devices that create new irritations as fast as new conveniences. But beauty that warms the heart and folly that tickles it are as provedly valuable as laughing gas and other anaesthetics. In fact, there is more than etymology in the kinship between aesthetics and anaesthetics, and both have been denounced as hellish by the godly.

Mem spent most of her day planning her second letter home and growing acquainted with that husband of hers. She used Tom Holby as a model, reluctantly, yet for lack of better material.

She had supposed that writing fiction must be as easy for its manufacturers as spinning webs is for spiders. But constructing character was exhausting work for her; perhaps spiders grow weary, too, and suffer temperamental stringencies.

She learned that the author must wrestle with the invisible as Jacob with the angel, and that the angel could dislocate a joint at a touch.

Mr. Woodville eluded her maddeningly, and her sketch of him was so inconsistent that her father, when he received her second letter, found in its very befuddlement an evidence that she was losing her wits over the fellow.

Doctor Steddon was pleasantly alarmed. Every man is afraid of every man who interests his daughter. Yet he wants some man to capture her.

The train carried Mem deeper and deeper into the soul of Mr. Woodville, and in the dark hours she spent in her berth, reclining on an elbow and gazing at the incredible landscape, everything unreal grew real, and her mystic bridegroom began to take form and voice, eyes and integrity.

She had great trouble with his trade or profession. This is always a complication with authors. Most of them in despair ignore the matter entirely or give the character some craft with elastic office hours and income.

The landscape was an incessant interruption. Just as she was about to settle on something, an amazing butte would slide past her window, or a captivating flat-roofed adobe hovel infested with little human cooties of Mexican extraction would delight her. The squalor of foreigners is always picturesque and it is typical of the artistic mind to find more poetry in an alien garbage heap than in a familiar temple.

The desert was beautiful to this girl because it was unusual. Its cruelty was romantic, since she had not encountered its monotony.

The next day the train came to an abrupt halt. A driving bar on the engine had broken and dropped; it had torn off the ends of the ties for hundreds of yards before its drag had been noticed by the engineer and the engine stopped. If the train had not been puffing slowly up a steep grade it would have been derailed and sent rolling like a shot snake; some of the passengers would probably have been mangled and killed.

It was a long while before the passengers found this out, and they reveled in the delight of averted disaster. Mem thought how fitting it would have been for her to have suffered a death so closely akin to Elwood's. There would have been an artistic grandeur in the pattern of their fates.

And yet she could not help being glad to be alive. She had ridden a thousand miles and more, spiritually as well as physically, away from Calverly.

Nobody knew how long the train would be delayed. All were like people on a ship becalmed in mid-ocean. They could not go on until a new engine was secured. A trainman had to walk to the next block signal tower, miles ahead, and telegraph back for another locomotive.

The passengers settled down to hours of deferment, cursing delay and comparing it, not with the speed of the pioneers who agonized across the wilderness, but with the velocity of yesterday's express.

Viva and Mem wandered about, looking at the cactus and the sagebrush and deliciously expecting a rattlesnake under every clump. Viva returned to the car to sleep, but Mem strolled farther and farther away.

She saw Tom Holby set out for a brisk walk. He climbed a ragged butte with astonishing agility, winning the applause of the passengers. He had the knack of acquiring applause.

The other passengers dawdled about, but Mem went farther and farther. She wanted to see what was on the other side of that butte as much as mankind has longed to see the other side of the moon. When she got 'round she found that the other side was much like the other side: more desert, more buttes, utter dissimilarity, yet the complete resemblance of chaos to chaos.

When she started back the cool of the shadow made her rest awhile. The heat and the hypnosis of the shimmering sand sea put her asleep in spite of herself. She woke with a start. The train was moving, a new engine dragging it and its broken engine. She ran, fell, picked herself up, limped forward.

She was alone in the wilderness, and the train was already a toy running through a gap between two lofty buttes, one a grandiose Tower of Babel; the other a deformed and crooked, writhen diablerie. Both mocked the girl unendurably and she stood panting in a suffocation of fright, her hands plucking at each other's fingernails, which was about as profitable as anything else they could have found to do.

Then for the first time Mem understood what the desert meant to those who had seen the last burro drop and found the canteen full of dry air.

# CHAPTER XII

FOR A TRANCE-WHILE Mem made a perfect allegory of helplessness on a monument. She heard a voice laughing, with a kind of querying exclamation:

"Hello?"

The word was as unimportant as could be and it came from what she had just decreed the most useless thing on earth, a handsome moving-picture actor.

His next word was no more brilliant. He touched his hat and said:

"Well!"

Mem had not yet even found that much to say. And he went on garrulously to the extent of:

"Here we are, eh?"

There was no denying this, and it was the first thing Mem's paralyzed brain could understand, so she nodded briskly.

Tom Holby laughed at fate as in his pictures. He said:

"I've nearly died of thirst in the desert half a dozen times, and I've gone mad twice, but there was always a camera or two a few yards off and a grub wagon just outside. And the heroine usually came galloping to the rescue and picked me up in time for the final clinch. I see the heroine, but the grub wagon's late."

"Wh-what are we going to do?"

"Well, I'm not going to act, anyway, as long as there's no camera on the job. Let's sit down and wait."

"For what?"

"Oh, I guess the train will come back, or another one will come along and we can flag it in plenty of time. Sit down, won't you?"

Mem was almost disappointed at having her epic turned into a commonplace. She resented the denial of a noble experience, now that his coolness reassured her.

She hated him a little more than ever.

He brushed off a ledge of rock with his hat in movie fashion and said:

"Sit down on this handsome red divan, won't you? I'm Mr. Holby, by the way."

"Yes, I know," she said, and, feeling that she ought to announce herself, she stammered, "My name is Steddon, Remember Steddon."

"I always will," he said.

"Oh, that's my first name! Remember is my first name."

"Oh! What a beautiful name! Especially for such a, such a... Mmm, yes."

He caught from her eyes that where she came from a compliment from a stranger was an insult.

"Do sit down," he begged, "at least so that I can. I'm all out of training and I'm dog tired."

She sat down, and he dropped down by her. There was so much room elsewhere that this struck her as rather presumptuous, but she could hardly resent it since it was not her desert.

There was a long silence. Then he mused aloud:

"Remember, eh? Great! Robina would have preferred that to the one she chose. Do you know Robina?"

"I've seen her."

"On the screen?"

"On the train."

"Oh, then you haven't seen her. That isn't the real Robina that walks about. That's just a poor, plain, frightened, anxious little thing, a Cinderella who only begins to live when she puts on her glass slippers. She has to be so infernally noble all day long that you can hardly blame her for resting her overworked virtues when she's off the lot. I used to be a pretty decent fellow, too, before I began to be a hero by trade. But now gosh! how I love my faults! When there's no camera on me I'm a mighty mean man."

"Really!"

"Oh, I'm a fiend. I'm thinking of playing villains for a while, so that I can be respectable at my own expense outside the factory. But I'm so mussed up between my professional emotions and my personal ones that it's hard to keep from acting, on and off. Now look at this situation. If the camera gang were here I'd know just what to do. I'd be Sir Walter Raleigh in a Stetson and chaps. But since there's just us two here and I have you in my power or you have me in your power I don't know just how to act. It depends on you. Are you a heroine or an adventuress?"

"I don't understand you."

"Are you an onjanoo or a vamp?"

"I don't speak French."

"Then you must be an onjanoo," he said. "In that case I suppose I really ought to play the villain and... But here comes the train. Dog-on it! just as we were working up a real little plot. I hope I haven't compromised you. If you're afraid I have, I'll have to go back and hide 'till the next train comes along. Or you can, for I imagine it's Robina that reversed the engine. She probably missed me and suspected that I was out here with a prettier girl than she is — pardon me! Shall I go hide?"

"Oh no! no! I couldn't think of it. Nobody knows me. It can't make any difference what they say about me."

"Gosh! what an enviable position. Stick to your luck, Miss Steddon. May I help you down?"

# CHAPTER XIII

THAT WAS A CHAPTER in Mem's life.

Holby had guessed right. Robina had looked for him, not found him, and had set the whole train in an uproar. She bore down on the helpless conductor, and while he protested against the sacrilege of stopping and reversing the Limited when it was already late, she pulled the rope herself.

She knew the signals, having played in a railroad serial, and she soon had the train backing at full speed.

She had half suspected that Tom Holby had a companion in the desert, and when she looked out and saw him with the pretty chit whose magazine he had picked up, she was tempted to give the signal to go ahead again.

She preferred to give poor Holby her opinion of him. Mem crept back to her place, shivering with her first experience of stardom and its conspicuousness.

Viva made a great ado over her and had to hear all about it. She sighed over the tameness of the incident as Mem described it.

"But then that was what was to be expected, dear-ree. Us movie people gets so much excitement on the scene that we're all wore out when anything happens with no director around to tell us what to do."

Mem escaped and took up in haste her daily bulletin for home consumption. Mr. Woodville grew more vivid in her letter and his resemblance to Tom Holby was amazing. She even put in a little bit of her adventure and told how Mr. Woodville with marvelous heroism saved her from a rattle snake that charged at her with fangs bristling and rattles in full play. She confessed that she had never met such a man and that she really owed her life to him.

She thought this would lead up excellently to the proposal he was to make in the next day or two. She gave this letter to the porter, who dropped it off at the next stop.

The train made up so much of its lost time that it was only two hours late when it drew into Tucson.

Mem was bewildered when she found that Tom Holby was getting off there, too. And so was Robina. But they were only stretching their legs. Holby paused to say goodbye to Mem just as she was tipping her porter a quarter for two days inattention.

She did not see the porter's face. It was hardly as black as Robina's when she was compelled to wait while Tom made his *adieux*.

He left Mem in a whirl. But her faculties went round in the mad panic of a pinwheel when a strange, somber person spoke to her in a parsony voice:

"Miss Steddon?"

"Yes."

"I am Doctor Galbraith, pastor of the First Church, here. Your father telegraphed me to meet you at the train and look after you."

"Do you know papa?"

"No, but he found my name in the Yearbook, and I shall be only too glad to serve a brother in the Lord. I have found a nice boarding house for you, and my wife and I will look after you as best we can."

Mem was struck violently with the thought, "But what becomes of Mr. Woodville now?"

She followed Doctor Galbraith as if she were the prisoner of his untimely kindliness, as indeed she was.

# CHAPTER XIV

A DISASTROUS, PERHAPS a ruinous, blow had been dealt the girl. And by the last hand she could have foreseen it from. And with the kindliest motive.

It was all Ben Franklin's fault. The French praised him because "he ripped the lightning from the sky and the scepter from the tyrant." But he placed the lightning as a scepter in the hand of everybody and made everybody the tyrant.

And now no one can travel so fast that he cannot be overtaken and prevented by a telegraphic or telephonic message. The swiftest airship is a snail.

Mem had flown by express for two days and two nights and left her father at home, yet here he was in the proxy of a telegram, waiting for her at the station, smiling benignly and throwing the complex machinery of her plan into complete disorder.

Doctor Steddon had never for a moment suspected that his daughter was fleeing to the West to keep from breaking his heart. The dear old soul fretted over the loneliness she must face and the dangers of inexperience.

She had hardly vanished in her train when he had a sudden inspiration. He did not know a soul in Tucson, but there must be a church of his denomination there, and a pastor to that church. The Yearbook contained a list of all the clergymen, and it was easy to find the name of the incumbent of the Tucson pulpit. So he shot off a long telegram describing his daughter and pleading that she be met.

He chuckled over his foresight and called himself a stupid old dolt for not thinking of it before. And his wife praised him and slept easier. She knew Mem's plan to become "Mrs. Woodville," but she had not imagination enough to foresee the effect of this new embarrassment.

Mem had anticipated almost every other surprise but this. The main charm of Tucson was to be her anonymity there. When she heard her name called, and by a clergyman, of all people, the gentle providence of her father landed like a bomb-shell. Tucson rocked under her feet and her plot fell to pieces in her hand.

She would have to be under the eye of Doctor Galbraith, who was already promising not to let her out of his pastoral care, and warning her that his wife was waiting inside the station.

In her desperation she caught sight of Tom Holby, who had walked briskly to the head of the train and was striding back to his car. A frantic whim led Mem to say, very distinctly, as she passed him:

"Good night, Mr. Woodville."

Holby had already lifted his hat and made her a gift of one of his high-priced smiles before he heard what she called him. He stopped short with his hat aloft as if in a still picture. He could hardly believe his ears. He was so used to being recognized by total strangers that it stunned him to be called out of his name by this girl with whom he had been briefly cast away in the desert.

But he recovered his native modesty, laughed to himself, "This is fame!" and went on.

The Reverend Doctor Galbraith had paused for a backward glance, but Mem urged him along, saying, "That's an old friend I met on the train." And now she felt that she had established the existence of her Mr. Woodville. She was already unconsciously "planting" characters.

"Oh!" said Doctor Galbraith. "His face looked familiar; but I guess it wasn't."

The reason it looked familiar was that lithographs of it were pasted up all over Tucson. Holby was to appear there in a picture. If Doctor Galbraith had been more acutely observant, or had had a keener memory for faces, he would have caught Mem in a tangle of lies. But he was thinking of other things.

Mem hated Mrs. Galbraith with enthusiasm until she met her, and then she turned out to be not at all the preacher's wife as Mem understood the species, but a joyous Western woman raised on a ranch and of a loud and hilarious cordiality.

Still, Western hospitality is the most despotic in the world, and sometimes takes the form of lassoing and hog-tying its victim.

Mrs. Galbraith embraced Mem and cried, "Isn't she pretty?" She was distressed and ashamed because she could not take Mem into her own little home, which was spilling over with children. Mem blanched to think what would have happened to her plan if she had been incarcerated in a parson's household. The boarding house the Galbraiths had selected for her was all too near them, as it was. They commended her to the care of the landlady and left her. And the landlady drove Mem almost to insult by trying to mother the poor, lonely thing.

Mem was so beset by human kindness that she was about ready to murder her next benefactor. She longed for a bit of refreshing selfishness and indifference.

Her room had been occupied by various predecessors who left various traces of themselves; one left cigarette burns on the edges of all the tables and the mantel. But somebody had left a few novels. They were frightfully tempting.

There was an electric light over the head of the bed, a very marvelous affair. A twist of the key turned it on, and one could lie and read till sleep drew near, then merely reach up and switch on the blessed dark with a snap of the key.

After a hot bath and a vigorous scrubbing of her hair Mem yielded to temptation and enjoyed all the pleasant anguish of a major sin when she lay outstretched in her nightgown, with her hair spread out on her upright pillow and a romance on the desk of her knees.

Cleopatra could hardly have felt so luxurious on a golden divan covered with silk and fanned by slaves as Mem felt in that boarding-house bed. Cleopatra had perhaps novels enough to read, since the Egyptians were ardent story tellers, but she could not have tasted the sweets of stolen fruit or had her delight heightened by a struggle with an overtrained conscience.

The novel that held Mem spellbound was Thomas Hardy's *Two on a Tower*, that epic of two souls against a background of stars, against that starless "hole in the sky" which astronomers believed in when Hardy wrote the book.

This parson's daughter began her fictional education at the top. She lost many of the signals by which discreet authors indicate to sophisticated readers that things not to be mentioned are going on. But as she read and read, growing wider and wider awake and panting as if her body were running as swiftly as her mind, it gradually dawned on her what had happened to the heroine of the story, the haughty lady who lingered too long on the lonely tower with the young astronomer for companion and only the stars for duennas at a most unrespectable distance. When the astronomer sailed for Australia in ignorance of the plight of the lady, Mem's heart jumped almost out of her mouth, for she realized the similarity of her problem to that of the heroine. Her own lover had sailed away to a farther port than the Antipodes, and even more irrevocably.

She raced through the succeeding pages to see how the heroine would solve her doubly harrowing riddle of having yielded to a plebeian and of paying the most plebeian penalty. When she found that Mr. Hardy's heroine, who had been vainly besought in love by an old bishop, simply wheedled him into a renewal of his proposal and married him in haste, Mem gave up. She could get no help from the book. No bishop was courting her. Even if she had been willing to dupe a trusting lover, she had none to dupe.

The next morning, when Mrs. Galbraith called to take her for a ride, Mem was looking more jaded than the evening before. The parson's wife advised her to get out into the desert as soon as possible, and told her, for her encouragement, how her own husband had hardly lived through the long journey West and had been laid down like a sack of bones on the sands. Then the desert magic had begun, and now he was hale and vociferous "and his doctors all dead." So strange a thing is water: a little too little and the body shrivels away from the soul, a little too much and the body coughs the soul away.

But Mem was not cheered with promises of life. There was too much life in her and she could not manage her future. She could not dream of the sacrilege of suicide, but she would have been glad to be told that she would pine away swiftly and beautifully.

Mrs. Galbraith, chattering incessantly and as braggart as a guide, drove about the city, spread level in a circus ring of gray granite mountains. Everything far-Western was picturesque to the mid-Western girl; the sorriest and tamest Mexicans were swart bandits of dark capabilities; the Santa Rita Hotel in its Spanish architecture was something out of the Alhambra. The old mission dating back to 1687 was an astonishment to her. (The oldest building at home in Calverly was proud of its 1887.) The mountain devoted to the Botanical Laboratory was a cubist landscape, a vegetable zoo. She could not understand the science that was taking lessons humbly from the cactus, learning how to live on next to nothing a year, and teaching mankind how to turn the bleakest desert into a paradise. That was just what she might do with her own life; but she had no heart for it and she did not want to look like a cactus.

On the way back to her boarding house she noted many of Tom Holby's portraits on the billboards. He was not the star of the picture. Robina Teele was the star. Yet in one gaudy poster she cowered helpless and wide-eyed while Holby was shown fighting with a human gorilla. She was a dance-hall girl in the Yukon, it seemed, kept miraculously pure, like a medieval saint amid temptations and devils. And Holby was an Argonaut who believed her innocent because he was himself innocent.

Mem felt a longing to see this heroic picture. But Mrs. Galbraith would not leave her for a moment, and the night was prayer-meeting night.

Mem attended the evening devotions. There was nothing strange to her in the drowsy, cozy atmosphere, the sparse company singing hymns and bowing in prayer and finding a mystical comfort in the thought of sins forgiven and an eternal home beyond the grave.

Doctor and Mrs. Galbraith took her back to her lodgings and left her. They had no objection to moving pictures and attended them often, but Mem did not know this, and she felt like a thief when her worse self compelled her better self to a dark dishonesty. Both selves went to the movies!

If the cinema store had been an opium den Mem could not have sneaked more guiltily into it.

She was so ignorant of the conventions that when she put down her money and a ticket sprang up at her out of a slot, and her change came tobogganing down a little chute, she jumped and had to be told what to do.

When she had found a seat in the dark hall she was so illiterate in the staples of fiction that she tingled with excitement over hackneyed situations that left many a sophisticated child yawning and gave never a pause to the swaying jaws of the gum-grinding crowd.

There were both novelty and conviction for her in the pseudo-Alaskan snow scenes, the bloodcurdling escapes from death at the hands of desperadoes or the fangs of wolves, the blizzards that snarled the sledge dogs into tangles of hopeless misery and confronted the wayfarers with hideous death.

Most of the audience knew the actors and actresses in the picture by reputation, had seen them in other pictures, and read more or less fabulous stories of their personal lives.

The familiar situations rehashed and warmed over had the charm of old fairy stories remodeled again and again by fatigued parents for insatiable youngsters.

But Mem was experiencing an agitation such as she had not known since first her mother told her about Little Red Riding Hood and growled like a wolf, showing long white teeth.

One thing impressed Mem amazingly. She had just seen a handful of sleepy people at the once-a-week prayer meeting. Here she saw a packed house, the fifth packed house that day, and it had been so every day of the week.

It was inherent in certain natures to be solemnly convinced that whatever draws crowds should be stopped; whatever a great many people want to see or do must be put out of their reach. The principle is simple and direct; the public is a naughty child that cannot be trusted a moment; the moralist is nurse and must take away from it everything it reaches for, and force it to take whatever is supposed to be good for it.

Hissing and reproach are the portion of the man who resists the altruistic cruelty of zealots who would save his soul in spite of him. The zealots have always been even more cruel than the despots, for the czars have worked only for their own aggrandizement, but the zealots have the terrible fault that they labor meekly for the glory of their God.

The late war of the nations was followed in America, as elsewhere, by a recrudescence of the eternal war between enforced morality and liberty. Having closed the saloons, the busy agents of vicarious virtue ran about closing moving-picture houses on Sunday, clipping whole scenes out of films and subjecting them all to the whimsical approval of hired censors; assailing tobacco as a devil's weed and forbidding school-teachers to smoke even in their own homes. The cigarette, of which billions had been consumed by the triumphant soldiers, was actually banned in many states. In Kentucky, preachers and mobs of zealots demanded a law against teaching the infamous doctrine of evolution. In Illinois, a religious community forbade the teaching of the atheistic idiocy concerning the roundness of the earth and its revolutions about a distant sun. No lie was ever too ridiculous or unjust, no slander too vicious, no invasion of human rights too outrageous, for those who pretended that they were saving souls.

And while the moralists were denouncing the moving pictures for their wickedness, the critics were despising them for their triteness. But Mem was neither moralist nor artist; she was a young woman watching an epic unfolded.

She was seeing Tom Holby risk life and limb in the defense of beauty. She was seeing chivalry defying the cruel North and glorifying womanhood with knightly reverence and service.

There was something Homeric in the plot, if one could forget its age. In Homer's work a war was waged for a woman, and women walked through all the pages, the ox-eyed, the laughter-loving goddesses and their shining daughters, Helen and Iphigenia, Cressida and Andromache, Nausicaa and Penelope.

In a later day, Vergil would show a hero who ran away from a languishing queen, but Homer's warriors fought for women. Where Vergil began, "I sing of arms and a man," Homer cried,

"Sing, Goddess." The Greek tragedies and comedies were about women. The medieval romances concerning them, the plays of Shakespeare, Racine, Moliere, and all the others devoted themselves to the woman problem. Even Dante celebrated an ideal townswoman, and the most poignant scene in his "Inferno" was the coupled tragedy of Paolo and Francesca da Rimini. Sex had always been, as it must always be, the main theme of nine-tenths of fiction. To attempt to fetter its discussion was only to emphasize it by repression and change the symbols without altering the meaning.

Mem's soul was young; it still inhabited the golden age of épopée. Simple, direct anxiety of sex, for sex was new and wonderful to her. She was astounded at the courage of Tom Holby. It wrung her heart to see him plowing across white Saharas of snow, to see him challenge the barroom bully and beat him down and stand, torn, bleeding, and panting, over him. It melted her soul to see his tenderness with the girl, the waif of fortune, whose indomitable purity had withstood years of life in a gambling hell.

Being a woman, she was not quite convinced of Robina's supersaintly innocences, but she had no doubt of Tom Holby as Galahad. And when he begged the soiled dove of the Klondike to honor him with marriage, Mem wondered if such a parfait, gentil knight might not be waiting somewhere to rescue her from ignominy to bliss.

When the picture was irised out upon Tom clenching Robina to his big chest, and the lights went up in the theater, revealing an Arizona audience instead of an Alaskan solitude, she sighed and rose to face her lonely boarding house.

# CHAPTER XV

AS MEM WENT SLOWLY out with the straggling crowd she was overwhelmed with a loneliness for life, for love, for some-one to fight for her and uphold her in the deep waters; and then for a taste of the spiced wines of romance.

She cried aloud in the silence of her room for Elwood Farnaby to come back and help her, to come back and claim his right to the splendor of existence. Grief sprang at her like a puma leap-ing down from a tree and tore her with claws of anguish, set fangs into her heart and shook it.

In her room as she took off her clothes with listless hands she remembered her parents. She had not written to them for two days, and she had not carried Mr. Woodville forward.

She sat down and began a letter. Everything she could think of to write involved some difficulty. She described her arrival at Tucson, her surprise at being met by Mr. and Mrs. Galbraith. She squandered reckless praise of her father for his ever-watch-ful protection and the comfort of feeling that he and his prayers were always on guard. She praised the Galbraiths for their thoughtful attention.

Then she flung the pen down in disgust at the hypocrisy of her words and in revolt at the deep damnation of her whole plan. But rebel as she would, she must go on. She could not turn back now. One thing was certain: she must free herself from the Galbraiths; she must get out of Tucson. She must become Mrs. Woodville at once.

Life would not wait for her. She was like a serial writer at whose shoulder a nagging editor stands insisting. She was like Dostoieffsky, sick and confused, but unable to escape the necessity for filling the pages as fast as the ink could run, unable to recall any written page since it was printed almost before the next was written. And the title of her serial was also "Crime and Punishment." Her crime was not ruthless murder, but reckless creation. She had not driven an old woman out of the world, she was reluctantly dragging a child into it, yet society was as eager to find her out and disgrace her as the slayer.

For a night and a day she paced the jail of her room and beat her brains against the iron bars of her problem. She could not break through. She could not worm her way through. She had no imagination, no inventiveness. She was just an ordinary girl who wanted to keep from hurting anybody and was finding it mighty difficult.

She was tempted to send Doctor Bretherick a confession of failure and ask him to revise his continuity, but she was afraid to face the telegraph office with such a message and afraid to have it received at home. She dared not wait a week for a letter to come and go; and, besides, her author was at such a distance that he could not understand the emergency. It is well for authors to keep in close touch with their plays and pictures in the making.

She would probably have given up trying if a bit of luck had not befallen her. It was her habit of mind to credit it to a relenting Providence. When things went wrong she blamed herself; when they took a turn for the better she blessed Heaven. She saw divine purpose in the very bungling of circumstance that kept her frantic with uncertainties.

On the fourth morning of her suspense Mrs. Galbraith rode over in haste and distress to explain that her husband and she had to leave Tucson for a few days to attend his father's funeral. She promised to hasten back, and begged Mem Steddon's forgiveness for deserting her.

Mem was not quite sure that Heaven had slain the elder Mr. Galbraith just on purpose to help her out of her difficulty, but she had a hard time to keep Mrs. Galbraith from realizing how glad she was to be rid of her and her husband.

And as soon as Mrs. Galbraith had gone, she assailed her problem with a new ardor. It was plainly a time for quick and decisive action.

She threw caution aside and forbore to regard the perils of inconsistency. She wrote her father and mother a hasty letter to which the lilt of hope unconsciously contributed an atmosphere of bridal bliss.

MY DARLING MAMMA AND PAPA, — Well, you have lost your daughter not by fell disease, but by fell in love. You may say it is good riddance of bad rubbish, but it hurt me to lose the noble name of Steddon even for the beautiful title of Woodville, for that's what I've been and gone and done — yes, I'm married now. I meant to break it to you gentler but it popped out. So I'll leave it.

You see, Mr. Woodville — John — was so attentive and kind and considerate and respectful — almost reverent, you might say — and he's so big and handsome and fine and noble, and I was so small and lonely and so far away for so long that oh, I just couldent resist.

He stayed in Tucson (by the way, it is pronounced tooson, not tuckson) for several days longer than he planned because he said he couldent tear himself away from me but finally he had to leave for Yuma and he said he couldent live without poor little me. I felt I couldent live without him. And why should I deny myself a protector and the highest glory of womanhood?

So he begged me to marry him and go to Yuma I had about decided that Tucson was not the right place for me, anyway. My cough is much better but not enough better to quite suit, so I consented to marry John. Dr. Galbraith was awfully nice to me but he was called away by the unfortunate death of his father so he couldent marry us so we were married by Rev. Mr. Smjxns [here she wrote a name illegibly].

I havent time to write you more, for John is waiting and our train won't. I'll write a longer letter when I have the liesure.

I do hope you will be happy as I am about it. You havent lost a daughter but gained a son. We leave at once for Yuma, so address all your letters to me as Mrs. John Woodville, General Delivery, Yuma. Doesnt it sound grand, though?

I dont know how long we shall be there as John is looking over some properties and doesnt know just where to settle yet.

I wish I could write you that he is terribly rich, but while he hopes to be some day, he is very poor just now. But he is such a noble man and noble hearts are better than cornets, as the poet saith, and I shall try to be a help to him and some day we will pay back the money I have taken away from you poor darlings.

Well I must close for the present. Dont stop loveing me just because I have a husband. But send us your blessings.

Your loveing, loveing daughter
MEM.

She was exhausted by the soul strain and she had to rest mind and body before she could undertake the task of writing the Galbraiths a similar letter with the necessary changes. It was only herself that she had to conquer, since she did not have to look the recipients in the eye.

There was a kind of mischievous hilarity in the tone of her letter to the too-kind clergyman and his oversolicitous wife:

DEAR DR. AND MRS. GALBRAITH, — What you will think of me I can well imagine. Ingrattitude is the least thing you will think of. But I dont mean to be ungrateful.

You see it is this way: on the train as I wrote Mamma and Papa I met an old friend he was terribly nice to me and I cant understand why but he fell in love with me. I can tell why I should fall in love with him, though. Anyway we did so we expected to get married some day I wanted you to meet him but he was awfully busy and then you had to leave and then John had to go away and he said he couldent live without me and I dident want him to die so as he had to leave at once and he asked me to marry him right away I did so and now I am Mrs. John Woodville, if you please.

John has some properties to look over so we dont know just yet just where we will settle down so you will have to address me at General Delivery, Yuma, Mrs. John Woodville.

I can never never thank you enough John says to thank you for him and hopeing to see you soon again.

Yours most gratefully
REMEMBER STEDDON WOODVILLE.

Mem laughed as she wrote and sealed this letter, and was most grateful to the Galbraiths for their absence.

But her landlady had to be dealt with face to face or she could not get her trunk away. The landlady had expected to keep her guest for a long while, and as usual worked both ends of the game. When she had rented the room to Mem she had explained that her prices were high because of the heavy demand; when Mem wanted to unrent the room, the landlady complained that she would lose the use of it, as the demand had died.

Mem had to pay for the balance of the month and this took important dollars from her scant funds; but it gave her the strength to be curt when the landlady gasped at her instructions that any letters coming to Miss Remember Steddon should be readdressed to "Mrs. John Woodville, General Delivery, Yuma, Arizona."

The landlady's natural cackling over the unearthing of a romance was rigidly suppressed by Mem with as much calm as if she had been getting married every few days.

She was not so stolid when she set out upon her next errand. She had to buy her wardrobe for the third act, her widow's weeds. She was going to save a lot of money by purchasing no bridal gear at all, no veil, no orange blossoms, no trousseau, for her honeymoon was to be as imaginary as her wedding. But her mourning must be visible.

As she moved slowly down the Tucson street to a dry-goods store to buy a crape dress and hat and veil, she was dogged by a feeling of dreadful foreboding. To pretend to get married was a pleasant little comedy, but to put on false mourning was to carry the lie into the realm of grisly crime. A superstitious dread assailed her that if she put on the inky suit of woe she would soon have a real reason for it. Someone dear to her would die, and she would somehow be to blame for it.

She glanced over her shoulder timorously and felt a something at heel. She felt as one might who, lost in the wilderness and struggling with weakening steps to reach safety, sees a famished wolf following at a little distance, sees overhead an impatient buzzard making slow circles across his path.

But she must go on and cheat the wolf and the buzzard if she could. She had such distaste for the business that she was not quite ready for the natural questions of the saleswoman who met her demand for a mourning costume. Was it first or second mourning, half mourning? Did she wish very deep mourning, and what size? Was it for herself f or a relative? For herself? Oh, that was too bad! And was it a father she had lost? Not a husband? Oh, how sad! Was it very sudden? An accident or an illness? Mem had not yet decided which it was to be, and her guilty confusion might well have been taken for a confession of murder. That was what she felt it must be.

The saleswoman's curiosity was quickened to torment by the evasiveness of Mem's mumbled answers, and when Mem declined to have the things sent to her address, and asked to have them put in a box for her to carry, the saleswoman could not conceal her agitation. Mem caught her glance as she looked for a wedding ring on Mem's bare hand.

This frightened Mem and increased her despair of success, but she had to hold herself in control long enough to march out as a dazed relict of blighted hope. It was hard to manage this and carry a large bundle, too; but she reached the sidewalk somehow.

The saleswoman's suspicions had given her a hint. She stopped at a jewelry store and bought herself a plain gold band. She wore it out of the store, explaining that she had lost her first ring.

When she returned to her boarding house the landlady, whose inquisitiveness was still simmering to a boil, let her in. As Mem locked glances with her defiantly she saw the landlady's eyes go to her hand and widen with recognition of the wedding ring.

Mem let the box of mourning fall to the floor. If it had broken open! The landlady gasped:

"You ain't married a' ready?"

"Yes."

"Lord o' mercy! That's the quickest work I ever did see! Where's your husband?"

"Minding his business, his own business!"

She regretted the unwarranted insolence instantly, but it served to put the landlady on the defensive and taught Mem the value of bluff, and the military rule: when your position is weak, leave it and attack.

The landlady fried in her own fat trying to figure out what sort of creature Mem was, but the next morning she was gone. A few days later a letter came for "Miss Steddon." Before readdressing it, the landlady could not resist steaming it open. It proved to be a message of love from the girl's father. Among many expressions of uneasiness for the poor child was a pleasant word for Mr. Woodville; also a pious hope that the splendid gentleman would be a real protection and comfort to the little wanderer.

Thus one dupe dupes another and the fooled father fooled the landlady by confirming the lie Mem had told her. With all doubts as to the girl's honesty allayed, the mistress of the boarding house crossed out "Miss Steddon," wrote, "Mrs. John Woodville, General Delivery, Yuma," and glued the flap down again.

# CHAPTER XVI

THE EARLY MORNING TRAIN from Tucson would deposit Mem at Yuma in the midafternoon. The railroad was never far from the Mexican border and the desert was stinging hot.

Yet Mem suffered an inner chill and her flesh crept clammily at what she had to do; for on that journey she was to get rid of her husband.

He had been vague before, but as she made ready to slaughter him he became fearsomely real. She went through the experience of a bravo who had lightly accepted a commission to assassinate a stranger, but, on meeting him and coming to know him, found him likable, lovable, and his destruction abominable.

The scenes the train swept her through were as damned as her deed: a famine-land of stunted growth or none.

John Woodville sat beside her in the train. He vanished as soon as she turned to look his way, but when she gazed with unfocused lenses through the window at the blurred sand and sage his presence was almost palpable.

When she closed her scorched eyes she could almost feel him leaning against her shoulder, his breath stirring the little curls at the nape of her neck. He took in warm, strong ringers, her cold hand lying idle at her side. In the dark of her shut eyes he put his arm about her shoulder and drew her to him and kissed her cheek, whispering, "My wife!" He turned her head and pressed on her pale mouth so masterful a kiss that her lips reddened and quivered.

She tried to summon her dead lover to the defense of his rights in her possession, but Elwood was more unreal now, more remote, than the mirage of this conqueror.

She tried to fling him off by opening her eyes and re-establishing the other passengers in the crowded car, but the somnolence of the burning morning dragged her back to the weird world of sleep.

As her eyes closed she caught sight of a cowboy racing the train on a plunging bronco, and when she fell asleep she fell into the saddle of a pinto alongside John Woodville's mustang. And she rode with him across the sage-spotted sands, toward the brown mountains, and found there a cabin in a dark grove. And it was their new home. She was the mistress of it, but he was the master of her, a ruthless, laughing husband, who would not be denied, but mocked her fears and made her his wife, broke her to his will as he broke the wildly resisting bronco.

She ran, pursued but overtaken, and woke with a start, spent and panting, and stared at the drowsy passengers.

She was astounded and a little disappointed to find herself still on the same car. His hot cheek against hers was only the sun-baked windowpane tinkling with the rain of the blown sand.

She fought off the swooning drowsiness that dragged her back to a siesta of fancy, and devoted herself to the stern task of arranging a plausible death for her short-lived bridegroom.

Fear of discovery was as acute in Mem's heart as if she were planning genuine homicide. Some authors have wept over the slaughter of their creatures; some have rejoiced in their murder as a fine art. But Mem was a beginner, a bungler. She was bound to make a bad job of it, and she could not trust her imagination.

After an hour or two of deep study that only increased her sense of hopeless floundering, she went to her luncheon in the dining car. It was hard to play executioner on an empty stomach. On her way back to her place she saw on an empty seat a newspaper. The owner had plainly finished with it and tossed it aside. He was not visible and she resolved that theft was a proper prelude to a greater atrocity.

So she snatched up the paper and carried it back to her place. It was the *Los Angeles Times*, an enormous budget filled with the proud expression of the fastest-growing city in the world, a city tumultuous with prosperity at a time when nearly every other city and town was cowering under the aftermath of the World War.

Mem found (as is to be expected in any newspapers but those curious documents built to suit the ostriches who believe in concealing reference to crime and other departures from monotony) many accounts of murders, robberies, accidents, and other manifestations of human fallibility.

Magnificent burglaries were properly chronicled. Nearly every day somebody seemed to loot a mail train or a bank messenger of the ransom of a dozen dukes. Highway robbery was bringing back the glorious days of Dick Turpin, Jonathan Wild, and Claude Duval. Those who stood quietly behind their counters had drama brought to them on the tip of a pistol; those who motored along quiet roads or city streets were hailed from other cars by fleeting highwaymen or highwaywomen; or they discovered with their search lights somber gentlemen (or ladies) whose watchword was becoming a national greeting "Put 'em up!"

It seemed as if one half the world had its hands in the air while the other half went through its pockets, cash drawers, suitcases, or mail pouches.

Los Angeles, as one of the busiest cities going, naturally had its share of this industry; furthermore, its thronged streets were superior to every other city's in the number of people killed and maimed by the floods of automobiles.

Mem thought of Los Angeles as the missionary thinks of Benin, Somaliland, Milan, or Shanghai, or some other center of crime, though none of the foreign murder mills has ever approached the American grist.

In the *Times* she discovered a number of suggestive deaths. Here was the story of a man who slipped into the swollen Colorado River, which was running one of its annual amoks. Here were a hundred people in Colorado State swept out of their homes and drowned by a torrent. Here was a rich man whose neck was broken in an overturned car; here were a score effaced in a collision between an auto bus and an electric train. Here was a New-Yorker shot dead in his pajamas as he sat with a lapful of morning letters. Here was a man found buried in his own cellar; here was a mid-Western gentleman for whose murder his wife and his stepdaughter were being tried, the allegation being that they had filled him with arsenic taken from fly paper. Here was a man who hired a hobo to play a practical joke on his wife and pretend to hold them up in their doorway; then the amazing dramatist shot the hobo dead, shot his wife dead, and announced that he had taken part in a pistol duel with a highwayman. The cynical police found a few flaws in his glib story and wrung a confession from him.

He was a very religious young man, too, and superior to all small vices. And the jury at his first trial disagreed as to his guilt, since he repudiated his confession. A second jury found him guilty, but he pleaded insanity and deferred the penalty. Altogether an original genius in crime. Mem envied him his ingenuity.

There were instances enough and too many of death's activities in the newspaper. Here was an aviator doing a moving-picture stunt whose ship caught fire and brought him down burned to a crisp. Here was a man killed in his automobile by a big tree falling over him.

There was such an embarrassment of riches that Mem could not select a single method of doing away with Mr. Woodville. She forgot him utterly for a while in a page devoted to the gossip of moving-picture studios. She saw that Robina Teele and Tom Holby had come back to Holly wood from a dash to New York for local color, and would soon be going out again "on location," wherever that was. She saw that Viva d'Artoise and her husband had reopened their beautiful bungalow in Edendale. She saw that Miriam Yore had arrived and taken a palatial house for her stay. Maurice Maeterlinck had come out on a special train. Many English men and women of fame were on their way, and herds of authors who, being American, were unimportant. Domestic goods are always shoddy, and imported elegant.

Mem reverted to her plot. She had her mourning all ready to put on. But here was a new complication. If she arrived in Yuma as a widow she must don her mourning in the train. She would have to retire to the narrow cell of the women's room and make the change there. That was inconvenient, but not impossible — it was the only thing to do.

Yet if she went in a maid and out a widow, people might notice the change and wonder; for she had been well-observed by the other passengers. A few of them had remarked that it was hot, or asked her if it were not hot. "Pretty hot, what?" one woman had said. Mem had thought peevishly what a funny thing it was the way folks used "pretty"; "pretty hot" meant "hideous hot."

She knew that women were like cameras for snapshotting other women's clothes at a glance and remembering them like a photograph. Men didn't notice such things much; yet men had noticed her, two men particularly; one of them a flashy, impudent creature with hard, exploring eyes that fairly nosed her like a pig's snout; the other a lonely deer-eyed thing pleading for pity with a woman-hungry stare.

Mem had a flash of unusual cynicism toward the moralities. Why is it that we feel so sorry for the loneliness of the timid man and so disgusted with the loneliness of the bold man? The loneliness must hurt both of them about the same. But she did not dwell on the thought. Humanity is never going to give the sympathy to the hyena that it wastes on the more destructive rabbit.

What settled Mem's debate was the realization that if she donned her crape on the train it would cause a stir among the people in whose flying parlor she had sat for seven hours or so. And some of them would doubtless be getting off at Yuma.

She wondered if somebody would come up to her at the station, as at Tucson, and announce himself as the deputy of her father. She hoped not. He could hardly have divined that she was bound for Yuma. Yet she could not feel sure. For all she knew, the first person she met might be somebody from Calverly.

Another point decided her. If she wrote to her father that she had left Tucson as a wife and reached Yuma as a widow, it would be necessary to push her husband off the train or wreck the train or something; and that would be hard to verify.

There were other reasons for giving herself a little longer experience of wedded bliss. This marriage was for a purpose.

She grew frantic with indecision. The train seemed to be exerting itself to fling her into Yuma before she could make up her mind. Nothing was easier than to tell a lie, but, great Heavens! How difficult it was to foresee all the things that would happen to it as it went along accumulating complications. Like other works of art, a lie must be all things to all men or be strong enough to endure their idiosyncrasies and their attacks.

Doctor Bretherick had told her to hold her head up and run, yet not to run. He had thereupon shipped her West to a land of strangers; yet she could neither break away from the ties at home nor break through the nets ahead of her. She was running as fast as she could, but she had leg irons on. She had not left pursuit behind, and the path ahead was all brambles and pitfalls.

The train went whooping into a low, loosely built town as she oscillated from one plan to another. A hoarse voice bawled: "Yew-my! Yew-my!"

# CHAPTER XVII

NOBODY STEPPED FORWARD to call Mem by name. But she almost wished that somebody had, for she was in a foreign world indeed.

The town had nothing of Tucson's quality. It was still a frontier post in the eternal battle with the savage desert. Nearly a century and a half ago Spanish missionaries and soldiers had been massacred here by the Yuma Indians.

Indians were all about the station now, and they frightened the girl who knew of them only as demons of cruelty. The heat was savage, too.

There is a saying that "only a sheet of paper stands between Yuma and hell." Mem could have believed it as her thin soles winced at the oven-lid platform, and the sun bored through her hat and her sweaty hair into her very brain.

She was solicited to go to the hotel, but she could hardly afford such splendor. She inquired about a boarding house. The baggageman recommended one, and she rode thither, fearing to trust herself to wander about the sun-smitten streets.

They were torrid, those streets, but fascinating, since everything was foreign to her experience. The shabbiest adobe hut was picturesque to her because cooked mud was new to her; the "stick-in-the-mud" houses made of plastered willow poles were artistic, somehow.

Date palms and mesquite trees and fuzzy cottonwoods, pepper trees and domesticated cacti, made her cry out with delight.

But the Indians were the main charm. They gave the dusty, dreary town a festival look. They reminded Mem of the days when circuses had come to Calverly. She had never been permitted to go to them, and it had hurt her father's confidence in her when she showed a desire to see the free parades. But now she was inside the circus, part of the troupe. She expected to see an old stagecoach swing into the street, pursued by shooting Apaches.

Yuma was filled with Indians. An Indian school was there, and a reservation. The Indians had their own shops and farms. They were tamed now and no longer matched torture and treachery with the soldiers and the pioneers.

They were subdued to agriculture and petty commerce. Their barbaric souls found expression only in raw, flamboyant colors. The squaws went down the street in cheap fabrics, high in the neck and low in the hem. They wore mainly blue-and-white Mother Hubbards aided and abetted by capes of colors that massacred one another and tortured the beholder. The hot wind flapped their clothes about them with a ruthless draftsmanship that emphasized what it concealed. There was no question as to the conformation of these squat, stodgy figures.

The red fillets about their brows would have been more effective if the faces beneath had been more attractive or the lawless hair better kempt.

Even the young squaws had little to commend them to admiration, and the contrast between their gold-crowned teeth and their shoeless feet was not to their advantage.

The men were better looking and better carried. They were mainly tall and lithe and haughty. They had also a passion for color, for bandannas and loud shirts. They wore their hair longer than the squaws wore theirs.

Tribal custom forbade them to braid it and it fell in long strands sometimes to their waists, with no confinement except perhaps a piece of colored string.

Mem could hardly believe her eyes when a long, lean buck flew past on a bicycle, his hair streaming out like a young girl's.

She passed one boarding house in whose front yard was a signboard boasting the stormlessness of the region:

Free Board and Lodging
Every Day in the Year that
The Sun Don't Shine

In such a persecuting heat as this Mem thought the legend on the sign more of a threat than a promise.

When she reached the boarding house selected for her, she rejoiced at the sight of shade. But here lurked another landlady to be lied to. Mrs. Drissett greeted Mem hospitably and asked, "What name, please?"

Mem managed to check the name "Steddon" coming up her throat and changed it hastily to "Mrs. Woodville."

"Your husband ain't with you?"

"Er, no. He, he's coming along later." And now her heart sank. How could she kill off Mr. Woodville here when he had not yet arrived? How was she to arrive him?

"You'll want a double room, then," said Mrs. Drissett. "Yes, of course, er, yes."

And now she had to pay extra money for a ghost!

As she moved up to her allotted room the sad-eyed man she had noted on the train came up and asked for "'commodations."

It was well that Mem had not put on her mourning. She would have been caught indeed. She rested in her darkened room to escape the afternoon blaze, but when she came down to supper she was placed next to a woman who frightened her worse than a tarantula, by the petrifying remark:

"Small world, ain't it, Miz Woodville? My husband's folks on his mother's side was Woodvilles. What part of the country does your husband's family hail from?"

Mem choked sincerely on a bread crumb, but prolonged the spasm while she tried to plot an answer to this perilous question. She had never expected to be cross-examined on her husband's family or habitat, and had never equipped him with either.

So she excused herself and left the table, strangled in throat and mind.

She could not endure the jail of her room, and stole out for a walk. The desert twilight was turning the tin roof of the sky into a heavenly ceiling where invisible spirits were wielding brushes of divine splendor.

The town's one ambitious building, the courthouse, broke the horizon with a cupola that was a palette of reflected pigments.

She wandered down along the swollen Colorado, a stream of blood in the sunset. An old stern-wheeled steamer fought its way up from the California gulf noisily and ominously, like some primeval water beast returning to its lair in the Grand Canyon.

The mountains in the distance were piled up in mournful dunes against a sea of gleaming light.

But she was afraid of the Indians slipping noiselessly about on innocent errands. She could not believe that they were not planning a massacre. This was the old Apache country. Yet the Indians and the Mexicans, whose children played about as naked as the other pigs, were not dangerous to her. They made little trouble over an unauthorized child or two.

She hurried back to the main street where the Indians were mere loafers and small-town sports, smoking cigarettes and ogling the giggling girls in the evening mood of other small towns.

She was faint with hunger and entered a drug store for refreshment. She bought herself a nut sundae as at Calverly. On either side of her was an Indian brave treating an Indian girl to the same pale-face medicine. The braves wore head dresses of gaudy color almost as gaudy as the shirts on the young white beaux who were taking their sweethearts to the movies.

Mem followed the crowd and paid "two bits" to sit with the aristocrats, while the Greasers, the Hopis, and Navajos went in at the other door for ten cents.

The Indians had learned to spoon in the dim light, and they laughed at the low comedy and sighed at the low pathos. They could read the first universal language, and romance was warming their dreary lives.

Mem smiled to think of her father's wrath at the movies as the weapons of Satan, for she could not but realize how much safer from temptation these spectators were here watching the unfolding of almost any imaginable fictions than they would be wandering in stealthy couples along the gloomy river banks or left to the mercy of their own devices in the dark of their wretched homes.

She blushed suddenly with the thought that if she and Elwood had spent that Sunday evening in a moving-picture house, instead of mooning on the home porch, she might have escaped this shameful exile.

She went back to her boarding house relieved a little from the monomania of her own problems by watching the weaving and unweaving of pictured problems.

When she reached her new home she found the yard full of beds, and most of the beds occupied by a sprawling populace with hardly so much as a sheet to mask its night-wear.

She stole through the camp to her own room, and found it bedless. She stood at her door bewildered.

The woman who had frightened her away from her dinner by her genealogical interest in the Woodville tribe appeared ghost-like in nightgown and a toga'd sheet and, seeing her perplexity, explained the custom of the country.

"You'll suffercate if you try to sleep in your own room, honey. Get into your nightgown and bring your bedcloes down with you, like I'm doin'. Your bed is in the yard next to mine. You'll sleep good and feel right refreshed in the mornin.'"

There was nothing for Mem to do but follow suit. To one who had never seen a bathing beach or gone in bathing undressed among a crowd, the ordeal was terrifying. She dreaded it as an early Christian martyr might have recoiled when the Romans tore off her clothes and thrust her into the arena; as those three Quaker women must have shuddered when the good Puritans of Boston stripped them to the waist, tied them to the tail of a cart, and lashed their bare backs through the snowy streets of eleven towns for their souls' sakes; just as the good Puritans of 1920 lashed the bare reputations of the moving-picture producers for the good of the community.

Fortunately for Mem's tranquility, her Woodvillian relative by marriage was already asleep and asnore when she slipped wraithlike out into the yard and, after a pause at the brink, ran to her bed and crawled under a tent of mosquito netting and nothing else.

She lay staring up at familiar stars in a most unfamiliar world, and shame and loneliness smothered her, as she smothered her sobs in her pillow lest she wake the neighbors. The hot breath from her own lungs was cooler than the night breeze, and the bed beneath her was so warm that modesty battled almost vainly with nature to keep as much as a sheet over her.

She wondered why she had come to this Gehenna where she did not purge herself of sin, but committed more and more sin. She wondered why anybody was here at all. Having learned to distrust her own wild capabilities for passionate impulse, she wondered how long she would endure the penance.

Here she lay, tossing like a frying fish in a skillet, trying to atone for a moment's rapture with a lifetime of woe, while other women had glorious times and fame and luxury; and did what they pleased, and were fawned upon by the whole world. That Miriam Yore! She got ten thousand a week in spite of the fact that people said she had had two children outside the law! Was she popular in spite of that fact? or because of it?

In such insane brooding Mem fell asleep at length.

She fell asleep so late that she slept on far past the daybreak, and when the sun's rays finally flailed her eyelids open she sat up with a start, thinking that someone had moved the house out from under and over her.

Her darting eyes met the bleary gaze of the sad-eyed man, lolling a few beds away.

He smiled and drawled, "Good mawn'n." This was really quite too incredible. She did not answer him, but hid under the sheet until she was sure that he had scrambled out and, wrapping the drapery of his couch about him, had marched into the house.

Then she gathered up her bedclothes and ran.

She bathed standing up by a washbowl on a washstand, and the cold water was already so warm, her flesh already so tingling with the early heat, that she dreaded to get into clothes.

And, of course, she was suffering nausea every morning; her body was as sick of the complexities of life as her mind. The relentless machineries within herself seemed as bent upon her punishment as the relentless machineries of human society without. Her soul stood aghast between the persecutions of the devil inside her and the deep sea of the people outside.

She grew so distraught with trying to justify the peculiar ways of God to man, and especially to woman, that she felt afraid of her own rebellious soul. She feared her room and herself, and ran down to breakfast.

She was glad to see that the old woman who asked about the Woodvilles was not in her place. But she came in later, and with the kindliest spirit took up the question again.

"I was askin' you about the Woodvilles when you had a chokin' fit last evenin', and you didn't git to tell me about your husband. I'm a Rodman myself, or was till I married Mr. Sloat. But his mother was a Woodville like I told you, and finer folks never was. It would be funny if you and me was related, kind of, that away, wouldn't it?"

"Wouldn't it?" Mem echoed; and, like Echo, contributed nothing helpful to the conversation.

"Just where did your husband come from?"

"I don't know!"

"You don't know!"

"No."

"But he must have come from somewhere."

"No, he didn't. That is, he was an orphan."

"But even orphans have folks. What part of the country was he born in?"

"He doesn't remember."

"Land alive! Child, are you tryin' to have fun with me? You're not ashamed of the Woodvilles, are you?"

Naturally, anyone would have said, "No! Oh, no!" So Mem, being in an unnatural frenzy, answered, "Yes."

This stumped Mrs. Sloat completely. It was her turn to choke. When she regained the vocal use of her windpipe she began again, half to herself:

"So you're ashamed of the Woodvilles, eh? Well, well!

Who'dv thought it? Still, o' course, there's a black sheep in all families. Where'd you say your husband — Oh, he was an orphan, wa'n't he? I'd like to talk to him when he gits here. You're expectin' him, I believe you said."

"Did I?"

"Well, didn't you?"

"Maybe. I'm liable to say anything when it's so hot."

"Say, you'd better go lay down. You're talkin' awful funny. Go out and set on the corner the porch. They's usurally a breeze there if they's anywhurs."

"Thanks, I will."

Mem had a keen desire to go to her room and laugh uproariously. She had found a madwoman's glee in bewildering old Mrs. Sloat with her evasive answers. But in her room her insane self would be waiting to nag her with more baffling questions than Mrs. Sloat's. So she went to the porch and sat in the rocker at the corner and found a little nepenthe in watching the tremulous beauty of a pepper tree, all soft foliage and shadow. It seemed to be draped in old shawls with embroideries of deep red.

By and by the sad-eyed man came clumping along the porch and took a chair. He was evidently pining for someone to talk to, but he nearly lost his audience on the first question:

"'Scuse me, ma'am, but landlady says your name is Woodville. That right?"

Mem nodded, and her heart began to beat her side so hard that she wondered if he could not see it leap under her light waist. She made ready to escape again, but he allayed her panic:

"Reason I ast was, I knowed a man o that name no, dadgone it! his name was Woodward. That's right. His name was Woodward or no, it was well, anyways, it prob'ly wasn't his real name at that. I called him Woodie or Woodhead." He sat chuckling to himself over his reminiscences. "Woodie was a nice enough feller. Not much sense, but meant all right, I reckon. Many's the mountain him and I prospected, the Chocluts, Sooperstitions, all of 'em round these parts. See that big peak up there all by itself like a Gyptian obalisk? That's old Picacho. Used to be so rich in gold that a miner who didn't wash three hunded dollars of gold a day was fired for a no-count. Now it's all abandoned, towns and camps. There's gold there yit, but it's sure hell to find.

"Well, this Woodville, or whatever it was, seems like him and I went over every inch of this country with a pick and a spyglass.

We like to died a dozen times water give out. Once we got to a water hole so deep down our rope wouldn't just quite reach it, and we couldn't climb down. There was a big rattlesnake there at that. We was both black in the mouth. One of our burros had fell off a ledge and died, and the other n shook off his pack and bolted. And we was too weak to chase him. Then Woodie went plumb crazy. He throwed away his blankit and his cloes and took off his boots and flung 'em down the water hole at the snake, and would've jumped after 'em, only I helt on to him. I was some feeble m'self, but I got him roped and tied.

"Then he cert'ny give me and Gawd about the best cussin' out either of us ever got, and we both been swore at considable. Well, my brain begun to dry up and go crazy, too. I was startin' to throw away my things when a prospector found us. He had water and a string of burros, and he brought us in. After that I told Woodie I was goin' to keep away from the desert. He laughed hisself sick, and says he, Bodlin — my name's Bodlin — Bodlin, I'll bet you fifty dollars you come back before the year's out. I took him up, and I lost and won. Woodie went in again and stayed."

"He stayed?" Mem mumbled. "You mean he's still there?"

"He shore is, Miz Woodville! When we say a feller stayed in the desert we mean he ain't never comin' back at tall. There was a piece in the Tucson paper about Woodie. Pore old skate, he went back once too often."

"Did he die of thirst?"

"Not him. Not this time. That ole desert has more ways n one of eatin' you up. It was Woodie's luck, after dyin' of thirst a hunded times, to git drownded. Yessum, the desert is fuller of jokes than anybody you know. Take them miradges, for instance; when you'd give your soul for a spoonful of wet scum you see a lake and a river and a waterfall playin' away just ahead of you. It ain't there, and you know it. And yet you know it is and you just can't be pushin' on to see if it ain't there this time.

"But Woodie he made his camp in a dry arroyo bed, and durin' the night they was a cloudburst, and he must a been hit by a regular river before he knowed what struck him. They found him in a pile of brush the river had gethered up. When they found him it was as dry as ever and his canteen was empty.

"And now I'm forty dollars ahead, for I can't pay him his bet. I was braggin' about how smart I was to git out and stay out. But here I am goin' in again as soon as I can git a couple of burros and a few things. Once the desert gits you, it's got you. It's like some of these women you hate and can't git red of. They don't love you and they rob you and torture you and you know they'll kill you some day, but you just can't quit 'em for keeps."

Mem thought a long time before she spoke. Then she said:

"Do women ever go into the desert, Mr. Bodlin?"

"Sometimes; not often. Sometimes."

A wild look came into her eyes and she nodded unwittingly. The vassal of the desert said:

"Was you thinkin' of goin' in?"

She smiled curiously, and even he who knew so little of women read a yes in her smile.

"With your husband?" he mumbled.

She smiled again.

"He's a mighty lucky man, a mighty lucky man! The desert is a tough place on a pirty little lady. It'll lose you that white skin and them soft hands. But it would be a grand thing for a man to have a woman to talk to and to take care of, to share a canteen with and to find gold for. Or, if you didn't find gold, you'd have her. Under the stars and in the cool of some of them caves and they's canons up there where you find palm trees growin', like you was back in the Garden of Eden."

He was fairly writhing with his vision of such a pilgrimage. He sighed like a furnace:

"Your husband's shore one lucky man. Tell you what, Miz Woodville, if you ever git tired of him, just lea me know and I'll push him off a clift for you or punch a hole in his canteen. Anyways, I'll be on the watch for you. I can't give you no address. We don't git mail very reglar on the desert, but everybody knows Bodlin. Gosh all hemlock! But your husband's shore one lucky man!"

He got up and walked away, as if to escape the temptation to covet his neighbor's wife. The girl was so beautiful in his eyes that he would have been ready to commit murder to get her if that would fetch her. His visions of her companionship were too fiercely vivid to be borne in her demure presence.

But it was Mem who was going to do the murdering. She had found the way to be rid of her husband for the satisfaction of her people.

Now if she could only find a way to be rid of herself.

And that way came to her before the long day had burned itself away. She had hidden from the sun in her room. The drawn curtains kept out the light and the sun-steeped wind; but the still air inside the room seemed to have thorns. It stung her flesh with nettles where she lay supine on her bed in as little garb as her schooled modesty would permit.

She heard two waitresses talking in the dining room below as they set the tables for supper.

"Who was that letter you got, from? some feller?"

"Nah! It was from a lady up to Palm Springs, askin' me was I comin' back up there this season?"

"Are you?"

"Nah! Too quiet for me. Yuma ain't no merry-go-round, but Palm Springs, my Gawd! It's just a little spot of shadder in the desert. Nice and cool in the season, but what does cool get you if you're cut off from all the world? Would ya b'lieve ut, there ain't even a movin' pitcher there. When I want to hide from the worl I'll crawl into Palm Springs, but not before."

"This lady offer you a job?"

"Yes. She's on her knees to me. Mrs. Randies her name is. Husband's got a ranch. Nice little hotel there, too, with jobs goin' beggin'; but not for me, thank you. I'm through with them retreats. I'm tryin' to work my way to a real city. Gimme folks and plenty of 'em. How'd you like to go there and take my job at Randies's."

The other voice moaned: "Me? Not much. I run away from home to git love and excitement, and look where I've landed! My Gawd! but I wisht I was back in Wichita!"

The voices died in a clatter of plates and knives and forks. There was melancholy and thwarted ambition everywhere, evidently.

Mem had never heard of Palm Springs, but she was looking for just such a place. And a ranch! She had always wanted to see a ranch.

The heat here was like a madness upon her, but most of all she abhorred this eternal facing of questions. Mrs. Sloat was a nuisance, a menace. Writing letters home and getting letters from home had become an intolerable burden on her soul.

She wanted to get away from everybody that had ever known her. She wanted to find some deep, dark cave. She was the prey already of the instinct that Doctor Bretherick had spoken of, the instinct to crawl away and hide during the long, ugly phase ahead of her and the fearful climax at the end of it.

There was a blaze of mutiny in her heart against the whole business of her life. She understood why Bodlin's overloaded, overdriven burro had kicked off its pack and bolted. This pack of lies that she was carrying and adding to at every step was bound to crush her sooner or later. Why be a burro for other people's burdens? It would profit her none. What reward could she hope for?

Heat and fatigue whipped her into hysteria. Her soul vomited up all the precepts it had been fed upon. She found energy enough for one last desperate letter home. Then she would declare her soul bankrupt and face the world free of responsibilities to the past.

DARLING MAMMA AND PAPA, — By now you have probably ceased to be surprised at anything I do. You'll think I've gone clean crazy and I guess I have, but as long as I'm getting better and happier every day you won't mind.

I've been too busy to write you all about John as I promised. He is out here scouting for a famous mine and is going prospecting for it right away. It is a famous lost mine that got abandoned on account of some old littagation and was nearly forgotten. So he's on the hunt for it and we're going out to hunt for it together. It means losing ourselves in the desert and the mountains for a long while, there's no telling how long but it will be terribly romantic and fine for my health and when next you hear from me I may be so rich I'll send you a solid-gold sewing machine, mamma, and papa a solid-gold pulpit.

There's no mail delivery where we're going and no way of reaching us, but don't worry. If anything happens, I'll let you know. If you don't hear from me for a long while you'll know everything's all right. You can send your letters to me here and I'll find them when I get back. Don't send me any more money.

So goodbye and blessings on your darling heads. John sends his love.

Your loveing, loveing, loveing

MEM.

As she finished the letter she thought grimly of what Mr. Bodlin had said. She was not quite sure just what was going to happen to Mr. Woodville. In her morbid humor and her resentment at her own allotted torture, she had a leaning toward the most gruesome fates for her husband: a death from thirst or a rattlesnake's fangs or a fall down a precipice.

One thing was sure, John Woodville was going into the desert to "stay!"

She envied him the calm certainty of his fate. The main solace to her pride in her self-obliteration was the thought that she was going to cease to be a drain on the flat purse of her poor father. He and her mother had gone through life like two sad desert burros, carrying burdens. They should no longer carry hers.

Villager though she was, and used to housework, she had been brought up in a certain pride. To be a chambermaid or a waitress was a dismal come-down, but she must accept it. What right had she to pride?

She would go to Palm Springs and toil humbly as long as she could, and save her wages and pretend to be a widow. She would go there in mourning and bury her heart in sack cloth and ashes. And perhaps in that thief's crucifixion to which she was carrying her own increasingly heavy cross she would die unknown and be lost to the too many miseries of this world.

And so she fared into the desert to "stay." She went there to find obscurity and concealment, to embrace poverty and humility.

But everything went by contraries, and from that oasis she was to be caught up into a fiery chariot, for all the world to behold as it rolled her round and round the globe on an amazing destiny.

Everything that had tortured her and was yet to torture her was a schooling.

# CHAPTER XVIII

THAT A LIE NEVER prospers is a lie that always prospers. It is discouraging for lovers of the truth to review the innumerable and eternal untruths that are told for the truth's sake.

Mem broke away from Yuma with an unusual economy of falsehood. Her trunk was the only difficulty. It had followed her from Tucson to her boarding house in Yuma. But she could not check it further without giving her destination.

After a vast amount of thought Mem decided to ask her landlady to hold her trunk for her until she returned for it. She put into it everything that she could spare. She was going to travel light and forage on the country. There was an old shed in the back yard, and the dry air would serve as a perfect preservative for her belongings in case she ever came back for them. She told the landlady the same story she embodied in her farewell letter home, and asked her to hold any mail that might come. Then she slipped away while Mrs. Sloat was not looking.

She went to the station with her old suitcase and took the train into the Imperial Valley. To her it was as pathless and mapless and as filled with strange beasts as to the first prospectors. Only, she was not looking for gold or adventure. She was looking for peace. And, like the usual pioneer, she was sure to find almost everything but what she hunted.

In her ignorance Mem bought her ticket to Palm Springs station, instead of to Whitewater, where an auto bus would have met her.

She was a little more accustomed now to the desert, but she took no interest in the miracles that had tamed the wastes of sand and the Salton Sea and put the idle, sterile welter to work upon a vast garden; had built enormous dams to impound the stray water, and endless channels to carry it where it was needed when it was needed.

Mem was deposited at the lonely station, and fear smothered her as she watched the train vanish into the glare. But a rancher, almost as shy as she, offered her the hospitality of his wagon. He was rough, unshaven, and unkempt, the very picture of a stage robber. Still, she preferred him to the solitude, and he turned out to be almost as silent.

He was too timid to ask her questions and she was grateful to him for that. He said that he was going past the Randies's ranch anyhow, and would leave her there. And he said nothing more.

When the ranchman had helped her into his wagon he un-hitched the horses and made a dash for the seat. The horses began the journey with a take-off from the ground that hinted at a voyage through the air rather than along the road. Then they settled down to their ordinary gait. Mem would have called it a runaway, but the driver did not even haul in on the lines.

After a time, Mem saw ahead of her a shimmering lake and trees and a waterfall.

"That's Palm Springs, I suppose," she said.

"No ma'am, that's a miradge, a maginary miradge. They's nothin' there at tall, no ma'am."

And now Mem had learned that her own eyes could lie to her with convincing vividness. She wondered if they deceived her when they showed her sagebrush and crippled trees bent in rheumatic agonies. She thought she saw Lilliputian alligators scuttering here and there. They were chuckwallas, but she did not dare ask about them.

Suddenly, as the road led them within eyeshot of two vast hills of sand unspotted with vegetation, she saw what she was sure was pure mirage, a scene that must have come from her memory of a picture in an old volume of Bible stories. She would almost have sworn that she looked into the desert of Araby, for she seemed to see a train of camels in trappings, and, perched upon their billowy humps, men in the garb of Bedouins.

She rubbed her eyes and scolded them, but they persisted in their story. Having been so perfectly deceived by the equally visible lake and cascade that were not, she did not mention the camels to her host, who gave no sign of wonder.

Then the horses seemed to suffer from the same delusion, for they grew panicky and began to buck and back and leave the road. The driver yelled at them and tried to force them ahead, but as they drew near the camels they went into hysterics.

They refused to obey yells or reins or the whiplash or even each other's impulses. But at length their insanities coincided; they slewed in the same direction, carried the wagon into the side ditch, and overturned it.

Mem found herself gently spilled in the soft sand, so little injured that her only thought was for pulling down her skirts.

She lay still, reclining, not in pain, but in wonderment, as the wagon slid on its side, the driver stumbling along and still clinging to the lines as if he tried to hold giant falcons in leash. The caravan grew restive, too, and Mem was consumed with perplexity as she saw one of the animals forced to its knees not far from her. The sheik, or whatever he was, tumbled from the saddle and ran to her.

A brown face looked out from the hood, and from the scarlet lips surrounded by a short beard came a voice startlingly un-Arabic.

"Miss Steddon! Miss Remember Steddon!"

She was so dazed that she could only stare into the mysterious face, doubly dark against the blinding sun. The Arab smiled and laughed.

"You don't know me? Don't you recall Mr. Woodville?"

This frightened her and confused her unbearably.

"Who are you?" she gasped.

"As a matter of fact, I'm only Mr. Holby, Tom Holby, a common movie actor out on location. But the last time you saw me you called me Mr. Woodville."

"Oh, did I? I was thinking of my husband."

"Your husband! You were Miss Steddon a week or two ago."

"Yes, but..."

"Oh, I see! You have taken the fatal step since then. Is that Mr. Woodville playing tag with those dancing demons out there?"

"Oh no! He's dead."

"Dead, already! and you only married a few days! Why, what on earth —"

She dropped her head. She could not face the rush of sympathetic horror in those famous eyes. She could not think in the nailing sunbeams pounding her aching head.

Holby read this as grief and sighed.

"You don't want to talk about it, of course. Forgive me. But you can't stay here."

# CHAPTER XIX

THEY SAY THAT THE Magdalen was not really a Magdalen, that tradition has forgotten the text and mixed her with a woman of Bethany, just as Potiphar's wife is carelessly branded with the deeds of another woman.

But Mem, as she cowered on the sand, felt as humble as the Magdalen in the pictures, though the man who looked down upon her so tenderly had never posed as a Galilean, even in the Miracle Play they give every summer in the canon at Hollywood.

Tom Holby's profession was the opposite of a preacher's. He tried to show how people actually did behave, not how they ought to. His authors would not let him be very real, but always forced a moral, and that is the true immorality of the moving pictures; not that they present wickedness so that innocent people may imitate it, but that they present life as if it punished wickedness and rewarded virtue; which is a pretty lie, but a lie nonetheless.

While Holby had an instant suspicion that Mem was not telling him the truth, he felt no call to rebuke her or to wring it from her. He thought: "She's pretty. She's in trouble. My business is to be as nice to her as I can."

He lifted her from the sand, brushed her off, and went for her suitcase, which had been dumped into the stunted stubs of a cholla cactus, that vegetable porcupine whose frosty barbs were fiendishly ingenious in creeping into his skin. Holby brought away a few spines that would cause him long agony until with a knife and pliers he should gouge them out. The darts of Cupid might have been plucked from the same bush; and Holby found the thoughts of this shy girl like cactus spines embedded in his thoughts tormentingly.

As he lugged the suitcase back to the road he tripped on the long skirts of his Arabian burnous. He had practiced walking in it when he was before the camera, but he was thinking of Mem now.

He was thinking: "She was not married when I met her on the train; a week later she is a widow. She has gone through two earthquakes in quick succession: a honeymoon and a funeral. I have found that, whenever a calamity occurs to anybody, lack of money adds to the horror of it."

His instinct was not to save her soul, but to make her body comfortable.

And so when he set the suitcase down by Mem, he asked her to rest upon it, and stood between her and the sun while he spoke very earnestly.

"Tell me to mind my own business if I'm impertinent, but may I ask you one question? Did your husband leave you any money?"

Mem was so startled that she mumbled:

"A little."

"Not much?"

"Not much."

"Enough?"

"For a while."

"Have you come here to be with your parents or friends or relatives?"

"No. I'm looking for a position as a chambermaid."

"My God! You!"

Her eyes were amazed at his horror. He cried, again:

"You with your beauty! Oh no!"

She had been brought up on a motto, "Praise to the face is open disgrace." She snubbed him with a fierce toss of the head.

He laughed aloud. He had been a small-town youth and had known that motto, but he had been so long among women who were of a quite opposite mind that he was amused by the quaint backwoods ideal of regarding charm as a thing unmentionable in polite society.

While he was trying to keep his face straight, as he apologized, a sharp voice broke in upon them. A man in a pith helmet, dark goggles, and a riding suit had steered a restive horse close to them and was complaining:

"Say, Holby, do you realize you're keeping the whole company waiting in this ghastly heat?"

"I beg your pardon, Mr. Folger. Just a moment, old man. Let me present you to Miss—Mrs. Woodville."

The director touched his helmet and nodded curtly. As he whirled his horse to ride back to his caravan, Holby ran and, seizing his bridle, led the horse aside and talked to Folger earnestly.

"Look here, old man. That girl is a friend of mine and beautiful as a peach. She's got the skin and the eyes that photograph to beat the band. She's just lost her husband and come out to this hell hole to be a chambermaid! It's too outrageous to think of. Give her a chance, won't you?"

The director twisted in his saddle and stared at Mem with expert eyes, then laughed at Holby:

"Is she a sweetie of yours?"

"None of that, now! She's as nice as they make 'em. But I can't stand the thought of her working on a ranch, making beds and wrestling slop jars. Give her a test and put her in the mob scene or something. And don't tell Robina I told you to, in Heaven's name."

Folger was puzzled. Robina Teele was a troublemaker in the company. But she made profitable trouble in the hearts of the public. Just now she was smitten with Tom Holby, and she had dealt fiercely with one or two minor actresses he had been polite to.

But it was bad studio politics to encourage these tyrannies. Stars had to be disciplined with care, like racehorses, yet curbed somehow.

If Holby could be freed from Teele's domination, even by the sharp knife of jealousy, it might be a good thing for the next picture.

Folger cast another look at Mem. There was a fresh meekness about her, an aura of gracious appeal. It would do no harm to try her out. If she were a failure no one would know it. If she were a discovery, he would get the credit. It would not hurt him to do Holby a favor, for the director's own contract was under question of renewal and a good word from Holby would not come amiss.

"All right," he said, "I'll take a chance. Two of the extra women keeled over this morning from the heat. I'll have my assistant take her to the wardrobe woman and get her fitted out and made up. She can appear in the famine scene, and I'll bring her forward for a close-up. If she looks good in the rushes, we'll keep her on. And now, for Heaven's sake, get back on your camel, for the camera men are just about ready to drop."

He set spurs to his horse and rode across the field, with his megaphone to his lips as he bellowed his orders.

The caravan resumed its plodding advance, and Holby turned back to say to Remember:

"I've taken a great liberty. I can't bear the thought of your working as a servant when there may be a big career before you in the pictures. The director saw you and he wants you to help him out. There is a shortage in the company for the big scene, and you'd be a godsend. Try it and see if you like it. If you don't, there's no harm done and you'll be paid well for your trouble. If you do like it, why... But to please me — I mean the director — do this, won't you?"

He knew people well enough to glean from the first glance into her eyes that Mem was appalled at the prospect of playing in the movies, and that his one hope was to put his gift in the form of a petition.

Before she could quite realize what she was doing, Mem had said:

"Well, of course, if it would be doing you a favor."

"An immense favor."

"I don't know anything, you know."

"That's all the better. You have nothing to unlearn. Here's Mr. Ellis, the assistant director. He'll take care of you. I've got to go."

He introduced a young man who rode up and dismounted

with all the meekness of the meekest office on earth, that of assistant director. In a tone of more than vice-presidential humility Ellis explained to Mem what she was to do.

She was aghast at this sudden plunge into the deep waters of an unknown sea. She turned to tell Tom Holby that she really could not accept. But he was in no position to hear her. He was in every position. As his camel rose to its knees, Holby was flopped about in the air with a violence that threatened to throw his head afar like a stone in a sling. When the camel had established itself on its four sofa-cushioned feet it moved off with an undulating motion as sickening as an English Channel steamer's.

Mem turned to appeal to the man who had promised to drive her to the Randies ranch. But he was standing far out in a sea of sage and cactus, dolefully regarding his wagon, which lay on its back with three and a half wheels spinning in air and the other half of one scattered about the desert.

While Mem floundered in the sands of her own uncertain ties many camels went by, and horses in gorgeous trappings. Then followed a string of light automobiles loaded with machinery that she did not understand, with lighting equipment, with airplane propellers to kick up a sandstorm, and with paraphernalia of every sort.

After these walked and rode a great crowd of men and women in Arabian costumes, their faces and hands painted in raw colors. Ellis checked one of the cars in which sat a woman, Mrs. Kittery, to whom he introduced Mrs. Woodville, explaining what was to be done with her.

"Get in here, my dear," said Mrs. Kittery.

And before Mem could protest Mr. Ellis had flung her suitcase in, helped her to a seat, slammed the tin door on her, swung into his saddle and away.

The car kept to what road there was, and Mrs. Kittery soon learned how abysmal Mem's innocence was. But she was used to the ignorance of extra women and she was glad that Mem was not a Chinese, a Turk, or an Indian. She could at least understand English.

After a long and furiously jolty passage over the sand the caravan of motors and the mob of suffering extras came to a halt on the shady side of a cluster of Arabian tents.

Mrs. Kittery asked one of the extra women to make up Mrs. Woodville while she found a costume in the hamper. This amiable person was still unknown to fame as Leva Lemaire, really Mrs. David Wilkinson, whose husband had been killed in the war, leaving her with three children whom she supported by this form of toil. She preferred it to her previous experiences as a school-teacher and a trained nurse.

She made from forty to fifty dollars a week, and sometimes more, and she led a life of picturesque travel from nationality to nationality: a Mexican one week, a Hindu another, a farm wife again, a squaw, or a harem odalisque. Mem felt that the extra woman's life had its fascinations.

The art was "the business" to Mrs. Wilkinson, and she called it that. She was generous with grease paint and information, and she had a village mind that translated to Mem's village mind these foreign customs in a language she could understand.

Only such a steady-souled person could have kept Mem from bolting in panic before the ordeal of having her face calcimined and tinted, her eyelids painted, the lashes leaded, her eyebrows penciled, her lips encarnadined, and red dots put here and there to give depth. To her the decoration of the face with any color from outside had been hitherto an advertisement of eager vice. And now she was a painted woman, too!

Mrs. Wilkinson's own face was decorated like an Indian warrior's, including certain blotches of carmine, which she explained:

"My nose is too broad and flat, so I paint the sides of it red and that photographs like a shadow; and I have a double chin which disappears in the picture, thanks to the red; and I narrow my fat cheeks the same way. But you don't need any of that modeling. You're perfect."

Mem was dazed by this constant reference to her beauty. At home it had been a guiding principle that praising children made them conceited. These first compliments came like slaps in the face. But she was beginning to find them stimulating.

By the time Mem was varnished, Mrs. Kittery had arrived with gaudy costumes, earrings, necklaces, and bracelets. Mem was soon so disguised that when Leva Lemaire offered her a peek in the mirrored top of her make-up box she could not recognize herself at all. She looked like a cheap chromo of somebody else.

"There's two things you'll learn about the business, if you stay in it," said Leva; "you've got to get up at an ungodly hour and break your neck making ready on time. And then you've got to sit around for hours and hours with nothing to do. Half the time they don't reach you all day. And most of the scenes you're taken in are cut out of the final picture. Otherwise it's a nice life."

And now that her pores were stuffed with paint which it was disastrous to mop with a handkerchief, Mem had the task of waiting while the hot wind brought the great drops of sweat to her skin and the blown sand kept up an incessant scratching.

In the distance, in the relentless flagellation of the sun, the principals of the company enacted before a group of cameras a drama that Mem could not understand. The camels defiled slowly, then galloped back and defiled slowly again and again. There were long arguments; the director and his assistant dashed back and forth, trumpeting through their megaphones.

The camels alone revealed artistic temperament. They began to fight one another. A group of two dragged their terrified passengers hither and yon and knocked over a camera. One of them fled and, dumping his belfryman, got clean away. He was not found until the next day, and then in Palm Canon, where he reveled in a perfect duplicate of a homeland oasis.

Leva explained to Mem what all the bother was about:

"You see, they take everything first at a distance — long shots, they call them. They have three cameras here, but something always goes wrong, or looks as if it could be improved; so they make a lot of takes. Then they come closer and take medium shots to cut into the long shots. Then they take close-ups of the most dramatic moments. All these have to match — though they usually don't — so that they can be assembled in the studio for the finished picture.

"The camels go by one way to show they're passing a certain spot. Then they go by the same spot in the opposite direction to show the return. But in the finished picture that won't take place till a week later. But they take the things that happen on the same spot at the same time, no matter where they occur in the picture. It keeps the actors awfully mussed up in their minds. They don't know whether they're playing today, last month, or two years from now. That's Robina Teele on that biggest camel. She's earning her money today by the sweat of her whole system. She's sweet on Tom Holby and as jealous of him as a fiend. She's an awful cat, but he's a mighty nice boy, not spoiled a bit by being advertised as the most beautiful thing in the world. I was in a scene with him once; he was just as considerate as if I had been Norma Talmadge or Pauline Frederick."

While the extras waited and simmered their luncheon was served. The property crew went about among them, dealing out pasteboard boxes containing sandwiches wrapped in oiled papers, a bit of fried chicken, hard-boiled eggs, a piece of cake, and a Californian fruit: a peach, a pear, grapes, figs, a banana, or an orange.

There was a cauldron of coffee for those that wanted it hot, iced tea, and bottles of pop.

Mem had never been on a better-fed picnic. The women and men squatted on the ground and ate, swapping fruit and repartee. Some of the jokes sent blushes flying beneath the layers of paint on Mem's skin. There was a vast amount of caustic fun made of the principals, the director, and the management. But Mem tried to remind herself that the sewing circles at home were just as busy tearing down the reputations of the neighbors, only with a holier-than-thou contempt entirely lacking here.

There was a gypsy spirit in this company that Mem had never met. The gaiety was irresistible, and she managed to control her horror when she found that she was almost the only woman who refused a cigarette. Even Mrs. Wilkinson dug up a package from her desert robes.

The principals had their refreshments taken to them, and snatched it between scenes. Robina did not eat at all. She lived in an eternal Lent, since she had to fight a sneaking tendency to plumpness. She suffered anguishes of fasting and privation like a religious zealot, but from the opposite reason: the zealots crucified the flesh because it was the devil's lure; she in order to give it allurement and keep time's claws off her as long as possible.

So now, in a heat that drove the desert Indians into the shade and idleness, these dainty actresses and actors invited sunstroke and labored with muscles and emotions at full blast in order to make pictures and minimize the appalling overhead expense of every wasted hour.

After a time the extras were called forth from the comparative shelter of the tents to the scene of action. It was like being tossed from the red-hot stove lid into the very fire.

To Mem it was all incredible phantasmagory. She could not believe that this was she who stumbled across the sand, twitching her skirts out of the talons of the cactuses, carefully dabbing the sweat from her face with a handkerchief already colored like a painter's brush rag, and jingling, as she walked, with barbaric jewelry.

The mob went forward slowly and she recognized Tom Holby on a camel. She hoped that he would not recognize her, but he studied all the faces and, being used to disguises, made her out and hailed her with the password:

"How you standing it?"

She called up to him:

"All right, thank you."

There was vast interest in her from now on. The leading man had singled out an extra woman for special attention, and the gossip went round with a rush as of wings.

Mem did not know that she was already a public property. She would have fled as from a plague if she had known. Later she would come to realize that these people loved to believe the worst, forgive it, and absolve it with a forbearance met hardly anywhere else except in heaven.

The director massed the extras together and addressed them from his horse:

"Ladies and gentlemen, you are supposed to be an Arabian tribe driven from your homes by the cruel enemy. You are wandering across the desert without food or water, dying of hunger and thirst. Later in the afternoon, if we can reach it, you will be overtaken by a sandstorm and many of you will perish miserably. It's hard work, I know, but if you will go to it we'll be out of this hell-hole tomorrow and there will be more comfortable work in the cool night shots. So make it snappy, folks, and do what you are told on cue, with all the pep you can put into it. I thank you!"

The company was then divided into groups, with business assigned to each. Long shots were taken again and again. Small groups were posed with as much care as if the sun were benign instead of diabolic.

Close-ups of individuals were taken, the most striking types being selected and coached to express crises of feeling: "You go mad and babble, old man, will you? Tear at your throat and let your tongue hang out? ... You, miss, will you fall back in your mother's arms — you be mother, will you, miss, and catch her — you are to die, you know; just roll your eyes back and sigh and sink into a heap. And you, mother, wring your hands and beat your breast and wail. You understand Oriental stuff, eh? ... And I'd like somebody just to look up to heaven and pray for mercy, somebody with big eyes. Let me see, no, you're... I'm saving you for the... You, the young lady over there, will you step out? Please! Come on, come on! I won't bite unless I'm kept waiting; it's warm you know, folks. Come out, please. Oh, it's Mrs. Woodbridge, isn't it? I met you this morning. Here's your chance. Do this for me, like a good girl, and give yourself to it. Look up to heaven; if the sun brings tears to your eyes, all right, but let them come from your soul, dear, if you can. You see, you have seen your people dying like flies about you, from famine and hardship. You look up and say, O God, you don't mean for us to die in this useless torture, do you, dear God? Take my life and let these others live. Won't you, dear God?

"Something like that, you know. Don't look up yet. You'll blind yourself. Wait till I get the camera set. Here, boys, make a very close close-up of this."

Mem stood throbbing from head to foot with embarrassment and with a strange inrush of alien moods. The fierce eyes of the director burning through his dark glasses, the curious instigation in his voice, the plea to do well for him, quickened her magically.

The camera men set up their tripods before her, the lenses, like threatening muzzles, aimed point-blank; then they bent and squinted through their finders, and brought tapes up and held them so close that their hot hands touched her when they measured her exact distance, then adjusted the focuses. One of them lifted the fold of her hood a little aside from her brow. The director stared at her keenly, then put out his hand and asked for a powder puff. He dusted her face gently to dull the glistening surface.

They treated her as if she were an automaton, and she became one, a mere channel for an emotion to gush through.

Folger took her by the arm and murmured:

"Just once, now, dear, before we make the take. Remember what I told you. Let your heart break. Give us all you've got. Look round first and see your dying people. That's your father over there just gasping his life out. Your mother lies dead back there; you've covered her poor little body with sand to keep the jackals from it. Your own heart is broken in a thousand pieces. Can you do it? Will you? That's right. Look round now and let yourself go."

She felt herself bewitched, benumbed, yet mystically alive to a thousand tragedies. Her eyes rolled around the staring throng. Some of them were helping her by looking their agony; others were out of the mood, adjusting their robes, freshening their make-up, or whispering and smiling. But the gift of belief, the genius of substitution, fell upon her like a flame, and nothing mattered. They had brought music out into this inferno: a wheezy organ, a cello, and a violin that cried like the "linnet that had lost her way and sang on a blackened bough in hell."

Her heavy eyes made out Tom Holby gazing down at her from his camel and pouring sympathy from his own soul into hers. Then she flung her head from side to side in a torment of woe, cast her head back, and heaved her big eyes up into the cruel brazier of the skies, seemed to see God peering down upon the little multitude, and moved her lips in supplication. She felt the words and the anguish wringing her throat, and the tears came trooping from her eyes, ran shining into her mouth, and she swallowed them and found them bitter-sweet with an exaltation of agony.

She did not know that the director had whispered, "Camera!" and was watching her like a tiger, striving to drive his own energy into her. She did not hear the camera men turning their cranks. There was such weird reality in her grief that the director's glasses were blurred with his own tears; the camera men were gulping hard.

She did happen to note, as her upward stare encountered Tom Holby's eyes on high, that tears were dripping from his lashes and that his mouth was quivering.

The sight of his tears sent through her a strange pang of triumphant sympathy, and she broke down sobbing, would have fallen to the sand, if Leva Lemaire had not caught her and drawn her into her arms, kissing her and whispering:

"Wonderful! Wonderful!"

She felt a hand on her arm and was drawn from Leva's arms into a man's. Her shoulders were squeezed hard by big hands and she heard a voice that identified her captor as the director. He was saying:

"God bless you! That was the real stuff! We won't make you do it over. We had two cameras on you. You're all right! You're a good girl! The real thing!"

Then she began to laugh and choke, became an utter fool.

This was her first experience of the passion of mimicry. She was as ashamed as glorified, as drained yet as exultant, as if a god had seized her and embraced her fiercely for a moment, then left her aching, an ember in the ashes.

The director was already calling the mob to the next task. She could not help glancing toward Tom Holby. His camel was moving off with the crowd, but he was turning back to gaze at her. He was nodding his head in approval and he raised his hand in a salute of profound respect.

# CHAPTER XX

THAT AFTERNOON THE SANDSTORM was to be "pulled off." Dynamos mounted on trucks carrying airplane propellers were gathered toward the two great dunes piled to the northeast of Palm Springs, hiding who knows what under the sands heaped by winds that have roared down San Gorgonio Pass for aeons.

Toward the greater of them, a mass whose color had now the chatoyant luster of an opal five hundred feet high, a hillock whereon no more vegetation grows than on an opal, and whereon the light plays milkily through all the gamut of tinges, the caravan moved. The desert was to represent Sahara in the picture, and these actors and actresses were to convince the throngs that they were really a tribe of misery on whom fate heaped a cyclone of sand to crown their martyrdoms of hunger, thirst, and weariness.

As the straggling hirelings of art trudged across the shifty floor of sand, panting between the heat that beat down from the sky and shot up from the glassy meadow, the air stood still and they cooked as in a fire box. Their feet fried and their hearts staggered.

The suffocation sent a few of the crusaders to the ground, gasping like fish in a creel. These were gathered up and carried half dead to the shade, where a physician restored them. They were humiliated and grieved at the treachery of their own faculties.

The others hardly so much marched as tumbled forward. Mem was aided somehow by the ardor of her little success. She felt that if she could only keep to the fore she might be offered another draught of the new wine of art.

By and by she overtook Tom Holby, who checked his camel to have a word with her:

"I'd ask you to take my place up here, but I'm afraid you'd be as seasick as I was the first time I rode one of these wallowers. But hang on to that strap and it will help you a little."

Mem seized a pendent strap and was hauled along. She did not know, and Tom Holby did not care, how much this interested the neglected multitude.

After a time, as they slackened their pace to mount the dune in whose soft surface her feet sank above the ankles, Mem noted that the smothering hush of the air was quickened with little agues of wind. Gimlets of sand rose and twisted, ran and fell. A fiendish malice seemed to inspire them and they were vicious as devils at play.

Then the sky ahead was blotted from sight by a vast yellow blanket. It came forward as if giants were carrying it to spread over the terrified pilgrims. Ahead of it darted and swirled spinning dervishes of sand.

The blanket, as it approached, became a wall hurrying, a vast dam driven by mountain floods in the rear. The crest of it was a spume of sand. The menace of it was as of a Day of Judgment.

The actors had never seen anything of its sort, but they could guess what the camels knew: that it was of dreadful omen.

A few years before, a herd of cattle rolling up from Yuma had been caught in such a sandstorm, and when it passed they were all dead and buried.

The camels began to betray the terror that the people surmised. They grew frantic with panic, but knew that flight was vain. They were at the mercy of whatever god it is that beasts adore. Tom Holby's mount, without waiting for command, dropped to its belly and stretched out its neck and closed its eyes against the peril.

But the camera men set their tripods and began to turn their cranks. They had the instinct of the trade and were hopeful that if they themselves did not live their pictures might.

Tom Holby dropped from his post and gathered Mem into the shelter of the earners bulk. She did not know or care that his arm was about her as they stood peering across the parapet of the camel's back at the onset of the advancing Niagara. Other women crowded to the same camel. The rest of the crowd flung themselves down and dug their arms to the elbows in the sand lest they be swept away.

A courier gale leaped upon them in a yelling charge, with whips of fire that flung the tripods over, and the camera men with them. But still they persisted, and, shielding their lenses with their own bodies, turned them this way and that, grinding the cranks and picking up what groups they saw about them.

The torrid blast dashed the sand in shovelfuls upon the groveling crowd. The great robes fluttered, flapped, bellied, and, ripping loose, went whooping.

The gliding precipice of sand arrived and hid the sun in a gruesome saffron fog. And then precipice was avalanche. With abrupt chill, a brown cold mountain fell on them, stopped the breath, and played shrapnel on the skin in a maelstrom of dagger points that stabbed from every side.

Tom Holby wrapped his burnous about Mem as they cowered in the lee of his camel. The sand broke over their bulwark as breakers leap across a rock. They were drowned in waves that did not recede. The sand found them inside their robes; it filled their nostrils, their mouths when they gulped for breath. The breakers of sand swept round upon them, broke back over them, and with a grinding uproar that threatened to split the ears they packed with sand.

Tom Holby kept struggling to fling off the hillock that formed about them, kept lifting Mem's head above the mound that grew. Sagebrushes ripped from their places shot by, tearing the skin they touched. Roots of old mesquite went over like clubs, prickly pears and masses of cactus hurtled past in the torrent.

Suddenly the sand tide was gone. But a sea of rain followed it, cruelly cold and ruthless. It turned the mounds into gobs of wet sand, slimy and odious. What had been a world of drought in frenzy became a lake in a squall. What garments the wind had not wrenched free grew sloppy and icy and loathsomely sticky.

For half an hour the deluge harried the dismal caravan.

Then in an instant the rain was over. The hurricane of sand pursued by flood passed on up the valley, to rend the orange groves and tear the fishing boats from their moorings.

The sun resumed his own tyranny and lashed the thrice-wretched army back to its camp.

But the camera men retrieved their instruments from the rubber covers they had wrapped about them with a mothering devotion, and the director checked the retreat and formed it in groups for record.

The airplane propellers that had come forth to imitate the frenzy of the storm had yielded to it and were torn from their axles, lost here and there beneath the new surface of the blinking opal.

# CHAPTER XXI

THE FOOTSTORE AND SADDLESORE moving-picture people fell back upon Palm Springs like a defeated army.

The village, a cool shadow on a bleak waste, had known nothing of the storm except as a distant spectacle. The skirts of the gale had set the palm leaves to rattling together as in ancient staff play, and the limber towers of the tallest trees swayed and shuddered, but not one of them had fallen, nor been struck headless by lightning.

The village was alone. The winter visitors had "gone inside," that is to say, had departed to the cool seashore at San Diego and Los Angeles and the community had drawn itself together for its long summer nap.

There was room for the moving-picture people and Leva Lemaire invited Mem to share her room in one of the hotel bungalows. The sun sank early behind the vast barricade of the San Jacinto chain, rising sheer from the sand and piling height upon height to the crest ten thousand feet in air.

The mountains were blessed now with a mist of light that the aerial prisms gave the effect of down. The brutality of the sky became grace; the stark nakedness of the place was here covered with a flesh of earth, with grass and flowers, and with the larger flowers we call trees. Mem had known the oleander as a tubbed captive at home. Here it was a giant, spreading arms in a benediction of fragrant shade and dangling bouquets that brushed her hair and caught her hat. Palm trees of vast bole hung out umbrellas of somber green. Wan cottonwoods held up pallid limbs drooping with fuzz. Pepper trees let their tresses droop. The ancient and honorable black fig trees of the famous San Gabriel lineage, date palms, roses, flowers, and shrubs, massed and running wild about the rambling gardens, seemed miraculous to Mem, who had almost forgotten, in the dreary hell of the desert, that green things had ever been invented, and who found herself walking deeper and deeper into a revel of tropical luxury.

There were Indians here, too, the little company of Cahuillas; one old buck, with hair as black as tar drip and as long as his hat brim was broad, stood gravely watering hollyhocks with a garden hose; a clump of broad squaws worked at basket weaving; darting through the streets young Indian girls with bobbed hair flopping and gingham skirts flying, bestrode the wide horses of this village.

White people rode, too, cowmen from the ranches beyond and children. One half-naked little girl bounced along the lane on a monstrous horse so flat of back that she might as well have been riding a galloping plateau. Yet she was chasing home a troop of horses as big as her own.

"I was never on a horse," Mem sighed.

"You'd better learn to ride," said Leva Lemaire. "It comes in mighty handy in this business."

"But I'm not going into the business!" Mem protested, hardly able to push one foot ahead of the other. "I've had enough for the rest of my life."

"That's what my poor husband used to say every time he recovered from a spree. And he never took another drop till he got the first chance."

But Mem knew better. She was too tired to eat. She wanted to lie down and never get up. Leva guided her to the bungalow and left her.

Just to be cool, just to be still, were paradise now. After a time a porter brought her her suitcase. Leva had managed to find it. But Mem was too weary to change her clothes. She dropped into a chair by a window and watched a tiny boy drive home a few cattle, watched the last red plumage fade on the breast of the mountains, watched the first star suddenly shimmer as if a jewel had been tossed from somewhere on the sky. Other stars twinkled into being here, there, there, like the first big drops of rain, and soon the whole sky was spattered with them.

The moon that had lurked in the blistered air all day unseen turned up her lamp and carried it somewhere into the sea beyond the shore of the horizon, carried the sky with it star by star. The moon went reluctantly, but the Milky Way seemed to gleam with added radiance when she was gone. The lights in the homes made stars on earth and gave companionship to the dreamy night.

At length Leva came along the path, a shadow detaching itself from other shadows. She was full of high spirits. There had been great hilarity in the dining room of the Desert Inn. She was still restless, and she urged Mem to come with her and bathe in the hot springs of the Indian reservation.

Mem was enough restored by now to feel the distress of the sand that filled her hair and her clothes. The project had a tang of wild adventure, and she went along, taking clean clothes over her arm.

They walked through the double night of the foliage-shrouded streets, the palms muttering over them and blocking their way on the irregular paths.

At the reservation an old Indian admitted them with an utter indifference to their thrill of terror. Inside the cabin, lighted only by candles, they undressed and stretched themselves in the warm water thickened with sand. It crept about them with an uncanny tingling where the stream bubbled from the depths. It was a weird, a spooky bath, but it sent them forth clothed in skins reborn.

When they drifted past the hotel they heard song enriching the night. A man's voice carried the burden of the tune sonorously, and a woman's voice oversoared it like a hovering nightingale's. Or so Mem thought, until Leva whispered:

"That's Robina Teele singing. Pretty voice, hasn't she?"

"Beautiful!" said Mem, but begrudged the praise with a jealousy that surprised her.

"The man is Tom Holby, I think," said Leva. "Awfully nice fellow. Seems to have taken a great shine to you."

"Nonsense!" said Mem, oddly quickened by the thought and a little alarmed by her own delight.

"Well, we might as well move along," Leva grumbled. "We're only extras and we don't belong with the big folks."

Humbled and outcast, but without resentment, Mem followed through the heavy gloom, suddenly smothered with loneliness and uselessness, yet panting for something to do, something brilliant and tremendously emotional, like the moment of desperate passion she had enacted in the desert.

She wondered what the photograph would look like; wondered if she would ever see it, if anyone else would ever see it; or if it would be cut out as Leva had suggested. A terrible thing to feel fiercely and be cut out, snuffed like a candle flame that yearns and leaps and is forever as if it had never been.

When she reached the cottage she was very weary again. But she could not sleep and Leva wanted to read. There were two beds in the room and Leva sat propped up by a little bed light that painted her in bright vignette against the dark.

After a long stupor, Mem abruptly wanted to know something.

"Are the moving-picture people very wicked?" she heard herself asking.

Leva stared into the dark where Mem lay, and she laughed: "Very."

Mem sighed. She was sorry to hear it.

"In fact," Leva went on, "I don't know a single moving-picture person who is above reproach." She finished the page and turned it before she went on. "But then, neither do I know a single person in any other walk of life who is above reproach. Everybody I ever heard of is full of sin. The Bible says that we all fell with Adam and Eve. So I suppose it's only natural that movie people should be as faulty as everybody else is. But I can't see that they're any wickeder than anybody else."

"Really?" Mem cried, hoisting herself to an elbow.

"Really. Most movie people are stodgy and untemperamental and nice, everydayish, folksy souls. They work hard when they can, and save their money, and raise families, and have children and spats and diseases and petty vices like everybody else. A few wild ones make a splurge and get in the papers.

"But if you read the papers you see all the professions and trades represented in the scandals. The other day the front page told about a preacher who ran away with a girl in the choir and left a wife and several children behind him. But nobody spoke about the danger of letting girls sing in choirs. Yet choirs are dangerous, Heaven knows."

She could not see how Mem trembled at this random arrow that struck home. Mem was sorry she spoke and asked no more questions. But Leva needed no further prompting.

"I've tried a lot of trades: stenographer, nurse, canvassing for magazine subscriptions, clerking in a store, and just plain home life, and there was mischief everywhere. Don't believe all this talk you hear, honey, or put it in its proper proportion. There were no movies twenty-five years ago, but Satan is a million years old, and he hasn't taken a day or a night off yet. I used to know a piece about Satan finds some mischief still for idle hands to do, but he has enough left over for busy hands, too. Are you thinking of staying in the movies?"

"No."

"Afraid of them?"

"No-o."

"You've got a good start. You've made a hit with a star and a director the first day. Lord! I've been at it two years and still dubbing along. Better keep at it."

"No, thank you."

"Don't thank me!" said Leva. "I'm nobody. I couldn't be of any help except to find you a good boarding house and an agent. But if you ever come up to Los Angeles, I'll give you the address tomorrow. Don't let me forget."

"I won't."

Leva returned to her book, the turning of every page slashing Mem's mood like a knife. She was thinking that she was not good enough even for the movies.

Her sin had led her to the edge of this paradise, and then drawn her back by the hair. She was doomed to spend a certain time in increasing heaviness, and then to die or to go about thenceforth with a nameless child at her breast or trudging at her side, holding on to her hand and anchoring her to obscurity.

# CHAPTER XXII

WAKENED BY THE SOUND of rushing waters, she ran barefoot to the window. There was no sign of rain in that hard, marbled sky. The mountains looked as if rain had never dampened them.

She could not think just what their color reminded her of for a time. Then she recalled the burnt sugared almonds heaped in the window of Calverly's one candy store. How she had loved them! But this scorched, mottled-brown mountain range had no sweetness, only inconceivable bulk.

Still the crater gurgled. She saw that the yard about the bungalow, soft and dusty last night, was now a shallow lake with waters dancing everywhere. She thrust her head out of the window and drew it in again, for a Jap was shutting the water gates of an overflowing trough extending as far as she could see.

It was an irrigation ditch. He was flooding the ground before the sun could turn the water into burning lenses. She was to learn that the desert irrigated yields more richly than rich soil untended; just as common human soil responds with miracles to lavish floods of encouragement.

A boy from the main building of the hotel came skipping across the lawn to waken Leva, who must be up betimes. Mem would not yield to her appeals that she should come along and resume the moving-picture work. She would taste no more of the forbidden cup.

She put aside especially the temptation to be near Tom Holby and to taste the wine of his approval and his thoughtfulness.

Temptation, like love, follows who flees.

Mem went back to bed, but, goaded by discontent, rose, bathed, and dressed, and went to the hotel for breakfast, determined that she would inquire at once the way to the Randies ranch and take up her humble future before her funds were further diminished.

The dining room was deserted save for one man, and that was Tom Holby.

"Hello!" he cried. "Come sit with me. You're not working? Neither am I. I'm a gentleman till this afternoon. They're taking shots that I'm not in, so I slept late. Our poor star, Robina, is out in the gas stove, turning herself into a fricassee while I loll at ease.

"She is being kidnaped today by a roving band of bad Arabs. I was just starting to rescue her yesterday, disguised as a sheik or something, when I fell in with the famine mob. I rescued her last week up on the lot in Los Angeles."

Mem looked so bewildered that he explained: "You see, we built a whole Arabian street on the lot, and I broke in and broke out and broke up all the furniture, tearing Robina from the villains. Then we came down here to take the scenes of her capture. You'll get used to this upside-down business when you've been in the movies a while longer."

"I've been in them as long as I'm going to be!"

"Oh no, you haven't!" Holby laughed. "I wouldn't blame you for quitting if every day were like yesterday, but you got the worst of it at the first. I've never known a day like yesterday, but you'll not be likely to have another in a thousand years."

"I loved it."

"Then why are you quitting?"

She could not tell him the truth and no lie occurred to her, so she simply drew a veil across her eyes and left him to his own surmises. It was not his nature to persist when a woman rebuffed him, even though that was a rare experience with him. He waived the mystery as her own affair, and spoke up cheerily:

"Order a good breakfast and come with me to the Palm Canon. They say it's glorious. It will buck you up and save me from the horrors of solitude."

He took an unfair advantage of her by appealing to her charity again. It was the best way to tyrannize over her.

She consented for lack of ability to imagine a polite excuse, and finished her breakfast while he went in search of a car.

He came back with a rusty flivver which he drove himself.

There were seven miles of road winding in all directions, especially up and down. She praised Holby for the skill with which he kept his hands and feet playing.

"I had to drive one of these in my last picture," he said. "You have to handle nearly everything in the pictures. I've driven a stagecoach pursued by Indians through canons; and a coach and four down Fifth Avenue; and a donkey chaise in a London scene; and a side car in an imitation Ireland, a motor boat, a street car, a caterpillar tractor, an airship, a chariot, and a steam shovel. Talented lad, eh? Look! Did you see that?"

Mem had seen it. A long rope of scarlet silk ran across the road and threaded the sagebrush as if a red lasso had learned to flee of its own volition. It was a scarlet racer.

"Lots of snakes along here, but mostly harmless," he said. "Robina loves snakes. Do you?"

Her shivering repugnance answered for her.

After a time they passed a patch of ground a little drearier than the rest of the landscape. It had been cleared once, and a wooden cross erected there. Holby answered her questioning stare.

"That's probably the grave of some poor fellow who died of thirst. A villager was telling me last night that only last week a man was found dead within a mile of his ranch. He was that near to good water, but he couldn't make the distance. Out of his mind, probably. They said he was almost naked. Men who are dying for water have a queer mania for tearing off their clothes."

Mem was startled. She had heard this very fact from the man in Yuma. She had decided to let Mr. Woodville die of thirst. It seemed odiously cruel now to subject even an imaginary man to such a death. This reminded her that she had not yet explained to Mr. Holby the puzzle of her name.

He had evidently dismissed it from his mind, for he was running on:

"I don't suppose the pictures can show anybody dying of thirst now, with a censor in full power. They believe in clothes and lots of 'em. It looks as if they'd make the moving pictures die of thirst just in sight of the promised land. Just as the hard times are coming on, the censors rise up like a sandstorm and blow from all directions. You can hardly find a story that can stand their sand blast. They eat away the plot till it falls with a crash just as — see that telephone pole chewed away by the sand that blows all the time against it? Well, that's what the censors are doing to the picture game. If they don't topple the whole thing over it won't be their fault. But what will they do for salaries, then?

"In some of the states they cut out all reference to expected children. Would you believe it? They cut out a scene where a workingman came home and found his wife making little clothes and rejoiced and was proud! Was ever anybody on earth as indecent and filthy-minded as a prude? All crime and sin are pretty well forbidden, also. Hideous, isn't it, that grown people in a grown-up country called the land of the free and the home of the brave should be bullied and handcuffed till we can't even tell a story? We can't play Shakespeare, of course, or the Bible stories, or any of the big literary works any more.

"And they do it all in the name of protecting morals! As if girls and boys never went wrong until the movies came along; as if you could stop human beings from being human by closing up the theaters and telling lies to the children!

"But there's no use whining. We'll have to take our paregoric. The crookeder the politician the more anxious he is to win over the bigots. If he'll give them the censorship and a few other idiotic tyrannies they won't interfere with his graft."

Soon they arrived at Palm Canon and ran the car well up into the gorge, along a water that descended a winding stair with little cascades and broad pools. In some of them water snakes could be seen twisting shadowily.

But the wonder of the place was the embassy of stately palms that had marched down the ravine to the edge of the desert and greeted the visitor with the majesty of lofty chieftains in great war bonnets of green plumes. Some were tall and slender, with headdresses of fronded glory. Others were short and fat and so shaggy of trunk that they resembled the legs of giant cowboys in chaparajos.

There was a little cabin halfway up the canon, but it was locked and deserted. On a bulletin board were placards begging for mercy to animalkind and praising nakedness as akin to godliness.

"He ought to be on a censorship board," said Holby.

The hermit who kept this retreat was making good his creed, for when Mem and Holby got out of their car and stared from the edge of the barrier down into a stream meandering through an Eden of shade, they saw him naked at his bath.

Both pretended not to have noticed him and turned away. Before long he came up the steep path in apostolic garb with robe, rope girdle, sandals, and staff. He wore a beard and long chestnut curls as in the tradition of the Messiah.

"How easy it is to look like the pictures of Christ!" Tom Holby said. It angered him a little to meet a man whose ideals and practices were so contrary to his own.

The hermit lived on next to nothing, took no part in the activities of mankind, hid himself in obscurity, and led a life of sanctified indolence. He did not mortify his flesh, and he did not follow the medieval theory that baths are diabolic and dirt divine. He was neat and even his nails were manicured with care.

But he made no use of his body for the public good or gayety. He abstained from beauty and suppressed his emotions. Tom Holby, by the very opposite ambition, treated his flesh as an instrument of many uses; he diverted millions of people, and his prosperity was gauged by the delight he gave in quality and quantity. He was so far from seeking oblivion that his very postures were multiplied and sent about the world.

The ambitions of the two men were of mutual criticism and reproach.

Yet Holby was polite to the polite hermit who invited the wanderers into his neat little cabin, sold them postal cards with views of the canon, then with a most unhermit-like skill played them love tunes on an Hawaiian guitar of his own making. He held in his right hand a bar of steel with which he gave his melodies a quaint sliding tone, an amorous whimper of a squirrel-like pathos.

From this cozy retreat Holby led Mem down to the center of the palm haunt. He was thinking aloud:

"Funny business, being a professional good man. That sort of fellow hates the world and is afraid of it and retires to the desert to save his soul. Always seemed to me there was something lacking in that idea of being good. Save your own soul and let the world go to the devil! It means nothing to the hermit whether there is war or peace, famine or prosperity. He doesn't help any lonely people to smile; he doesn't feed anybody, or give any money to anybody; he doesn't build any railroads or cathedrals or theaters, paint any pictures or write any songs or vote or make shoes or anything. He doesn't commit any sins, maybe any of the crowd sins but he doesn't commit any good deeds, either.

"Still, if a man is so excited about his soul, it's better if he will go away by himself and save it than to spend his life trying to save everybody else's soul by censorships and foolish laws about tobacco and Sunday and art and everything."

In the depth of the canon the palms were densely congregated; their branches interlaced into a roof of murmurous green. Mem was in a mood of beyond the world; she felt bewitched as she walked over the dried fans of fallen leaves and listened to the birds that made a lyric caravan sary of this haven. It was a realm of Arabian magic, with no hint of the American magic that our familiar eyes ignore.

Mem dropped wearily down upon a stone by the brook in a thatched tent of palms. Tom Holby, though there was a place at a distance, sat down at her side.

This threw her heart into a flutter. His own heart was evidently on the scurry, too, and there was a fierce debate within him whether he should speak or not. Finally he said:

"You've got me at a terrible disadvantage here. I'm all alone with you, and helpless. It wouldn't do me any good to scream and I'm so weak that you could overpower me with a look."

She could not make him out at all. He had to explain, baldly:

"You know when a woman lures a man out to a solitude like this…"

"Lures?"

"Well, use any word you like, just say 'goes with a man anyway,' she sets the poor fellow to guessing mighty hard. I wouldn't annoy you for worlds. I've got a queer hankering to be of some service to you. But I can't place you anywhere.

She did not know his language.

"Can't place you at all. You have a sweet, innocent, beautiful face and your eyes are as gentle as a dove's. But that has been the case with some of the daintiest little desperadoes that ever tore up society. The first time I met you you told me your name was Remember Steddon. You called me Mr. Woodville when we said goodbye in Tucson. A week or two and we meet again, and you are Mrs. Woodville and your husband is dead and you're going to be a chambermaid on a ranch.

"It's all possible, but it isn't a bit convincing, and you've got me puzzled. If you've committed a crime and are hiding out — you'd better get into a bigger crowd, because you're as conspicuous out here as old San Jacinto peak. If you've committed a crime, I'm sure you had a good reason to and I'm no informer. But I wish you would tell me whether you are the cleverest adventuress I ever met or just a poor scared little lonely lost child."

Her confusion was that of a child. He could see no trace of insincerity in her panic and there was a wedding ring on her finger. But this did not impress him much; he had seen too many married actresses take off their rings to play maidens, and too many unmarried actresses put them on to play wives. He had seen wonderful sincerity in impersonation. Robina could make him weep almost at will in her scenes of hapless innocence. He broke out impatiently when Mem did not speak.

"Tell me honestly one thing: Is there a Mr. Woodville? Were you ever really married to anybody?"

She turned frightened eyes upon him and spoke with a parrying evasion:

"Why, why should you doubt it?"

He stared at her sharply; then his eyes softened and he mumbled:

"You poor little thing! What on earth are you up to? What are you running away from? Why should you come to this place out of season under a false name with a wedding ring you bought yourself?"

She carried her other hand to conceal the ring as if it were a shameful baby. The instinctive gesture convinced Holby that he had guessed well.

Now she fell into an ague of terror. She looked this way and that, as if for a door of escape. But she knew that on all sides of her was a wilderness of mountains and desert. She was horribly afraid of Holby; he had the domineering, demanding manner of a police officer.

But instead of denouncing her or arresting her, he suddenly took her two trembling hands in one of his and with the other pressed her to him and held her tight.

She struggled fiercely, yet with the feeling of a lamb in a shepherd's clasp. She knew that he was no enemy, yet she could not accept him as her friend on so short an acquaintance. Friendships were not made at such speed in Calverly.

So she fought until he released her. Then she rose and staggered along a crackling path, scattering little lizards that seemed rather to pretend than to feel fear.

She began to weep, ran blindly into one of the palms, and fell, but into Holby's arms again.

"Tell me the truth," he pleaded. "Let me be your friend. I want to help you. If it would help you most to let you alone, I'll do that. If it would help you to be held tight and hugged hard and kissed and loved, I'll do that, and mighty gladly. But in Heaven's name, don't stand there and have chills and fever and not speak!"

She felt a mad yearning to tell him the truth. She felt that he would be very merciful and wise and everything wonderful. She felt that he would not be shocked. Those actors and actresses could not be shocked by anything, probably. And yet a kind of snobbishness even in humiliation locked her jaws on her secret. She was a clergyman's daughter, after all, and it would be an appalling come-down from all her teaching, to make a movie actor her confidant and accept his advice and help and Heavens! She was already accepting his caresses!

Mem was a princess of the parsonage, and she was suddenly recalled to her pride of estate.

"Please!" she said, quite haughtily. "Oh, please!"

Tom Holby writhed when his generous motives were flung back into his face. He was filled with rage, and yet he pitied her more than ever. He pitied her as the vagabond pities the hidebound Puritan who sets him in the pillory.

He longed for such freedom and equality as he enjoyed in his wrangles with Robina Teele, who swore at him and struck at him with a manly vigor.

He controlled himself and groaned an ironic:

"Forgive me!"

When she ingenuously answered, "I do," he almost suffocated with tormented wrath and sardonic amusement.

He dumfounded her by speaking in the jargon of his craft:

"They say that when Griffith wanted to get the final grimace of agony in Lillian Gish's face in the scene where her illegitimate baby dies in *Way Down East*, you know they photographed her face while he held her feet and tickled them. I don't know how true the story is, but I feel just that way. Do I look it?"

He was so interested in expression that he actually thrust his face close to hers for her verdict on his mien. She had still another baffler for him:

"Who's Griffith?"

This heathenish ignorance of the first god of the American cinema, took his breath like a blow on the solar plexus and he could only whisper, huskily:

"Let's go back."

# CHAPTER XXIII

WHEN THE MOVING-PICTURE caravan left Palm Springs, Mem lost the courage that had led her to refuse to go with it.

Tom Holby rather coldly advised her to take up the moving pictures as a career. The director praised her and promised not to forget her. Leva Lemaire begged her to come to Los Angeles, where it would be cool and profitable, and warned her not to risk her life in the desert. Also she collected for Mem the day's wage of seven dollars and a half for her work as an extra woman. This thrilled the girl with her astonishing earning powers. At that rate she could earn as much in a week as her father earned in a month. Even she!

But Mem would as soon have followed a pack of gypsies or a circus troupe out of Calverly. It was only when the movie people were gone that she realized how much they had filled the scene, how empty and little the stage was, now that the picture crowd abandoned it.

She found a place as maid in the home of a storekeeper at such wages as he could afford. She began the sordid routine of her tasks, but, contrasting them with the glamour of playing tragic roles, she felt herself entombed.

Then the summer heat began and grew so fierce that her employer's wife and children went "inside" to the seashore. This left her in a position of embarrassment and terror. She was an embarrassment and terror to her employer, too; for she had a beauty that she unwittingly flung over him like a net. Her beauty stung him in his thoughts. It filled his honest soul with poisonous desire. He tried to summon courage to send her away, but the sorrow in her eyes made it impossible to dismiss her. Finally, being as wise as he was good, he determined to flee from the temptation to tempt and took shelter with his wife.

Mem had not watched him well enough to note her influence upon him. She went about in a daze, with heavier and heavier heart and tread.

She spent much thought upon the letter home that she had not yet written, that she must write if ever she were to go home again. The whole purpose of this long, long journey into loneliness was to be able to write that letter; and it had not yet gone.

Every time she made the beginning her hands flinched from the lying pen. But when her employer left the village for a few days with his family at the coast, one night in a frantic fit of histrionic enthusiasm she dashed off her fable, sealed it in an envelope, and dropped it after dark in the mail box.

DARLING MAMMA AND PAPA, —

How can I write the terrible news? I can hardly bear to think of it, let alone write about it. But my darling husband passed away in the desert. I cannot write you the particulars now, for I am too agitated and grief stricken and I do not want to harrow you with details. I know your poor hearts will ache for me, but I beg you not to feel it too deeply, because I am trying to be brave. And I remember what you taught me, that the Lord giveth and the Lord taketh away.

Poor John did not find the lost mine he was looking for, and he did not find the water hole he expected, for, after I had waited for him a long time in our camp by a little spring, another prospector brought me word that he had found him and buried him. The poor boy had torn all his clothes off in the thirst madness and had been dead for three days when found.

I cannot write you more now. I am in no need of money and I will come home when I get a little stronger. The climate is doing my health wonderful good even if it has broken my heart.

But don't you worry. I'll be all right and I'll send you a long letter as soon as I settle down somewhere.

All the love in the world from

Your loveing

MEM.

After she had slipped the letter irrevocably into the mail box she realized that the postmark of Palm Springs would be stamped on the envelope. Her place of concealment would be disclosed.

Still, it would not matter. She was a widow now in the minds of her people and she could go back to them and face the future in calm. But, she would have to go on playing a part all her life and playing it once more in the monotonous theater of her own home.

She had a fierce desire for her mother's help in the approaching ordeal, but how could she endure it to begin lying again in her dear old father's trusting face?

Her soul wanted to run and climb, leaden as her feet were. She was a bit flighty in her head at times, nowadays. A longing for cool waters and icy waves assailed her. The Los Angeles paper which came to the house every day spoke of Santa Monica as the place "where the mountains meet the sea."

That phrase had an hallucinative influence. She imagined the vast herd of mountains crowding down to meet the radiant breakers that the Pacific flung upon their shining horns as they bent to dip their muzzles into the surf.

The ocean was so near to Palm Springs that her employer spoke of having breakfasted once on the beach and reached home long before dinner time. And that was by the winding motor roads to the Northwest.

The fantastic notion came to her that she might climb the San Jacinto sierra and cross it to the ocean as the eagles did, or at least catch a glimpse of blue waves.

The mountains had a beckoning look always, and on this afternoon, when a clouded sky gave a little shelter from the sun, she set out to follow her vagary as far as her strength would take her.

She crossed a strip of sand as soft as deep-piled velvet, and came to a path that slanted up a rounded cliff lifting a granite wall right aloft from the unrippled surface of the desert.

The exertion of climbing was more than Mem had bargained for. She was weaker and weightier than she had thought. The steeps that looked so inviting from a distance were ragged and forbidding. The burnt-almond mountains were hot and sharp-edged gridirons to her feet. When she was high enough to look down on the leafy thatch of the little village she grew dizzy and afraid.

The loneliness up there was grisly. Something said, "Go back!" She fought the everlasting tendency to retreat from everything she undertook, but gave up and decided to return.

And now, as she stared at the swift descent before her, she grew more afraid of climbing down than of climbing up. She hesitated, then mounted a few steps with pain and struggle.

She had not the strength to go on, nor the courage to go back. The sun came blazing forth and seemed to spill upon her a yellow hot mass of metal that slashed her about the head and rolled over her shoulders in blistering ingots.

The fiends of height swirled round her. She tried to call for help, but whence? A stone rolled under her foot and shook her from her balance. She wavered, clutched at nothing, whirled, struck, bounded from the hard rock, fell and fell, and then a smashing blow, blackness, silence.

# CHAPTER XXIV

A YOUNG INDIAN GIRL chasing her stray pony about the sand had noted the figure climbing the side of the cliff, and had studied it, wondering at its erratic behavior.

She had seen Mem stumble, then fall; had heard the thump of the body on the cushioning sand; had run to the nearest house and told what she had seen.

A man there came out and followed the Indian girl. When she pointed to the height where Mem had stood when she slipped, he said:

"That's all of sixty feet. She's dead for sure."

But she was not, though she was lifeless enough when they reached her, and more than one bone was broken.

A woman had tried to kill herself a few weeks before by jumping from a far higher cliff, and, landing on sand as soft, had wakened, to her keen disappointment, in this world instead of the other, with a few more bruises and anguishes than before.

The Indian girl dispelled the natural suspicion that Mem had attempted suicide. Her first outcry when she was brought back to consciousness was a shriek of terror that resumed her thoughts where they had left off.

She was recognized and taken home. The village doctor was fetched, and he did all that his skill could do to hasten the repairs that nature began upon at once.

Though Mem had never dared to visit the doctor, he knew of her, and knew of her as a widow. The wedding ring on her finger forestalled even a thought of the truth.

When she was strong enough to be talked to he prepared her for bad news.

"Am I to be crippled for life?" she cried.

"No," he sighed. "You will bear no marks of your accident. But... you will not... but your other hopes and expectations will not be realized."

She was dazed and he was timid, and he had some difficulty in making her understand his bad news: that she would not be a mother.

She bore this blow with a fortitude that surprised him.

Before she was able to be up and about, the family came back and ministered to her with a kindness that punished her. One morning she was terrified to receive a letter from home. It was addressed to "Mrs. John Woodville" and it was written by her mother, with a long postscript from her father. Her mother's letter was a labored effort to pour out sympathy for her daughter in the loss of a husband who, she knew, had never lived and could not die. Her expressions of horror at his demise were written for the sake of her husband, but she was never meant for a dramatic author and Mem could feel the artificiality of her language. But her father was completely deceived and mourned sincerely. His postscript was all pity and loving sorrow; he told of his prayers for her strength to bear her cross and pleaded with her to be brave. He said that he had prayed for her in church and the congregation sent her loving messages.

Mem could see him on his knees imploring Heaven, pacing his room with the tread she had heard so much in her childhood, and stretching his clasped hands across the pulpit Bible as he solicited mercy of Heaven.

Remorse came upon her again with the suffocating fury of the sandstorm. She felt that she could never face her father or her village again. Now that her accident had annulled her excuse for being here, her conscience forbade her to go home again.

Now she felt an exile indeed, and an unutterable loneliness, without her lover, her child, her own people, or even the familiar scenes that might have given her inarticulate consolation. The old trees about the old house would have waved their arms above her, and murmured mysterious broodings over the mystery of despair. The very trees here were foreigners.

On an impulse she wrote a long letter to her mother, enclosed it in an unsealed envelope, and enclosed that in a sealed envelope addressed to Doctor Bretherick. After the letter was mailed she wished she had never sent it. It could only carry dismay into her lonely mother's soul. But it was as impossible to recall as a scream shot into the air. She imagined all consequences but the one that came about.

The last of her money went to pay the doctor's bill, and she was a sick pauper. She resumed her menial work gradually as her strength returned, but her distaste for it grew to loathing. The Reddicks, her employers, were kind to her, but they were master and mistress, and their own lives were hard.

She was weak and woebegone, at the bottom of the cliff of life. She had never climbed very far, but she had fallen far enough to give both soul and body an almost fatal shock.

She was ashamed of her past, and her future was as dismal as the desert and as full of cactus. She was a drudge in a poor family in a scorched settlement abandoned by all that could get away.

The only inferiors she could see were a young widow named Dack and her five-year-old boy, Terry. Mrs. Dack took in washing. During the winter she was overworked; during the summer she was undernourished.

She did the heaviest laundry for the Reddicks, and when she called for it she usually brought her boy along for lack of someone to leave him with. The child had the infantile genius for improving the world by imagination, and made a brilliant adventure of the errand. He owned a rickety express wagon left behind by some visitor child; and it gave Terry all the uplift of a fiery chariot. His mother would set the bundle of wash in the wagonette, and immediately it became a magnificent truck, an automobile, or an airship, and the boy a team of horses, a motor, or a winged aviator, as his whim pleased.

His mother caught a little cheer from Terry's inexhaustible rapture, and Mem, seeing them move along the road to their shack, felt such pity for them that she gained a little dignity from the emotion, since pity is a downward-looking mood.

Her sympathy was quickened, perhaps, by the frustration of her own motherhood. Nature had begun to prepare her spirit as well as her flesh for maternal offices, and somewhere in oblivion was a half-completed little child doomed to perish before it was born. That tiny orphan wailed in the porches of Mem's heart, complaining that its destiny, begun in romantic shame, was ended in unromantic catastrophe. Famished of love, Mem fed upon the widow's boy.

It hurt Mem to see how sorry a future Terry Dack could expect. The children of the Indians were less unlucky, because, like the children of negroes, they entered a world that made them no promises.

But every American white child has a chance at wealth and the Presidency of the United States as his inalienable birthright. Yet Terry Dack began with no inheritance but handicaps.

He would have no opportunity in Palm Springs for anything but the humblest future. He would grow up to a few scraps of public-school education. His father was already dead and his mother only half alive. She had been a pretty thing once, and she loved to tell Mem of her life on a ranch near Whitewater. As a little girl she had owned her own horse and ridden it. As a young "sage hen" she had been the belle of ranch picnics and parties. She had married a glorious young cattleman, whose father went broke because his herd of cattle was smothered in a sandstorm. The son had soon after been torn to pieces by the teeth of a vicious horse he had tried to break to the saddle.

Then all the joy and velocity had gone out of Mrs. Back's life and she had become the bent slave of a washboard, her arms forever elbow deep in suds.

The boy Terry was of the Ariel breed. His fancy girdled the earth in forty minutes. The world was a stage to him; an old boot as effective as Cinderella's glass slipper; the clothesline was a private telephone wire.

He mimicked birds and animals and often covered his mother with terror and amused chagrin by imitating her clients with uncanny skill.

He had an eye for mannerisms of walk or posture. His vision owned a photographic detail, his ear a phonographic skill for record and repetition.

Ignorant and young as he was, he could merely sketch the emphatic features of the people he cartooned, but in the outline there was always a likeness that made his mother or Mem cry out the name of the subject at once. Terry would usually preface his performance with a:

"Looky, mamma! This is the way old Miz Reddick walks. This is the way you do, mamma. This is what the old Indian squaw does when she weaves baskets with her hands and uses her feet to work the rope that scares the birds from the fig trees. This is the way, mamma, you wash cloes and wring 'em and hang 'em up to dry."

Sometimes his mimicry was terrifying. He would repeat things he had overheard in the street from careless men; he would imitate some deviltry he had learned from an Indian or Mexican or American boy or girl, or from the little devil that curls and fattens in every child's own heart, as the worm in the apple.

His mother and Mem would look at each other in the dismay that comes to grown-ups when they see the ignorance of baby-hood vanishing like down from a peach. They were afraid of what life in their wicked little world would do to their little idol.

Terry would weep with vexation at an inattentive audience or at his inability to express what bubbled inside his little kettle of a chest. He would weep when angered, but at no other time. Pain, grief, disappointment, terror, loneliness would bring no tears, no sobs.

Once the child caught cold in all that heat! And Mem sat by his bedside through several smothering nights, while the back-broken mother slept. Mem, all alone in her vigil, found that imagination was good company. She constructed little plays. She pretended that Terry was her own baby; and, like him, she enriched a sordid existence with the rich tapestries of pretense. She had been forced to be a play actress for so long that the ordeal had become a pleasant habit, a necessity.

She exercised her acquired skill in making up little dramas to while away the tedium of the long nights and to keep the wakeful child's mind from his cough.

Among all the rich nights of human experience, from the perfect night that Socrates praised, the more than royally luxurious night of dreamless sleep, to the glittering revelries of a Trimalchian banquet, no nights are more precious than those somber hours a mother spends at the bedside of a sick child.

It was during this long heartache that Mem received the second letter that found her in Palm Springs. This was from Leva Lemaire, saying that she had just seen in an old paper a paragraph describing Mrs. Woodville's fall from the mountain and her miraculous escape from death. Leva expressed the utmost sympathy and prayed that her beauty had not been marred. She added:

"But if it has, you can still find something to do in the movies. I've given up trying to be an actress and taken a position in the laboratory projection room, correcting the films. It's cool and dark and interesting, and far better than that miserable oven. I think I can get you a place, if you'll come up. Los Angeles is the only town in the world that's alive these days, and there's no excuse for a woman of your education and charm wasting her sweetness on the desert air. Do come! I've sent my three children out to their uncle's ranch. You could live here with me and my friends."

The thought of working in the dark and the cool was a hint of Paradise to Mem, but she would not leave Terry Dack while he was ill.

Early one evening she went to the drug store to fill a prescription, and found a stranger there sprawled across a showcase, talking.

His voice startled her, though it was so slow and lazy that the druggist found it almost a soporific.

"I been out on the old Picacho mountain pros-speck-tin. I went over it once with an old pardner o mine name of, well, I always called him Woodhead. He went batty on me count of a water hole not havin' no water into it."

Mem stood for a moment, petrified, all but her heart, which was scurrying like an alarm bell in a steeple.

This was the man Bodlin she had talked to in Yuma! She had told him that her husband was alive and that she was going into the desert with him.

He would recognize her the moment he saw her. He would ask about the husband he had so frankly envied. All her duplicity would be revealed. She would probably be stoned out of the village.

# CHAPTER XXV

HER CHIEF DISMAY was her inability to get rid of the lie she had begun. She found it always ahead of and about her with new demands; always behind her with new reminders.

She stole out of the drug store with the prescription unfilled and, hastening down the street, asked a young Indian girl who came along to finish her errand for her. She waited in the shelter of a fat palm tree, ready to take flight if the Yuma man should come out and follow her.

But he was evidently still telling the weary druggist his un-solicited experiences, for, after a time, the Indian girl returned, bringing the medicine and explaining that her delay was due to the much palaver of a man who would not stop talking.

On the way back to the Dack cottage Mem thought fast. She had hidden herself in a tiny hamlet, the nearest thing to solitude. She had hidden herself in vain. The only other hope was to seek concealment in a crowd, as Tom Holby had suggested.

And now coercion was added to the allurements of Los Angeles. She told Mrs. Dack and Mrs. Reddick that she had received a call to go to Los Angeles at once.

Mrs. Reddick protested and pleaded with all the hospitality that is bestowed on a good servant where servants of any sort are hard to get and keep. Mrs. Dack could only regret her departure, and her meek desolation of mien almost overcame Mem's resolution. The boy Terry was out of danger, but his arms around Mem's neck were withes she could hardly break. The soft hands, the dewy cheeks, the lonely eyes of the child were fetters cruelly tyrannous.

The next morning Mem lugged her old suitcase to the starting point of the auto stage. It carried her and a few other passengers across a badlands, pallid as a convict's cheek and with the same unshaven look.

At Whitewater she caught a train that sped her gradually into the vales of plenty, through leagues of citrus groves in flower and in fruit at once.

Seeing orange blossoms abloom in leagues, she blushed to think that she had never worn them. She marveled at the alleys of green, polka-dotted with golden oranges, with lemons and grapefruit hanging like gifts in tinseled Christmas trees. Long reaches of walnut groves went by in wheel spokes. The walnuts made the neatest and shapeliest of orchards. There were olives, almonds, roses blowing in red miles along the country roads. She was coming up into Eden.

And eventually she reached the new Babel, which her father had denounced as the last capital of paganism. No city could be so wicked as her father and she had thought Los Angeles, and be anything else. And Los Angeles was everything else.

Scanty as her resources were, Mem had to pay a taxi-cab to take her to Leva's home. It was the first taxicab she had ever ridden in, and she was hysterical with fear as it shot and spun through streets so thick with traffic and so wild that this city's record of accidents had achieved supremacy in the world.

The driver mauled his gears so recklessly that the cab was incessantly snarling and spitting, a very beast of prey. Yet Mem was almost more afraid of the taximeter, as she watched it adding dimes to her fare at a spendthrift rate. She was likely to be destroyed by bankruptcy if not by collision.

The street slid through a long, long tunnel and then swooped up and away to Sunset Boulevard (she loved the name), then gradually into a domain of tiny houses with large gardens, each of a luxuriance that struck Mem as almost fantastic. All of these people must be grand viziers the way they surrounded themselves with tropical splendors.

The Spanish names of many of the streets made literature to her eye and she was dazed by the number of them. She thought that Los Angeles must have extended its limits almost to San

Francisco. San Franciscans often made the same accusation.

Suddenly the car swerved to the right and scooted up a little avenue of low houses, not white only, but pink or mauve or yellow, with roofs of varicolored tile and awnings of gaudy stripe.

In a city so widespread, and made up of so many small houses so far apart that, when the man was at his work and the wife in the kitchen or shopping, there was nobody visible, she had the impression of Los Angeles that Arthur Somers Roche expressed: "a million white houses and not a soul going in or coming out of one of them!"

The cab jolted to a stop before a tiny palace of four or five rooms. Mem got down, paid the pirate her ransom, and toted her suitcase up to the quaint little door.

This was Leva's home! She had a palm tree, a pepper tree, a few truculent cactuses, grass, and a fountain. Along the walk stood a row of palms, their trunks studded or lapped in many facets where leaf stalks had been cut off. A gorgeous vine of bougainvillea was flung up over the cornice with the effect of a vast carnival shawl.

Leva was not at home. A servant who opened the door said that "she would not git back from the stoodio befo six or happast."

Mem asked permission to wait, knowing nowhere else to turn; she studied the bright rooms as if they were chambers in fairyland. She could hardly comprehend the patio, and the walls of concrete (she did not realize that she could almost have poked her thumb through them), the garden built into the house, the frail and many-tinted furniture, the photographs of famous paintings that she had never heard of. The whole spirit of the place was foreign to Mem. It looked genie-built.

The servant was glad to relieve her loneliness with chatter. She explained that Miss Lemaire lived there with three other ladies, all of them in the movies, and none of them getting their pictures took.

They lived here with no more thought of chaperonage than a crowd of bachelors. Mem's greatest shock was the abrupt arrival in a world where the enjoyment of life was made its chief business. She had been brought up to believe in duty first in self-denial, abstention, modesty, demurity, simplicity, meekness, prayer, remorse. Here people worshiped the sun, flowers, dancing, speed, hilarity, laughter, and love.

They worked hard, but at the manufacture of pretty things, of stories, pictures, paintings, music. To her there was an inconceivable recklessness of consequence. They thought no more of respectable appearance than South Sea Islanders.

Yet they seemed to be as happy as they tried to be. They had their disappointments, jealousies, scandals, gossips, griefs, and shames, but so had the gray village people she had left. These Utopians had no winter in their climate or in their souls, only a little rainy season, a bit of chill.

When Leva and her friends came in at dinner time they came like young business men home from offices, tired of shop, yet full of its talk; eager for amusement, knowing no law except their own self-respect for health or reputation or efficiency. The first one in set a victrola to playing a jazz tune before she noticed Mem. The second one in joined the first in a dance. They quarreled over a new step with laughing violence.

Mem was aghast at their contempt for conventions. They despised the Puritans who abhorred them. They snapped their fingers at appearances and regarded caution not as an evidence of decency, but as a proof of hypocrisy.

They had in their time known all of Mem's compunctions, but had abandoned them one by one as a soldier throws off all baggage that hampers the freedom and range of his march; as a swimmer in strong currents casts away everything that weighs, including clothes. She would learn that many of those who loved to break the rules of outward propriety were solid as white marble in their standards. She had already learned at home that many of the most spotless exteriors are only whited sepulchers.

She would conform herself with trepidation at first and with much backsliding into respectability as she understood it. But she would soon embrace the new paganism with desperation and finally with gaiety, adapting herself like a beach comber to the customs of a tribe of self-supporting women who compromised themselves so freely that the critic gave them up as hopeless. One does not fret much over the conventionalities of gypsies.

At first she supposed that all Los Angeles was Hollywood. But she would learn that to a large portion of the city's population the word "Hollywood" was a synonym for riotous outlawry, a plague spot, a kind of spendthrift slums. And in Hollywood itself she would find a large, old-fashioned village element dazed by its gypsies. Furthermore, the city, which her father had damned with such wholesale horror, was nine-tenths composed of mid-Westerners like himself, people who had brought their churches and churchliness with them. There were hundreds of thousands of Iowans, Missourians, Kansans there; and they held picnics constantly, enormous reunions which differed from the camp meetings and barbecues of the mid-West only in the fact that the groves were not of maple and oak and hickory, but of eucalyptus and palm and pepper.

Whether Mem had come to her ruination or her redemption, she had come to a new world. Before she learned how freely, with what masculine franchise, these women conducted their lives, before she could recoil from such perilous associations, she was entrapped in their cordiality, their vivacity, their lavish kindliness.

Leva, the third one home, welcomed Mem as if she were a returned prodigal sister instead of a passing acquaintance met in the desert. She would listen to nothing but the unpacking of the suitcase and the acceptance of a little bed covered with a gaudy Navajo blanket. There were flowers at Mem's plate in a lavish heap. And a big basket of fruit was set in her room. Californians are prompt and frequent with gifts of flowers.

The other women came in variously. One walked. One drove her own car up into a garage just a little bigger than the car. One was set down by a big studio touring car that 12 delivered its passengers of nights and gathered them up again of mornings, for Los Angeles is a city of maleficent distances. Every place is a Sabbath-day's journey from every place else. And there is no Sabbath — at least no legal Sabbath. Yet the people seemed to be extraordinarily good and kindly. They seemed to get the sun into their lives. Their hearts felt as big and golden and juicy as their own oranges. Even the lemons had a sweeter acridity than at home.

At home "California fruit" had been a byword for bigness, high color, and insipidity of taste, something a little better than Dead Sea fruit. The smaller, plainer native apples, pears, and peaches had possessed a better flavor.

But California fruit had reached Calverly after a long, dark journey, and it was eaten in a foreign air. Out here, however, where the oranges could be lifted warm from the tree, the figs sliced fresh for breakfast, the peaches stripped of their downy silk while their wine was new, there was no lapse from the joyous promise of their advertisement.

If the sunlight was of a gold refined and somehow enriched, the shadow was also of a deeper cool. Just inside its edge the sun was walled out. The first builders had not known this. They had set above their houses the roofs of wintry climates, and one might still see in older Los Angeles obsolete homes whose slanting shingles were excellently arranged to let the snow slide off. Since there was no snow to slide, they served as furnaces for the hot sun.

Next came the low roof with the wide, flat eaves, casting a heavy shade about the windows. But this made the houses chilly, and the new school brought the tiles just to the brim of the walls; and these walls were not often glaring white as before, but brown, dove gray, salmon, shrimp, olive.

Where the shadows lay along the lawns or the walks they were of unusual design, not dapplings of rounded leaves as in the mid-West, but the long scissored slashes of palm fronds, the thready reeds of papyrus, the pepper's delicate flounces.

Even in this Eden, however, there was distress, anxiety. The hard times that were freezing the outer world were threatening the raging prosperity of Los Angeles.

Studios were closing overnight. Supposed millionaires were departing abruptly in search of funds to meet their payrolls. Stars who had been collecting ten thousand dollars a week or less were left stranded in the midst of unfinished pictures and unfinished mortgages and jewelry bills. The lesser fry were being cast ashore in heaps, like minnows after a tidal wave's recession.

The girls at Leva's were wondering how long their jobs would last. A mere cut in salary would be a welcome mercy, a respite from a death sentence.

This was devastating news to Mem, for she had landed on this tropical isle in the expectation of at least a breadfruit tree. Her blanched face told her story to Leva, who held out more hope than she inly entertained.

"Never say die, Mrs. Woodville," she said. "There's always a chance. The companies are turning off their oldest, most experienced people in droves, but every now and then they take in a newcomer. I'll speak to the laboratory chief. Anyway, your board and lodging won't cost you anything as long as we've got either here, eh, girls?"

The girls agreed. Their adventurous spirit included a reckless hospitality and they put off care till tomorrow in the hope that it would never come.

After the dinner the victrola was set whirring again and Mem was invited to forget her troubles in a fox-trot.

She gasped at this. She had never learned even a lamb-trot. Her father's church did not permit dancing, and, while it overlooked the sin in certain of its parishioners, there would have been scandal indeed if the parson's daughter had ever lifted her foot in aught save solemnity.

But Mem was not allowed to explain. She was dragged from her chair and forced to copy the steps set before her. It would have been impossibly priggish and insulting for her to plead religious scruples, and she put her best foot foremost.

The dance mood was innate and she had a natural grace of rhythm that had languished unheeded. The steps were simple, and their combination at the whim of the dancer who led.

Mem was soon whirling about the room, with more or less awkwardness which only made for laughter, and with a swimming intoxication that left her panting and dizzy, but strangely, foolishly happy.

She had learned a new alphabet of expression. She misspelled the words and jumbled the syntax, but she was getting along somehow on a new planet.

When three or four men drove up in a car and invaded

the house with invitations to a dance at the Hollywood Hotel, Mem declined, of course. Her refusal was ignored as of no importance.

"It's Thursday night," said Leva, "and it's our religious duty to show up at the Hollywood. Everybody's there. You might meet somebody who'd give you a job."

Mem begged to be excused. She could not dance and she was very tired.

"That's when you're at your best," cried Leva, who was an entirely other woman from the shrouded Arabian that Mem had met at Palm Springs.

While Mem protested Leva motioned one of the men, a young actor, to make her dance.

In spite of her struggles she was snatched from her chair into the arms of this faun whose manly beauty was his stock in trade. It was the first time any man except her father and her brothers had embraced Mem since Elwood Farnaby had thrilled her with his love. She did not count the brief duel with Tom Holby in Palm Canon, since he had made no effort to overwhelm her resistance.

But this laughing satyr, Mr. Creighton, held her tight and compelled her to dance.

Giddy with the whirl and sullen with the outrage, Mem's anger blazed into open disgust. Creighton said he was horribly sorry and only meant it in fun, and by his abject contrition made Mem ashamed of herself. She did not know what to do or say.

This was her first experience of the confusion that comes from being too respectable on a holiday. To escape from the scene of her kill-joy boorishness (as it looked to her now) she went out into the moonlit patio. The moon seemed to make life simpler. It has a way of blotting the material details with dumb shadow and spreading a love light over dreamy surfaces.

From a house somewhere near and drowned in foliage came a music of guitar and ukulele and young voices.

An automobile went by, trailing laughter in a glittering scarf. Over her head a palm tree waved an aromatic fan, as over a daughter of Pharaoh. Along the northern sky the mountains were aligned, built of some soft-tinted cloudiness as if they were a wall decreed between this Xanadu of all delights and the harsh, respectable realms of the East, a barrier between the woeful lands of shagbark and mock orange and this garden of almond trees and roses.

In a radiance so amorous that it seemed almost to coo, Mem felt that the great needs of her soul were love, tenderness, rapture. This yearning was divine in this light. In the bright lexicon of the moon there was no such word as "Don't!" Everything wooed everything. In Mem's downcast eyes her bosom was silvered with the glamour and gathered into the same thought that mused upon wall and flower and tree, upon the depths of the sky, and upon the nearest vine leaf aquake with the ecstasy of being alive at night.

The air was imbued with a luscious fragrance that delighted her nostrils and drew her eyes to an orange tree, almost a perfect globe in symmetry, and curiously forming a little universe whose support was lost in the gloom beneath. In the round night of its own sky hung moons exhaling perfume and temptation.

Like another Eve, she yielded to the cosmic urge and put her hand forth to the tree of knowledge, plucked the fruit that was not hers, and made it hers.

She did not peel the cloth of gold and divide the pulp, but, as she had seen these Californians do, buried her teeth in the ruddy flesh, tore out a hole, and drained the syrup.

She was too well schooled in biblical lore not to think of Eve. There was, however, no Adam for her to involve in her fall; so she took the whole fruit for herself. But then, instead of feeling shame as the scales fell from her eyes, shame itself fell from her and she laughed. Eve had become Lilith for the moment.

She felt in her heart that there was something wrong here in this new life. But then there had been so much wrong in the life she had led before. This was a city of peril, but she had not escaped peril at home.

She breathed deep of the new freedom. She cast off her past, resolved to bend her head and her back no longer under remorse, but to stand erect, to run, and dance, and to be beautiful and rich and famous.

Like Eve, she felt that the first necessity of her new era was clothes. If she had had any she would have called a taxicab and dashed away to the Hollywood Hotel. She felt that she could dance with anybody or with nobody. She could be Salome and dance herself into half a kingdom, dance everybody's head off, including her own.

But it has been so arranged that whenever a woman is set on fire with a high resolution to do some glorious thing, an elbow demon always brings her back to the dust by whispering, "You have nothing fit to wear." Otherwise the conquest of the world would not have been left to blundering, hesitant males.

Mem went into the house. The moon was all very well for beautiful moods, but it was impracticable; it did not provide the wardrobe for the deeds it inspired.

She went into the house like a prisoner granted a little exercise in a walled yard, then driven back to her cell. She was awake in her perplexities when Leva and her friends came home. The young men raided the ice box, then went their way.

Leva was so drowsy that she could hardly get her hair down, but she sat on the edge of Mem's bed and discussed the future.

Leva advised new duds by all means, and offered to have them charged to her own account until Mem could find a job and begin to pay. It was harrowing to Mem to think that she must take on a burden of large debt before she could hope for small wages. But the need was imperative.

The next morning Mem acquired on tick the brief trousseau of a little business bride. Then she went to the studio with Leva and was assigned without delay to the laboratory projection room at twenty-five dollars a week. A hundred pretty actresses got no jobs at all, for they were seeking glory and wealth.

The size of the studio astounded Mem. It was a vast factory. This company's assets were thirteen million dollars; its last year's gross income: eight million. In a score of years a toy unknown before had become the fifth largest industry in the world, a mammoth target for every sort of critic.

And now Mem had entered the machine shop, if not the art.

# CHAPTER XXVI

ALL DAY SHE SAT in a dark room and ran a little projecting machine that poured forth moving pictures before her on a little private screen. She must watch out for typographical errors, a "to" for a "too," a slip of grammar, a mistake in an actor's or a character's name. Her common-school education was good enough for this, though it was by no means so marvelous as Leva had told her employers it was.

Later Mem was permitted to study the films for blemishes, scratches, dust specks, bad printing, bad tinting, bad assembly, bad any one of a score of things.

There were five other young women besides Leva engaged at the same task, each with her little projection machine and her little screen and her little picture racing ahead of her past the continual night of the laboratory. At one end of the projection room was a larger screen for the laboratory chief (a learned scientist) and his assistants and occasional directors who came with problems of photography requiring immediate solution.

The conversation was in a foreign language to Mem, but the jargon grew gradually familiar and she kept an eager ear alert for information. She decided to master the trade in every detail.

It was fascinating at first, a strange and fairy business.

Like a chorus of girls at spinning wheels these maids sat and unrolled from the magic distaff romance unending and of infinite variety.

Mem was supposed to keep her mind on her own screen, but it was impossible not to glance at the other pictures. Now there was a glittering flood of waters roaring almost audibly through a canon, and in them a spun and tormented canoe that finally flung into the waves a fugitive woman and cast her on the rocks. Someone told her that so great an actress as Mary Alden had spent thirty minutes in those icy waters while they photographed the scene. This went by again and again in different "takes" by different cameras, as if Miss Alden had been killed and brought to life again repeatedly to respond to encores of death.

Over against this tremendous rush of nature there appeared suddenly a yet more thrilling cataract of human passions, a battle in a Chinese den, where frenzied criminals, Chinese and half-castes and policemen, struck and stabbed and shot and broke over one another's heads furniture of exquisite carving or hurtled from ornate balconies and splintered embroidered screens and jeweled idols; Lon Chaney leered and bled and let demoniac thoughts flicker across his mask.

Parallel with this flowed a torrent of luxury, a reception in a home of wealth, designed by Cedric Gibbons, lover of arches and interlaced perspectives; beautiful women in gleaming dresses danced or listened to love stories or let tears drip like diamonds upon their fans of white peacock feathers.

A vast mountain range shouldered the clouds aside and a posse of vigilantes chased a pack of desperadoes on desperate horses or desperadoes chased Tom Mix as a fugitive hero who sent his broncho leaping, sliding, galloping down cliffs and up ravines, a swallow darting away from falcons.

In a close-up of huge detail, Will Rogers's whimsical face twisted with cowboy impudence and embarrassment and pathetic wit.

In another, the cinematographic features of Helene Chadwick exploited her subtlest moods in a language that could not be misunderstood; or Claude Gillingwater's Jovian brows struggled with big emotions or Richard Dix's stalwart humor flourished.

He was whisked away, and a low comedian took his place with high antics of most ancient glory, the horseplay that the new critics have always denounced and the classics have always adored: the knock-about assaults on dignity, the physical satires on pomposity that delighted Aeschylus no less than Aristophanes, Cervantes, Shakespeare, Goethe, all the big men who were not afraid of fun and understood that there is less wisdom in a strut than in a caper. Then the sensitive beauty of Colleen Moore rolled by tremulous to every least emotion as an aspen leaf.

Before all these windows Mem looked into countless phases of life and emotion and character. It occurred to her that she was getting a divine purview of the world. Life to her looked much what life must look like to God. He must see billions of souls unrolling their continuities before him in all varieties of grimace, frenzy, collapse, appeal for pity or laughter. Humanity must dance before him as before her until each life was cut off or vanished in its final fade-out.

She wondered more and more why the moving pictures should have been greeted with hostility and contempt or fear. She did not understand that they were to teach the world a new language, or open a new world, or bring golden gifts of any sort to the people are always crucified at first by the Pharisees. Later, their converts become Pharisees for new Messiahs.

She was ignorant of the primeval eternal habit of the critic mind to lash out at all that is alive and eager. Why lash the dead? They cannot feel the sting of the whip.

She knew only that the moving pictures were abhorrent to multitudes and it seemed to her pitiful that this should be so. All these actors and actresses and photographers were merely trying to illuminate life, to pass dull hours away, to quicken the spirits of the lonely and the weary.

The artistic beauties of the pictures made her inarticulately happy. She knew nothing of painting or sculpture or architecture. She loved sunsets and moon dawns and light on leaves and the textures of fabrics embracing shadows in their folds. She loved the war of gloom and glow. She found the pictures overwhelmingly beautiful to her eyes, kaleidoscopes of leaping masses and lines, symphonic tempests of shape and color.

For a time Mem was in a heaven of tumultuous ecstasies. But gradually the delight turned to torture, the torture of envy.

She was young and she had been told that she was beautiful. She had realized with shame and anger and disgust at first that she seized the eye and charmed it. Now, as in almost every other way, she was so revolutionized that what had hitherto seemed to her odious was beginning to seem admirable. What had been her evil was her good and her good her evil.

If God made her pretty it was because he delighted in beauty and wanted it known. He did not grow flowers in cellars. He was not afraid to squander the sunshine.

If the art of mimicry was a God-given gift, it must be meant for use. She had acted once before a camera, there in the desert. She had felt the possession of an alien agony. She had shot tears from her eyelids. She had brought tears to the eyes of strangers. She had tasted the sweet poison of vicarious suffering. It was accounted divine on a cross; why diabolic on a screen? She was an actress by divine intention.

She sat in a dark room and watched other people's pictures flow by. It seemed wrong, wicked, cruel.

Yet she was educating herself unconsciously in the complex technics of acting, learning dramatic analysis and synthesis.

Fools who knew nothing about acting spoke of it as if it had no intellectual element. They thought that the common-enough ability to write impudent scurrilities about the brainlessness of actors was a proof of brains.

Mem came to see how difficult a science, how bewildering an art the mimetic career requires. She would learn the anguishes of self-control and self-compulsion that must be undergone when the actor's soul squeezes itself into the mold of another character. She could already see how many ways there were of thinking, holding hands, of looking love or hate, of kissing, crying, laughing, rising up and sitting down.

She was mad to act.

# CHAPTER XXVII

AMONG THE PROCESSIONS of types that marched past Mem's eyes as she sat at her magic window in the projection room among the innumerable American types, good and bad, rich, poor, foreign, native, rural, urban, the aliens of every clime and age and costume, the animals and the birds, the plunging horses of the cowboys, the lions, the wolves, the rattlesnakes, went many children in rags and tags and velvet gowns.

She saw Booth Tarkington's "Edgar" family and the other tiny artists of the colony; exquisite Lucille Ricksen; the essence of boyhood, Johnny Jones; the plump Buddy Messenger; the adorable Robert de Vilbiss. She saw at the movie houses the little master of comedy, Wesley Barry, with his skin a constellation of freckles; and the all-conquering Jackie Coogan.

On the lot she saw the children, and they were always happy. The mothers were with the little ones. Going to work was going to play. They lived an eternal fairy story. They did not have to wait till bedtime to coax a worn-out fable from a jaded parent. They went through great adventures in magic-built castles. They had an infinite number of new toys and new games, and, greatest bliss of all, they had importance.

Mem was told that five-year-old Jackie Coogan had made his mother a present of a big touring car costing seven thousand dollars! That he had a salary of seventeen hundred and fifty dollars a week! She thought of little Terry Dack and his second-hand express wagon, helping his mother to pack her bundled wash home to bitter toil. He had a dismal life on the desert's edge, illumined only by his own unconquerable fancy and his dramatic gifts. His was the home life of multitudes of American children. He had far more of mother's love than most of them. Yet the stage child and the movie child were spoken of with pity!

Mem decided that it was well worth a child's while to accept such pity as a rebate on the fat blessings of such a life.

She wrote Terry's mother, urging her to come to Los Angeles without delay; to beg, borrow, or steal the necessary funds; to seize the chance to rescue the divine child from poverty and oblivion, and to earn luxury by giving the world the sunshine of his irresistible charm.

She had not meant to let anyone in Palm Springs know where she was, but she took the risk of embarrassment rather than risk the boy's future. Her motherhood had transplanted itself to that other child, and his welfare was vital to her.

As a final inducement she promised to introduce Terry to the management of her own studio. She permitted the impression that she was a rather important person on the staff.

And the day after she mailed the letter she lost her job.

The tide of hard times had engulfed the studio where she was engaged. All but two or three companies were laid off. The laboratory force was reduced to a skeleton. She went home one night and did not come back.

And now the dark room that had come to be a prison cell was as dear a home as the shut cage of a canary that cannot get in again.

She was homesick for the many-windowed gloom; for the black wet chambers with the big vats of "soup" where the endless tapes of minute pictures were developed; the lurid red rooms where the printing machines chattered; the drying rooms where the vast mill wheels revolved with their cascades of film.

The gates of the "lot" were closed against her as the gates of Eden against Eve.

There was no pleasure in lying abed of mornings. There was no comfort in omitting the stampede to beat the time clock.

The pay day came around no more, either. She had debts to absolve for clothes no longer fresh. She had tomorrow's and next week's hunger to dread. The girls at her house were equally idle and their hospitality lost its warmth for lack of fuel.

They tried to make the best of idleness. They wore the records to shreds and danced together all day long to pass the time away.

Young men who had no money to spend on excursions came to the house of evenings and helped to dance away the tedium.

It became a commonplace for Mem to jig about in young men's arms. She learned to dance. She learned to play a little golf, a little tennis. She even gained a bit of familiarity with the saddle at the home of an actress who owned horses and had built a riding ring on her estate when she was flush, and was glad now to have her friends exercise themselves and her stable.

Mem went also on her first beach picnic. If she did not learn to swim, she learned at least to add the paganism of the ocean to the paganism of the canons, the deserts, and the palm-blown plains.

The Pacific-coast civilization surpassed all the other coasts in its return to the pre-figleaf days. On the leagues of sand variously named Coronado, La Jolla, Laguna, Re-dondo, Hermosa, Santa Monica, there was as much care free, clothes-free gaiety as in the Marquesan and Tahitian realms that Frederick O'Brien found, or made, so Elysian with his fragrant pen.

The first day of Mem's visit to the shore was terrifying. As the automobile in which she rode threaded the long and narrow lane of Venice, a woman darted across the path, dragging a child by the arm. Mem thought at first that the mother must be fleeing from a fire that had surprised her in her tub, and that in her confusion she had put on her husband's undershirt and nothing else.

But hundreds of others were seen hurrying from that same fire in much the same costume.

The girls she was with parked the car in a little blind alley ending at the walk along the sand. Mem had come at last to "where the mountains meet the sea."

The blinding blue desert of the Pacific, almost as calm as the sky it met and welded with, the twin blues overwhelmed Mem for a moment with vastitude. Then she caught sight of the margin where the waves broke lazily in long cork screwing lines of green fringed with white froth. Among the billows and in front of them swarming human midges leaped, swam, ran, walked, squatted, burrowed, flirted, lunched, nursed babies, slept.

The sand was abloom with umbrellas, a monstrous poppy field. Along the endless walk miles on miles of little shops were aligned, with piers thrusting out into the ocean, bridges that led nowhere and were loaded down with pleasure shops. Giant wheels, insane railroads that made a sport of seasick terrors, every ingenuity for making happy fools of the mob bent on unbending.

As far as the eye could see along the vast scythe blade of shore thousands seethed, all so lightly garbed that if Mem had met any one of them in Calverly she would have fainted or fled. She was stunned. But the enormity of the multitude gave the exposure an impersonal aspect. It was like looking into a can of fishing worms wriggling unclothed in anything but a light nuptial band of color.

As she stood benumbed Leva nudged her and said, "Hurry up; we mustn't miss a minute."

"Am I expected to go in there like that?"

"Of course!"

"Not me! Not today! No, thank you!"

She could not be persuaded. She hardly consented to sit on the sand and wait. While she waited her eyes were whipped with such sights that she was anasthetized by shock. Fat mothers, fat fathers, scrawny matrons, and skeletonic elders paraded among infants and boys and girls in all stages of growth, and none of them was decently clothed according to any standard Mem knew.

Here and there Apollos and Aphrodites moved in perfection of design and rhythm, their beauty and their grace appallingly revealed. Mem bent her head, averted her eyes, felt sick at the stomach. But the coercion of the throng was more potent than any other influence. She began to think herself a ninny to be the only one out of step with this army. She compelled herself to look without flinching and, she hoped, without curiosity.

By and by the sanity, the beauty, the higher morality of it began to convert her from the immemorial folly of making a virtue out of a physical hypocrisy.

The world had come a long distance from the period when a law was passed in Virginia in 1824, making it a misdemeanor to take a bath in private, except upon the advice of physicians, which advice was usually against such a dangerous practice.

The world had come a long distance from the ideal of wearing one's graveclothes and one's grave expression while still walking about the earth. There were still loud howlers and sincere pleaders against the infamy of letting other people see one's epidermis, against letting mankind know that womankind was biped. But the dear old ladies and gentlemen with their brooms could not sweep back this oceanic tide.

Here and there they arrested or mobbed some woman or man who took off an inch or two too much of the mysteriously permitted, ever-varying minimum. But millions bathed in public and sought the fountain of youth not in dark forests, but on the sun-gilt ground where sea and land debated boundaries.

By the time Leva and her company came leaping out to join the revel, Mem was a little better. Seeing her friends, whose good sweet souls she loved, was a fresh shock, but she survived it and envied them their ability to fling off their solemnities with their other garments.

Before the afternoon had slipped into twilight she was able to laugh when she saw them playing ball with sunburnt young men of their acquaintance. When they gathered about her and sat in a crisscross of brown and white legs, she had to reconcile herself to South Sea standards. The sky was too bright to stare at all the time. They ate peanuts and popcorn and introduced her to that wonderful meal composed of a roll split open like a clam and stuffed with cleft sausage, dill pickle, lettuce, and mustard, a viand so irresistibly good that it lent a grace to its shameless name, "hot dog."

A few days later Mem might have been seen in a bathing suit of popular brevity, substituting a general coat of tan for the forty blushpower slio had abandoned.

She was not sure whether to call herself a lost or a newfound soul, but she was sure that she was an utter changeling from the remorseful girl who stole shamefast out of Calverly to hide herself from human eyes.

She was already publishing her bodily graces to the world and she was devoured with ambition to give her soul also entire to the millions. She wanted to attitudinize her soul upon a film as public and as huge as the sky and compel mankind to watch it and admire.

Mem in a way was an allegory of all recent womanhood. She had dwelt in Puritanical respectability as in a kind of mental harem, with a yashmak on her demure mind and a shapeless black robe of modesty over her bundlesome clothes. Her thoughts had been her father's to direct until he should guide them into a husband's fold. Something had gone wrong. Her thoughts had contained black sheep that strayed and fell into the dark ravines.

But now she was out of it all, joining the vast hegira of humanity from the dark ages of ritual and ceremonial and uniform into the new era of all things good in their place, and concealment of the truth, the one irretrievable evil.

Her soul and her body were her own now. No, they had gone beyond even that. Her soul and body were the public's. Beauty was community property. She was committed to their fullest development into such joyous acrobatic agility and power that they should give joy and a delightful sorrow to the public. For which the grateful public would pay with gratitude and fame and much money.

# CHAPTER XXVIII

IN SWIMMING, DANCING, MOUNTAIN climbing, horse-back-climbing, motoring, singing, laughing, days and nights reeled by. But gaiety as an ether against the pangs of idleness was a heavy, an almost nauseous, drug. She looked back on her earlier existence at home as a slothful indolence at best, a waste of gifts, a burying of genius in a napkin and the napkin in the ground where it must rot, yet never lift a flower from its corruption. To be busy, to achieve, to build her soul and sell it: that was her new passion. She gave up all thought of going home to Calverly. She would never be content with village life again.

One day she loitered through Westlake Park and watched the visitors feed the wild fowl that grow tame there. The man or child who had bread crumbs for largess was almost mobbed. Overhead the chuckling seagulls made a living umbrella, careening and dipping to hook the morsels tossed in air. From every quarter birds of various pinion gathered, swerved, darted, flung backward on wings that were both brake and motor. About the feet others scampered or stalked, pecking, gobbling. On the nearer ripples ducks, terns, and geese moved like little ferryboats; coots scooted, and swans, black and white, thrust up their periscopes from the reedy banks where they moored.

Mem loafed about until she grew too weary to stand. Her despondent soul drifted as lazily as the swans, and felt almost as willing to beg for bread. She sat down on a bench on the Seventh Street side, and by and by was hailed by a sturdy mid-Western voice.

"Well, as I live and breathe! If it ain't Miss Steddon!"

"Why, how do you do, Mrs. Sturgs!"

It was a mid-aged woman who had been a member of her father's church and had gone West — Mem had now to say, "come West," because of her husband's lungs.

Mem's first impulse was to welcome anyone from home. Her second was to fear anyone from home. But Mrs. Sturgs was already squeezing her broad person into the remaining space on the bench.

Her life in this Babylon had not changed her small-town soul, body, or prejudices.

Mem's wits scurried in vain to bring up protecting lies. Mrs. Sturgs was too full of her own opinions and adventures to ask any embarrassing questions beyond a hasty take-off for her own biography: "And how's your father and your mother and your whole fambly? All well, I hope. And so, you're here! Well, well! Well, as I was sayin' yestday, everybody on Dearth gets to Los Angeles sooner or later. It's a nice city, too, full of good, honest, plain — o' course those awful moving-picture people have given the town a... But there's plenty of real nice folksy folks here; and the town growin' faster than... Well, as I was tellin' m' husband last week, it takes all kinds to make a world and the Lord may have had some idea of his own when he made movies; of course, I enjoy seein' 'em. You just can't help enjoyin' the terrible... But the people that make 'em, well!

"Such stories as they do tell about their... Why, that Hollywood is just a plague spot on the earth! The gentman we used to rent from... We own our own home now, or will soon when a few more installments are... And the prices here! my dear! oh dear! But he said that friends of his who had rented their homes to movie people... Why, would you believe it? some of those cowboys one day on the ranch, next day earning a thousand dollars and buying jewelry on credit, wrist watches with split diamonds for crystals and they rent a nice house and ride a horse in the dining room and shoot the china right off the... It's a fact! And some the women little pink ninnies that don't know enough to come in when they get fortunes for just making eyes at the camera, and they rent nice respectable homes and hold, well, orgies is the only word, orgies is just what they are.

"It's a sin and a shame, and if something isn't done about It... Why, young girls flock there in droves, and sell their souls and bodies for... It's simply terrible."

"A gentman who claims to know was telling m' usband and he told me that there isn't one decent woman on the screen, not one. Would you b'lieve it? Every one of them has to pay the Price to get there at tall.

"He says to m' usband that it's the regular thing. Before a girl is engaged she has to... Those directors... Why, any pretty girl who is willin' to lose her immortal soul can get a chance if she'll only... And if she won't, why, they turn her away.

"I declare it makes my blood run cold just to... Don't it yours?"

"I don't believe it," said Mem.

She had heard a vast amount of gossip, but she had not heard of anybody paying such an initiation fee. She had seen a great deal of joy and some of it reckless, but with a childish recklessness. She had seen no vice at all.

Mrs. Sturgs flared up. There is nothing one defends more zealously than one's pet horrors.

"Don't believe it? Well, that's only because you're so innocent yourself, speaks well for your bringing up so strict and all. You naturally wouldn't believe folks could be so depraved, but if you'd heard what I've—Why, it's true as gospel! My husband had it from a man who knows whereoff he speaks. They sell their souls for bread, and, as the Bible says, their feet lay hold on well, you know. Any girl that's too honest to pay the Price don't get engaged, that's all, she just don't get engaged. Of course there may be some decent ones, old ladies that play homely parts, and but if a young girl wants to succeed in that business she's just got to — Oh dear! That's my car. There's not another one for half an — They run out to our place only every — Goodbye! I hope to see you again soon. Wait! Hay! Hay!"

And she was gone into the infinite purlieus of Los Angeles. She caught her car and it slid off, gong banging, and bunted a passing automobile out of the way with much crumpling of the fender and the vocabulary of the driver, but no fatality. Which was unusual. Mem did not regret the abrupt departure of Mrs. Sturgs. She was glad of the woman's breathless garrulity.

It had not only left her with her secrets intact, but it had given her a hint. Mrs. Sturgs had substituted faith for facts and had spoken with that earnestness which is more convincing than evidence.

Mem accused herself of blindness instead of charging Mrs. Sturgs with scandal. She felt that the alleged wickedness had escaped her notice because she was too stupid to recognize it.

But Mrs. Sturgs's accusations had the same perverse effects as her father's jeremiads. His sermon had made her long to see Los Angeles. Mrs. Sturgs had suggested an answer to her own riddle.

She wanted to act. She was determined to act. She needed money. She must have money. It had never occurred to her that a pretty woman is merchandise. She had given herself away once, and now she found that there was a market ready, and waiting, with cash and opportunity as the price. She had wares for this market. She could barter them for fame and future. Since she could, she would.

She sat on the bench and noted with a new interest that some of the men who passed her and stared at her had question marks in their eyes. Up to now she had shuddered at the vague posing of this eternal interrogation. She had not taken it as a tribute of praise or as an appeal for mercy, but as a degrading insult. Now she thought of it as a kind of sly appraisal, a system of silent bidding, auctioneering without words, the never-closed stock market of romance and intrigue.

These men, who swept their eyes across Mem's face and tacitly murmured, "Well?" had nothing to offer but a little sin or a little coin. She had no notion of the rates. She wanted none of their caresses or their dark purposes. She wanted the light of glory, opportunity; so much fame for so much shame.

She grew grim as she meditated. "The Price" was only a vague phrase, but she was ready to pay it, whatever it was. But to whom?

She brooded a long while before she thought of a shop to visit. She smiled sardonically as she remembered The Woman's Exchange at home where women sold what they made: painted china, hammered brass, knit goods, cakes, and candies. Well, she would sell what God had made of her for what man might make of her.

At the studio she had met the casting director, one day when the commissary was crowded with stars in their painted faces and gaudy robes and with extra people portraying Turks, Japanese, farmers, ranchers, ballet dancers, society women, Mexicans. He had been introduced to her as Mr. Arthur Tirrey when he asked if he might take the vacant seat at the table where she sat with Leva and another girl.

He was an amiable and laughing person with an inoffensive gift of flattery. When he learned that all the girls worked in the laboratory projection room, he had exclaimed:

"Why waste yourselves in that coal cellar? I'll put you all in the next picture."

The others had not taken him seriously. Indeed, they had no ambition to be photographed. Mem had often wondered at the numbers of pretty women she knew who had no desire to have their pictures published. It balanced somewhat the horde of unpretty women who had a passion for the camera.

After the lunch she had learned who Mr. Tirrey was and what the duties were of a casting director. It was he who said to this one or that one, "Here is a part; play it, and the company will give you so much a week."

He was the St. Peter of the movie heaven, empowered to admit or to deny. He was the man for her to seek. He had seemed a decent enough man, and he had looked at Mem without insolence. But you could never tell. Mrs. Sturgs had it on the best authority that the only way to success in the movies was "the easiest way."

Mem took a street car home. She was glad to find the house empty. Leva and the others were out on a canon hike, dressed in high boots and riding breeches, and braving the perils of rattlesnakes as well as the frightful men who lurked in the thickets or who sprang out of motors and kidnaped women every now and then.

Mem pondered the costume appropriate to her new errand. She was going to lure Lucifer, and she was afraid that he would be too sophisticated for her. But her problem was solved for her by its simplicity. She had only one very pretty gown, so she put that on.

She studied herself a long while in the mirror, since her eyes and her smile must be her chief wardrobe, her siren equipment. She practiced such expressions as she supposed to represent invitation. They were silly and they made her rather ill. The face in her glass was so ashen and so miserable that she borrowed some of Leva's warmest face powder; and smeared her mouth crudely with the red lip stick.

It was a long journey to the studio, with three transfers of street car. She reached the lot late in the afternoon, just before the companies were dismissed and the department forces released.

The gatekeepers knew her, smiled at her, and let her in. She went to the casting director's office and found him idly swapping stories with his assistant. He spoke to her courteously, and when she asked if she might see him a moment he motioned her into his office, gave her a chair, closed the door, and took his own place behind his desk.

The telephone rang. He called into it: "Sony, Miss Waite; that part has been filled. The company couldn't make your salary. I begged you to take the cut, but you wouldn't. Times are hard and you'd better listen to reason. You'd have had four weeks of good money, and now you'll walk. Take my advice next time, old dear, and don't haggle over salary... All right. Sorry. Goodbye!"

He turned to Mem and started to speak. The telephone jingled. He had a parley with a director who could not see a certain actor whom Mr. Tirrey was urging as the ideal for the type. They debated the man as if he had been a racehorse or a trained animal. Tirrey spoke of him as a gentleman, who could wear clothes and look the part. He had been miscast in his last picture. He was willing to take three hundred a week off his salary because his wife was in the hospital and one of his daughters was going away to boarding school.

Another telephone call: an agent, evidently, for Tirrey said: "We took a test of Miss Glover. She's terrible! Her mouth is repulsive, her teeth ought to be straightened, her eyes are of the blue that photographs like dishwater. We can't use her. Don't tell her that, of course. Tell her, we're not certain about the picture; we may not do it for months. Give the poor thing a good story."

This was a discouraging background for Mem's siren scenario. But she was determined to carry out her theory. Mr. Tirrey's eyes looked her way now and then as he listened to what was coming in through the wire.

When he looked away, Mem, in all self-loathing, adjusted herself in her big chair to what she imagined was a Cleopatran sinuosity. She thought of her best lines; secretly twitched up her skirts and thrust her ankles well into view. She turned upon Mr. Tirrey her most languishing eyes, and tried to pour enticement into them as into bowls of fire.

She pursed her lips and set them full. She widened her breast with deep sighs.

Tirrey seemed to recognize that she was deploying herself. He grew a little uneasy. Before he finished the telephone talk, his assistant came in to say that another of the directors had decided to call a big ballroom scene the next day, and fifty ladies and gentlemen must be secured at once.

"He wants real swells, too," the assistant said. "He says the last bunch of muckers queered the whole picture."

Tirrey groaned and said, "Get busy on the other wire." He took up his telephone again, used it as a long antenna, and felt through the city for various extra people. He advised several actors and actresses to lay aside their pride and take the real money rather than starve.

His patience, his altruistic enthusiasm for the welfare of these invisible persons, touched Mem with admiration. She could not see where or when this Samaritan could find time or inclination to play the satyr.

He was a bit fagged when he finished his last charge upon the individuals and the agencies. But he was as polite to Mem as if she had been Robina Teele.

"What can I do for you?"

"I want a chance to act."

"What's your line?"

"Anything."

"Anything is nothing. What experience have you had?"

Mem had not come here to offer her past, but her future. She was suddenly confronted with the fact that all actors must offer themselves for sale: not the pretty women only, but the old men, too, and the character women.

Actors are much abused for talking of themselves. Few of them do when business is not involved, but when it is they must discuss the goods they are trying to sell. Shoe merchants talk shoes: railroad presidents, railroads; politicians, politics; clergymen, salvation. Each salesman must recommend his own stock and talk it up.

So Mem had to grope for experience and dress her window with it. And she had had so little she lied a little, as one does who tries to sell anything:

"I was with the company that Tom Holby and Robina Teele played in. I took the part of an Arabian woman. Mr. Folger, the director, er, praised my, er, work."

"Well, he knows," said Tirrey, "but he's not with us, you know. Have we your name and address and a photograph outside in our files?"

"No."

"Well, if you'll give them to Mr. Dobbs, with your height, weight, color of eyes and hair, and experience, we'll let you know when anything occurs. Everything's full just now, and we're doing almost nothing, you know."

He was already implying that the interview was ended. She broke out zealously:

"But I've got to have a chance. I'll do anything," she pleaded. He looked sad, but rose and shook his head.

"I'm sorry, my dear. I can't give you jobs when there aren't any, now can I? I'll introduce you to Mr. Dobbs and he —"

He moved toward the door to escape from the cruelty of his office, but a frenzy moved her to seize his arm in a fierce clutch. She tried to play the vampire as she had seen the part enacted on the screen by various slithy toves. She drew her victim close to her, pressed tight against him, and poured upward into his eyes all the venom of an amorous basilisk.

"I'll pay the Price. I know what it costs to succeed, and I'm willing to pay. I'll do anything you say, be anything to you. You can't refuse me."

She could hardly believe her own ears hearing her own voice, though her pride in the acting she was doing lifted her from the disgust for the role.

He looked at her without surprise, without horror, without even amusement, but also without a hint of surrender. His only mood was one of jaded pity.

"You poor child, who's been filling your head with that stuff? Are you really trying to vamp me?"

The crass word angered her:

"I'm trying to force my way to my career, and I don't care what it costs."

Tirrey's sarcastic smile faded:

"Sit down a minute and listen to me. A little common sense ought to have told you that what you've been told is all rot. But suppose it wasn't. Suppose I were willing to give a job to every pretty girl who came in here and tried to bribe me with love. Do you know how many women I see a day? A hundred and fifty on some days; that's nearly a thousand a week. I happen to have a wife and a couple of kids and I like 'em pretty well at that. But suppose I were King Solomon and Brigham Young and the Sultan of Turkey all in one. A hundred and fifty a day really, you know. You flatter me! I won't ask you how I could do any office work or how long my health would last, but how long do you suppose my job would last if I gave positions in return for favors? And if you won me over you'd still have to please the director and the managers and the author and the public. How long would our company keep going if we selected our actresses according to their immorality?

"It's none of my business what your character is off the lot except that your character will photograph, and a girl can't last long who plays Polyanna on the screen and polygamy outside.

"Just suppose I gave you a job for the price you want to pay and collected my commission, and then the director refused to accept you, or fired you after the first day's test. What guarantee could I give you that you could hold the job once I recommended you for it? And what would the rest of the women on the lot and off it do if such a business system were installed here? What would the police do to us?

"There's a lot of bad gals in this business and there's a lot in every other business and in no business. But put this down in your little book, my dear: there's just one way to succeed on the screen and that is to deliver the goods to the public.

"The danger you'll run in this business is after you get your job. The men you associate with are mostly mighty nice fellows, magnetic, handsome, good sports, hard workers; otherwise the public wouldn't look at them. Well, you'll be associated with them very closely, and you'll feel like a bad sport, maybe, sometimes, if you try to be too cold and unapproachable when they're in a friendly mood. But that's a danger you'll meet anywhere.

"Forget this old rot about paying the Price. Good Lord! If you could sit here and see the poor little idiots that come in here and try to decoy me. I get it all day long. Your work was pretty poor, my dear. I congratulate you on being such a bad bad woman. But I'm immune. You'd have failed if you had been the Queen of Sheba. Now go on outside and tell Mr. Dobbs your pedigree and we'll give you the first chance we get, and no initiation fee or commission will be charged. How's that? A little bit of all right, eh? You're a nice child, and pretty, and you'll get along."

He lifted her from her chair and put his arm around her as a comrade, and slapped her shoulder blades in an accolade of good fellowship.

She broke under the strain and began to cry. She dropped back into her chair and sobbed. It was good to be punished and rebuked into common decency by the way of common sense.

Tirrey watched her and felt his overpumped heart surge with a compelling sympathy. He resolved to move her up to the head of the endless army of pretty girls pleading for opportunity, the bread line of art.

When he had let her cry awhile, she began to laugh, hysterically at first, then with more wholesome self-derision.

Her eyes were so bright and her laughter so glad that they impressed a director who pressed his face against the screen door. Mem had been so deeply absorbed in her plan that she had not observed the other door standing wide open save for its screen.

Tirrey asked the director in as he opened the inner door for Mem's exit. But the director checked her with a gesture. Tirrey presented him as Mr. Rookes. He had to ask Mem's name. She gave it, from habit, as Mrs. Woodville.

Mr. Rookes said to Tirrey:

"I've got to let Perrin go. She's no good at all: no comedy, no charm. She's supposed to play a village cutie and she plays it like Nazimova's Hedda Gabler. This young lady looks the type. She's very pretty, nice and clean looking."

Mem was aghast at being so discussed, yet it was thrilling to be considered. She did not even note that the director had neglected to demand virtue as the Price. It was almost more embarrassing to have him demand her experience.

Her story improved with repetition:

"Oh, I played a bit for Mr. Folger. He said I was wonderful."

"Was it comedy?"

"Well, not exactly. It was character." She was trying to talk like a professional.

"Would you mind giving me a test?"

She was not quite sure what he meant, but she was there to pay any price, so she said:

"I'd love to."

"It's late," said Rookes, "but I'm desperate. Come right over to the set before the electricians get away."

He hurried her through the screen door, across the grass to one of the vast warehouses, and there under a bombardment of grisly lights, with a camera aimed at her point-blank and under the eye of various men in overalls, he asked her to smile, to turn her head slowly from side to side, to wink, to laugh aloud, to flirt with an imaginary man, to indicate jealous vexation at a rival.

Rookes was fretful over the snarl this small role was causing in his big picture. The delays and shifts it had compelled had already added several thousand dollars to the expense account, since the overhead and all totaled nearly three thousand dollars a day even with the recent cuts in salaries.

He assumed that Mem knew the rudiments of her trade and could use the tools of it, which were her muscles. He gave her no help, painted no scene, did nothing to stimulate her imagination.

In the desert, among the famine-wrung people in costume, under the fiendish sky, it had been easy to lift her eyes in prayer and to weep.

She found out all of a sudden how much harder it is to be natural in one's own clothes than to play a poetic role in costume; how much harder it is to be funny than to be tragic.

She could not smile at command. Her lips drew back in a grin of pain. Her wink was leaden.

The camera caught what her face expressed and it expressed what she felt, which was despair. She had her chance and she was not ready for it.

She knew that if she had been droll and mischievous, the director's face would have reflected it as Mr. Folger's eyes had grown wet when she wept in the desert. But Mr. Rookes was merely polite; the camera man was mirthless; the props and grips stole away.

The test was short. Mr. Rookes said: "Very nice. Ever so much obliged. Mr. Tirrey will let you know how it comes out. Thank you again. Good night!"

And now she must find her way out. Tirrey was just driving away in his car as she sneaked through the gates, feeling that her Paradise was gone again.

She had so little hope that she did not mention the experience to Leva. She had no ambition to promulgate her failures. It was success that she wanted.

For once, her gloomy forebodings were justified. And ever after she trusted her gloomy forebodings, often as they fooled her.

The next day passed with no summons from the studio. But the mail brought her a letter from Mrs. Dack.

It was written in such script as one might expect from a hand that clutched a cake of soap or a hot boiler handle or scrubbed clothes against a washboard all day six days a week. It said:

> DEAR MRS. WOODVILLE. I was awful glad to
> get your letter. Been meaning to anser it but trying
> to fix up my afairs sos I and Terry could come up
> to your city. Yesday I was to Mrs. Reddicks and she
> said she had a tellagram for you but had no adress

and so could not forword it. It said your mother was so worrit not having had no anser to her letters she was comeing out on the first train and would reache Palm Springs day after tomorow. Hopping to see you soon ether there or here,

MRS. P. DACK.

P. S. Both I and Terry send you lots of love.

Mem was petrified. Nothing could stop her mother from coming. The first blaze of joy at the thought of the reunion was quenched in the flood of impossible situations her presence would create.

Alone with her skyish ambitions, her contempt for village standards had been sublime. But that was in the absence of the village. It made an amazing difference in the look of her new ideals and practices that they must be submitted to a mother's eyes.

Her mother did not know Los Angeles.

But then, Mem did not know her mother. Daughters have not all been mothers, but all mothers have been daughters.

Mem's courage turned craven before the wilderness of her problems, unemployment, poverty, ambition, Terry Dack to launch, and her mother to educate.

# CHAPTER XXIX

REMEMBER STEDDON WAS NOT exactly a runaway. She was a walkaway. She was not included in the pitiful beadroll of the sixty-five thousand girls who vanished from American homes that year and caused a vast bother, though girls have been running away from home since girls and homes were.

They have followed the cave men, the barbarian invaders, the Allied troops, the caravans, the argosies. They filled the primeval factories and the places of merriment, the Corinths and Alexandrias. Some of them became slaves and some sultanas, priestesses, royal favorites, empresses, tsarinas, queens of song and art. Some starved, some flourished.

Mem felt that to go back would condemn her to ignominy and futility, while to stay away promised a chance for wealth and glory. She heard voices calling her, saw spirits summoning her to the skies, no less than Joan of Arc did, and perhaps with no more insanity.

But now her mother had found her out and was pursuing her. Her mother would be as grave a problem to her as she to her mother.

The fall from the cliff that did not quite free Mem's soul from her body had quite freed the little parasite soul that was to have been her conspicuous fardel to bear through life. But the tiny leech had begun to drink her blood and in its death it tore open a wound that would never quite heal. Her soul had bled and she had been stricken with awe before the two miracles that fastened a life upon hers and then wrested it from her before it was quite a life.

The letter she had written her mother then had been the instinctive cry of a child beset in the dark by some enormous presence passing overhead.

Just as instinctive was the compulsion that drew her mother to her across the continent.

Old Mrs. Steddon had raised a family and been habited to a mother's slumber, light and fitful and broken with frequent dashes to bedsides troubled by bad dreams or imagined burglars or mere thirst or a cough. Mrs. Steddon had always flung out of her own warm covers to run to the call. If her hasty feet found both her slippers or one or neither, she hastened as she was. She would not have paused for a wolf, an Indian, a murderer, a fire, or an earthquake.

Mem was still her baby in the dark, and it did not matter whether she lay needful and terrified in the next room or beyond the deserts or the seven seas. The mother's one business was to get to her. Her telegram was her old night cry: "I'm coming, honey. Don't worry. Mamma's coming to her baby." She shot this cry across the continent and called Mem "baby," although Mem felt as old as night.

The Reverend Doctor Steddon had wished that he might go along, but his church tasks held him and he could not find the money for two fares. The lies he had been told had succeeded to perfection.

Mem's efforts to hide herself and support herself in the wilderness he assumed to be her usual unselfish and characteristic unwillingness to be a bother to her father and mother.

Doctor Steddon agreed with his wife that she must set out at once for Palm Springs. He raised the necessary funds by lifting still more of his little savings from the bank and drawing pauperdom closer. His only regret was that he had not more to sacrifice.

And now Mrs. Steddon was following Mem's train route, with all the difference in the world: Mem, a young and beautiful girl, had had all her fate before her and a heart of growing audacity and reckless ambition. Mrs. Steddon, an old and shabby parsoness, had all her hope behind her and that not much, and a heart full of inexperience and of timidity before everything except self-immolation.

When Mem learned that her mother was already on the train, she could devise no plan for turning her back. Somehow she had to be met and provided for.

Every one of the women of Mem's Hollywood household was out of work. She who had savings was lending them to her who had not. One of the women in the bungalow gave up the fight and, putting up her little car for security, borrowed from Leva money enough to pay her fare home to the village and the scornful relatives she had sworn never to return to except in triumph. The servant had been released and the stranded women were cooking their own food, such as it was.

It was this dire confrontation with bankruptcy that had goaded Mem to her insane idea of pawning her virtue for an opportunity. When the casting director had given her a sermon instead of a *quid pro quo*, she had found herself abject indeed; even her shamelessness repulsed and her last trinket proved nonnegotiable.

And now her mother! "In every deep a lower deep!" But Leva responded to her panic by an almost hysterical bravery. She laughed, "I'll dig a little farther down in the sock," and added the trite old bravery: "Cheer up! The worst is yet to come!"

With a few dollars from Leva's waning resources Mem took the train to Palm Springs, her one remaining hope being the confidence that when she returned she would find a letter from Mr. Tirrey saying that she was engaged.

She reached Palm Springs in time to have a little talk with Mrs. Dack, who was closing out her business and good will as a washerwoman and preparing to take her boy Terry to the golden city of Los Angeles. This was a gamble, indeed, and Mem was frightened by what she had set on foot. She found nothing so terrifying as having her advice accepted. She had not realized what an army of children was already quartered in Los Angeles.

By working all the time and never spending much Mrs. Dack had accumulated a pittance that looked like a fortune to her. She would find that Los Angeles prices were not scaled to keep retired laundresses in luxury for an extended period. But that was for the future.

She and her boy and Mem stood on the platform, waiting for the up train, and when Mrs. Steddon dropped off the steps Mem put her right back on again. She ran forward and persuaded the baggageman to carry Mrs. Steddon's trunk on to Los Angeles. It was only when the train was flying once more through the desert that she and her mother found a chance for real greetings and then they were restrained by the presence of other passengers.

At least Mrs. Steddon was restrained. Mem was stimulated.

This simple, familiar matter of a mother and daughter meeting again after a long parting revealed the gulf between them. Mem had crossed the gulf. She had dwelt in the blazing sunlight, in a bright, a gaudy bungalow with noisy friends. The house was made to look well from the street. The toil of all the inhabitants was toward publication, the entertainment of the public. Mem's new ambition was to parade her emotions before the world and storm the world's emotions. There was far, far more in this than mere conceit or ostentation. She wanted to help mankind by educating and exercising its moods, as even the most ardent evangelist is not without anxiety for public attention, for the meekest has his pride and his greed of notice from his God if not from his public.

So now Mem felt that it would be a shame to let these strangers think she did not love her mother tremendously. She devoured the little old woman with kisses and caresses, and she did not keep her voice inaudible. That was her new ideal of devotion. She was advertising her love a little, but no more than religious people flaunt their creeds.

Mrs. Steddon was no less aglow with joy in the recovery of her lost lamb, and no less aware of the audience, but she felt quelled by it and under an obligation not to disturb it by her personal emotions.

At home she lived in a dull old house as devoid of architectural fripperies as of graces. The blinds were always down and the ideal of that house was that the neighbors and passers-by should never know of its existence. Good houses were seen and not heard.

She was troubled by Mem's voluble enthusiasm, her warm clothes, her careless rapture, her demonstrative affections. She did not mar the festival by rebuking her child, but she grew a little more quiet and reserved, as if to give a hint, or at least to lower the average.

Mrs. Steddon's body had traveled thousands of miles, but her soul had not budged. She was just what Mem had left in the village, looking, indeed, a bit more village in her bonneted shabbiness than before. But to the mother Mem was altered almost beyond recognition.

Her spiritual wardrobe had been enormously enlarged and the clothes upon her body were of another world.

Los Angeles has fashions of dress that are all her own. Many of the moving-picture people are conspicuous anywhere by their sartorial differences. Even the wax figures in the shop windows of Los Angeles have a challenging spirit unlike any other waxworks. The dummies attitudinize, beckon, and command attention by their uncanny vivacity, where the indolent wax figures of shops of other cities are content to stand still like clothes racks and make no effort to sell their wares.

Mem had acted a role in make-up before cameras; she had learned to dance and swim and ride, to compete with young men in athletics, business, repartee, and flirtation. Her body was no longer a hateful shroud of the spirit, but a finely articulated, galloping steed for the soul to ride and put through paces.

She was so changed outside and in, from coiffure to foot gear, that at first her own mother had not recognized her in the young actress who swept down upon her, flung her back on the train, and treated her as a fresh-air-fund waif. Later she realized with embarrassed admiration that this brilliant butterfly was what had come out of the dun chrysalis that she had named Remember. She had loved the child, but had never suspected her of being so capable of so many metamorphoses.

The swift journey from the mountains and through the desert into the orange gardens was repeated for her in the journey she made now with Mem's soul.

The girl's first questions were eager demands for news from home; but then her talk turned all to herself. She was "selling" herself to her mother as she had tried to sell herself to the casting director.

Mrs. Steddon had been prepared to find a scared and sickly child in a shack in Palm Springs. She had come as a rescuing angel. She found that her wings and halo were old-fashioned and her child doing better without her than ever she had done at home. As Mem's tongue outraced the train, the dazed mother learned that her baby was now a fearless adventurer upon the paths of ambition; that she was actually one of those appalling creatures known as an actress, and a movie actress above all things! A movie actress below all things!

Mrs. Steddon's comments were simple gasps and reiterated "Well, well's." Mem's autobiography was hardly finished by the time Los Angeles was reached.

And now the abashed immigrant that Mem had been when she faced the crowded streets and the taxi comets was as sophisticated as if she had been a native daughter of Los Angeles. She sheltered her mother as if her mother were a new-come immigrant of immature mind.

They left Mrs. Dack and Terry at the home of a cousin, then sped on to the bungalow.

Leva, who ran out to whisk Mrs. Steddon into the shrimp-pink residence, found her calm and serene. But it was the calm of chloroform.

She made no resistance to Leva's disposition of her and her things. She accepted the vacant room and made no demur at the decorations left by its late occupant: snap shots of rollicking beach parties, of horseback rides through canons, of Greek dancers, of postal cards with queer photographs and queer jokes, portraits of stars and others, all in a high state of excitement.

During the train ride and Mem's chatter Mrs. Steddon had been doing some earnest thinking in a little private brain room just back of the auditorium. Her husband had pledged her to write him frankly how their poor child was and how soon she would be strong enough to be brought back home. Mrs. Steddon had promptly realized that Mem was far too strong to be brought back home at all. She realized, too, that if she wrote her husband frankly just how Mem was and what she was up to, Doctor Steddon would probably fall down dead in his study, or have an apoplexy in the pulpit when he stood up to scourge the sins of his congregation and felt his whip hand stayed by the fact that his own sheltered pet had gone wronger than any girl in town of recent memory.

Mrs. Steddon did not want to commit murder. She was not like that ancient monster of self-preservation who said that if all mankind stood on a balance to be dumped into hell unless he told a lie, it was his duty to tell the truth.

Mrs. Steddon was one of those craven wretches who would have told a million lies to keep one poor soul from being dumped into hell. She had never quite understood the extraordinary precedence the truth had usurped over love, mercy, courtesy, and convenience. She never lied in her own behalf or to save herself from blame. She sometimes lied to shift blame to herself from her children. She lied to the children about Santa Claus, about how quickly bad children are punished and how inevitably good children are rewarded; about how infallibly right their father was, and such commonplace household perjuries. She lied to her husband incessantly about how wise he was, how eloquent. She applied untruth generally as a kind of arnica, a first-aid panacea.

Her only hesitance now concerned just what untruth it was safest and most satisfactory to tell him.

She was a wicked old woman, and it was small wonder that she rapidly lapsed into enormous popularity among the lost souls of Hollywood.

Fortunately, her daughter left her alone for a while and she had time in her bedroom to work out an attractive lie. She must say that Mem was well. That was a good, solid fact to rest the springboard of fancy on. She must explain that Mem had left Palm Springs for Los Angeles. Why? Well, because she had a chance to improve her position and her doctor had said that Palm Springs was too full of palms or something. A doctor's advice was the best bet, because a doctor was the only human power that her husband recognized as superior to his own impulses.

Next, what was Mem doing in Los Angeles to support herself? She had written that she needed no more money from home. It would be fatal to say that she had entered upon a cinematic career. And it would be adding humiliation to infamy to admit that she had lost her job even in that inferno.

Mrs. Steddon chewed the end of the penholder into pulp before a light from some place inspired her. Old Increase Mather, in explaining how old witches did not always sink when thrown into the water, observed that the devil can also work miracles, and it must have been Beelzebub who upheld this old witch of a Mrs. Steddon in the deep waters about her.

But the miracles of hell, like those of heaven, confer only a temporary benefit. Doctor Steddon would accept her falsehoods without suspicion, but woe unto her when he should learn the hideous truth.

For the moment, however, Mrs. Steddon was inspired to write to her trusting husband that she found Mem in very good health and engaged in nice, light, ladylike work in the public library at pretty good pay, considering the cost of living; also that she was boarding with some right nice ladies also in library work at the address given. She closed with some remarks on the beauties of California, a land the Lord had been awful partial to.

As she finished this letter Mrs. Steddon felt dizzy. She wondered if her giddiness might be the first symptoms of whatever it was that carried off Sapphira and her husband.

But, remembering that Sapphira had fallen down, she decided to lie down first. She fell asleep, and did not know that Leva Lemaire, peering in and seeing her there stretched out, white haired and benign, had looked upon her as a tired saint and, tiptoeing in, had spread over her a Navajo blanket of barbaric red and black.

While her mother slept Mem wept, more freely and copiously than in all her life before.

# CHAPTER XXX

NO WORD HAD COME from the studio as to the result of Mem's test pictures. There was no telephone in the bungalow to ring a verbal message in or take one out.

Mem could have gone to a drug store and telephoned from a pay station, but she was afraid to hear her fate come rattling out of the little rubber oracle. She wanted to meet her destiny face to face and make a battle for it if the issue hung in doubt.

She simply had to have work now because she had her mother as well as herself to support. She was still too new to realize that need is not a recommendation or a substitute for ability. Insofar as it has any bearing in the case, being hard-up is an argument for disability. Jobs are offered most promptly to those that already have them, and those who have work to offer rarely seek those who are idle.

As Mem hastened along a palm-lined avenue to her street car she was hailed by the man she had refused to dance with, the handsome Mr. Creighton from whose arms she had fought herself free in rage and terror the first evening of her arrival in Hollywood when he tried to make her dance.

Another evidence of the distance she had traveled was the fact that she had danced with him often since, and that when he invited her to step into his automobile she hailed him as a taxi-angel and ordered him to rush her to her studio at top speed.

He had bought himself a new racer, a long underslung craft of desperate mien. "I can't afford a car," he confessed, "and it's all bluff, but when you're hunting a job it makes a great effect to roll up in your own roadster."

The impudence was contagious and Mem calmly remarked:

"I must get me a car. What do you think is the best make?"

The two non-capitalists blithely juggled thousands of dollars and hundreds of horsepower.

"What effect do you want to affect?" said Creighton. "If you're going to play ingenues you'll want a shy and virginal auto; if you're going in for adventuresses and heavies, you'd better get a bus that's a bit sporty."

Mem thought she was nobly conservative when she said:

"I shouldn't like to be too conspicuous."

"That's right, the gaudy old days are over," said Creighton. "The pioneers out here went in for plaids and gold brocade upholstery and everything outrageous. Then Jeanie MacPherson made a sensation by having her car painted plain black, and now almost everybody is very sedate except Roscoe, of course. He is so big he has a Jumbo car."

Mem was good enough actress to conceal from Creighton the fact that her interest in the makes of cars was a mere windshield to the cold gale of anxiety playing on her nerves. She was in a panic lest she should not be engaged at all. Her immediate problem was not the selection of an automobile, but the assurance of food and raiment.

Creighton rolled her up to the studio gates and waved her good luck. She faltered when she entered the casting office. She almost fainted when Tirrey's assistant told her bluntly that there was "nothing doing." Mr. Tirrey had so many hearts to break, so many hopes to sicken with deferment, that he avoided the ghoulish task when he could. He had warned his assistant to save him from undergoing another of Mem's assaults upon his emotions.

When Mem received this curt facer through the little window in the door between the waiting room and the outer office, she blanched and fell back.

The room was full of anxious souls, each with its desperation. There sat a hungry fat woman whose bulk had kept her employed when sylphs had had to wait. Next her was a gaunt creature who could play Famine or a comic spinster with equal skill. A brace of sparrows with yellowed curls that looked like handfuls of pine shavings waited with their mother. Three beautiful young men with the eyes of dying deer perused their fingernails for lack of more exciting literature. An assortment of villains, first and second murderers, and more or less aristocratic extra folk stood about, hoping against experience.

Scattered among the laity, they would have passed for ordinary folk, but, grouped here, they took on a curiously professional mummer's air.

Mem stared at them and a hot resentment thrilled her. She would not accept a place in this mob of nonentities. She went back to the window and motioned to the assistant casting-out director. She pleaded for just a moment of Mr. Tirrey's time. The assistant said he was busy; but he could not snub those eloquent eyes. And that patient man, Mr. Tirrey, with a Samaritanism that should win him through Purgatory, accepted the ordeal, invited her in, and braced himself for the familiar business of the undertaker, the old sexton in the graveyard of art.

"I don't think you realize how much this means to me, Mr. Tirrey," Mem began. My mother has unexpectedly arrived. I've just got to support us both now, and it is more important than ever that I find work."

Poor Tirrey had heard this so often that it ought to have bored him. But he could never quite protect himself from these expressive, passionate individuals who refused to become mere generalities. He was like one of Saint Hoover's men doling out food about the world. Hunger was hunger no matter how frequent. But he was unable to perform miracles and feed hungry thousands with a few loaves and fishes. When his loaves and fishes gave out the baskets were empty, and the rest of the sufferers must go vacant.

He said he was sorry; and he was. He would keep her in mind. He would not forget. Something might turn up. When Mem failed to go, the busy wretch was tormented into a slight impatience. He stooped to self-defense.

"You don't seem to get my angle of it, Mrs. Woodville. I can only hand out what jobs there are to the people that fit them best. You came in the other day and said you were so ambitious and determined that you would, er, sell your honor for an opportunity. I told you why I couldn't make the exchange. Now you come in and try to sell me your poverty. That is even less, ah, marketable. There's a big line of scared and hungry people always forming and falling away out there. Some of them are old veterans with children, artists who have done fine things for us. But we have to turn them away. If an old lady with sixteen starving babies asked me to let her play a young girl's part I couldn't give it to her, could I, now?"

"No, but I'm not an old lady with sixteen children," Mem persisted, stupidly stubborn.

"No, but you don't suit the director and he's got the final say. Mr. Rookes gave you a test. He saw the result and says you haven't got comedy, at least not in that part. Comedy is difficult. It takes twice as much skill and experience as romantic drama. You may have it, but you didn't show it."

"The test wasn't fair!" Mem protested. "I didn't have any help. He just told me, 'Turn your head, smile, laugh, wink, flirt.' Who could do anything worthwhile like that?"

"I know, but it cost the company about fifty dollars to make it. It's the test everybody has to go through. Another girl went through the same ordeal and she made good. She got the job. I'm mighty sorry, but the only job there was is gone."

Mem struggled to her feet and turned to the door. But the sight of that plank, that coffin lid, made her recoil. She could not go out into the wilderness. She could not go home to her mother and confess failure, accept despair. Her lips wavered childishly. She found things in her throat to swallow. Her eyelashes were full of rain. Her diaphragm began to throb.

She cried beautifully, honestly. She was not artful about it, or insincere. It was a gift. She suffered with exquisite ease and grace.

She was one of those pretty things it is hard not to caress, in whose wail there is a keen and compelling music.

Tirrey found himself more dangerously wooed by her grief than by her proffer of love. Her shoulders were pitifully round; her hands groped for other hands to help; her eyes, seen blurred and monstrous with woeful tears, were more beautiful, somehow, than when she had tried to fill them with seduction.

His heart ached to draw her into his bosom, kiss away her tears, take her upon his lap, and soothe her like a child, one of those terrible children that Satan pretends to be when he is most insidious.

Mem was a dangerous weeper. This would be learned in time and turned to her great profit and the blissful agony of the multitude. She was not acting now. She was reacting to the anguish of the bitter world, its cruelty, its bleakness, the favoritisms of fate, the willingness of Providence to let the willing lie idle, and the ambitious starve.

Tirrey paced the floor, promising Mem all sorts of wonderful futures. He managed hardly to keep his hands from her by entrusting them to each other to hold clenched behind his back. But his sympathy only fed Mem's self-sympathy with new fuel.

At the screen door that opened on his office appeared Mr. Rookes, the director who had rejected Mem after the test. He did not know who was crying, but his emotional soul heard the call and he peered in through spectacles already misted.

Mem saw him and ran to him, imploring, "Please, oh, please, Mr. Rookes, give me a chance!"

Mr. Rookes had a priestly regard for his altars. A work of art was as solemn and as chaste a burnt offering to his god, the Public, as the oblation of any other priest before any other deity.

It was just as sacred a duty to him to secure, somehow, laughter for the comic scenes as tears for the pathetic. The Public, that shapeless, invisible ubiquity, needed its mirth as well as its lamentations. It required not only its hecatombs of human sacrifice, but also beeves and bullocks, sheep and lambs, doves and wrens and swallows.

Rookes knew as well as Shakespeare knew, that the pathos and the tragedy suffered if there were no attendant buffoonery, no relief of tension, no tightening and releasing of the springs of laughter.

If an actor could not command laughter, he must not be entrusted with comic roles, however serious his necessities. Rookes would have let his mother or his daughter die rather than give her a part she could not play.

Only those who know little or nothing of the dramatic world, or whose own hearts are so hard that they do not care whom they wound, pretend that the world of mimic emotions is cold or cruel. It is amazing how much of the theatrical or cinematical time is spent in easing the inevitable griefs of the vain suppliants. Mem's sobs so agitated Rookes that he finally said: "You come and see the test yourself, and then, if you think you ought to have the part — Well you come and see for yourself."

He opened the door for her and led her out into the lot. He called to a man smoking on a short flight of steps:

"Heinie, have you that reel of Mrs. Woodville's test I took the other day?"

"I guess so."

"Put it on, will you."

"Sure! Go in Number Two."

And now Mem, who had seen so many faces flow by in the laboratory projection room and had been so free with comments and criticisms, was to see her own soul unreeled. She felt a sudden rush of regret for her harsh judgments on those poor creatures who had had to fight for their artistic lives with their features.

Rookes escorted her into a small cell, dimly lighted, a screen at one end; at the other a few seats against a wall perforated for the projection machines.

The operator in his room at the back snapped off the one lamp on the wall, and then played a long stream of light upon the screen. Every portrait was a record of some mood of Mem's.

It was weird to see herself over there flat and colorless, yet fantastically alive. She was face to face with herself for the first time. Science had answered the prayer of Robert Burns, "Oh, wad some power the giftie gie us."

Mem had studied her mirror and still photographs of herself, but now she met the stranger that was herself as the world knew her. She had never realized her features as they were; nor her expressions. She could look at her own profile. She could coldly regard herself in laughter and in an effort at flirtation.

The miracle of miracles was that her very thought was photographed. She could see her brain pulling at her muscles, as one who stands behind the scenes at a puppet show sees the man aloft and the wires that depend from his fingers jerking at the jointed dolls.

She had to admit that her smile was artificial; her lips drew back heavily and mirthlessly from her teeth. Her lips were prettier than she had supposed, and her teeth more regular, but her smile was a struggle. Her arch expression was clumsy. Her glance askance was labored, and when she executed the mischievous wink her eyelid went down and up as delicately as a cellar door.

She shook her head and wasted a blush of shame on the dark. She could not blame Mr. Rookes for rejecting her. She told him so, and he was grateful for that.

"I've learned a lot," she said. "I wish I could have another try."

"I wish you could, but the part is filled for this picture. Another time I'll remember, but it's too late for this picture."

He heard her catch her breath in a quick stab, and he was afraid that her prayers would be renewed. He hastened to say:

"Let me show you the girl who got the part. Let's see what you think of her." He called out, "Oh, Heinie, put on that test of Miss Dainty."

"Sure!" came the hail from the man at the wheel.

And then the white beam shot forth a serial portrait of a successful rival. This girl was pretty where Mem was beautiful. She was superficial and frivolous where Mem was deep and important. But she had the *vis comica*. She was as sparkling as a shallow brook. Her eyes danced, mocked, flitted. Her lips twitched with contagious mockery. Mem hated her, but smiled in spite of herself, giggled in spite of her wrath.

This girl had chosen the name of Dainty to replace the misnomer her parents and her forbears had fastened on her. She lived up to her name or down to it.

She looked pink even in the brown medium of the film. She looked round and mellow even in the one dimension of the screen. Her soul danced back of her eyes, and the hand she raised to peek through was like the lithe hand of a Bacchante in whose grasp life is but a bunch of grapes, spurting wine at the least pressure. Her very fingers were tendrils and her hair about her head was a vineyard wreath.

She had her sorrows, perhaps, and her woes. It was probable that she was heartbroken because she had been denied a tragic mask and doomed to make people happy instead of profitably sad. But whatever her private woes, she shed gaiety. The dark and ultraviolet rays were lost in the prism of her soul and she reflected only the narrow rainbow of good cheer.

"I see why you took her," Mem sighed. "I don't wonder."

"It's fine of you to say that," said Rookes, and squeezed her hand in grateful compliment. The kindliness of this set the girl's regrets off again.

She went out into the sunlight convinced and beaten. But being convinced of one's unworthiness and confessing one's defeat are not consolations; only added sorrows.

Before Rookes could escape she was crying again. She loathed herself for her weakness, her poltroonery, before a disappointment. She called herself names, but sobbed the harder for her self-contempt.

It chanced that the president of the company was returning to his office from a visit to one of the stages. This was the man whose name was familiar about the world. Every film from his factory was labeled: "Bermond presents"; "Copyright by the Bermond Company"; "This is a Bermond picture"; The slogan of the company was, "This is a Bermond year."

When a picture succeeded, the star, the author, the director, the photographer, the art director, the continuity writer, the distributors, divided the praise, the size of each slice depending on who awarded it.

When a picture failed, the producer had a monopoly of the blame and the entire financial loss.

He was the commercial demon, the fiend of sordid mercantile ideals. Yet Bernard Shaw, with his intuition masked as satire, had said to him, "There is a hopeless difference between us, Mr. Bermond: you are interested in art; I am interested only in money."

As a matter of truth, he was the most passionate of idealists, compelled to keep the ship afloat. Like the captain of a ship, he had all the final responsibility for the cargo, the passengers, and the shifts of wind and weather, he must study the mystic barometer of public favor and disfavor and keep the prow forging ahead in calm and in head gale.

He had to build the ship, feed the crew, the stokers, and the prima-donna passengers, and keep them all from mutiny. If the ship sank, they would all desert him and he would go down with it alone. In the hard times he must sacrifice much of the cargo, cut down the pay and the rations, shorten sail. Otherwise, the ship would founder; yet none would thank him for taking the necessary measures to keep it alive.

The critics would blame him for many things, but they would never forgive him for letting the ship sink. Success would be both his crime and his condemnation, but failure would be no atonement.

Like most business geniuses, he was far more emotional, sensitive, responsive, audacious, than the bulk of his artists or his critics. He could not pour out his emotions in song, verse, impersonation, or gesture; he must pour it out in capital. He must dig the capital with grim toil, and he must scatter it like a spendthrift heir.

With him, and contrasted with him in build, manner, and spirit, was Jacob Frank, vice-president, the immediate master of the crew, whose ideal was calm judgment, a happy ship, a smooth and economical voyage. He was a gentle ruler with a twinkling eye.

When Mr. Bermond heard Mem crying, his heart hurt him. He did not like scandal, disorder, confusion, or grief on his lot.

He asked the distraught Rookes what had happened. Rookes explained: "A bit of temperament. She wants a part she can't play, and she's all cut up."

"Oh, that is too bad!" Bermond groaned, and his voice took on a mothering tone. He went to Mem and tried to console her. He took her hands down from her contorted face and forced her to look at him. Seen through the cascade of her tears she was strikingly attractive, appealing.

He tested the public always by his own reactions. He judged artists by their influence on him. He felt that Mem was somehow an artistic weeper. His brain was alert to make use of ability wherever he found it.

"Don't you take it too hard," he said. "You never know your luck in this world. Many an artist gets thrown out of one job into a much better one. I knew a young singer and dancer who was fired because he was not good enough to come into New York with a cheap show. Two days later he was engaged for the biggest part in the most beautiful musical piece in years, and ever since he has been a star.

"If the first manager had not fired him the second would never have given him his chance. If you had played that little village vamp you would maybe have played it so badly we should never have engaged you again. But now you go home and wash the red out of your eyes, and any day now we'll be sending for you to play a big part. Sarah Bernhardt failed in her first play, you know, and you may be a second Sarah someday. Just you wait. Now that's all right."

Mem's eyes were filling with rainbows. A bystander drew Bermond aside. Claymore was a dramatist who had had a few successes before he established himself in the moving pictures as a director. He believed in the eternal verities of dramatic expression and motive, and he was skeptic of the rituals of the parvenu priestcraft of the movies.

"That girl has the tear," he said to Bermond. "That woman you've given me for my next picture is God-awful. I've spent two days trying to make her cry. She has the face of a doll and she's as tender as a billiard ball. She's a confirmed optimist. She couldn't even shake her shoulder blades as if she were crying.

"Let me take this kid and give her a real test. She might have just what we want."

"Sure! Fine! Go to it!" said Bermond, and hastened to Mem with the good news that Mr. Claymore — the great Mr. Claymore — was going to give her a chance.

So Mem left the studio shod with the ankle wings of hope, those tireless pinions that carry the actor lightly along such dreary miles of barren road.

As she hurried through the gate, one of the studio cars drew out and the driver paused to offer her a lift. He was taking home

Miss Calder, an actress of much fame as an impersonator of women of various ages. In the picture she was then engaged in she carried the character from young motherhood to ancient grandmotherhood.

She was tired as a pack horse, and small wonder. She explained to Mem that she had been called at six in the morning in order to be breakfasted and made up for a nine-o'-clock appearance on the stage. The dressing of her hair and the filling of it with white metallic powder that would photograph as really gray was a long and wearisome process. The preparation of her features was another.

She had given herself to racking emotions and much physical toil since nine. It was now six and she had not yet had time to remove her make-up.

Mem stared at her in the twilight. She was as multicolored as a sunset, patches of white, blue, yellow, green, and red gave her face a modeling in the monochrome of the negative that could not be imagined from her present barbarous appearance. To complete the palette she had painted her eyelashes lavender to soften the flash of her keen irises.

When she got home she would take off the laborious fresco and struggle with the removal of the powder from her hair, because on the morrow she must go back for a day of retakes to the period of her young and rosy black-haired bridehood.

She would be lucky to be in bed by ten in order to be up again at six. She had given up a dinner party and a dance that night, and had known no recreation for a month; was not likely to know any for a fortnight longer.

For this toil she was paid, as Mem later learned, four hundred dollars a week. But it was not much compared with the ten thousand a week that Miriam Yore was known to have been paid.

Mem's ardor for a screen career was not to be blunted by any account of overwork. Artistic toil was what she craved, and when the car stopped at her bungalow she ran to her mother rejoicing, as if she brought home certain wealth instead of a gambling chance for grueling labor.

She paused at the door, suddenly realizing that her mother was not a woman of theatrical traditions, but the devoted wife of a preacher who abominated the moving pictures all the better for never having seen one, and whose horror of every fiend connected with them was the more unrestrained for never having met one of the fiends.

# CHAPTER XXXI

MEM ENTERED THE HOUSE dreading that she would find her mother as dismayful as a stolen child flung in the corner of a wagon filled with gypsies. She found her presiding over the house with a meek autocracy.

Mrs. Steddon might not have been so daring if her daughter had been there to quell her presumptions. She had stayed in her room until she heard the racket and caught the savor of dinner getting. Then she slipped into the kitchen where Leva and two other girls were bustling about. She stared at them a moment and announced that she was going to do the cooking and the housework herself. They tried to shoo her back to her room, but she amazed them by her gentle obstinacy and her irresistible will.

"You children need a mother more'n most anything else," she said, "and I'm going to be one to you. I can't be an artist, but I can raise a family."

By the time Mem arrived the girls were calling her "Mother." Sundry young men who drifted in that evening were soon calling her Mother. In a week they were kissing her when they came in and kissing her when they left, bringing to her the troubles that no one ever gets too old to want a mother's eye upon.

Before the week was gone Mrs. Steddon was going to parties, to dances, to beach picnics.

She had begun her downfall by writing her husband a ghastly and elaborate lie. When Mem learned of this first result of her mother's association with the new world, the girl felt that her father's opinion of its malign influence proved his insight. But then, daughters are apt to agree with their fathers in theory if not in practice.

Mrs. Steddon, however, was mother first, last, and all the time. She acted upon impulse, and it was always an impulse of adaptation to circumstances as they arose, and she always chose the role of protecting her own.

Like a bird on a nest, she spread her wings over her young and fought for them as best she could, while she sheltered them from rain or wind or any threatening hand, even though it might be the divine hand.

What, indeed, is the whole duty of a mother whose daughter is uncontrollably unconventional or worse? Should the matron abandon her wayward child to go a ruinous way alone, or should she go along with her, hanging back as a brake, exerting a little restraint, being present to lift her when she falls, or comfort her in her shame or remorse? Mem's mother was suddenly confronted with this problem. Her village child was at large in Los Angeles!

Her chick was a duck, already far out on the pond! Mrs. Steddon could not swim in that puddle, but she could keep close to the water's edge. She did not even cackle remonstrances or warnings. She just waited and clucked and offered the eaves of her wings as a shelter.

And so the old village parson's wife abruptly found herself or made herself a theatrical mamma. This sort of mother has been often presented, but rarely without caricature, almost never with understanding.

Because she is apt to grow a little stagy and to forget her years and the solemnity expected of them; because her daughter is pretty sure to be unmanageable, she is dealt with more harshly than the more familiar mother who persuades her daughter to become a housewife and to marry a substantial husband instead of a romantic lover; than the mother who keeps her daughter from suing an adulterous or a cruel husband for divorce, than the mother who fears the gossip of the neighbors more than the smothered infamies of a hypocritical home; than the mother who endures every drudgery, skulduggery, and shame, and destroys her own birthright to deceive her children.

These others are familiar ancient mothers dwelling wretchedly in a sordid martyrdom. Sometimes they are saints of patience and their long agonies are rewarded. Sometimes their devotion has a morbid, almost an obscene and witchlike, aspect.

But the theatrical mother must share the limelight of publicity with her public child. She must seem to approve or connive in the real or alleged indiscretions of her own child, and she is liable to the accusation of being a procuress or a corrupt and odious shield. Sometimes, indeed, she is a grafter, a blood sucker, a vender of her child's future, renting a tot for wages and spending them on herself instead of investing them for the child's future.

But the movies did not invent wicked parents. Since time was, children have been driven to the streets, the mines, the looms.

The movie mammas, at least, at worst, did not drive their children into the dark, to grimy toil and heartbroken obscurity, but to sunlight, beauty, play, fame, and infinite praise.

Many a movie mother had been what Mrs. Steddon had been. Mrs. Steddon would in time be as harshly criticized as the worst of the others.

Her own daughter was the first to feel uneasy. Mem had expected her mother to be horrified by the new surroundings. She had braced herself to defend the art life against prejudice. She was disappointed of the support that criticism gives. To break rules and to disobey and shock the elders are among the chief fascinations and consolations of having to endure youth.

But when the parents and the oldsters fail to make rules or to protest against infractions of the rules they make, the young are robbed of something precious.

When the elders go farther and join the young in their rebellion against old dignities, then indeed are the young outraged.

So Mem was shocked because her mother was not. Mem could have grown eloquent in upholding the bohemian standards of behavior; she had superbly denounced the village hypocrisies and pruderies. But when the villager accepted bohemia and reveled in its revels, what was a daughter to do?

One thing was soon evident. Mrs. Steddon would not go back to Calverly; she would not urge Mem to go back; and she prepared to do in Rome as the Romans did.

Mem could not imagine what a task it all was to her mother, because she had never been a wife, a parson's wife, in a small-town church. She had not known the sickening monotony of a life devoted to avoiding life, to couching even the terms of normal connubial raptures in pompous terms of religious exaltation. She had not known how wearisome devoutness becomes when it is made a trade, a merchandise, a livelihood.

Mrs. Steddon had been a girl, a wild young female with natural instincts and gaieties and a natural impulse to kick over the restraints of the respectable. She had fallen in love with a man whose passion was dogma and whose prime study was the whims of a mystic Deity before whose vague edicts he prostrated himself. She cared nothing for doctrines and hair-splitting interpretations of ancient texts, but she gave herself up to the prison of the parsonage with bravery and good cheer. She suppressed her wrath against the pious frauds and the cruel niggards who made her husband's life a treadmill of unrewarded ambitions. She bore her children and did her best to coax them toward the ideals their father thundered about their unruly heads. She might have been a nightingale or a skylark, but she consented to be caged and to chirp a little song and forego her wings.

Now, however, the cage was opened. She had been decoyed into a garden where birds of rich plumage flung from branch to branch in a pride of wings and rhapsodies of song.

She was too old to dart and carol, but she would not build a cage about herself and continue to mope.

The freedom, the franchise of the sky, the glory of liberty that art gives its practicers and their companions, were hers, and the drab little woman accepted a tiny corner of this heaven as her very own.

At first a mother is only a gangplank for souls to cross from nowhere into this world. Once ashore, the mother can do less and less for the child. If she can become the companion, philosopher, and friend, that is much. But it serves the child no good purpose for the mother to give up all interest in her own career and accept inanition. The best of a woman's life may well be that part of it which follows the departure of her last grown child from the home. Let the mother follow her flock out into the world.

But Mrs. Steddon's emancipation was for Mem to discover with amazement gradually. For the moment she was too much absorbed in her mad hopes to consider her mother's belated debut into the full light of day.

The next morning found her at the studio betimes, borrowing mascaro and advice from Miss Calder, who experimented with her skin as in a laboratory and delivered a scientific discourse on the epidermis and its preparation for the camera.

Claymore was waiting for Mem when she came down the steps from the long gallery of the women's dressing rooms. She was daubed, smeared, lined, powdered, rouged, mascaroed, and generally calcimined for duty. Her heart was beating in alternate throbs of fear and frenzy. Her feet were at the brink of the Rubicon.

# CHAPTER XXXII

THE SCENE OF HER endeavor was to be a drawing-room built and decorated for an unfinished picture whose company was now in the Mojave Desert practicing art on the edge of Death Valley.

Claymore had provided a cameraman, a few men to handle the electric lights, a property man, and even a pair of musicians: a violinist and the treader of a wheezy little portable melodeon. Where the ceiling of the drawing-room should have been was a platform on which a number of downward-pointing spotlights were arrayed in the charge of a man called "Mike." From the scaffoldings above hung great dome lights, the "ash cans." In the windows and doors other spotlights were ambushed, each group with its attendant, and, where the fourth wall was removed, tall iron frames held rows of Cooper-Hewitt tubes like harp strings, and sun arcs, Winfield, and Kliegl lights, and other instruments of torture connected by cables to various switchboards.

The concentrated radiance burned out the eyes in time, or brought on a painful temporary blindness. To the newcomer there was an insanity about the extravagance of glare. But the finished result reduced the flame to a twilight and explained the necessity, for each picture could be exposed for only the sixteenth of a second, and in its tiny frame of hardly more than a square inch it must compress enough definition to cover, when projected, a screen thousands of times its size.

When Mem walked on the great stage and followed Claymore into the little space allotted to her, she noted the waiting crew of spectators and her heart faltered. How could she give her soul to emotions in the presence of these strangers? It would be like stripping herself and dancing stark before a band of peeping Toms. But needs must when ambition drives.

Claymore marched her into the scene and asked her to stand while the camera man made his set-up for a long shot. The electricians trundled their batteries forward and turned them on her; the camera man advanced upon her with the tape measure and went back to squint at her through the finder. He stared at her through a color filter of deep blue and discussed her hair and her eyes. Claymore came forward, carrying a rouge stick he had borrowed from somebody's forgotten make-up box, and gave Mem's mouth a little extra length, put a dot next the inner corner of each eye, and, taking a powder puff, dusted her brow lightly where the perspiration of terror was beginning to shine.

Then he gave her a little of what he called footwork.

"Go back to that door and come forward to this spot. Shake hands with, er, with your lover, er — Well, no. Let me see. That's too simple. Let's get down to business.

"You've a — Oh well, just for instance, you've been, er, betrayed and your child has died and you've been accused of murdering it and you're now being called before the judge and the jury. Do you get me? You're coming into a courtroom under a charge of crime; you feel your shame, but you're innocent of the charge, yet you're overwhelmed with guilt for your fall, and the father of the child was killed in the war, say, and you don't much care whether you live or die; so you're in despair, yet defiant. That's a triple layer of emotion for you and I don't suppose you can get much of it over, but just try to give the atmosphere of it. Now back to the door. Walk through it once."

Claymore was as much embarrassed as Mem, for his invention was not in its best working order so early in the morning. He felt as silly as a man badgered by a peevish child to tell a story.

But his trite plot stirred Mem amazingly. He could not know how close his random shots had come home to her and flung her back from the forward-looking artist to the lone fugitive who had stumbled into California laden with disgrace.

She was all atremble and her eyes darted, her fingers twitched. Claymore marveled at her instantaneous response to his suggestion. There were born artists who shivered on the least breath of inspiration and suggestion.

His first impression of Mem was that he had found a genius, and he fought against the obstacles he encountered later with the zest of a man digging toward known gold.

In a kind of stupor Mem obeyed his commands like the trained confederate of a hypnotist. She went to the door, came in reluctant, shamefast, doomed. She advanced slowly till she reached the edge of the rug he had indicated, then halted, and with a fierce effort hoisted her head in defiance and braved the lightning of the judge.

She heard Claymore call to her: "That's fine! Now we'll take it!"

She started back, but was checked by the cameraman's "Wait, please!" He ran forward and shouted directions on all sides for lights.

"Hit those spots! Throw the ash can on her. Bring up that Kliegl. Put a diffuser on that Winfield. What's the matter with the second spot? Your carbons are flickering. Mike! Mike! Trim those carbons on the second spot! Pull 'em!"

Then the lights went out and there was a wait while Mike ran along the gallery parallel, with tweezers in his gloved hands. When Mike was ready the cameraman shouted: "Hit 'em! All right, Mr. Claymore!" Mr. Claymore called, "Music, please!"

And Mem found herself in a sea of blazing radiance, tremulous with a shimmer of music.

She went back to the door and nodded when Claymore's "Are you ready?" penetrated the myth realm from far away. She heard him murmur: "Camera! Action!" and she heard his voice reciting an improvised libretto for her pantomime.

"You've come from your dark cell! The light blinds you! You begin to see the angry public, the cruel judge. You flinch. You fall back. They are going to sentence me to death! They are hissing me because I loved too well! But my little baby! They said I killed him! They can't know how I loved him! How I felt his little hands on my cheek, his lips at my breast! How I suffered when his cheek grew cold! O God! I prayed for his life even though it meant eternal shame! But he is gone! My lover is dead! What is this world to me! Wring your hands! Look up at the judge! Draw yourself up! Defy him! That's it! Now let the tears come! My baby, I am coming to you! My baby!"

She heard his voice wailing and trembling like the *vox humana* stop the village organist used to pull out for the sake of pathos. It was maudlin, unforgivably cheap and trashy, yet it was the truth for her, as for millions of other girls. It was trite because it had broken so many hearts.

She felt a fool, a guilty fool. The music, the lights, the director's voice all, all was insanity. But it swept her heartstrings with an Æolian thrill and they sang with a mad despair.

She vaguely knew that the camera crank had ceased to purr; she heard the clop of the levers shutting off the lights; the music was ended. But her suffering went on; she could not stop crying.

Her head bent, her taut body broke at the waist, she was sobbing into a corner of her elbow and dropping to the floor when Claymore caught her and upheld her, eased her to a chair, and stood patting her back idiotically and saying, "Fine! Fine!"

She looked up to see if he were mocking her, and saw that his cheeks were streaked with tears. The cameraman was doleful as if he mourned, and the property man was turning away to blow his nose.

Mem began to laugh the laugh of triumph. Yet she felt that she had cheated a little. The director had stabbed an old wound by accident and unsealed an old fountain of tears.

He had exhausted her dramatic experience of life already, and he would find her imagination unschooled, her mental and physical agility all to seek.

But he had touched her once. She had responded once to the call and had given the strange authority of reality to a feigned adventure of her soul.

"She's got it in her!" he mumbled to the camera man.

And the camera man, with eyes still murky, grumbled: "The real thing!"

Now Claymore cast about for the next test.

"You've got the gift of tears," he said. "Now let's try a bit of drama! Let's exaggerate and chew up the scenery and tear a passion to tatters, for it's easy to tone you down when you overdo, but it's hard to pep you up if you're flat."

He cudgeled his brain for an excuse for ranting, towering rage. He chose one of those scenes innumerably done in the moving pictures, a sordid pattern common enough in real life through the ages, but all too crowded in the movies, infinitely multiplied and repeated until it became boresome to the frequenters of the films and nauseated the moralists, gave them excuse for a general assault on the whole art and industry.

Claymore took up a heap of tarpaulin and piled it on a chair to represent a man, found a screwdriver left on the scene by a carpenter, and gave it to Mem for a pistol. Then he outlined a scenario startling and bewildering to her, and utterly uncongenial to her character and experience:

"This tarpaulin is a terrible villain. He has decoyed you from your home and tired of you; he has put you on the street and made a drug fiend of you, and now you have seen him with another girl, and you plead with him not to desert you; he laughs at you; you turn on him like a tigress and, when he goes on laughing, you creep up on him with a false smile and suddenly shoot him with this pistol."

The novice stared at him like a dumb thing that had not understood a word. She looked at the screwdriver. It had no resemblance to a pistol, and if it had suggested one she would have dropped it in horror. She stared at the pile of yellow canvas and could get nothing human out of or into that.

"I don't believe I quite understand," she faltered, suddenly reverted to childhood days when she was asked to read a page she had neglected to study.

Claymore missed the instant result of his first appeal to her imagination, as he thought; to her memory, as she knew. Her eyes were a fogged mirror now and gave back neither light nor image.

He played the bit for her. None of the spectators thought it funny or silly. It was part of the familiar routine factory commonplace to see a fat, bald-headed director striding about, clutching his heart and sobbing.

Mem had hidden in her father's study once and watched him rehearse a sermon, had seen him beat his desk for a pulpit, raise his streaming eyes to the ceiling for heaven, and repeat phrases in various intonations in search of the most effective stop.

She was not amused or disgusted by Claymore's antics. She was simply baffled. Unable to feel why he did what he did, she tried to remember his actions.

When he finished she took the screwdriver and repeated his gestures with neither accuracy nor spirit. She merely gave a girl's poor imitation of a man's poor imitation of a poor girl's frenzy.

She shook her head in confessed failure before Claymore shook his head and scratched it and said, patiently:

"That's hardly it. You didn't quite get the spirit. You see you're a...," etc., *da capo al fine.*

The cameraman sat down. The rest of the crew turned aside to gossip about more interesting topics. They knew that they were in for a long wait.

# CHAPTER XXXIII

CLAYMORE WRESTLED WITH the girl's flaccid soul. He went and walked her through the scene again and again. He sat on the chair and pretended to be the villain. He laughed with very hollow mockery. He played the part himself. He said:

"If you'll give it more voice you'll give it more spirit. Call me a beast with all your power!"

"You're a beast!" she faltered so feebly that Claymore laughed and she had to join him. He said to her, "Look me in the eye and with all the venom and volume you've got snarl, 'Agh! you beast!'"

He roared it so full-chestedly at Mem that she quailed before him. Then she nodded, understanding, and gave back the words. It was like an oboe trying to echo a trombone. She shook her head in discouragement. He would not give her up.

"Fill your lungs and hurl your whole body into it!"

She tried again and again, but her voice was stringy, stinted, reedish. He spoke bluntly, in good old English:

"You've got to get your guts into it!"

She did not know that she had any, and he had to explain that he really meant her diaphragm.

He asked her to scream at the top of her lungs. She emitted a feeble squawk. He shook his head. He let out a shriek of his own that pierced the high rafters and seemed to rattle the glass roof. She did a little better on a second try. Claymore's patience was wonderful. "What are you most afraid of?" he said.

"I don't know," she giggled, sillily.

"What's your favorite nightmare?"

She pondered. "Well, I, I —"

"Falling off a cliff is one of the most popular," said Claymore.

"I fell off a cliff once," said Mem, almost boastfully.

"Really! And did you survive?" Claymore gasped, then grinned at his own imbecility. "I know one actress who dreams that she is caught under a wrecked automobile and can't get out and is being crushed to death."

To Claymore's amazement the blank mien before him was suddenly shot through with anguish, the features knotted and whitened with streaks of red like a clenched fist.

Once more he had thrust his hand into one of her experiences. She felt the presence of Elwood Farnaby, her almost forgotten first love, and last. The ghastliness of his death under a runaway automobile flashed back before her. She felt a regurgitation of all the terrors that had churned in her heart in those hideous days and nights.

Claymore, never dreaming what the random hint had evoked in her soul, was happy at finding her responsive once more. He called to the camera man:

"Come on, Johnny, we'll take a close-up, a big close-up! Be as quick as you can."

While Mem hung back saying: "Please! No, no! I couldn't! Don't make me!" Claymore was hurrying the crew to seize this precious excitement before it died.

The crew closed in upon the camera with a mass of blazing lights. Claymore pushed a chair close up to the lens. The camera man spread and shortened his tripod and got on his knees. He made one of the crew sit in the chair while he sharpened the focus and perfected the lights. He did not want to fatigue the priceless heights of agitation that he could see in Mem's wide eyes as she stood wavering before the sudden gust of emotion.

Protesting and reluctant, yet too palsied for flight, Mem permitted Claymore to lead her to the chair and place her in a cowering position.

"Close your eyes, to save them," he said. "Don't open them till I tell you to. Then open them suddenly and see the automobile upon you. It's on fire. You can't move. You struggle in vain. I'll hold on to your hands to pinion you down. When you see that you are crushed and caught, give me the wildest cry you can scream! All ready, Johnny? Hit the lights! Take the camera from my nod. Now, my dear, you're in the car, the brake is broken! It's dashing over a cliff! It's turned over! You are under it! It's on fire! When I say the word open your eyes and face death and die with one terrible shriek!"

She felt through her clenched eyelids and on her shivering cheeks the flare and heat of the focused calciums. She felt his hands dragging her helpless wrists down till she was all huddled upon herself. She seemed to feel in his taut and frenzied grip the weight of the engine that had slain her lover. Then she heard the quick word, "Now!" She opened her eyes and saw a chaos of wrecked iron and steel about her. Terror knifed her and her whole body was wrung with a mad howl of affright.

She heard her voice go leaping into the high spaces. Her hands were free. They went to her left side where her heart rocked like a fire bell. She opened her eyes in wonder. The lights were off. The crew was staring at her with white faces. The camera man was breathing fast. Claymore was mopping his blenched brow and saying, "Whew!"

It was so inadequate a word for the awe still shaking their little world, that everybody laughed but sickishly.

Claymore brought forth his most valued word saved for rare occasions.

"By God! That was authentic!"

And the others said, "The real thing!" A strange phrase for a perfection of imitation.

Claymore was encouraged again. He had found another nugget in the rubble. He would continue to work the mine.

If he had known Mem's life and the things she had experienced, few but fearful, he could have brought forth expressions of intense amorous possession, of desperate surrender, of groveling shame, of mad grief, of craven hypocrisy. But he groped in ignorance and did not realize that her two successes had been due to memory rather than interpretation.

Another failure trailed at heel of this other victory. Claymore returned to his little drama of the street. He tried to get energy in a gesture, in a walk, a stride, a quick whirl, a flaunt of arms, a fierce charge.

But Mem had been schooled all her life to keep her hands down and to avoid flourish, to take short steps and to keep her waist and hips stolid. Though the fashions of the day gave her short, loose skirts, no corsets, free arms, she might as well have been handcuffed and hobbled and fastened in iron stays, for all the freedom she used.

Claymore made her run, with longer and longer stride, bend and touch the floor, fling her arms aloft, take the steps of a Spanish dancer and a Spanish vixen. But she was unbelievably inept.

"I wish I had the courage and the kindliness to give you a Belasco training," he said. "You know he testified in court that when he trained Mrs. Leslie Carter for her big war-horse roles, he had to break her muscle-bound condition first. He threw her down stairs, throttled her, beat her head against the wall, and chased her about the room. She told me herself that she learned the Declaration of Independence by heart and spent hours and hours repeating it as glibly as she could. Every time she missed an articulation she went back to the beginning and recited it all over again hundreds and hundreds of times. That's how she learned to deliver great tirades with a breathless rush, yet made every syllable distinct. That's how she learned how to charge about the stage like a lioness.

"To be a great actress is no easy job. You've got to work like a fiend or you'll get nowhere. You've got to exercise your arms and legs and your voice and your soul. If you will, you've got a big future. If you won't you'll slump along playing small parts till you lose your bloom of youth, then you'll slip into character parts and go out like an old candle."

Mem was beginning to wear down, to understand the joys of a pleasant housewifely career, the luxuries of obscurity.

But Claymore hated to give her up. He made one more desperate effort to unleash her soul and her body from the shackles of respectability.

He set her to denouncing the tarpaulin villain again. He made her pour out before that heap of wrinkles a story of shame and disprized devotion and degradation. He put her against the wall and made her beat upon it and lament her turpitude. He made her fling herself to the floor and pound it with her fists and laugh in mockery. Then he made her draw the screwdriver and fire five shots into her canvas betrayer.

Her imagination flagged so dismally in this scene that he decreed the screwdriver a stiletto and made her stab the man to death. He laughed at the blow she dealt and forced her to slash and rip and drive the blade home until she fell down exhausted with the vain effort to be a murderess.

Claymore was as exhausted as she and he wasted no film on taking pictures of her failure.

"Let's go to lunch!" he said. "We've earned a bit of chow."

# CHAPTER XXXIV

THE UPSHOT OF THIS ordeal by fire was that Mem was recognized as a star yet to be made if, indeed, her nebulous ambitions should ever be condensed into solid achievement.

Claymore felt that she had a future. He told her so. But he told her that a period of hard labor lay between her and that paradise. He compared the development of an artist with the slow human miracle that had rescued so much of California from the grim bleakness of the desert, the desert that yields and reconquers, retreats and returns.

Great reaches of the fairest home realm of Los Angeles had once been barren sand. Irrigation and intensive farming had made a pleasance of it and one could see everywhere the industry of the little pioneers pushing the wasteland back, as if humanity were feeling its way like a shapeless amoeba or a groping vine putting its tentacles forth and fastening them wherever sustenance might be found.

Claymore was one of those developers of talent who feel a passion for searching out gold where it lies, building roads, as it were, to hidden hearts and giving them expression, making a traffic and commerce of expression.

He found in Mem such a temptation. Her beauty was evident, but empty-faced beauty was as cheap and useless as iron pyrites with the glister of gold and no other value.

The studios were infested with pink pretties, insipid and characterless, doomed to hold up faces as faultless and as charmless as the petunias and morning-glories that flaunt their calico in vain about country gardens and porches.

In Mem he felt the ore. He did not know that it had gone through the smelting fires of tragedy, but he felt that she was capable of tragedy, and he wanted to instruct her in the mechanisms of transmitted grief.

As they left the stage he watched her out of the corner of his eye. She did not really know how to walk, though there was unconscious grace in her carriage. What he wanted was conscious grace expert enough to mask its understanding, the art that conceals art and knows its genius all the while the deft, strong hand of the driver of a trotting horse who gets the ultimate speed from the racing machine without ever letting it break into a gallop or bolt into a mad run.

Claymore talked to Mem of herself and her body as frankly as a father confessor dissects a soul before a believer's eyes. She was thrilled with the almost morbid sensation of being the subject of such remorseless analysis. She was like one of the victims of the new-fashioned operations by local anaesthesia who sits up and in a mood of hysterical fascination chats with the surgeon even while he slashes the skin open, lays bare the nerves and arteries, discloses the deep penetralia of the temple.

The director asked her if she would practice at home what he had told her and shown her on the stage, and then some day let him give her another test.

She consented with delight, and appointed the morrow as the nearest day there was. She had only one somber thought: that she must go home again without a promise of work, with neither income of money nor outgo of art to expect.

But Claymore asked her to wait while he spoke to Mr. Bermond. She loitered on the green lawn, watching the made-up actors and the extra people and the others moving about their tasks. Some day they must gaze at her with respect and whisper, "That's Miss Steddon, the great star."

By and by Mr. Bermond came out bareheaded to see her. He had a way of meeting candidates out of doors. It was easier to remember an engagement and dash away, than to pry the more tenacious ones out of his office chairs.

Bermond shook Mem's hand warmly and said, with as much enthusiasm as if he were the beneficiary of her hopes, as of course he might be:

"Well, Mr. Claymore tells me you have much talent. That's fine! But he says your work is spotty, immature. You have little technic. But that's all right. Everybody has to learn. He has a small part in his picture, and if you want to take it, all right. The part won't stand much money, but you will get experience and that's what you want, yes?"

Mem could have hugged him. He was beautiful as the dawning sun on the hills of night. Later she would come to hate him and fight him as a miser, a penny squeezer, a slave driver, but so Christopher Columbus and Cortes were regarded after their brief moments of beauty as discoverers.

Bermond was a believer in "new faces." He had found that the audiences would forgive immaturity of art rather than maturity of figure when it had to choose. The part he offered Mem was a role of girlish pathos with a wistful note and a few moments of village tragedy. She would adorn the screen without being able to do much damage to the story at worst.

Mem felt that in passing from director to director she was undergoing a series of spiritual marriages and divorces. There were such intense emotional communions that it was far more than a mere acquaintance.

But before she left the lot that day she had signed her name to a long document which she pretended to read and understand. About all she made of it was that she was to have a salary of seventy-five dollars a week during the taking of the picture, and that the company might exercise an option on her services thereafter if it chose.

Mr. Tirrey was delighted in a paternal fashion. It was a sunbeam in his dark day when he could open the door to youth and hope.

Mem went home elated, and was greeted so royally that she forgot how diminished her hopes were from the immediate stardom she had imagined under Claymore's first frenzy.

The next day the star of the picture arrived on the set in a large hat. When Claymore told her that she was not to wear it during the scene she exclaimed that her hair was not dressed.

There was nothing to do but send her to the coiffeuse. This meant a delay of an hour. The company and the throng of extras and the crew must lie idle at the cost of nearly a thousand wasted dollars to the picture.

It was with such unavoidable blunders that Bermond's cup of grief was filled. No system of efficiency could be installed to prevent the individual slip. An alarm clock that failed to ring, a telephone out of order, a letter misaddressed, and thousands of dollars of time and overhead went *pouff!*

The company's disaster was Mem's good luck, for Claymore, seeing her lurking in the background waiting for instructions, called her over to him.

Everything was set for a test and he dismissed the rest of the company for an early lunch, while he sent Mem through her paces again.

He had a canvas partition drawn round a corner of the scene and once more put Mem at bay against a wall with a camera and a nest of light machines leveled at her.

She had spent the evening before at mad spiritual gymnastics in the bungalow, with her mother and Leva as audience and critics. Claymore found that her soul was wakening and her limbs throwing off their inertia. He set her problems in mental arithmetic like a tutor coaching a backward pupil for an examination.

It was an exceedingly curious method of getting acquainted. Teacher and student became as much involved in each other's souls as Abelard and Heloise at their first sessions.

When the star came back with her hair appropriately laundered, ironed, and crimped, and the rest of the company gathered, Mem could see that Claymore gave up his task with her reluctantly. And that sent a shaft of sweet fire through her heart.

Late in the afternoon Claymore offered her a lift home in his automobile. It was quicker than the street car, but it seemed far quicker than that. They chattered volubly of art theories and practices. They did not realize how long the car stood in front of her bungalow before Mem got out, or how long he waited after she got out, talking, talking, before he bade her the final good night.

Her mother realized it, peering through the curtains, and Leva exclaimed:

"Good Lord! The minx has the director eating out of her hand already. She'll get on!"

She said this to Mem when the girl came skipping into the house, and shocked her with a glimpse of how their high spiritual relations looked to the bystander.

Leva taunted her all evening, and the next morning called after her, as she set out to school:

"Aren't you going to take a big red apple to teacher?"

Mem took him two of them in her crimson cheeks.

She had met none of that traditional demand for her honor as an admittance fee to the art. Tirrey had refused her flat. Bermond had not invited her to love him, and Claymore had talked nothing but art. Yet Claymore occasionally gave her a scene with an actor as a foil, talked to her of the arts of embracing, kissing, fondling, rebuking, accepting, denouncing, battling.

But sometimes he seemed to take more than a professional interest in the demonstrations. Sometimes he drew her arms about himself, and she felt that even if he did not clench her tight or hold her long, he wanted to.

The cameramen, the dawdling light crew, and the props and grips were chaperons, but they were becoming as unimportant as the scenery. Sometimes she thought they were aware of a something in the atmosphere. Perhaps she caught a glance shot from one to another, or an eye turned away a little too indifferently.

But that only enhanced the excitement, and on one occasion when Claymore tried to teach her bigness of wrath and compelled her to scream and strike at him, there was such an undertone of affection in the pretense of hate that she felt fairly wrenched apart.

She met Tom Holby on the lot one day. He had been asked to come over and talk of a possible contract with the Bermond Company. He greeted Mem with effusive enthusiasm, and she warmed at the pride of his recognition. Then she felt a little twinge of conscience, an intuition that she had no right to be so glad to see Mr. Holby, since now she belonged to Mr. Claymore.

This was an amazing and slavish reversion to primeval sub-missiveness for an emancipated woman. But there was a tang of wild comfort in the feeling that she was owned. And then she wondered if she did not owe the priority to Mr. Holby. This was a complication!

It is the custom to regard such confused romances in the dramatic and other artistic realms with scorn as the flippant amours of triflers; but they are of exactly the same sort, as earnest, as pathetic, and as reluctantly entered into as the countless entanglements that doctors and churchmen encounter in their equally emotional relations with souls in turmoil of one sort or another.

Literature used to be packed with the disastrous affairs of churchmen and their communicants, but the silence has been profound of late, except when a sensational explosion bursts into the newspapers. And there has been little disclosure at any time of the secret chambers to which the physician's *passepartout* admits him.

The stage and the painter's world have had too much attention and too little sympathy, and shortly the moving picture was to be assailed by a tornado of national disgust and wrath, an eruption of hot ashes and lava from a deep resentment stored up unknown against the magic development of the new art into Titanic power.

But no one foresaw the accident that was to turn a commonplace carousal into a cataclysm.

For the present Mem had no greater anxiety than the peculiarly masked flirtation with her director and the battles with little artistic problems as they arose.

Her life had regularity again. She got up on mornings with a task before her. She had hours of waiting for every minute of acting, but she was one of the company and she could study the work of others. Her textbooks were the faces of the actors and actresses, the directions of the directors.

The mere learning of the language was an occupation in itself. She felt puffed up when visitors were brought upon the stage and permitted to see pictures taken.

It was surprising how fascinating the thing was to the outsiders. Kings and queens, princesses and princes, foreign and native generals, ambassadors, opera singers, plutocrats, painters, gathered humbly in the backgrounds of the scenes and marveled at the business of drama and photography, the morbid blue lights and the surprising calm and graciousness of the process. They had evidently expected noise and wrangling and tempestuous temperament.

One day when a little scene was being filmed in which she was the only actress, the rest of the company being excused for a change of costume, a visitor from overseas was brought upon the set, a great French general.

The publicity man, whose lust for space never slept, suggested that the general might like to be photographed on the scene. He laughed and came forward with a boyish eagerness. He displayed at once a terror he had not revealed under bombardment. On one side of him stood the director, on the other Mem, thrilled and thrilling.

The still cameraman took several pictures and the incident was ended, it seemed. The general kissed Mem's hand and left her almost aswoon with pride. The publicity man gave her one of the pictures and she set it up on her mantel as a trophy of her glory.

Whether the general really said it or really meant it, only the publicity man knew, but when the picture appeared in newspaper supplements about the world it was stated in each of the captions that the great warrior had said, "Remember Steddon is the prettiest girl in America."

More amazing yet, Mem first learned of this astounding tribute from her astounded father.

Soon after she began to feel a pride in her art and to take home to her mother little compliments she had heard, and to feel that she was launched at last upon the illimitable sea of the greatest, as the newest, of arts, and the most superb of all livelihoods, the storm broke upon the moving-picture world.

An actor involved in a dull revel, of a sort infinitely frequented since mankind first encountered alcohol, was present at the death of an actress. The first versions of the disaster were so horribly garbled that the nation was shaken with horror.

All the simmering resentment against the evil elements and ugly excesses of the "fifth largest industry in the world" boiled over in a scalding denunciation of the entire motion-picture populace.

For a week or two the nation rose in one mob to lynch an entire craft and all its folk. Editors, politicians, reformers, preachers, clubwomen, all of those who make a career of denunciation and take a pride in what they detest, drew up a blanket indictment against thousands of assorted souls and condemned them to infamy.

Doctor Steddon had been one of the loyal leathers of the moving pictures, and he surprised himself in the jeremiad he launched at his little congregation back in Calverly. A newspaper man happened to be present, the rain that morning denying him his usual worship on the golf links and he published a column of Doctor Steddon's remarks.

The proud father sent a clipping to his wife and daughter, never dreaming that the moving pictures were furnishing them their bread and butter, boots and beatitudes.

They cowered before the blast and understood the emotions of Adam and Eve after they had eaten of the tree of knowledge and heard the Voice in the garden.

They debated the hateful problem of confessing the truth, but could not bring themselves yet awhile to the disclosure of their fraud.

And then a letter came from the man they loved and dreaded. As Mrs. Steddon's fingers opened the envelope in the awkwardness of guilt, two pictures fell to the floor. They were in the brown rotogravure of the Sunday supplements. They were alike except in size; one was from the *New York Times* and one from the Chicago *Tribune*. Both presented Mem standing at the side of the French general. Both stated that he had called this promising member of the Bermond Company "the prettiest girl in America."

Mem and her mother gathered themselves together as if they had been dazed by a rip of lightning from the blue and waited for the thunderbolt to smash the world about them. They read the letter together. It began without any "Dear Wife" or "Dear Daughter." It began:

The enclosed clippings were sent to me by members of my congregation who were sojourning, one in New York and one in Chicago. It is hard for me to doubt the witness of my eyes, but it is almost harder to believe that the wife of my bosom and the daughter reared in the shelter of our home could have fallen so low so suddenly. Before I write more I want to hear the truth from both of you, if you can and will tell it.

# CHAPTER XXXV

THE REVEREND DOCTOR STEDDON was something more than a father to his daughter, something more than a husband to his wife; he was also the high priest of their religion.

The daughter had fled from his face after her sin, and had found a new paradise, a new priestcraft, a new religion beyond the desert. She had come to believe in an artist God, loving beauty and emotion and inspiring his true believers to proclaim his glories through the development and celebration of the gifts and graces he had bestowed. She felt that he required of her hymns of passionate worship instead of the quenching of her spirit, the distortion of her graces, the burial of her genius. The Mosaic Ten Commandments contained no "Thou shalt not commit dramaturgy." She felt a consecration, a call to act, to interpret humanity to humanity. What her father had deemed temptations and degradations she now considered inspirations and triumphs.

And yet she could not feel quite sure of herself. High as she might rate her career, she had come at it by stealth and had been led to it by a dark path of lies and of concealed shame. The overseeing heaven and the pit of hell yawning for unwary feet still terrified her.

Her mother had a different excuse; she had come hither to protect her daughter and redeem her from calamity. Her deception had been a form of protection. What if she had deceived her husband? It was all for his comfort, and she had never sought her own. If one may die for another's sake, why may one not lie on an alien behalf?

Besides, Mrs. Steddon had grown up with her husband and had seen his tempers goad him to too many mistakes. She was merely angry at him now for a burst of wrath, while Mem cowered before him as an inspired prophet.

Mrs. Steddon was all for retorting to his letter with another of defiant rebuke. But Mem advised delay. She was not quite sure of herself or her art.

Torments of doubt, conflicting remorses, profound bewilderments are no more familiar to religious zealots than to artists in every field. And Mem could not orient herself in her new world. But she would not give up her career. That much was certain. She had drained the family savings already for her mother's overland journey and her own. She must earn enough to pay back the draft somehow; and here was her one chance.

Fifteen dollars a week was all that her veteran father earned. She could support him and the whole family better than he had any hope of doing. She was the true bread winner now, and she must not quarrel with her bread. She had a warm desire to take her father's poor old gray poll under her wing, to give him rest from his long toil and repose in the new Eden, almost to mother him and nourish him even as Lot's daughters had nourished their father. But she could imagine the horror with which Doctor Steddon would be thunderstruck at the hint that he should step down from the fiery chariot of his pulpit and bask in the shadow of a motion-picture actress. The letter that suggested such a thing would be as fatal as one of the infernal machines that people were sending through the mails to shatter the recipient.

Yet she could never give up her career and go back to the grave of Calverly. It was too wonderful to play a scene on the set, to revel in a moment of dramatic power, throw out a tragic gesture, look a mute appeal, then, next day, to sit in the black projection room and hear the small group of witnesses murmur at her sorrow and praise her graces.

This precious harvest of her toil was too dear to relinquish. She had just dropped her sickle into the edge of the golden wheat and she must go on.

On the evening of the arrival of Doctor Steddon's letter two callers dropped in: Claymore and Holby.

The subject of all moving-picture talk was still the Arbuckle case, a *cause célèbre* that monopolized the headlines of the newspapers for weeks, especially in Los Angeles, where two hostile camps were formed and the enemies of the free film took new heart and determined to chain and tar the beast once for all.

"Woe unto the world because it must needs be that offenses come, but woe unto him by whom the offense cometh."

Since man had cumbered the ground there had been hilarious groups and drinking bouts of more or less gayety. They had been called festivals, Bacchic revels, or disgusting debauches, according as a poet or a preacher described them.

After the prohibition law became law in the United States the enormous amount of liquor still consumed, the appalling tidal waves of crime, had been matter for jokes or sermons or hot debates, the same arguments proving opposite contentions for both sides.

On a certain day when there were probably ten thousand similar guzzling coteries, a certain moving-picture comedian of Falstaffian girth and vast popularity entertained in his hotel rooms at San Francisco a number of men and women; one of the women fell ill and died a few days later and another woman told a story so garbled at the start that the nation shuddered with the pain and the ugliness of it. The story was soon contradicted in almost every particular by the prime witness herself and by all the other confused and confusing witnesses. But the tide of national wrath could not be recalled.

An ambitious district attorney resolved that the comedian should be tried for murder in the first degree. Two juries and a judge declined to go so far with him, but the pulpits and the editorial columns, the legislative halls and forums and the very street corners, roared with a demand for somebody's destruction.

All this was pitiful, hateful, lamentable, everything bewildering and depressing, but it was also very common in human history. The same avalanches had been started by a whisper and had engulfed whole races, religions, political parties, reigning families, churches, lodges, charitie and what not? Just as now the entire motion-picture world was smothered in a welter of abuse and condemnation.

With all the logic of a mob reveling in a chance to realize its mob lust, it was assumed or pretended that there was something specifically of the moving-pictures in the affair at San Francisco.

Drunkards, bootleggers, and respectable millions who smuggled liquor into their homes without scruple expressed horror at a motion-picture actor for having liquor in his possession.

The cry for censorship arose with renewed fury, and there was no stopping the superstition that all human wickedness was somehow due to this new devil.

By a coincidence, while this one motion-picture clown was drawing all the lightnings of the sky upon all the motion-picture people, the churches were contributing to the criminal courts an extraordinary number of cases. A Protestant minister in Alabama was on trial for beating a Catholic priest to death; another preacher was being found guilty of drowning his wife in a lake; another of flogging his own child to death for unsatisfactory prayers; a white-robed faith healer was indicted for manslaughter on account of a pious laying on of hands so violent that an elderly patient died in an agony of broken bones; the next most spacious murder case of the day was charged against a man whose father was a minister and whose wife was the daughter of a bishop.

Yet nobody dreamed of assailing religion as an incentive to murder; no one warned the young to avoid churches or suggested a censorship of sermons.

It struck nobody as ludicrous or contemptible to blame a twenty-year-old art for evils that had flourished during ten thousand years of recorded wickedness.

The public was in a lynching mood and would not be denied.

A whole art was being tarred and feathered and tortured in every cruel and fantastic manner. Bankers withdrew money from companies with pictures half finished. Audiences fell away in the picture houses everywhere. The motion-picture Goliath, already weakened with the malnutrition of hard times, staggered under a shower of stones from the slings of myriad Davids.

While they lasted those were dramatic days for the bright children of the moving pictures. They felt like gypsies riding caroling through a summer landscape and suddenly assailed by farmers with pitchforks and abuse.

The newcomer, Remember Steddon, was especially aghast. The delectable mountain she had essayed to climb was abruptly fenced off as a peak of hell.

# CHAPTER XXXVI

DOCTOR STEDDON HAD CONSTANTLY besought from his pulpit forgiveness for his flock's woeful sins of omission and commission. He had cried to heaven that his people were miserable sinners incessantly backsliding into every wickedness. Yet it was somehow different when a motion-picture player growled, as Claymore did now, "Well, we are rotten, rottener than any outsider knows, and we're only getting what was coming to us."

Claymore was always the apologist. What he loved he distrusted. His wife had left him on that account. He had felt compelled to correct her faults and lovingly chastise her. He had been a director in the theater and had gone about shamefaced on account of the misbehavior of so many of its people, the alleged low standards of the successes, the lack of appreciation for Shakespeare, the absence of a true sense of art in all Americans, the mysterious genius for art in all foreigners.

As soon as he had been decoyed into the motion-picture field the theater borrowed enchantment from distance. It was as noble as antiquity. And now all his wailings were against the trash the motion-picture trade turned out and its base commercialism compared with the lofty accomplishments of the theater.

He was a priest at an altar, but he always praised the elder gods. So now he growled.

"The motion pictures have been riding for a fall. It's all due to a sudden rush of money to the head. Cowboys were yanked off the ranch and sent loco with the effort to spend a thousand dollars a week. Brainless village girls and artists models were plunged into enormous publicity and dazzled with fortunes for making a few faces every day at a camera.

"They acted like drunken Grand Dukes before every Jeweler's window. They gave parties that were nothing but riots. The vampire was developed as a special attraction. The press agents magnified the wickedness of their clients. Divorces were considered good advertising.

"There are sots and dope fiends among us, and immorality enough to sink a ship."

Tom Holby was of another character. What he loved he adored, fought for, would not criticize or permit to be criticized.

"Hold on a minute, Claymore," he broke in. "Is there any part of the country where booze parties are unknown? The dope fiends aren't all in Hollywood. Every other town has about the same quota. East and West and North and South, in Europe, Asia, Africa it's the same.

"I tell you the average morality is just as high in Hollywood or Culver City as anywhere else in the world. We're a bunch of hard workers and the women work as hard as the men. They're respected and given every opportunity for wealth and fame and freedom. The public has been fed on a lot of crazy stories. A few producers have kept up the idea.

"A lot of bad women are at large in the movies, but most of 'em were bad before they came in and they'd have been a lot worse if they had stayed at home. The moving picture did more to keep girls and boys off the streets than all the prayer meetings ever held. They drove the saloon out of business more than any other power. The screen is the biggest educational and moral force ever discovered and it hasn't got a fault that is all its own. I tell you it's a cowardly shame to throw dirt on it. I hold my head just a little higher than ever, and I am shouting just a little louder than before, that I'm a movie man."

Mem looked on Tom Holby with new eyes. She had never thought of him as a fiery patriot in his art. His hot zeal was vastly becoming to him and cast into the shade the revering affection she had gained for Claymore, the inspirer and encourager of her personal skill. Her art was bigger than herself and she was thrilled with almost reverence for Holby.

To the surprise of everyone, the most ardent defender of the movies was the least expectable of all in such a gallery: Mrs. Steddon, the minister's wife.

Her demure, shy soul kept her quiet for a long while, but finally she struck out with all the wrath of the patient and the long-suffering. She was, indeed, now a Hollywood mother. She was the mother of all the movies and she lashed forth in an abrupt frenzy like an enraged kitten.

"Well, I think it's a crying shame for everybody to begin picking on such lovely people who work so hard and have such good hearts and do so much to make the world brighter. And if you make it brighter you make it better. You children mustn't take it so much to heart.

"This is a lynching country and every once in so often they've got to have a victim, no matter where they find him. When I was a girl the people that wanted to free the slaves were treated worse than what movie people are, and when our church was young the other churches used to treat us terribly. The things they said about our early preachers and did to them: jail and whipping posts and abuse, good gracious! You'd never believe it!

"Look what they did to Admiral Dewey: one day the nation's pet hero, and the next a yellow dog. They gave him a house for a gift, and when he put it in his wife's name, just to make sure of it for her, the people rose and treated him worse than they treated Guiteau. And all he had done was to be nice to his wife!"

From her, of all people, came even a word of compassion for the object of the nation's wrath.

"And that poor young man who got into all the trouble, he couldn't have meant to do any harm. He was just a big, overgrown boy, and he made too much money too soon, and he drank too much. Oh, the terrible sufferings people go through who can't help drinking too much when they find what they've done.

"There was a deacon in our church, a good man as ever was, but now and then he'd go mad for liquor, and he never knew what he might do. Once, after a long period of being perfectly nice, he tasted the communion wine and left the church and went mad crazy with whisky and oh dear, how he wept and prayed! Even my husband was sorry for him. Christ was sorry for everybody, even for the people that crucified him.

"And that young man, so big and fat and funny all the world laughed at him and paid fortunes to see him act. And now people are after him like wolves, and nobody says a good word for him.

"Even if he had done what they said he did, how broken-hearted he would be now! It seems to me that most of the people who howl for his life are making themselves crueler than what they say he was.

"Nobody seems to know just how that poor girl came to her death. But suppose the worst that's said was true. It's not half as bad as thousands of cases that have gone on in this country.

"Why, in our peaceful little town there was a terrible thing happened. I hardly dare speak of it, but there was a pretty young girl, a wild thing, but awful pretty, and some young fellows got a lot of liquor, and she was alone with them, and after terrible goings-on why, she died the next day.

"And that happened right in our home town of Calverly long before moving pictures were even thought of. And not a line was published in a single newspaper, not a sermon was preached against it, and nobody ever dreamed of prosecuting one of the five young men who really killed that poor, foolish young girl. Two of the men were members of my husband's church. They were terribly sorry and repentant and it seemed the right thing to hush it up and not talk about it.

"I guess there isn't a town in the world that hasn't had things like that happen. A preacher's wife gets to know the most pitiful things. If all the preachers and doctors and mothers and fathers would tell all they knew, oh dear, what revelations!

"And so I say, why should everybody act like this young man was the first one that ever did anything terrible? Why should they say it had anything to do with the business he was in? Why should they persecute the dear, good, nice people in the moving pictures? I think it's just frightful and if I was in the movies I just wouldn't stand it."

Mem throbbed with love of her mother for her ardor, but she bent her head, realizing her own secret. Claymore stared at the flaming little matron with gleaming eyes of approval. Leva Lemaire squirmed, ashamed of her own acquiescence in the storm of abuse.

But Tom Holby rose from his chair and, going to Mrs. Steddon, bent down and kissed her on the hair and wrung her little hand and kissed it.

And in that tribute he wooed Mem more compellingly than in any other possible wise.

Mrs. Steddon clung to Tom Holby's big hand and patted it, then rose and left the room. When Mem would have followed, she was sent back. Then Mrs. Steddon, in a fine frenzy, went to her table and wrote her husband an answer to his letter.

> DEAR HUSBAND, — I am ashamed of you for writing such a mean little note. Yes, I am proud to say that my daughter is an actress and is doing fine work. If you are not proud of her it is because you don't know enough to be. You will some day, you'll see.
>
> She is working hard and earning lots of money, and I'm going to stay with her as long as she needs me. I guess you can get along without me awhile. If you can't, come on out and see for yourself how wrong you are. I hope your next letter will be an apology. Mem would send her love if she knew I was writing.
>
> Your loving WIFE.

When this tiny bomb exploded in Doctor Steddon's parsonage it produced an astounding effect. The old devil fighter was not afraid of all the legions of hell. He could even face his richest pewholder without flinching; he could oppose his bishop or a whole assembly of fellow ministers.

But he was afraid of that little wife of his. She alone could scold him with impunity and by the mere withdrawal of her approval cast a cloud across his heaven. He was in an abject perplexity now.

Mrs. Steddon was as much afraid of Mem as her husband was of her. She dared not tell Mem that she had written the letter until after it was mailed beyond retrieving.

Then she confessed, and Mem startled her by a sudden collapse into bitter grief.

"I have come between you and papa. I have disgraced the family and lied to him and dragged you away from him and set you against him. I have taken you away from the other children, and broken up our beautiful home, and I wish I were dead."

Mrs. Steddon poured out lies with spendthrift zeal in the effort to comfort her and restore her pride. "Your father needs a vacation, and your sister Gladys is taking better care of the house than I did."

But Mem's grief was irredeemable.

Yet there was a benefit even in this. Her heart was so abrim with tears that, in a scene next day when Claymore wanted her to weep, he had only to call for tears and they gushed in torrents.

And from this enhanced responsiveness and the aggravated sympathy it aroused in his heart came the great peril that Tirrey had warned the girl against: the peril not of having to sell herself, but of giving herself away just for the graciousness of the deed.

# CHAPTER XXXVII

ALL THIS WHILE THE boy, Terry Dack, had been troubling Mem's conscience. She had induced the mother to give up her safe and sane career as a washerwoman and undertake the peculiar offices of mother to a prodigy. But the prodigy had not yet found his chance to prove himself. The producers did not seem to be so eager to engage the boy as Mem had expected.

As soon as she was installed as an actress she ventured one day to ask Mr. Tirrey to see the child; he consented to make an appointment. Mrs. Dack laundered her son as carefully as if he were a week's wash. She starched and ironed him and rendered him generally unnatural. She was in a panic of anxiety, but the boy's reaction to this was one of stodgy reserve.

Tirrey kept a number of famous candidates waiting while he bent to receive the tiny petitioner. The child must have found something lacking in this effusive courtesy or some offense in its manifest condescension, for he refused even to shake hands and retreated into his mother's bosom like a frightened rabbit.

The more the mother scolded the more the boy froze. The casting director was patient, but plainly not encouraged. He gave up at length, and asked his assistant, Mr. Dobbs, to place in the files a picture of the boy, with a record of his age, size, color, and the ominous words, "No experience."

Mem and Mrs. Dack left the office disheartened. Mrs. Dack was too downcast to scold or punish. She could only ask the boy why he had misbehaved. She might as well have asked why his hair was the tint it was or his features so shaped.

He had simply not been in the humor, and he had not yet been trained to coerce his moods to respond to the call.

That night Mrs. Dack came to see Mem to say that she would have to go back to Palm Springs and her drudgery. She was afraid to attempt a washerwoman's *métier* in Los Angeles, though there was need enough for artists in her line. She suffered tub fright in a strange land.

The boy felt guilty. He had suffered keenly when his mother broke down at home and wept. He suffered now when his beloved Mem appealed to him frantically:

"Oh, honey, why were you so mean to the gentleman who wanted to be nice to you?"

"I don't know," said the artist in embryo. "Something inside of me just wouldn't behave. I wanted it to, but I couldn't make it."

Mem understood this language. She had once tried to smile and wink and laugh before a director, and had found her muscles lead. Terry's failure had not been an intentional insolence, but a kind of mental lockjaw.

Even the salesman cannot be at his cunningest with every customer; and shoes, jewels, lands, and creeds are as hard to sell as souls when the ecstasy is wanting.

While Mrs. Dack was trying to persuade Mem not to blame herself for the fiasco, urging that Palm Springs was a nice place and washing a good-enough trade, Claymore dropped in to call.

Mem and her mother and Mrs. Dack were in Mem's bedroom when Leva brought word that Mem had a caller.

Mrs. Dack said that she would be saying goodbye. When she put out her hand, like a hook, for the child, who was usually within reach, he did not affix himself to it. When she and Mem looked about for him they found him in the front room, perched on Claymore's lap and making violent love, child love, to the captivated tyrant. The boy's big fawn eyes were lustrous with affection, the little fingers were wrapping and unwrapping their tendrils about Claymore's hand.

The women stood back and watched the two, unnoticed. Terry startled Claymore by saying:

"Why do you scrooge up your eyebrows thataway?"

"Do I?" gasped Claymore.

"Yep, you do. Looky; this is how you go."

As Claymore flung back his head and laughed at the revelation of an unsuspected habit of mien, he caught sight of Mem in the embrasure of the door and demanded:

"Do I scrooge up my eyebrows? The little rat says I do."

"I hadn't noticed it, but you do," said Mem. Terry was hilarious with pride, and Claymore, who distrusted everything he loved, was a glutton for humiliation. He had chosen a profession in which it is frequent, public, and expensive.

"I wish I had this child on the lot," he said. "We're getting close to a big scene in this next picture where a child is ill and delirious. The boy we had in mind has just had two front teeth knocked out in a fight at school. That won't look pretty in the picture."

Claymore, director-like, loved to discover new talent, dig up gold quartz in chunks and refine them. He looked down at the up-looking boy.

"Would you like to act for me?"

"Yep; you bet."

"Would you do what I asked you to?"

"You bet."

His mother said, "He's an awful good little tike, never cries or —"

"Never cries?" Claymore gasped.

"Except when he's mad."

"Oh! Well, he'll cry for me, I guess, if I ask him to. Won't you, old man?"

"You bet."

"You come over tomorrow and see the casting director. I'll tell him to bring the boy to me, for a test. Does he know anything about make-up?"

Mem shook her head and answered, with professional calm, "I'll make him up, myself, tomorrow morning early."

And now there was rapture in the household of Dack. The widow was retrieved from the wash tub at the desert's edge. The son was rescued from the dull lethargy of a sage brush future. A scepter was put in his hand and he would be raised aloft to such glory and such empire as no infant monarch had ever known. If he succeeded, millions of men and women in every land would gaze up at his living moving portrait, and pay him the homage that greets childhood when it is beautiful in the sunlight.

Terry Dack was about to be struck off in innumerable portraits and showered upon a grateful world.

At the age of five he would commence his business career with a salary of two or three thousand dollars a year.

It was dazzling, yet some people called it a dull age in a dull world, and looked back to medieval France for romantic happenings.

And many exceedingly good people would hold up their hands in horror at such cruel treatment of a child. Turning from the hideous revelations of immemorial precocious depravity, from the ghastly records of the children's courts founded by Saint Ben Lindsey, from the loathsome spectacles of the streets and alleys of ancient and modern times where children were flung like garbage, good people would revile the movies as a degradation of children.

The police and the lawmakers would regard the studios with a jealous eye. If young Mr. Dack failed to receive at least four hours of schooling on any day; if he were permitted to work more than four hours on any day, the guilty director and everybody concerned would be liable to heavy fines and imprisonment.

But the Dacks did not realize into what odium they were descending. They felt that they were being lifted up out of despair into a cloud realm of bliss.

Mrs. Dack's gratitude was so dire that it put Claymore to flight. He went away raging. He had called to pay court to the fascinating Miss Steddon, and he had adopted a child and a mother whose silly enthusiasm drenched him like a capsized tub of warm suds.

Mrs. Dack scurried away to her bleak lodgings to unpack her bundles. Palm Springs might pine for its lost laundress, but the world would be the happier for its newfound lamb.

Terry was forever getting to sleep that night. He was telling his mother what palaces he would buy her, what silks he would dress her in; she should ride in two solid-gold Fords at once, with a policeman for driver.

The next morning the Dacks were at Mem's door before she was up. They sat on the steps, watching the red-faced sun rise yawning from his bed on the mountains. They saw the newsboy on his bicycle fling the morning paper on the dewy grass, and Terry decided to buy himself a gold bicycle.

His mother tried in vain to hush his prattle. Finally the rattle-snake *whirr* of an alarm clock within shook the bungalow from its repose and they made their presence known.

After breakfast, Mem made up her own face first in order to get it out of the way, and also as a model for Mrs. Dack to copy. Terry's hands clutched at the various pigments with all the primeval instinct of a savage desire for paint. He repeated the names of the various layers of grease and color as a most delightful lesson.

When Mem was ready to begin on his face he held it up like a little balloon for adornment.

Leva had taken over the automobile of the housemate who had gone back East to the Midwest. She drove the Dacks and Mem to the studio. The streets were full of actors and actresses in automobiles of every sort. Most of them made up their faces at home and some of them put on their costumes there.

The town had the appearance of a carnival's morning after, and strangers found the sight astonishing. But to the established populace it was nothing but the daily exodus to the factories of the working classes in their overalls and caps. The make-up boxes the toilers carried were merely their tool kits.

The iron grills at the studio entrance were wide open and a throng poured in. Automobiles were parked along the curbs, and famous artists, extra folk, cameramen, executives, cabinetmakers, electricians, chemists, scene painters, decorators, cowboys, Chinese, Arabians, cooks, waitresses, a small cityful flocked to the numberless tasks that combined to build a snow of pictures.

Claymore was waiting for his protege and carried him off to his set, where he put him through an ordeal he was too young and too eager to regard as anything but the pastime Claymore pretended it was.

The boy's magnetism was instant with everyone. Everyone smiled at the sight of him. He put a live coal in every heart to warm its cockles. The cameraman smiled and joked as he turned the crank.

Terry Dack had that which gives certain poems, dramas, paintings, statues, orations, an irresistible fascination. His wheedling pout might be known for a mere trick; cynics might resent his big eyes, his babyish prettiness, and rebel against his tears, but they would find their eyes moist, their lips quivering, their hands aching to caress him or spank him. He could not be ignored.

Mr. Bermond, on an early round of inspection, stopped to watch the test being made, to ask who the child was, and to mumble to Claymore, "Sign him up!" He paused also to shake hands with the young tyrant, to toss him in the air and hug him tight with a heartache he dared not confess.

And so Terry's fortune was made. Or, at least, it was assigned to him to get. It would not be so easy to earn as it seemed. He would not realize, himself, what intellect he was developing, what intuitional processes he was perfecting in the laboratory of his soul.

He was sent home that day with a promise of a verdict on the morrow. He left the studio with bitter regret and a gnawing terror. His fierce imagination dramatized the deferment as exile.

His mother took the contagion of fear from him, and they were in an anguish until Mem returned that evening with the glad news that the test film had been rushed through the laboratory and had evoked vast enthusiasm in the projection room.

It was always a problem whether the charm would photograph. In Terry's case the picture was beyond the reality. His skin had an incandescence. His emotions were graphic upon his features.

The next day was Terry's first birthday as an artist. Mem announced herself as his true mother, and Claymore said, "Then I am his father!"

They looked at each other with a kind of fright. They were already linked in a wedlock of art, and a child was born of the union of their souls. And this had terrifying implications.

# CHAPTER XXXVIII

IT HELPED TERRY'S ART somewhat to be told that he must play a little girl. That angered him and anger gave him pathos. His humiliation was only a child's humiliation, but the pint cup brimming with bitterness is as overcharged as a tun of malmsey.

His mimetic genius, after the first shame of being clad in a girl's bonnet, slip, and short socks, found delight in a satire on the poses and carriage of little womankind.

The stage was a magic playground to him. He had to have his schooling: they gave him a private teacher who put him through his spelling and sums in the environs of the scene where he was called now and then to enact his role. Work was recess to him, and he scampered from his textbooks to the set as to a wholesale toy shop.

The electricians told him all about the big light machines. The property men let him help them with their labors. The assistant director lent him the megaphone for a toy and he bellowed through it like an infant Stentor. The lady who had to make herself look very old with all manner of paint was as gentle an ogress as ever ate a child. The beautiful star held him in her lap, and he learned to keep his hands off her make-up and kiss her behind the ear. He was as close to heaven as a child may climb on this doleful footstool. He had even the supreme pride of condescension; for an even younger actor than he was in the cast.

He felt the dignity of a veteran as he watched the scenes in which his little baby "brother" was engaged. This child was too young to be asked to act. The scenes he played in had to be played as games and they were costly games, for every minute spent could be charged off as five dollars gone.

Even if Claymore had been a brute he would have found it necessary to dissemble, because little children cannot be coerced to drama, though they may be whipped, starved, scolded, or frightened with hell fire and bogies to be "good."

Claymore had the patience of a born mother. The baby's own mother was vexed and easily moved to anger. She scolded, yanked, and threatened, and Claymore had to protect the child from her and keep her out of sight while he conducted the strenuous pretense.

He lay on his stomach on the floor and devised seductive wiles while the camera men and the light crew watched for his signal to begin their record.

Part of this picture was a domestic comedy, and this baby was supposed to escape from its nurse and its anxious mother; to find a loaded pistol, play with it, look down the barrel, and bite the fatal muzzle. Of course the pistol was not really loaded, but it was hoped that the effect would give the audience that bit of blood curdle for which it loves to pay its best money.

Claymore would hand the baby a morsel of candy, drop another down the barrel for the child to peer after and try to extract. Then Claymore would scuttle backward out of the range of the cameras, motion the electricians to hit the lights and the camera men to crank.

He cooed to the baby in prattling terms, struggling to keep it so absorbed in its task that it would not look out toward the camera and betray to future audiences the presence of a coach.

Time after time something diverted the baby's mind. Just as the scene was rolling perfectly the child would look away and fling the pistol down, or wave its hand and grin at someone in front. Then the task had to be begun again. The child had an impish gift for giving the cameramen false starts and then ruining the most promising take-offs.

The director, groveling about the floor, would not despair, but returned to the toil with a persistence much praised in spiders and ants and other stubborn industrials.

The author of the continuity had to leave the set and tear his hair and curse to get rid of his nerves. The production manager, whose business it was to keep the picture going at high speed and low cost, fumed and figured the expense. He said to the director, "That damned brat has cost the picture three thousand dollars so far without a foot of film to show for it."

Claymore, whose sympathy was inexhaustible as long as there was an honest effort, resented the insult to one of his cast. And eventually he won his point, decoyed the baby through the scene, and caught it with two cameras. The audience would never dream of the toil or the cost as it smiled at the brief frivolity. But then it is the pride of the true artist to conceal his toil as something obscene, a disgrace if discovered.

Terry Dack had no such patience for his bungling junior as the director showed. He was impatient to get to his own scenes, and when at last they were reached he began life anew.

He romped and whooped with laughter during the long waits between the brief takes while the lights were being brought up, the camera angles discussed, the properties arranged.

The moment the word "Action!" rang out he became the earnest artist. Already he knew that, while tragic scenes may be played in a cheerful atmosphere, comedy must be approached solemnly. He agonized over his humor, but he did not lose self-control in pathos.

Once, between the first take and the second of a pathetic scene, he began to tell a funny story to the camera man.

Claymore said: "Don't laugh in this scene, now. It's very serious."

If a super had told Edwin Booth not to giggle when he went on in The Soliloquy, he might have received a glance of similar barb. Claymore apologized hastily.

But Terry's pride in his superiority to the bungling baby was doomed to fall. There was a scene where he and his brother painted each other's lips with their stage mother's rouge stick. There was a scene where they said their prayers at the actress's knee. In these he shone and in moments of childish pathos. But by and by the crisis arrived when Terry must play a lost and abandoned waif freezing in a dark doorway, and sobbing in lonely dismay as he groped blindly for his mother and called her name.

He had responded to all the demands upon his armory of smiles and glooms, but when Claymore appealed for tears they would not flow.

Terry tried and tried. He squeezed his eyes. He stared at the lights. He tried to think of sad things, but never a bit of brine responded.

Even the groping of his hands was awkward and unreal.

Claymore explained, "I want you to do just what you do when you are sick or afraid at night and you reach out in the dark and feel for your mother."

"Oh, but I never do!" said Terry, with a certain loftiness of demurrer.

This ended that. Claymore pondered. "Did you ever play blindman's buff?" "You bet!"

"Do you remember how you would put your hands out when your eyes were shut?"

"Oh yes! I see what you mean now. Like thisaway."

And he clenched his eyes and put his plump hands forth, stroking the air to find his mother's cheek.

"Great! We'll take it!" said Claymore. The cameraman called, "Hit em!" The glare poured from the concentrated arcs. The music struck up a sobbing tune. The director called: "Action! Camera!" And Terry groped pitifully.

So far so good. But next was the crying scene, and the weeping must be real. Glycerine tears would be an insult to both audience and actor.

Claymore tried to tune the actor up to the climax by explaining the situation. Terry nodded like an old scholar. But no tears rose. Claymore appealed to the boy's sympathies for the character, for himself. He spoke in his most tear-compelling intonations. But not a tear would well from the desert of Terry's dry orbs.

"Think of your mother being awful sick and dying, far away from you!"

But Terry was too much of an actor to take this bait. "What's my mother got to do with this movin' pitcher?" he asked, in fine sincerity.

Claymore took up other weapons. He hammered that usually malleable little soul almost raw. Three hundred dollars had gone to the waste basket already and not a foot of film was even spoiled yet.

Claymore did not lose his temper, for he could see that the child was wrestling with his own unresponsive tear ducts. But he grew anxious for his story. It was essential that the child should weep and thousands of feet had already been taken with this scene in view.

At length he remembered what Terry's mother had said, "He only cries when he is mad."

And now he shifted his approach. He made all ready for the shot. He pretended a deep disgust for Terry, put him off his lap with a curt: "You are a quitter. The trouble with you is that you're not trying."

"I am so trying!" Terry gasped, astounded.

Claymore enacted contempt. "No, you're not! You're just in an ugly, stubborn mood. You can see that we're all waiting here, the light crew, the cameramen. You know the picture can't go on till we get this easy scene finished. Mr. Woburn [the author] has to have this scene in his story or it's spoiled. But what do you care? Mr. Bermond has paid you money and wants to pay you more, but just to spite him and all of us you hold back your tears."

The injustice of this outraged the child's soul. He stamped his foot in protest. "That ain't so!"

"It is so, so!" Claymore snapped back, and again he flaunted the red rag. "You can cry as well as anybody. You know that I've been friends with you, and I thought you were friends with me and with the star and Miss Steddon, here. But you're worse than the little baby who wouldn't play with the pistol. He didn't know any better. But you, there's only one thing keeping you from crying."

"Wha-a-at?" whimpered Terry, his lips shivering, his chin puckering as with a drawstring, his throat gulping till Mem could hardly keep from dashing to his rescue.

Claymore snarled: "It's your meanness. You're a dirty little alley cat, a spiteful little alley cat."

"I am no-ot a nalley ca-at!" Terry sobbed.

"Of course you are. You don't belong on the screen. Go on back to your alley, you cat. Go on back to the desert with the other coyotes. We don't want you here, because you won't cry."

"I will so cry! Boo-hoo, I will cry!"

Claymore tossed his voice in scorn.

"Oh, you might make a lot of sniffles, but you wouldn't dream of crying like a lost child, I want my mamma!"

"I want my mamma!" Terry howled.

The flood broke from a suddenly blackened sky. Sobs shook his frame. Tears spilled and darted across his fat cheeks. The childish treble rang wild.

Carpenters working on distant sets paused with the heart stab a child's cry thrusts into the breast.

The electricians, the property men, the actors and actresses, gulped and clenched their hands.

Terry did not see the lights come on at Claymore's signal. He did not see Claymore tap the elbows of the cameramen nor hear the cranks scuttering.

He sobbed and sobbed while Claymore goaded him on, giving him his cue disguised as abuse, "I want my mamma! You alley cat!" in antiphony with Terry's increasing anguish.

"I want my mamma! Shut up! I want my mamma. I WANT MY MAMMA!"

There was something uncanny and cruel about it in Mem's mind. It was a form of torture, a Spanish Inquisition not after beliefs or confessions, but after stored-up emotions. Mem's blood ran cold at the shameful business of flogging that young soul to such old woes.

She was ready to rush into the sacred circle of the set and attack Claymore for his brutality. She would lose her own career, but she would escape complicity in such a low trade.

Just before she sprang to the attack she heard Claymore stop the cameras with the word, "Cut!" The first cameraman called to the chief electrician, "Rest 'em!" Then the relentless torturer, Claymore, ran forward, picked Terry up in his arms, hugged him to his heart, and kissed him, mumbling:

"That's my boy! That's the good, brave artist I thought he was."

The briny victim peered through the dripping eaves of his drenched eyelashes and said:

"Was at all right? Honest? Did I cry good?"

And when Claymore groaned, "Great!" Terry laughed aloud and twisted Claymore's ear, kissed him, and throttled his neck with his short arms as he yelled:

"Mamma! Mamma! Mister Claymore says 'at was great!"

Mrs. Dack ran forward to embrace him, her heartaches turned to aches of pride.

In the good old days children had been beaten incessantly; stout rods were spoiled religiously to spare the children from the perils of hell. Stories of goblins, of ogres, of child-eating witches and wolves, had filled the nursery books and the nursery talk. Myriads of children had been slain to annihilate their races. In Russia at this time children dead of starvation were heaped in windrows by the thousand. Endless armies had been sent to the coal mines, the factories, to the starvation and duress of foundling asylums, poor farms. In old England two little girls of eight had been kept in solitary cells for over a year, hundreds of children were hanged for theft. The babies of devout parents had been doomed to gloomy homes and dour repressions for their souls' sakes. Little children had been trained to sob and weep for the sins they inherited from Adam and for the fires of hell awaiting their least misstep.

This child had been constrained to weep in a game of pretense and perhaps a million people would weep because he wept, a million people would feel the pity of childhood, and thousands of children would be better cherished for the brief martyrdom of Terry Dack.

"He who would make others weep must first have wept himself." And Terry had learned the gentle art of altruistic tears. His heart had enlarged its education. To his technical equipment a great weapon had been added.

In a later scene he had to cry again, and now it was he that pleaded with Claymore in his anxiety for perfection.

"I'll cry all you want if you'll ony make me mad again. Call me a nalley cat. That makes me awful mad."

Obediently Claymore called him an alley cat and even a

gutter snipe; and he caterwauled magnificently with neatness and dispatch.

And so in many layers his little soul worked, striving to present a faithful transcript of child life, child comedy, child tragedy, in order to buy his mother pretty things and to save her back from the torture of the tub, and to buy himself learning, power, wealth, fame, and a future of boundless scope.

There was a divinity about it.

Terry was a veteran indeed now. He had been under fire. He had played a big scene, had shed and inspired saltwater, or, as the technical term was, he had "got the tear."

Yet, superior as he felt to his junior, the infant that had played with the pistol, he was himself a novice to a veteran who gave him much useful advice and comfort a girl of twelve, an old actress in a young art.

Polly Thorne had been a moving-picture actress since she was five. She belonged to a stepladder family of ten children, all of them on the screen, all of them wholesome, handsome, happy people like their parents, also filmers.

Polly was a figure of national importance. She had created a role in a long series of pictures of childhood.

But Polly, alas had been doomed to play the little minx and tattletale who always told on her brother. Famous little Polly and her mother had been sent on a long cross-continental tour of personal appearances at moving-picture theaters. She had returned in time to work in Claymore's cast.

But there was a sorrow in her heart. She had found that because of her brilliant impersonation of the spiteful little wretch, the stupid public confused her character with her characterization. In Minneapolis she had overheard a press agent say that he would not even escort her to the theater because she was such a vixen! She loved her public, and it was a bitterness to have it persuaded that she was unlovable.

Her eternal plea was now for some scene that would redeem her reputation. She longed to show before the camera the kindly spirit she revealed away from it.

But most of all she longed for what all actresses long for: a crying scene. Two things the normal actress desires above all things: to weep and to be murdered *coram populo,* as every actor wants most of all to play Hamlet, debate suicide, and be slain with a poisoned rapier.

Polly entreated Claymore incessantly:

"Oh, please, dear good Mr. Claymore, won't you, wouldn't you, couldn't you kindly please put in a little scene where I can cry?"

"I don't see how I can in this picture, Pollykins," Claymore protested. "I'll have the next picture written so that you can drown in your own tears."

"Oh, but the next one may never come!" Polly urged. "I'm getting too big to play little girls, and I won't be big enough to play *onjanoos* for two or three years. I may have to leave the screen for a while. Couldn't you just slip in a little bit? You know, when Miss Steddon is sick why couldn t'I go to her and pet her a little and cry over her?"

"I'll see the author," said Claymore, "or maybe you'd better."

Polly turned the witchery of her shining eyes on the author, wheedled him, flattered him, courted him, all for the boon of a little brine.

And finally she coaxed a promise from him that he would interpolate a scene with Miss Steddon and give Polly a good cry.

The news was glorious. She darted to her mother, squealing with delight. She ran back and kissed the confused scribe, who would one day boast that the great Polly Thorne had honored him with such a seal of approval.

Polly dashed to Mem and sat upon her lap, tremulous with the rapture of her promotion to the dignity of a priestess of grief. Mem understood the thrill. She was looking back already from an increasing remoteness upon the excitement of her own novitiate.

Strange people, these actors, who plead for suffering! Yet what else do the rest of us but cultivate misery, hug it to our hearts, run to embrace assured regret, make a habit of renewed remorse, resent all warnings and sign posts, and store up repentance in lavender, in old attics, in revisited scenes and haunted night thoughts?

Since we cannot always find grief enough at home or in the misbehavior of our neighbors, we have a gory newspaper dropped at our doors every morning. We snatch at extras, the bloodier the better. We buy magazines and books dripping with assorted woes for every taste; we have storytellers, songsters, fiddlers, poets, painters, players to make us writhe. We put tragic art at the top of the heap and pay him or her the most homage, and usually the most money, who wrings the most drops out of our twisted hearts.

The moving picture made its instant appeal because it brought the most agony within the reach of the masses at the greatest convenience with the least expense.

# CHAPTER XXXIX

HAVE A JOB AND get a job. To him that hath Remember Steddon's first picture was approaching its finish by a zigzag path, the scenes being shot according to their geography rather than chronology.

In one episode Mem was photographed stealing in through a front door and crossing a hall into a drawing-room. When this was rehearsed and taken several times, she was immediately required to return across the hallway from the drawing-room and carry with her the memory and the influence of what had taken place in the drawing-room.

But, as a matter of fact, the art director and his crew of carpenters and decorators had not yet constructed the drawing-room. It was still building on another stage, two hundred yards away, and the scene could not be taken for a week.

Furthermore, the preceding scene in the street had not been taken. It would be shot on location in a street several miles away.

The actress had, therefore, to recall what she had done long before she did it.

This was one of the inescapable difficulties of the technique. Every art has its absurdities and contradictions, and the moving-picture actor must perform incessant Irish bulls of sequence.

But all of Mem's anxieties concerning make-up and costume and interpretation were overwhelmed in the anxiety as to her future. She dreaded any hiatus in her career, another fretful hunting for more work.

She had been already acquiring a little name. Gossip of every sort was rife, and some of it was flattering. The word floated about that "Steddon was making good at Bermond's."

Other directors began to speak to her on the lot and at the luncheon table. The matron in charge of the dressing rooms told her that she had heard several people speak of Miss Steddon's fine work. The man in charge of a projection machine told her one day, "Very nice, Miss Steddon!" That was praise from a jaded expert. Some of the other actresses on the set had confessed that she had made them cry and choke up. She had "the stuff." She was delivering the goods. Her soul was getting over.

At home she found a note now and then asking her to call at another studio. Agents sent her proffers of their good offices and promised to enhance her opportunities and her earnings.

But the Bermond Company had an option on her services. This included the right to farm her out for single pictures to other companies. It was a flattering kind of slavery. Still more flattering was Bermond's reluctance to lend her to a rival.

Eventually, Bermond agreed to rent Mem to a new company that was to make Tom Holby a star. He had earned the elevation, and this meant that he and Robina Teele would part company at least upon the screen.

When Mem read of this plan on the motion-picture page of an evening paper her heart gave a hop, as if a fat frog had leaped in her bosom. She was not sure just what the excitement meant within her there.

She did not want Tom Holby for herself, yet she did not want to see any other woman land him.

Claymore obtruded upon her meditations. She was under the obligation imposed by his devotion.

It was certain that he and Mem must sever the relations they had established as director and directed, but a deep friendship, something deeper than friendship, had developed during their communion.

He had found her increasingly, irresistibly fascinating as he ransacked odd corners of her heart for emotional material; as he studied her expressions and postures; as he thought of her in her absence. Before him, she moved about to music, and that lifted them to another planet somehow.

He tried to be particularly aloof, professional, and directorial in his conduct with Mem, lest the company discover his infatuation. But his love was less and less content with courtesy alone. The very effort emphasized what he sought to hide, and the whisper went about that Claymore and Steddon were thicker than thieves. They gave the impression of a bride and groom pretending to be old married people and only advertising their infatuation by their aggravated indifference.

Mem was not blind to the look in his eyes, nor deaf to the overtones in his voice. She wondered for a while that so powerful a man should have selected so humble an apprentice and let the star glide by unworshiped.

Her heart was mellowed with a kind of upward pity for the great man that she was dragging down to her own meek level. But it was pleasant to be adored.

All day they labored over the mimicry of love and woe, and yet they gained no private immunity from its fever.

When he called on evenings, Claymore would make excuses to step out into the patio with Mem to show her a very remarkable moon.

He persuaded her now and then to stroll, anything to get her away from the eyes and ears of her mother and her housemates.

He never said anything, however, that he might not have said before a crowd. He never tried to hold her hand or snatch a kiss or filch an embrace. Mem was constantly set quivering with expectancy that he would make some advance, some gesture of endearment, yet always unable to decide just what she would do if he did. But he didn't.

She wondered at his curious shyness. For a man of such autocracy and such a habit of ordering her about before people, to be afraid to speak to her in solitude, it was funny.

She did not realize that his chief battle was with himself. He knew the perils a director runs who lets himself flirt with or favor one of his company. Even to deliver himself to bandied jokes was unbearable. He fought his love for the sake of his pride of office.

So he did not speak, but he ached, and he communicated his anguish to the very air.

The picture and its final retakes were finished on a Saturday afternoon. There was an evening's idleness ahead. Claymore asked Mem to take a drive in his car, a long farewell flight about the familiar and the unvisited roads. She accepted meekly. Something told her that this drive was important to her fate.

Something was always telling her something. Nine times out of ten it was false, but she forgot the failures and recalled the coincidences.

# CHAPTER XL

NOBODY HAD YET ASKED Mem for her self-respect as an initiation fee or an initiation rite. She was paid a weekly wage based upon her ability, her experience, and her usefulness. She was paid in the coin of the realm.

Her price would rise and fall according to the general market for moving pictures and her specific value. Her emotion and her beauty were commodities, and Steddon stock would be quoted on the Soul Exchange as the demand for it rose and fell, as the bidders for it increased or diminished.

She could not add to her artistic assets by incurring moral liabilities. If her sins were discreet or picturesque they would not affect the public esteem. If they were unlucky sins, she might find herself suddenly bankrupt, closed out, shut down.

Up to now she had met no more of those compliments which are called "insults" than any girl is likely to meet with as she goes her way through any community. Her mother had been with her almost all the time when she was not on the lot, and the lot was full of mothers of little children and young stars.

Claymore had been chaperoned by the company and his own reverence for discipline. But now she was outside his authority. Both were outside the Bermond inclosure.

The picture was finished. Claymore could offer her no more scenes, no more advantages, no more roles, not even the little tributes of special close-ups or flattering lightings or the tender privilege of being "shot through gauze" or out of focus.

And now they were as helpless together as any other twain

whom nothing restrains or separates in the undertow of passion. They were two emotional people without a barrier.

Among the countless things written and said about the hows and whys of women's surrenders, one motive seems to have been too much ignored, though it must have exerted a vast influence on countless women, must exert an increasing influence as women go more and more into the worlds of business, of art, and of freedom with only themselves for their guardians.

Good sportsmanship, a hatred of smuggery, a contempt for too careful self-protection, a disgust for a holier-than-thou self-esteem; these are amiable attitudes of mind that make for popularity. To be a miser of one's graces, a hypochondriacal coddler of one's virtues, is to be unloved and unlovable.

So many a man will gamble, break a law, risk his career, his health, his life, get drunk, steal, slay, and play the fool rather than face the reproach that he is a mollycoddle, a Puritan, a prig, a Miss Nancy, a coward, a Pharisee.

And many a woman who would not yield for passion or for luxury must have consented for fear of seeming to be over-proud, stingy, cold, prudish, disobliging, superhuman, subnormal, unsportswomanlike.

Mem had been swept once beyond the moorings by a summer storm of devotion to young Farnaby, her first love. Now she was to feel her anchors cut adrift by the gracious gesture of good fellowship with a colleague.

Claymore called his last "cut!" at four o'clock that Saturday afternoon. The last shots had taken less time than had been foreseen. Mem had told her mother that she might be kept at the studio till late in the evening.

The members of the company bade one another farewell as after a pleasant voyage. Mem hurried to remove her makeup and put on civilian clothes.

As she came down the steps from the long gallery of dressing rooms she saw Claymore coming from his office on the ground floor. He smiled.

"Othello's occupation's gone. I've got an idle afternoon on my hands. Why don't we take a little motor ride and get a bit of fresh air?"

"I'd better go home," Mem faltered, invitingly.

"Ah, you can always go home. School's over. Let's play hooky."

"All right!" she cried, with a childish eagerness for mischief.

She went with him to his car where it was parked outside the lot. He helped her in with a manner of possession, of capture. He sent the car spinning out along Washington Boulevard toward Venice. By winding ways they reached the vast amusement huddle and, passing the canals that gave it its name, pushed on to the pleasure streets of cheap and noisy merriment.

They loitered awhile on the sand, but it seemed a little late for a swim, and Claymore easily persuaded her to drive farther along the sea road after an early dinner at the Sunset Inn.

When they had finished their coffee the sun was low and huge. It blazed like a cauldron simmering with molten gold, searing the eyes and inflaming the sky about it.

The Santa Monica Mountains marching down to the sea grew lavender with the twilight. Ocean Drive stretched along a forest of palms like huge coconuts dark against the gaudy west. Then the road dropped in a long U down Santa Monica Canyon and out again, a canyon divided between strange neighbors, a Methodist camp meeting grounds and the paradise where the Uplifters Club gives its outdoor festivals, pageants of rare beauty, the forest deeps uncannily illumined with fuming mists of many-colored smoke.

As they turned out again at the ocean's edge the sun fell into the wide sea and was quenched, leaving along the west only a glow of powdered geranium petals, though the wet sands were a burnished kettle color where the ripples laved and smoothed them.

The automobiles of every make were so many that they were almost one long automobile, or at least a chain on which they slid as black beads. Their lights were coming out now like early stars pricking a twilit sky.

The waters grew dull, liquid slate, with patches of lapis lazuli. The light went out of the world as if it were a moisture withdrawn from flowers that drooped and shriveled. The lavender mountains were a dull mauve, growing dim and listless. The road sidled along high cliffs with little canyons folding them into long wrinkles.

Here and there on the beach knots of people gathered about darkling fires, cooking dinner in a gypsy mood.

Another, more solemn community was established here: a cluster of Japanese fisherfolk, earnest little people crowded out of their own islands and finding no welcome in California. But they toiled on, ignorant of the articles, stories, novels, and orations devoted to their denunciation as a menace and a promise of war.

The car rounded headland after headland, finding always another beyond. On one of these stood a lighthouse with a patch of bright sky shining through. When they reached it, it was a moving picture fishing village, Inceville once, now the R. C. Ranch Studio, an odd jumble of hollow shells, English huts, Western block houses, a church, a strip of castellated walls, all sorts of structures that a nimble camera could present as parts of great wholes.

The road fared on, cutting off the tip of one ridge and leaving a cone the color of a vast chocolate drop set up at the ocean's rim.

The next headland ended in a bit of sand where a few palm trees had been installed to represent a South Sea island vista. The very mountains in silhouette were like a strip of scenery.

Twilight was smothering the long and twisted gorge of the Topanga when Mem and Claymore turned their backs on the last glimmers of the ocean.

For miles and miles the highway mounted and writhed along the steeps of precipices, hugging the rocks to let pass car after car with lamps flashing in front of blurred passengers.

The road had been slashed through walls of stone, or of heaped conglomerate like enormous piles of cannon balls. The slopes, of increasing depth and majesty, were clothed with sage and stunted trees. Here and there stood the tall white spikes of the "candles of God," the yuccas de Dios, now in bloom. They had a ghostly glimmer where they hoarded the last rays of waning day.

Mem's heart was stabbed with terror at every sharp swerve around a beetling ledge, for the headlight swung off down the cliff, revealing the danger to be feared rather than the road to be followed.

In almost every bay where there was a bit of space a motor had stopped and drawn close to the cliffside in the dark. It was easy to imagine the purpose of these halts. Each car was a wheeled solitude, a love boat at anchor in a stream of cars ignoring and ignored.

All over the world it was the custom of the time to take advantage of such little solitudes. There was a vast outcry in pulpits and in editorial columns against the evil, and evil was undoubtedly achieved in immense quantity. It was no new evil, however, but the ancient, eternal activity that has never failed to find its opportunity in desert and in garden, in hut and palace, on porch and deck, in graveyard and cloister, in cave and on hillside, in chariot, palanquin, sedan, stage coach, buggy, Victoria, or donkey chaise as well as in auto.

It is an equally old evil to accuse the implement of creating the power that makes use of it, and would use another weapon if need were.

There was a strange influence in this recurrent mystery. Everywhere lovers were hiding themselves in conspicuous concealment. Mem felt disgust at the first dozen, amusement or contempt for the next fifty, tolerance for the next, and...

Claymore did not speak of them or of anything else. He was too busy twirling the wheel and gauging the little distances between the edge of the cliff and the cars that whizzed past.

Halfway up the canyon his headlight ransacked a black cove between two headlands and found no motor in possession of the estuary of night. And here, to Mem's dumb astonishment, he abruptly checked his car, swung in off the road against the wall of rubble, and stopped short with a sigh of exaggerated fatigue.

"Well," he groaned, "this is a drive! I'll rest a bit if you don't mind. Pretty here, eh?"

From their cavern of gloom they looked across a fathomless ravine to a mountain on which the risen moon poured a silent Niagara. In the dozing radiance a creamy shaft of yucca stood, a candle blown out in a deserted cathedral.

The night air was of a strange gentleness, and the cars that shot past threw no light into their retreat.

There was a long, long silence that rilled Mem with a terror she could not quite fail to enjoy. She could not tell whether she heard her own heartbeats or his, but excitement was throbbing in the little coach that had brought them so swiftly to this remote seclusion.

Claymore was dumb so long that Mem had time to cease to be afraid of what he would say, and to begin to wish that he would get it said, so that she could know what her answer would be.

She felt a baffling uncertainty of herself. She could not imagine what she might do or say. She had not had much experience of men, but enough to know that before long he would initiate the immemorial procedure that starts with an arm adventuring about a waist and a voyage after a kiss.

She told herself that the only right and proper thing to do would be to resist, protest, forbid, and prevent at any cost the profanation of her sacred integrity. If necessary, she must fight, scratch, scream, escape, run away, appeal for help to any passer-by, or, as a last resort, leap over the cliff and die for honor's sake.

But who was that She and who was that Herself who told each other so many things?

Herself told She that Mr. Claymore could not be treated as an ordinary ruffian, an insolent, outrageous knave, a fiend. He had treated her with most delicate courtesy from the first, he had given her opportunity for fame and money, he had taught her his art, he had given her his admiration, his praise, his devotion, his mute but evident affection.

If he loved her and revealed his love, she could hardly reward his patient chivalry with prompt ingratitude and violence and fear. That would make her the insulter, not him.

She must be very gentle with him and ask him kindly to forbear and not to spoil the pleasant friendship that she had prized.

But if he still persisted? He was sure to be gentle at worst. He would obey her with a sigh of loneliness and his heart would grieve. Somehow, as she foreshadowed such an acceptance of defeat, she could not but feel a little disappointed.

Thousands of years of ancestry had put it in her heart to enjoy being overpowered, over persuaded, captured. Women had been earning their own livings in various ways from most ancient antiquity and had never yet overcome their eternal tendency to play their part in the immortal duet.

If Mr. Claymore should propose marriage, that would make his caresses acceptable according to some canons, though not to all. But he could not marry her and she did not want to marry him. She did not want to marry anybody just now. She was a free woman in a free country.

She was not free, however, from the witchery of this night, this dream, the vast yearning of this mountainous beauty. She was not free of the disaster of desire, the hunger to be embraced and kissed and whispered to, the need to be kept warm in the cold loneliness of the world.

But her training kept telling her that only a wicked man of wicked aims could have brought her here for the damnation of her soul, the temptation of her flesh, and all the infernal risks involved.

Still, she could not hate him even in her imagination, though she tried. She could not denounce him for what he had not yet attempted, and she could not quite despise herself for not being unwilling that he should show a little courage.

Besides, what a hypocrite she would be to protest and rebuke him for sullying her honor when she had none! Who was she to be indignant because a man asked her for a kiss? How could she honestly deceive him by pretending innocence? How could she undeceive him by confessing her wicked past?

Her thoughts spun giddily in her mind, all entangled with a skein of romantic threads. She was young and pretty and time was wasting her flowerly graces. Someone ought to cull them while they bloomed.

While she debated with herself, as doubtless innumerable women have debated with themselves in like plights, Claymore's own mind was a chaos of equally ancient platitudes of a man's philosophy.

At length he found the courage or the cruelty to slip his arm about Mem's waist and to draw her close to him. He was almost more alarmed than delighted to find that she hardly resisted at all.

He took her hands in his and whispered, "Your poor little hands are cold!" Then he kissed them with cold lips that he lifted at once to hers and found them warm and strangely like a rose against his mouth.

He was as much amazed as if hers were the first lips he had ever kissed, as if he had just invented kissing. Then in a frenzy of wonder he closed her in his arms with all his power. He did not know that the wheel bruised her side, and neither did she. But she forgot to debate her duty or to think of her soul. She thought only of the rapture of this communion, and her arms stole round his neck and she clenched him with all the power of her arms.

As fire drives out fire, so evil evil. There was an evil flourishing then with an unheard of fury, a wave, a tidal wave of crime, of murder, theft, violence of every sort.

The highways and the houses of the world had gone mad with the enterprises of robbery. Nobody was safe at home or abroad, in palace or hovel, shop or mail car. Millions on millions of treasure were being carried off by thieves. Theft was ubiquitous. On one of the roads of Los Angeles, a month or two before, a couple locked in each other's arms had been challenged by a thug with a gun. He had robbed both man and girl, then carried the girl off in his car and later flung her outraged body down at the side of the road and left her. When the police had traced him and jailed him, he had fought with such fury that they had to kill him after he had killed one guard and wounded another.

It was a sorry time when thieves did not respect thieves and when even illicit love was not safe from criminal interference.

Mem, swooning she knew not where or whither, was awakened from her mad rapture by a low voice across her shoulder.

"Sorry to interrupt you, folks, but I need your money."

She turned and found herself blinded by the glare from a motor halted at a little distance. Dazzled as she was, she could see the gaunt hand that held before her a black pistol with a glint outlining its ugly muzzle.

She whirled and stared into the staring eyes of Claymore. It was not fear, but an infinite disgust, that she saw there, as his arms left off embracing her and rose slowly into the shameful posture of abject surrender.

# CHAPTER XLI

CLAYMORE WAS SANE ENOUGH to attempt no resistance, though he almost perished of chagrin. He endured the insolence of the masked stranger who thrust his free hand into every pocket, twisted the watch from the chain, stole the chain and a wallet and the loose silver, and cursed because there was no more to steal.

Claymore had next to witness the rifling of Mem's person, the clutching for earrings that were not there, the groping about her bosom for a brooch, the wrenching of her one poor perjurious wedding ring from her finger, the snatching of her wrist bag from her arm.

The blackguard had the venom to say:

"I'd ought to bean yous both for not havin' somethin' fit to pinch. You ain't worth the wear and tear on me conscience."

He held his clubbed pistol over Claymore's head a moment, then forbore to strike, and dropped from the step with a last warning.

"Sit pretty now and keep em up till I git goin or I'll…"

His car shot round the curve, but they sat petrified for a time. In the black dark he might be lurking still.

But at length Claymore brought down his aching arms. They were too much ashamed of themselves to return to their late post about Mem's shoulders.

Claymore was afraid to speak lest he begin to sob. He started the car and turned back down the canyon.

It was another realm from the one they had ascended in such

romance. The enchantment was sardonic now; the majesty was a Brocken ribaldry; the dim yuccas sarcastic candles of a black Sabbath.

The sea waited for the road wriggling toward it reluctantly, in an infinite laughter of contempt.

Claymore spoke when the silence grew unbearable:

"I tried to see something in that dog's eyes or his manner that I could identify him by, but I couldn't."

"Were you thinking of describing him to the police?" Mem asked.

"God, no! I just want to beat him to death privately. We can't afford to start explaining how we happened to be there."

It was a little too crass to word. Mem blushed in the dark. It was shameful to have gone on such an errand. It was somehow a little more shameful to have been thwarted and frustrated. A perverse remorse filled their souls with confusion; a remorse because of a wrong remorse, a disgust for an unaccepted temptation and for being so temptable.

# CHAPTER XLII

A WOMAN NEVER QUITE forgives a man for not dying for her at the first opportunity. She probably never quite forgives him for dying, either.

So the clever man evades the situation where a choice is required, as the virtuous man evades temptation while it is yet far off.

For weeks afterward Mem shuddered at the picture of what would have happened if Claymore had attacked the footpad and been shot to death. She would have been left alone in the titanic labyrinth of Topanga Canyon with a dead body to explain and her presence there to excuse. Yet it was not quite satisfactory that he should survive after surrender.

She was acquiring a habit of translating life into scenarios and continuities of ingenious complication and more or less thrill, and she spent days and nights juggling with possible conclusions to this adventure.

She had been dizzy with the swirl of Claymore's love storm and his inarticulate demands, when the gruff demand of the thug shivered her whole being as a boat that scuds before a gale and rounds a headland is smitten with an opposite blast.

The road, returning along the sea, was more populous than before with dark cars stranded in shadow. In the distance Venice with its countless lights lay like a constellation fallen in a heap upon the ocean's edge.

When they reached it, it was a cheap tinsel affair, darkly crowded. They left it and turned into Washington Boulevard, winding toward Los Angeles. Vast stretches of dark field were broken by brilliantly lit sheds where fruits and melons were for sale, now and then a roadside tavern, now and then a moving picture studio.

The Green Mill was eerie with green wheels studded with green bulbs. Dancing was the chief industry there.

Inside the classic portico of the Goldwyn Studio work was evidently going on, for the huge lot was alight. The Virginian mansion of the Ince Studio dreamed in snowy beauty. A little farther rose the curious whimsy of the Willat Studio with its fantastic architecture; next were the long buildings where Harold Lloyd made his comedies.

They crossed Wilshire into Hollywood through a dark forest of oil derricks invading the very heart of the thronged bungalows.

Claymore, brooding deeply in his earnest soul, felt that he owed Mem some atonement. He meant it nobly, but it sounded crude when he checked the car in front of her little home and took her hand and said:

"If you will let me marry you, I'll see that my wife divorces me."

These divorces of convenience marked the new-fashioned way of accomplishing an old-fashioned righteousness. He wanted to make her "an honest woman."

But the times had passed for that. Woman had come into the right to lose her own soul on her own responsibility. No man can make her an honest woman by any deed of his.

Mem laughed nervously.

"No, thanks!" It was as uninspired as possible, but then it is not easy to make a brilliant answer to a stupid suggestion. She felt that she must improve on it a bit, but she helped it little when she added: "Just as much obliged. Goodnight!"

She left him and went to face her mother. She had not the courage to tell of the robbery. She covered the nakedness of her ringless finger with her other hand and, yawning ostentatiously, sneaked off to bed.

And that was the end of her love story with Claymore. It had been a success in no respect as a love story. But as an education it had been invaluable.

He had taught her to know herself and the volcanic emotions within her, and how to release them at command. She was far from being a great or a complete artist, but she had the ambition to be one; she had some of the resources, and she knew what the others must be.

It seemed an ingratitude, almost a treachery, to take Claymore's inspiration and tuition and give him in return only a few kind words and an evidence of her frailty before temptation.

But while she could command herself to weep and to throb with enacted love, she could not scold herself into a genuine passion.

She felt degraded in the eyes of Claymore, and hoped that she would not see him again until the memory had blurred. But she was still more tormented with the problem of the thug who had found her in Claymore s embrace.

She would never know who he was, because his face had been masked. But he had studied her. He would know her any-where, and if she became famous, he would sneer as he saw her published face. He would sneer, and he would doubtless talk.

# CHAPTER XLIII

THAT WAS A DISMAL night in Mem's chronicles. She was humiliated before her own soul in a dozen ways and before the eyes of her best friend and the anonymous, faceless raider.

She could not sleep her accusing self away. The critic within her soul kept condemning her, and nothing was more odious than the fact that she had been caught.

Also, she could not sleep for the fever in her parched eyes. The last day at the studio had been spent in the furious circle of the lights. They had almost burnt her vision away, and she had been unable to face them in one of the final close-ups without gushing tears and stabbing pain.

During the night she had a mild onset of "Klieg eyes" and had nightmares of blindness. Her career would be blasted at once. Her terrors added to her repentances and her anguish made slumber impossible.

As she lay staring into the dark, the windows and the furniture began to wake from the black and take on definition. The world in the dawn was exactly like the film as she had seen it developed in the dungeons of the laboratory, a sudden faint revelation of outlines, a gradual clarity, and finally all the details.

She rose wearily from her bed, flung on a wrap, and stole to the window. The little garden and the orange tree were being developed likewise by the chemistry of the sunrise.

She felt an impulse to walk about, and, thrusting her bare feet into slippers, she went through the door as stealthily as an escaping thief.

The morning was as yet only a paler moonlight. She was surprised to find the mountains missing from the horizon. It seemed odd that a sierra should be removed overnight. It was a mist that hid them, so frail a thing to conceal such bulks!

As she watched, the veil was withdrawn into nothingness. The mountains rolled up their mighty billows. It was as if they had been created anew by the original edict or by that long squeeze the geologists imagine.

As they emerged sullenly from the void, the rest of the world opened shop. Flowers began to waken; vines to take thought of further explorations; birds began to whet their beaks, little butchers sharpening their knives for the market.

Somewhere a bird was singing. It is good poetry to praise the song of birds. But this one sounded like a squeaking wheel. Yet it would be ridiculous to liken an ungreased wheel to the pipe of a half-awakened bird.

In a vacant lot at the back, rabbits were sitting up and shivering their noses in a posture of amazed stupidity. Across the walks and the grass little herds of snails were returning to their corrals. They had the look of having been out all night and their knapsacks were tipsily awry. And they left shining wakes wherever they went, as drunkards leave footprints in the snow.

The flowers were putting on their colors like robes, or like makeup that night had removed. It was the light that restored their beauty of hue.

Light! They were its creatures and its voices. And she was a child of light. Darkness was her death, and all her speech was reflected radiance from the sun or from some of the little suns that tiny mankind had devised for its amusement and convenience.

In the yard next door blackbirds were breakfast hunting. She noted that each glistening male was nagged and bullied by a fat brown female. When he found a worm she ran and took it away from him. When he did not find one she nipped him with her bill or made a pathetic racket. If he tried to swallow one unobserved she made him disgorge it. If she stumbled over one as she waddled, she kept it herself. Her motto seemed to be the old phrase Mem had heard as a child: "What's yours s'mine; what's mine s'm'own."

No wonder the males were so sleek and crisply alert. No wonder their womenfolk were so obese and petulant.

Mem thought she saw the old-fashioned housewife in the female blackbird. She grew plump on the toil of her smart husband, and contributed little but an appetite and a number of new beaks for him to feed.

She was glad that she would not be such a woman. She would find her own food and pay her way, and she would pay it handsomely. She filled her breast with a deep draught of this pride. She had been wicked once by inclination, but then she had been wicked as an old-fashioned home-keeping girl. Now her wickedness was her own, at least, and she would not let Claymore take the blame; for when you take the blame you take the credit, too, and the control.

She would be no man's chattel to make or mar.

The blackbirds gave her a contempt for the ideal woman of old, an exultance over being a real woman of new.

She stood and watched the lustrous creatures for a long while. Vance Thompson had squandered some of the opulence of his style on the blackbirds of Los Angeles. Knowing the world as few men know it, he gave the city supreme praise, above Algiers, Tunis, Monte Carlo, or Palermo, "And yet," he wrote, "I've fallen in love with the birds. Especially those grave and beautiful blackbirds. There are a dozen of them on my lawn, I can see them from the window. The gentlemen wear blackly purple cassocks and the ladies are dressed in soft nun-colored brown. And they are so friendly, so clean-stepping, so busy and blithe, that they look like predestined citizens of Los Angeles. Symbols and types. Every city has its birds. Venice has its pigeons of Saint Mark's; Moscow its crows, those secular monks of the Kremlin; Paris has its sparrows, and Stockholm its swans, ah, those black swans of the Djurgården! And your California blackbird is the bird, ideal and appointed, of Los Angeles."

Musing upon the feathered bipeds, the high-stepping Othellos and the drooping Desdemonas of birddom, Mem's mind was soothed of its fevers. But her body grew chill. Her bare ankles brushed a dewy leaf and she fled into the house. The light scourged her wounded eyes.

# CHAPTER XLIV

TWO DAYS LATER SHE began work with Tom Holby's company in a new studio, a great establishment where one could rent space, scenery, all or any portion of a production from manuscripts to distribution.

A number of the farthest-famed stars occasionally made pictures there: Douglas Fairbanks and Mary Pickford, Betty Compson, and many others.

Mem had been lent out to Holby. If she were a slave, she was at least received as a captured Circassian princess might be received by a sultan who had bought her at a high price.

When she appeared on the lot Holby greeted her in person. He led her into his office and described the part she was to play, read her the big scenes.

He bemoaned the artificiality and triteness of the plot. It was warmed over like funeral baked meats. He had longed to do a story adapted from W. J. Locke's novel, *Septimus.*

Holby had wanted to play the simple Septimus. Mem, who had read no novels at all till recently, was horribly illiterate in famous names. But she was wondrously stirred by this story as Holby told it:

Septimus loved a girl who merely liked him. She loved another man, loved him "too well," as the curious saying is. He "betrayed" her, as another curious saying is, and when he had gone beyond her reach she found that she was to become a mother, still using the stock phrases.

Holby noted that Mem was all ashiver over the situation.

He never dreamed that it had been her own, her very own. He thought that he had frightened her prudery and he tried to soften his phrases still more.

But she was uncontrollably agitated when he went on with the plot and told how Septimus, for all his innocence, discovered the cause of the girl's dismay and, knowing all, offered to marry her so that her child might have a name, so that the girl he idolized might not be driven to desperation.

"Are there men like that?" Mem gasped.

Holby looked at her and interpreted her question as a cynicism.

"Oh yes," he answered, earnestly. "There must be lots of men like that. If I loved a girl and found her in such a plight, I think I would I hope I would offer to help her through it. It wouldn't be much of a love that would die at such a situation, would it?"

Mem fell to thinking. A ferocious temptation assailed her to confess to Tom Holby that she had been such a girl herself, but had never dreamed that such a man existed.

Perhaps when Tom Holby had courted her a little there in Palm Canon, if she had not rebuffed and despised him, but had told him the truth, he might have offered her his famous name; they might have been married and she might now be sitting with him in their own home with a living child at her quick breast. The vision shook her like a blast of hot desert wind. Her baby had never seen the world. She had never seen its face. Where had its soul waited and whither had it returned? Had it joined its father in that strange over-grave realm?

For a few mad moments Mem longed to be a wife and mother so insanely that she could hardly check the cry of protest at the denial. She forgot her brave independences of the early morning, her pride in her artistic self-sufficiency. She wanted to be an "old-fashioned woman," to be fed by her husband and to feed his children.

But while the tempest was raging inside her soul, she was so remote from her body that her face had not disclosed her thoughts at all.

What Tom Holby saw was a dreary smile, which he misread as mild disdain for such romantic nonsense.

When she spoke at last she merely asked:

"And why didn't you play Septimus on the screen, as you say you would have done in real life?"

"The censors!" he snarled. "They've got everybody frightened to death. In Pennsylvania and other states you can't even refer to approaching maternity. The producers don't want to make pictures with a big market cut off in advance, so we've got to be more prudish than a Sunday school library.

"The censors seem to feel that if they keep the motion picture audiences from even learning that babies are born of their mothers a great blow will be struck for morality. The books and magazines and newspapers can talk of twilight sleep and birth control and everything, but the poor movies can't even show a young wife sewing on baby clothes.

"But let's not talk of censorship. I froth at the mouth every time I think of the shame and the tyranny and the asininity of it. The story of Septimus would have been beautiful. It is as clean as the parable in the Bible about the woman taken in adultery, and that's given to little girls to read and it's preached in all the pulpits. But on the screen it would immediately send all the audience out to get into trouble. Anyway, I can't do the story and we've had to cook up this mess of denatured realism we're going to do. But, Lord! How I should have loved to play Septimus and have you play the pitiful little girl I would have married. In the story she married Septimus and came to love him so dearly that when she met the other man she hated him."

He fell into a silent while and Mem dreamed tremendous dreams, vain and already frustrated, but beautiful with all the elegies of the might-have-been.

People make love unconsciously at times and in the truest courtships never a word is spoken. Two souls travel mystic gardens together and come to deep understandings without the exchange of a syllabled thought.

Mem was so wooed by Holby. The mere brooding upon him as a lover, a husband, a protector who would once have solved an ugly problem into beauty, presented him to Mem in a light of compelling warmth.

She tried to shake off the spell, but from now on there was an aureole of chivalrous self-sacrifice about Tom Holby that changed him altogether from the flippant, too polite, and far too popular idol of foolish girls that she had rated him.

All through the taking of that picture Mem watched him as from a lattice that hid her from him, but disclosed him to her in the kindliest sun.

The picture had to be made in record time because the producers had limited capital and unlimited experience of the disastrous expense of leisureliness.

The director, Kendrick, was a slave driver, a worshiper of schedules. He demanded that the people be on the set made up, costumed, coiffed, and wide awake, so that the cameras might begin to grind at nine sharp. But he was not so punctual about letting the weary troupers knock off at five. He kept them often till nearly seven.

When Mem's day of toil was over she was so footsore, so soulsore, and had seen so much of Tom Holby and his manufactured love, that she had no inclination to see him of evenings, and he made no effort to see her.

She crept into her bed at nine when she was not kept at the studio for night work. She was called at six and began the day with a long and dreary building up of a false complexion, layer on layer, line by line.

She rarely saw Tom Holby's real face. He also was painted like an Indian brave.

But for all the fatigue and the artifice, there was a feeling of delight and of friendliness on the stages. Cooperation was necessary and it was the custom. The technical problems were innumerable and their discussions as scientific as laboratory debate.

The reward of rewards was the rapture of creation. Nearly all the members of the company would rather act than eat, rather play feigned sorrows than indulge in real joys. They sought for difficult tasks, they were grateful for demands upon their utmost resources. They sulked only when their toil was diminished or they were left out of a scene or not taxed to their limit.

Mem's affair with Tom Holby was settling down into the pleasant but drab relationship of two business partners. They were as friendly already as an old married couple without ever having known the initiatory rites.

But in this dull fact there lurked a resentful, impatient peril.

# CHAPTER XLV

THERE WAS MUCH SKYLARKING on the set, a childlike spontaneity of wit and cynicism, and an inexhaustible fascination of craft.

Mem was becoming something of a technician. The mechanics, the artisanship that sustains every art, the alphabets of expression, the wireless codes for the transmission of emotion, its creation in a transmitter, its preparation for the receivers all these things no artist can ignore and succeed.

The more eloquence the orator feels in his heart the more he considers his tones. The more earnest the writer the more piously he cons his dictionary. The more glorious the singer the more he studies his breath control, his coups de glotte, his white notes, his transition colors. The more fervid the composer the more he ponders acoustics and tone combinations and the inventions of new instruments. The more eager the painter the more he analyzes his values, the more he seeks new tubes, new brushes, new chemistries of color.

Only the amateur, the dawdler, the dilettante despises his craft and depends on passion or that egotistic whim he calls inspiration.

So the ambitious actor must experiment always with the tools of thought, the engines of suffering.

Once when Mem was shocked at a flippancy of Tom Holby's concerning his art, he rebuked her earnestly:

"You're not really well acquainted with your art unless you can joke about it. What's funnier than the idea that being funny is not as serious as being solemncholy? There was never a finer actor than Nat Goodwin, and I heard him say once, speaking of his Shylock: 'I was great in the last act. I knew I was great because the audience was weeping and I was guying it, and when you can guy a serious scene you've got to be great.'"

Mem began to understand also, but slowly, that making fun of one's serious emotions is a form of modesty, a covering of nakedness, a shy retreat behind a mask of smiles.

She began to be able to talk flippantly of her art and to talk of it in trade terms.

One day when she was posing for a big close-up of herself asleep, the director asked her to try to squeeze a tear or two through her great clenched eyelids. She startled even him by saying, with an elfin earnestness:

"What kind do you want? One great big slow teardrop, or a lot of little shiny ones?"

He was shocked, but he hid his own sense of sacrilege in a careless:

"Give me one large tear about five-eighths of an inch in diameter."

"Alright," she said.

And she did. It oozed through her long lashes and slipped reluctantly down her cheek into her hair. And, knowing what he knew of its control, he felt his own eyes wet, and the jaded camera man whispered, awesomely, "Great!"

In another scene, where more tears were required of her, he noted that while she waited for the camera setup she had her hands gabled at her lips and she seemed to be whispering to herself.

Curious, he asked, "What are you up to now?"

She gazed at him. "I was praying God to send me beautiful tears."

He shook his head and walked away, gasping.

One afternoon the chief financial power in Tom Holby's company saw Mem pacing up and down by herself at a distance from the set. He watched her and noted that she leaned against a canvas wall and hid her head in her arm. Her shoulders quivered and shook with forlorn woe.

His heart was touched and he could not resist an impulse to go to her and proffer his sympathy in her evident grief. He touched her on the arm and asked, with an almost mothering solicitude:

"You poor child! What's the matter?"

She whirled on him in surprise and stared through a shower of tears. Then a smile broke from her blubbering lips and she giggled:

"Oh, I'm just getting ready for a big crying scene."

He fell back as if he had touched a serpent. He was disgusted with himself for making such a fool of himself and wasting his precious pity on a little trickster.

The climax of Mem's shamelessness was reached one day when Robina Teele and the great Miriam Yore visited the studio and stopped for lunch in the commissary. Mem was put on her mettle by the grandiose condescension of Miss Yore and by the suspicious jealousy of Robina Teele.

The matter of tears for sale came up and Miss Yore spoke of how she got hers.

"I find that if I use the tone of voice intentionally which I use unintentionally when I am really crying, the tears come. It may be just muscle memory or it may be that I grow very sorry for myself. "

Robina did not know how she got hers.

"Margaret Anglin said she could cry at will over a fried egg or anything. So can I. I just imagine the scene and say to myself, 'Cry!' And I cry till the director says, 'Cut!'"

Neither of the famous women thought to ask the rising Miss Steddon how she manipulated her lachrymal art. Tom Holby, feeling that she was slighted, brought her into it by asking her her system.

"Prayer and brute strength," said Mem.

Robina was in an assertive mood, and, as one violinist might challenge another to a concerto or an orator propose a debate to another, she called for a duel of tears. She thought she could send Miss Yore back to the grand opera she had come from.

"Let's have a crying contest," she said.

"I should have to have music, " said Miss Yore.

"Come over on my set and we'll give you your favorite tune," said Holby. He dragged Remember Steddon along, though the two veterans did not take her into account.

Holby explained to the director that they were to have a field day of emotion, and he consented to defer the scene he was about to shoot.

Miss Yore wanted the theme of the "Liebestod" played over and over. The wheezy little portable organ made a sad mess of Wagner's braided harmonies, but the violinist caught the cry of the melody.

Robina could cry best for "Just a Song at Twilight," but she gracefully yielded the choice of music to Miss Yore.

Mem had never heard an opera, grand or comic. But the strangely climbing anguish of the tune caught her up on its pinions, and lifted her into that ether where the souls of imaginative artists fly in all disguises and assume all personalities.

The rest of the company and the crew stood aloof and watched in amazement as the two world-famous stars and the rising young asteroid, Mem, began to war with their own features like athletes tuning up or shadowboxing.

The three women walked apart for a moment, grimacing and forcing themselves into a state of agony. Robina achieved the first sob. She broke and flung herself on a couch and sobbed aloud. Mem jealously decided that she was cheating and rather looked down on her shoulder-work. It was pumpy.

She stared at Miriam Yore, an ambulant statue of heroic postures, lifting her hands to heaven, carrying them clasped to her fulsome bosom, and indulging in the despair of a Medea or a Cornwall princess whose draperies must also weep about her beautifully.

In Mem's eyes Miss Yore was as stagy as Miss Teele was screeny. Neither of them seemed quite human. Grief to Mem was a homely, unlovely, tearing, disordering thing. To cry gracefully was not to cry at all.

She was the realist, the small-town girl whose heart gives way, whose features crumple, whose eyes blear and reek with bitter, devastating brine.

The onlookers called Robina wonderful. They called Miss

Yore beautiful. They paid the untimely tribute of admiration. But when Remember Steddon abruptly flopped into a chair like a flung rag doll, and began to choke and snivel, to dab at her eyes and wrinkle her chin, to fight and hate the spurting tears, to sway her head in futile protest, to give vent to ugly little rasping noises that seemed to saw her throat raw and to grow extraordinarily homely and pitiful, the spectators felt a something familiar out of their own childhood, out of their own old lonelinesses and defeats. Their own faces puckered, their hearts were nests of pain, their eyes went dank and were blurred.

They gave her the ultimate tribute of sympathy and echoed her misery.

Miss Teele stopped crying to stare. Miss Yore ceased her magnificent stride. Both forgot to be artists. Before they realized that Mem had not really broken down in a genuine grief they had surrendered the battle and were crying with her.

And she, having set in motion the wheels of sorrow, could not stop them. There is so much to regret in this world and in any life, that it is perilous to start the tears rolling, lest they crush the soul.

Her triumph astonished Mem and all the witnesses. But she was almost destroyed with her own victory. She was sick and ashamed of the blasphemy of her abuse of such holy things as tears.

Afterward, however, she could laugh again, and when Tom Holby told her that she had wiped the earth up with her two rivals it was a thrilling thing to hear.

The contest was the talk of the whole studio, and the publicity man sent broadcast, to the enlargement of Mem's fame, her brilliant étude in tears.

It was all working toward her glory as a mistress of emotions.

# CHAPTER XLVI

THE DIRECTOR, KENDRICK, was in a desperate frenzy to complete the picture. The hard times were reducing the incomes of the producers and exhibitors at a terrifying rate.

The apathy that accompanies all financial depressions sickened the public appetite for everything. The critics were saying that the emptiness of the theaters was due to the stupidity of the plays, but just as stupid plays had prospered mightily when the boom was at its height. The critics were likewise saying that the moving pictures were unworthy of the patronage they were not getting. But the fault was with the public dyspepsia and not with the cooks.

In any case, the vast cinematic industry was in as serious a plight as the steel, the copper, the lumber, and all the other giant industries.

In spite of the ferocious slashes in salaries, wages, sets, most of the studios were declaring holidays of a month or more.

The orders had gone forth to rush the Holby picture to a conclusion. The big night storm scenes had been scheduled for the final takes. They would appear early in the story, but too many accidents might happen if they were shot in sequence. It would be lamentable if any of the actors were injured at any time, but it would be disastrous to have an arm or a head broken or a case of pneumonia in the middle of the work. It had happened. Actors occasionally died with extravagant inopportunity, or broke bones, or marred countenances that could not be matched or replaced. The expense of some of these mishaps was appalling, with an overhead of two thousand dollars a day.

On the final morning the first scenes were begun promptly at nine. Kendrick promised to let the company go at three to rest for the all-night grind, but delays of every sort occurred. A light would flicker during an important scene. In a close-up one of the characters would swerve outside the narrow space allotted.

When the actors were again attuned and the director was impatient to cry, "Camera!" one of the camera men would find that he had not film enough and a new magazine must be fetched.

Such inevitable, incessant delays were peculiarly irritating to a company on the razor edge of emotion, but there was rarely an outburst. Emotion, being property, was conserved. There is probably no class of people who act so rarely as actors.

The general opinion to the contrary is, like most general opinions, based on ignorance.


At three o'clock there were still many scenes unshot. The work continued and it was not until half past seven that the day's work was done. The "rushes" of the day before were still to be inspected in the projection room, whither the company scampered.

It was eight o'clock before anyone could stop for dinner. The actors were not considered, but the work crews had to be humored. Some of them were members of unions and it was a legal peril also to keep extra people at work more than eight hours in a day.

Tom Holby and Mem sought their dinner in a little shack near the studio. They perched on stools and ate T-bone steaks, fried potatoes, doughnuts, and coffee with the voracity of longshoremen.

At nine they went to the first of the sets. The Californian night was black and bitter cold. The night in the story was one of tempest and battle. Tom Holby must run an automobile into a ditch and make a desperate war against four brutes who were instructed to put up a good fight.

The public would not stand a mock engagement. Fists had to land. Heads had to rock, and when a man fell he must fall. He must go over with a crash wherever the blow sent him.

The actors wanted it so.

Tom Holby expected to end the night bleeding, bruised, tattered, and mud-smeared. He had cracked many a bone and lost a tooth or two on such gala occasions; and once he had splintered the bones of his right hand when his fist missed the face it was aimed at and struck the stone beneath it.

Mem's share in the hurricane was to run through the wildest of the storm and bring rescue.

Such scenes in the movies are often railed at as cheap sensationalism, yet they are heroic art. In an epic poem, or a classic drama, they are accounted the height of achievement. Winslow Homer's high seas, Conrad's gorgeous simooms, are lauded as triumphs of genius. The author rifles the dictionary and guts his thesaurus, the painter wrecks his palette and his brushes, and is celebrated as of the grand school. When the moving picture geniuses likewise exhaust a vocabulary of mechanical effects, and spread before the world visions of beautiful drama, the critics pass by with averted gaze.

Mem had five scenes to dash through. Her pilgrimage was to be a sort of *Pippa Passes*, but she was not to go singing; she was to be stormed upon as Sebald and Ottima were.

Each bit of scenery through which she was to flash had been made ready the day before. Three long perforated rain pipes were erected on scaffolds and connected with the standpipes, and they were reinforced by men who would play a fire hose or two upon the hapless actress. The gale was to be provided by an airplane engine and propeller mounted on a truck.

Mem, suffering the chill of the night especially because of fatigue and excitement, inspected the settings she was so briefly to adorn.

"Why do they build that fence around the wind machine? " she asked Kendrick.

To keep people from walking into the propeller and getting chopped to mincemeat," said Kendrick. "My assistant was engaged on three pictures where airplane propellers were used, and a man was killed in each one of them. In one of them an airship caught fire and fell during a night picture. He was the first man to reach the aviator. He picked up the poor fellow's hot hand and his arm came off. It was charred like Excuse me!"

Mem gasped and retreated from the rest of it, and she kept as far as possible from the giant fan. The propeller made a deafening uproar when it was set in motion, and it churned the air into a small vertical cyclone.

Caught in the first gust of it, Mem was driven like an autumn leaf with skirts whipping away from her.

In her first scene she was to dash from a house and down its steps. First, the men with the fire hose soaked the shell of the house, the porch, and the steps, and the ground about them till they were all flooded. Then the rain machine was tested and sent its three showers from overhead.

The wind machine was set in motion and the air was filled with sheets of driven rain. The lightning machine added the thunder of its leaping sparks to the turmoil.

Kendrick, in thigh boots and a trench coat he had worn in France, went to the porch to test the storm. In his hand he carried an electric button with a cable to the lightning machine. This rang a bell for the man in charge of it. The noisy wind machine was controlled by wigwag signals with his hand.

The director was a god in little. He could bid the rain rain, the wind roar, and the lightning blaze. He rode upon the storm he created.

At first the storm was too mild for his taste. At his command it was aggravated until he could not stand up before it. Gradually he achieved the exact magnitude of violence, and the men in control of the forces of imitated nature understood that thus far they must go and no farther.

Under a vast umbrella, and behind shields of black flats called "niggers," the battery of camera men stood arranging focuses and lights. Two of them used lenses that would make close-ups, while the others caught the long shots, for there would be no chance of taking special close-ups.

After an hour or more of harrowing delay the army was ready for the battle. Mem climbed up the scaffolding back of the palatial front door and porch. The assistant director explained the signal he was to relay from the director, and the storm was ordered to begin.

A gentle rain fell from the pipes. The fire hose, aimed up in the air, added its volume. The wind machine set up its mad clatter. The rain became a deluge of flying water and the lightning filled it with shattering fire.

Then Mem was called forth. She clutched her cloak about her and thrust into the tempest. It was like driving through a slightly rarefied cataract. She hardly reached the pillar at the edge of the porch, clutched it for a moment, caught a quick breath, and flung down the steps. And that was that. All this preparation for one minute of action save for a brief return to the porch to pose for still photographs.

She was dripping and so lost that she ran into one of the property men, who checked her. Kendrick came to her and gave her an accolade of approval. He patted her sopping shoulder and said:

"Fine! But in the next scene hold your cloak about you a little tighter. The wind was so stormy and your clothes so wet that there wasn't much of you left to the imagination. In some of the states the censors may cut the whole scene out. But we won't retake it."

When, two days later, Mem saw the rushes in the projection room, she could hardly believe that the storm was a matter of such clumsy artifice. The reality of it fairly terrified her. The rainswept porch and the fury of lightnings about the pillars gave no hint of human devising.

She felt a surge of pity at the bravery of the little figure she made plunging into the wrack on her errand of rescue. The gale flung her cloak and her skirts about her in fleeting sculptures of Grecian beauty. But when she paused at the edge of the steps and staggered under the buffets of the wind, she was aghast to see herself modeled in the least detail like the clay of a statue, all the more nude for the emphasis of a few wrinkles in a framing drapery. She felt her first sympathy for Miss Bevans' prudery and blushed in the dark projection room. She did not at all approve the groan of the director.

"Wonderful! It's like an ivory statue on an ebony back ground. To think that the dirty-minded censors will call it indecent, the blackguards!"

Mem hoped that the company's own censors would excise it before the outside world saw it; but she said nothing. She belonged to her art, body as well as soul.

But this revelation was for a later day. For the present, the director's caution to keep her cloak about her was alarming enough.

She was taken to a warm room and wrapped in blankets while the next scene was prepared. This was a matter of another hour's delay. Rain pipes had already been erected, but the lights had to be trundled into place, the cameras placed and protected, and a hundred details made ready before she was called out again.

Holby and Kendrick were solicitous for her and asked if she was chilled. She laughed. The adventure kindled her youthful arteries.

It was not so pleasant to stand still and have the firehose lifted above her. She was supposed to have run a long distance between the porch steps and this scene, and she must enter it wet.

She had a bit of chill in this shower bath and there was a hitch in starting. But at length she got her signal and went forward again, head down, into the wild storm. The propeller ran too fast and she could not proceed. She clung to a wall and tugged in vain. The blast carried her cloak entirely away and she had no protection from the ruthless scrutiny of the lightning or the unedited records of the cameras.

The noise was so appalling that the director ripped his throat in vain. He had to run to the wind machine and check it. The picture had to be taken over. Mem's cloak was recovered, and the mud washed from it. Then it was laid clammily about her icy shoulders and she made another try.

This time the result was better, and she returned to the room and her blankets for another hour. She could not seem to get warm. Her bones were like pipes in which the marrow froze.

When she went out again Kendrick asked her how she was. Her teeth chattered together as she said, "All right-t-t-t." He looked at her with sympathy and admiration, and he decided to cut out one of the most promising scenes, lest it overtax her strength.

During her absence a telephone pole and a tree had been brought down by the storm and photographed as they fell. It was her business now to clamber across the pole and push through the branches of the tree, and so fight her way out of the picture.

The rain pipes had been brought forward and set up in a new position. The cameras were aligned. Next them stood a truck containing a great sun arc. Next that was the lightning machine, abreast of it the wind machine.

In the preliminary tests it had been hard to find the right angle for the gale to blow from, and the wind machine had been shifted several times. The wind man in his confusion forgot to notice that the property men had forgotten, in their confusion, to set up the fence before the propeller. It was after midnight now and everybody was numb with cold, drenched with the promiscuous rain, and a little irresponsible. Their working day was already fifteen hours old and it would last at least five hours more.

The spectators who had gathered to watch the first scenes had been driven from the lot by the cold their thick cloaks and overcoats could not overcome. Tom Holby had been photographed in a climb up the wet sides of a ravine, and was half-frozen in his soaked clothes, but he stayed to watch Mem through this scene.

He was palsied in the bundled wraps about him and his heart ached as he saw Mem in her little wet dress throw off her blankets, put on the dreadful mantle of the wet cape, and go out into the distant dark beyond the range of the cameras.

The storm broke out anew at the director's signal. The wind bellowed and slashed the branches of the prostrate tree. The lightning snapped and flared and its flare winnowed the rain in flaming wraiths.

Then from the dark the little sorrowful figure of Remember Steddon appeared, a ghost materializing from the night. She struggled with the maniac hurricane, stumbled and fell across the telephone pole, thrust aside the wires, lifted herself and breasted the wind again, drove into the wreck of the fallen tree. The branches whipped her wet flesh cruelly. The lightning just ahead of her blistered her vision like the white-hot irons driven into the eyes of Shakespeare's Prince Clarence. The wind blew her breath back into her lungs. If she had not gained a little support from one stout bough of the tree she could never have reached the margin of the picture.

Kendrick's heart was glad with triumph as he saw her pass out of the camera range. He called, "Cut!" and the camera men were jubilant as each of them shouted "O.K. for me!"

Then Kendrick heard screams of terror, wild howls of fear. He ran forward and saw the blinded little figure of Mem still pressing on straight into the blur of the airplane propeller.

His heart sickened. She would be sliced to shreds. She could not hear the yelled warnings in the noise of the machine.

# CHAPTER XLVII

THE OPERATOR SHUT OFF his engine, but the propellers still swirled at a speed that made them only a whorl of light. The witnesses were paralyzed by the horror of the moment.

Tom Holby broke from a nightmare that outran the immediate beauty of the little woman walking forward to a hideous fate. He ran and dived for her like a football tackler, hooked his left arm about her knees and flung her backward, thrusting his right arm and his head beneath her, so that when she struck, her shoulders were upon his breast, her drenched hair fell across his face like seaweed.

She opened her eyes in a chaos of bewilderment. Just above her the flying propeller blades were glistening in the light of the sun arc.

They were still revolving when the wind machine man, leaping from the post where he had stood expecting her fate and his own eternal remorse, ran to lift her from the ground. Others helped up Tom Holby.

He had knocked himself unconscious when his head struck a rock in the road. His cheek was ripped and gushing blood.

He came to his senses at once and forced a ghastly laugh.

Mem screamed with fear for him. She had not yet realized her own escape. She was all pity for Tom Holby, and anxiety.

"It's nothing," he said. Then he staggered with dread of what Mem would have looked like now if he had waited an instant longer or missed his aim at her knees.

He drew her from the vortex of the propeller, which was subsiding with the dying snarl of a leopard that has missed its pounce.

Now Mem understood what her own adventure had been, and her knees weakened with an ex post facto alarm.

Kendrick came up and, after a decent wait for the incident to have its dignity and move on, he thanked and congratulated Holby on retrieving the girl from massacre.

"It wouldn't have meant only the horrible death of this beautiful child, but it would have meant also the horrible death of this beautiful picture; for hardly anybody would have wanted to see it if it were stained with blood."

"And all my beautiful art would have perished with me!" said Mem, with only partial irony. She had reached the estate of the creative soul who longs for the immortality of its work more than itself, and feels it a death indeed, a death entire, to have its record lost.

Just to have a book in a library, even if it is never read; just to have a painting on some wall; a tune in somebody's ears, a scientific discovery recorded somewhere — that is honey enough in the ashes that fill the mouth of the morituri.

Kendrick's next thought was one of dismay. Tom Holby had not yet fought his big fight, and yet his face was torn. How was this to be explained in the preceding scene where he was supposed to leave the arms of his sweetheart in her defense?

In the topsy-turvyness of film construction the scene in which Mem and Tom Holby were set upon by a pack of ruffians had not yet been taken, though Mem had already almost completed the scenes in which she ran to call distant strangers to Tom's rescue.

After a long while of puzzling Kendrick decided to make an effort to photograph Holby so that his damaged jowl should be hidden by Mem's face or by shadows. It would be hard to manage and the men who had promised to beat Holby up to the best of their ability would hesitate to pummel a man already so hurt.

But to put the fight off till the cheek was healed would cost the company a thousand dollars at least.

When Mem understood all the trouble it had cost to snatch her from destruction, she said:

"I'm not worth it."

Kendrick was in no mood for polite denials, but Tom Holby gave her a look that made the fishing worthwhile.

Mem was blanketed like a racehorse and taken to her dressing room once more. She slipped her wet clothes off and dried them and herself by the fire while she waited for the next foray into the storm.

After that was to come the attack by the desperadoes and her flight for help. She had seen many pictures in which the heroine stood about wringing her hands idly while her lover fought for her with some worthless brute. She had always despised a heroine who would not take up a chair or something and bash in the head of her lover's opponent instead of playing the wallpaper.

She protested now against having to run away from the scene, but Kendrick grew a trifle sarcastic:

"The company doesn't require you to rewrite the scenarios, Miss Steddon; only to act in them. Besides, there are half a dozen villains here, and I really think you'd better run out of the scene, seeing that we've already spent half the night and all of our nerves showing you going for rescuers."

Mem was sufficiently snubbed, and apologized so meekly that Kendrick was still furious.

"And for God's sake don't play the worm! The story is rotten and your criticism is perfectly just, but we poor directors and actors have to do our best with the putrid stuff the office hands us."

Men stood about and watched the fight. It was a magnificent or a loathsome spectacle, according to the critic. When Vergil describes an old-fashioned battle with wooden boxing gloves macerating the opposing features, it is accepted as of epic nobility. The movies give the real blood instead of nouns and knock out teeth with primeval dentistry.

The actors who assaulted Holby were tender of his raw cheek at first, but both he and Kendrick demanded action, and after Holby had smashed a few noses with the effect of knocking corks out of claret bottles, there was anger enough.

The one caution Kendrick shrieked through his megaphone was not to knock Holby senseless and not to knock him out of the camera's range.

The cameramen were tilting and panning their machines to keep the action within the picture, and they were howling contradictory messages to the fighters.

There was none of the arena ardor in Mem's soul. She was none of the girls who watched gladiators butchered, or thrilled to Inquisitional processions, or went to modern prize fights.

She was so sickened by the noise of the blows, and the spurt of blood, and that most desperate drama of all: when strong men batter each other in rage, that she had to retreat into the cold morning air out of sight and hearing of the buffets that seemed to land on her own tender flesh.

The dawn was just pinking the sky when the last of the night work was over. Everybody was dead-beaten. The crews would have to remain after the actors had gone, and the actors had finished a twenty-one-hour day of grilling emotion and physical toil.

The chauffeur who took Mem home in an automobile told her that he had already had twenty four hours of driving and would have four or five hours more. She expected him to collide with almost anything, but his eyes still attended their office.

It was seven o'clock when Mem crept into her bed, an hour later than she had usually wakened. Her alarm clock stared at her with rebuke, but she gave it a day off and slept till nightfall.

The next day the company gathered to see the rushes of the night stuff. Almost all of them were perfect, vivid, dramatic with the chiaroscuro of lightning upon midnight storm, and incredibly real.

A strange feeling came over her and over the others when they saw the various takes of the scene in which she clambered across the fallen telephone pole, pushed through the branches of the toppled tree, and pressed on into the teeth of the gale. For just beyond the point of her exit from the picture the wind machine was waiting. She had been hurrying headlong to destruction and never dreamed of her peril.

Kendrick sighed, "That came near being a portrait of you walking out of this world."

Tom Holby did not speak, but he reached out and, seizing Mem's hand, wrung it with an eloquence beyond words. He seemed to be squeezing her heart with clinging hands.

There were five takes of this bit, and Mem began only now to understand the hazard she had incurred, to comprehend how close she was to annihilation, to the end of her days upon this beautiful world.

It came upon her like a confrontation of death. What an unbelievable thing it was! For all of being the most familiar thing in life, the one experience that nobody could escape, man, animal, plant. As that tree had fallen so she would have lost her roots in the good earth. As the telephone wires of the prostrate pole had gone dead, so the thrill would have ebbed out of her nerves; everything beautiful, gracious, voluptuous, would have been denied her. She would have been void even of the precious privilege of pain.

The old Greeks joked about the simpleton, the philosopher, who had wanted to know how he looked when he was asleep and had held a mirror before him and shut his eyes. But she had seen herself asleep on the screen, and now she had seen herself marching into her grave.

The vision was intolerable to her. It assailed her like a nightmare. It drove her frantic to make the most of life, to taste every one of its sweets, its bitters, its glories and shames, each tang of existence. To experience and to make others experience! She must be quick about it, for who could tell what moment would be the last? For the sake of other people she must live at full speed from now on, act many pictures, briskly, brilliantly, hurriedly, so that she should not waste a grain of the sand speeding through the hour glass.

As she watched the last of the takes her heart surged with anguish for that strange girl she was there, struggling against the wind, fighting her way out of a little inconvenience into destruction.

It seemed to her that she typified all girl-kind, all womanhood, all humanhood, passion-swept, love-urged, braving obstacles, defying every restraint and stumbling on into the lightning, into the lurking horror, running blithely, blindly into the ambush that every path prepares.

She was consumed with an impatience to begin a new picture at once, and to be very busy with life and love, beauty and delight.

And yet there is always an "and yet." The yets follow in incessant procession, treading one another's heels.

And yet, when Tom Holby, after they had left the lot, asked her to ride with him for a bit of air, and swept her to the perfect opportunity of bliss, her soul balked.

He was handsome, brave, magnetic, chivalrous, devoted. He had leaped into danger to seize her out of it. He bore in his cheek a scar that would mar him for life, perhaps, as his badge of courage.

His big racing car, like a fleet stallion, had galloped them far from the eyes of witnesses into a sunset of colossal tenderness, with a sky flushed as delicately as a girl's cheek, yet as huge as a universe.

They sped along "the rim of the world" with desert on one side and the whole Pacific sea on the other. The world was below them for their observation and they were concealed by distance.

And yet, when Tom Holby told her he adored her and that she was adorable; when he courted her with deference and meekness and pleaded for a little kindness, her heart froze in her. She could not even accept a proffered beatitude.

She looked at him and thought and said:

"Too many people love you, Tommy. You belong to the public, and you couldn't bring yourself down to really loving little me."

"Oh, but I could! I do!" he cried. "Damn my public! I don't care for anything but you."

She was not quite serious and not quite insincere when she answered:

"But I haven't had my public yet, and I love it. I want it. If I ever grow as tired of it as you have done of yours, then we might see each other. But just now the only love I can feel is acted love."

"Then let's have a rehearsal," he suggested, cynically. But she shook her head and laughed. She could not tell why she laughed, but, having tasted mirth, she decided that that was what she had chiefly missed in life and what she needed most.

Her home had been nearly devoid of gaiety except of an infantile, ecclesiastical sort. Her father had been one of those who could never think of Christ as wearing any smile but one of pity or forgiveness. A laughing Messiah was incredible, horrible. And as her father's chief aim in life was to fill life with religion, hilarity with its inevitable skepticism had no part at home.

Since she had left her home on the most dismal of pilgrimages, Mem had given herself chiefly to the earnest, the passionate emotions.

And now she felt like a desert suddenly dreaming of rain.

"I want to laugh, Tommy," she cried. "Amuse me, make me laugh!"

But Holby was no wit. He had an abundance of wholesome fun in his nature, and he roared when he was tickled, but he was not a comedian, a humorist, or an inventor of risible material.

He shook his head and could not even think of a funny story, at least of none that he dared tell Mem.

He was as willing to escape from her in her present mood as she from him, and he said:

"There's the new Charlie Chaplin comedy. We might get in."

"Let's try," said Mem. "I've just realized that what I'm really dying for is a good laugh, lots of good wild laughs at I don't care what."

Holby swung his car round and returned toward Los Angeles.

"Tommy," said Mem, "what is comedy? What is it that makes a thing funny?"

"Search me!" said Holby. "I don't know."

"Neither do I," Mem pondered. "But I'm sick of all these crying scenes and emoting all over the place. I want to be a comedienne. Do you think I could be one?"

"I don't think so," said Holby, with scientific candor. "You never made me laugh. You don't laugh much."

"No, but I'm going to. I think if I ever love anybody really, it will be a great comedian. Do you know any comedians who aren't married, Tommy?"

"Lots of 'em," said Holby. "A sense of humor keeps a man from getting married or staying married long."

Mem laughed at that. She did not know why. Perhaps because he had said it so dolefully. Perhaps because it was a sudden tipping over of something solemn. She had spent her life getting ready for the holiness of matrimony. She had made a wreck of her ideal and had dwelt in a hell of shame and remorse for the sacrilege.

And now Tommy had implied that it wasn't so very sacred, after all. He had slipped a banana peel under a dismal ideal and it had hit the ground with a bump. The whole world looked gayer to her, as if someone had flashed on a light.

She hoped the automobile would not be wrecked before she had this huge laugh that was waiting for her. And somewhere in a clown's uniform was waiting, she was sure, the man or the career that would illuminate all her existence. A good laugher would be a good lover.

Making people cry and educating them in the agonies of sympathy was a silly sort of ambition. What fools people were to pay money to be tortured!

But to be made to laugh — that was worth any price. To make people laugh in the little while between the two glooms before birth and after death, to love and live laughing, that was to defy sorrow and to make a joke of fate.

# CHAPTER XLVIII

NOTHING COULD REVEAL the extreme youth and the swift maturity of the moving pictures like the career of Charles Chaplin. For a few years he was a byword of critical condemnation for his buffoonery, a proof of the low public taste. Suddenly he was hailed as one of the master artists of time. It was not he that had improved, or the public. It was the critics who were educated in spite of themselves to the loftiness of buffoonery and the fine genius of Chaplin. The public had loved him from the start.

He was at this moment in Europe meeting such a welcome as few other visiting monarchs ever got. Mobs blocked the streets where he progressed until the police had to rescue him. Their Eminences of literature and statecraft pleaded with him for interviews. Lloyd George begged for a comedy of Charlie's to help him, as Abraham Lincoln leaned on Artemus Ward.

And yet he was just out of his twenties and, only a dozen years or so before, he had left England as the humblest of acrobats and the least known of her emigrants, as ignored as he was himself ignorant of the new-born American-made art that was to lift him to universal glory.

His picture, *The Kid*, had been hailed as a work of the noblest quality, rich in pathos as in hilarity. Solemn editorials proclaimed him the supreme dramatic artist of his generation.

He was a household word about the world, a millionaire, and as familiar to the children as Santa Claus. He had become a Santa Chaplin to the grownups.

Yet numberless raucous asses who were quite as solemn as Charlie, but not so profitably or amusingly asinine, were still hee-hawing the old bray that the moving pictures were not an art, but only an industry. Of course it all depended on one's own private definition of the indefinable word "art," and it was quite overlooked by those who denied the word to the Movia that if it were only an industry, it was a glorious industry. Mark Twain decided that if Shakespeare's plays were not written by Shakespeare, they were written by someone else of the same name. So if the movies are not an art, they are something else quite as artistic.

To Remember Steddon they were her first language for expressing her turbulent self. To her they were philosophy and criticism of life; painting and sculpture given motion and infinite velocity with perfect record. They were many wonderful things to Mem as to the myriads of bright spirits that had flocked to this new banner, golden calf, or brazen serpent, as you will. And now Mem, having tasted of the sorrows of the movies, was athirst for the light wine. Clowning at its best is a supernal wisdom, and Chaplin's *The Idle Class* was full of laughter that had an edge, a comment on humanity, a rejoinder, if not an answer, to the riddles of existence and its conduct.

He played a dual role in this picture, both a swell and the tramp he had made as classic as Pierrot. According to what plot there was, the aristocratic loafer and tippler of the first impersonation forgot to meet his wife at the train, the train on which the tramp had stolen a ride to his favorite resort.

There was mockery not only of pompous toffery, but of serious emotion as well. When the besotted young swell receives from his neglected wife a letter saying that she will never see him again until he stops drinking, he turns away, and his shoulders seem to be agitated with sobs of remorse. But when he turns round it is seen to be a cocktail that he is shaking.

The jester was tweaking the nose of love and repentance and bringing all the high ideals off the shelf with a bang. The audience, bullied a little too well by trite nobilities, roared with emancipation.

Again when he dresses in a suit of armor for the costume ball, he cannot resist one more cocktail. But just as he lifts it to drain the glass the visor of his helmet snaps down and will not be opened for all his frantic struggles and the painful efforts of those who come to his aid. The least intellectual spectator shouting at his antics could not but feel the satirical allegory of all life, wherein the visor always falls and locks when the brim is at the lip.

But the triumph of joyous cynicism was the last flash. The big brute who has roughly handled and despised the ragged tramp repents of his cruelty and runs to humble himself in apology. The tramp listens to his beautiful self-abasement and everyone expects a gracious finish, but the incorrigible clown gives the penitent a kick in the behind, and runs away.

Bitter philosophy it was and shocking to the best principles, yet it was a flash of the pride that rewards condescension and patronage and mawkish charity with a kick in the tail and takes to flight. It pictured what everyone in the audience had often wanted to do in those resentful moods which are so very human because they are so far from divine. For the soul, like the body, needs its redemption from too much sweetness as well as from too much bitterness. There is a diabetes from unassimilated sugar that is as fatal as too much salt.

And that is the noble service that farce and clownery render to the world. They guarantee the freedom of the soul, freedom not only from glooms and despairs, but from the tyrannies of bigotry as well, from the outrages of religion, of groveling idolatries, all sorts of good impulses and high principles that ought to be respected but not revered, ought to be used in moderation but not with slavish awe.

Going to a farce of such a sort was, for Remember Steddon, going to a school of the highest educational value; it was a lessoning in life that she sorely needed.

She had been taking life and love and art and ambition and sin morosely.

Tom Holby found her already changed when they set out for her home. She had been restlessly unapproachable before the comedy, like a mustang that will not submit to the bridle, will not run far, but will not be taken; that stands and waits with a kindly air, but, just as the hand reaches out, whirls and bolts.

Now that she had seen the picture she was serene. She was genial, amiable. She snuggled close to Holby in the car, and yet when he spoke tenderly she made fun of him, giggled, reminded him of bits of the picture that had amused her. This enraged him.

"I'm going in for comedy," she said. "It's the only thing worthwhile. All this tears and passion business makes me sick. I'd love to have it so that when anybody hears my name he smiles. Wouldn't it be glorious to have a washerwoman look up from her tub and say: 'Remimber Steddon? Och, yis, I seen her in a pitcher once and I laughed till I cried.' Wouldn't it be glorious to have the tired business man say to his tired society wife: 'I've got the blues, and so have you. There's one of Steddon's pictures in town. For God's sake let's go see it and have a good laugh!' Wouldn't that be a wonderful thing to stand for?"

Holby made a grunting sound that implied, "I suppose so, if you think so." He added, after a silence: "Funny thing, though; more people get relief from a good cry than from a good laugh. If you have tears to shed, and you go laugh your head off at some damfoolishness, you'll find the tears are still there when you get home. But if you see Camille or Juliet or some pathetic thing, if you watch some imaginary person's misery and cry over it, you'll find your own tears are gone."

"That may be true," said Mem, "but all the same I'd like to take a whack at comedy."

Holby fought out in his soul a decent battle of self-sacrifice before he brought himself to the height of recommending a rival. "There's Ned Ling; he's looking for a pretty leading woman. He's not Chaplin, but he's awfully funny in his own way and he's getting a big following. He usually gets engaged to his leading lady; saves money that way, they say. If you're so hell bent on a comic career get your agent to go after him."

"Ned Ling," she mused. "Yes, I've seen him. He's funny. He might do. I may make a try at him a little later. Just now I feel all tuckered out. I want to get away from the studios, out into the high sierras. I believe I'll buy a little car and go all by myself."

But when she reached her home there was something waiting in ambush for her: a letter from her father. And this was not farce, nor to be greeted with a kick and a run.

"Oh, I was wondering if you would ever come!" her mother wailed as Mem came laughing in the door, still laughing at Chaplin's blithe rebuff to maudlin penances.

It was odd to be greeted so by the patient little woman who irritated Mem oftenest by her meek patience.

"I was so worried for fear you had had some accident. Why couldn't you have telephoned me?"

"I told you I might be detained at the studio, mamma, and not to expect me till you saw me," Mem answered, and had not the courage to tell the rest of the truth.

"Oh, I know! I oughtn't to a worried, but I'm a nuisance to myself and to you and to everybody."

There she was again! Taking that maddening tone of self-reproach. But Mem simply could not rebuke her for it. She embraced her and held her tight, instead.

"It was all because of a letter I had from your father. If you had come home sooner I wouldn't have mentioned it to you, maybe! Heaven knows you have trouble enough, and now I'm sorry I spoke. Just forget it."

Then ensued a long battle over the letter, Mem insisting upon reading it, fighting for it as for a cup of poison held out of her reach.

And it proved to be a cup of poison when finally she got it from her mother's reluctant fingers.

> DEAR WIFE, — The Lord giveth and the Lord taketh away. I have lost you and my darling daughter and my head is bowed in shame and loneliness, but I still can say, "Thy will be done."
>
> I think you should know, however, how things are here. Otherwise I should not write you. But I am afraid that the daughter that was once ours might tire of the husks of sin and wish to come home repentant.
>
> Bitterness filled my soul when I learned that she was leading a life of riotous mockery, and when I

saw the picture of her smiling in wanton attire at the side of that smirking French general, I had it in my heart to curse her. I wrote in my haste. I repented my hardness of heart and bowed my head in humble shame when I read your angry reply. I had lost your love and your admiration, but that was deserved punishment for the idolatry that had grown up in my heart towards you; and for the mistakes I must have made in not giving our erring daughter a better care.

But now it has pleased the Lord to pour out the vials of his wrath on my gray hairs. The old mortgage on the church fell due long ago, but foreclosure had been postponed from time to time. We gave a benefit to pay it off, but everybody was too poor to respond, and it did not pay expenses.

The manager of the motion-picture house here offered to share the profits on the showing of a picture in which, as he had the impudence to tell me, my daughter played a part. But while it would have drawn money for curiosity that would not have responded to a Christian appeal, I felt that it would be a compounding with evil, and I put Satan behind me and ordered the fellow out of the house.

Then I made a desperate appeal to our banker, Mr. Seipp, and he promised to do what he could for us. But the other day his bank was closed after a run upon it. He had previously mortgaged his house and sold his automobile, the one that killed the poor boy, Elwood Farnaby, whom you will remember as one of our choir. The banker was our only wealthy member and with him failed our last hope. The crops have been poor and the hard times have affected the local merchants so that pew rents have not been paid and the usual donations have been withheld.

There were no conversions at the last communion. Even the baptisms and the weddings that brought me an occasional little fee have been wanting.

The campaign we made to close the motion-picture houses on Sunday was lost at the last election. We are fallen on evil days.

What small religious enthusiasm is left in the town has been drawn away to other churches where there are younger ministers with more fashionable creeds and fresher oratory. I have not been spared overhearing carelessly cruel remarks that I was too old to hold the pulpit any longer and should give way to a fresher mind; but I have not known where else to go, as I have had no calls from outside. And I could not — God forgive my vanity — I could not believe that I was yet too old to toil in the vineyard of the Lord. I have endured every other loss but that, and now the vineyard is closed.

The church is to be closed. We had no fire in the stove last Sunday and almost no worshipers were present. The sexton was ill and his graceless son refused to leave his bed.

What I shall do next or how take care of the little children that still cling to our home, the Lord has not yet told me in answer to my prayers. I still have faith that in his good time he will provide a way or call his servant home, and I hope you will not take this letter as a plea for pity. It is only to explain to you that if you should plan to return to the fold you will find the fold a ruin. I could not even send you the money for your railroad fare.

There was a piece in the paper saying that the moving-picture studios were also closing for lack of funds, and I wonder if my poor daughter has been turned out of the City of Pleasure in which she elected to spend her life. The rain falleth alike on the just and the unjust.

My cup is full and running over, but my chief dread is that unhappiness and want may be your portion as well as mine, and that I shall fail you utterly after providing so scantily for you all your days.

I can only pray that my fears are the result of loneliness and age and weariness.

It has not been easy to write this, but it would have been dishonest not to let you know. For months I used to think, every time I heard the train whistle: Perhaps it brings my loved ones home. For the last few weeks I have feared that it might, lest I should have to welcome you to utter poverty. Even the oil is wanting to keep burning the lamp I used to set in the window every evening.

And now may the Lord shield you with his ever-present mercy, or at least give us the strength to understand that in all things he knoweth best.

Your loving

HUSBAND.

As she read this letter and saw back to the lines of her old father's heavy brows, saw the bald spot she had stared at from the choir loft, saw all the sweet wrongheadedness of the veteran saint, Mem's heart hurt intolerably. From her eyes fell streams of those tears that she had sold for so much apiece. Her face was blubbered and crumpled and soppy as in the crying contest for points.

Her old-fashioned heartache and eye shower ended in an old-fashioned hysterics of shrieking laughter, of farcical cynicism at the ridiculous sublimities of life. She startled her mother by crying, suddenly: "The Lord is another Charlie Chaplin, mamma! He's just planted another kick where it will do the most harm."

# CHAPTER XLIX

MEM HAD BEEN DEBATING what make of car to buy. Cars were cheaper in price now, and wonderful bargains were to be had in slightly used cars purchased by hardly used stars who could not complete the payments or keep the gasoline tanks filled.

She had cried herself into money—not much, but a good deal considering the hard times, the general unemployment, and her inexperience.

She had spent little of it. She had no time to shop or even to go down into the streets and stare in at the windows.

She had hardly found the time to read the advertisements and study the fashion plates in the Sunday supplements.

What car to buy and what new house to rent had been amusing conundrums for idle moments of musing. And now those conundrums were solved. Her mother sobbed:

"What on earth can I write the poor darling?"

Mem replied: "The answer is easy. I'm going to send him all the money I've got."

Her mother cried out against robbing one of her loves to pay another. It seemed a cruel shame to take the first bit of cake from her daughter and sell it to buy bread for her husband.

"You'll need it yourself. You may not have another job soon. You need new clothes and a rest."

"Rest and the clothes can wait."

Her mother kept a miserable silence for a long while before she could say: "Your father will never accept money that you have earned from the pictures. You know him. He'd rather die. He'd rather the whole world would die."

This gave Mem only a brief pause. She answered simply:

"Doctor Bretherick got me into this business by making up the pack of lies that brought me out here. Now he can make up a few more and save poor daddy from desperation."

She sat down at once and wrote the doctor a letter, telling him what he must know already of her father's helplessness. She enclosed a money order for two hundred and fifty dollars. She wrote a check at first, but she was afraid to have it put through the bank at Calverly lest her father hear of it. She instructed the doctor to make up another of his scenarios about a repentant member of the congregation wishing to restore some stolen funds or anything that his imagination could invent.

Then she set the wheels in motion to secure an immediate engagement with the next to the greatest comedian on the screen, Ned Ling, a man whose private life was as solemn as his public life was frantic and foolish; whose personal dignity was as sacred as his professional dignity was degraded; a man of intellectuality; a reader of important books; a debater of art theories; but above all a man afraid of nothing so much as he was afraid of love.

The Bermond Company was declaring another holiday, letting out such of its people as were not under contract, farming out such others as it could find places for in the shriveled market.

The public was not flocking to the pictures or to anything else. The exhibitors were losing money or closing down.

It was a period of dead calm and torpid seas. Wise men were trimming sails to the least breeze and jettisoning perilous cargo. The too courageous ones were sinking, vanishing, blowing up, dying of famine.

When Mem spoke to Bermond of her desire to play a comedy with Ned Ling, Bermond leaped at the idea. It would take her off his salary list for weeks and it would help her fame. He was not altogether selfish. He arranged a dinner under the pretext of a private preview of Tom Holby's new picture. It was not yet in its final shape, but the producers were glad to lend it to Bermond.

Bermond warned Mem to wear her best clothes.

There was a certain shame in her heart at baiting such a trap, but she felt now that she had a higher purpose than her personal ambition. She was working for her father and his church as well; and religious motive has always been a wondrous sedative to a conscience.

Bermond saved her the price of a gown by lending her a flashing Parisian miracle from his own big wardrobe. It was astounding to him as it was to Mem to find what a change clothes make in a soul. The simple things she had worn hitherto had once given her a simple modesty. In her first scenes she had been as bad as Miss Bevan, forever pulling her skirts down. Her muscles remembered when her mind forgot. Kendrick had yelled to her once, "In God's name, Miss Steddon, forget your knees and don't advertise them by always covering them."

When she saw herself before her mirror now in the Paris gown she recoiled in red horror. A tide of blood swept under her entire skin. Her bosom was bared in a great moony sweep, there were no straps at all across the shoulders, and her back was revealed to the waist. She had never known how beautiful it was until she stood before her mirror and looked slantwise across her shoulder at the creamy charm of the gently rippling plane.

She rose to the challenge of opportunity and clothed herself in audacity. The consciousness of her beauty gave a lilt of bravado to her carriage. She was happy in her self, and silenced her old modesties with a pious thought that the Lord never gave her such flesh for concealment. Her mother was pale with terror of the white swan this pretty duckling had grown to, but she let her sail away.

The unsuspecting Ned Ling came to the dinner and never dreamed that Mem was there to play the Lorelei. She shuddered at her own coquetry, but it was art for Art's sake and in Heaven's name besides.

She met the comedian with a mixed attitude of homage and of self-confidence. She made him proud and she made him happy. Best of all, she put him at his best. He said witty things, and her laughter was a final allurement.

After the dinner they sank into big chairs in the Bermonds' living room to watch the new picture. From a table behind them a little domestic projection machine sent a cone of light across their heads to a small curtain. And there a Lilliputian twin of Mem wept and fought and won through a tiny drama.

From the dark, the happy gloom Ned Ling kept crying out his enthusiasms for Mem's skill. He was frank enough in criticism of the picture as a structure. He groaned at the comic relief and he shouted in ridicule of the hackneyed situations. Bermond echoed his praise and his censure. The picture was not a Bermond creation, but Mem was.

In an interlude during a change of reels Ned Ling said, with all the earnestness of an earnest clown: "I love your tears, Miss Steddon! They make me weep. See how wet my eyes are!"

He leaned close and made her look into his melancholy orbs. Their melancholy was their fortune, for in his pictures he never smiled except when he was in a plight of comic despair.

"I love to weep," he went on, shamelessly. "Last Christmas. How do you suppose I spent my last Christmas? I stayed at home alone and felt sorry for myself. I did! Honestly! I just wallowed in self-pity. I sat for an hour before a mirror and watched the tears pour down my cheeks. And when they fell into my sobbing mouth I drank them, and loved them because they were so bitter. It was the happiest Christmas I ever spent. Next Christmas let's you and me sit together before a mirror and have a glorious cry and weeping duet. I can't imagine anyone else who would make me weep as lusciously as you. Will you come?"

"I'll be there," said Mem, half with pity and half with mockery.

Thereupon, as the lights went out again, he laid his hand on hers where it rested on the arm of her chair. When she moved it he clutched it eagerly and whispered, "Oh, please!" and clung to it like a lonely child.

He laughed aloud at the wonderful battle Tom Holby put up, but he cheered Mem's every scene as she dashed through the storm.

"How brave! How beautiful you are!" he murmured, leaning close. She whispered to him the tale of how near she was to death in the scene when she thrust her way through the tree.

And now he clung to her with both hands as if he would save her thus belatedly from danger.

"I was very near to death in my last picture," he said. "I was supposed to sit down innocently on a plumber's torch. I had on asbestos trousers, but somehow my coat tails caught fire and I should have burned to death if Miss Clave hadn't thrown a rug around me. Awfully nice girl. I could have gone on loving her, but she kept talking about marriage and I was afraid she'd get me to the altar someday. God knows I'm afraid of marriage. Aren't you? It sickened me when I heard the audience scream with laughter at the scene. We kept it in as it was and gave it a funny title. It had just the touch of obscenity that everybody loves. Too bad we Americans make such a bane of obscenity! A little wholesome smut never hurt anybody."

When the picture was finished he told Bermond what a genius he had in Miss Steddon and said he wished he had her himself. Bermond adroitly and coquettishly forced the card on his hand, and before Ned Ling quite knew it it had been arranged that Mem should be lent to him at a figure far above her Bermond salary.

"I stuck him for the extra money," Bermond laughed afterward, "but I love to make Ned Ling pay. It hurts him so. I'll split the bonus with you, my dear."

# CHAPTER L

TOM HOLBY CALLED ON Mem the following evening. He had so earnest a face, so longing a manner, that she had not the heart to tell him at once of her triumph over Ned Ling and her engagement to play the leading role in his next farce.

But Holby seemed to realize that something had happened to take her a little farther out of his parish. There was a fugaciousness in her manner, an independence of him, that terrified him.

He grew as flat-footedly direct and simple as one of the big, bluff he-men he so often played. He actually twirled his hat, running his fingers round and round the brim as he did when he was a cowboy making love to a gal from down East. He was as sheepish as Will Rogers playing Romeo, but not so shriekingly funny.

His very boorishness pleaded for him, and if Mem had been free of this new hunger of hers for a taste of comedy she might have taken pity on him lovingly.

But she was in a mood of deferment at least, and her smiling, teasing manner baffled him. In his confusion he noted a bundle of letters in his pocket, and for lack of another topic pulled them out.

"This is a pack of letters that came to the studio just as I was leaving," he explained. "I stuffed 'em in my pocket. Haven't had a chance to look them over. Mostly mash notes, I guess."

He took out the lot and riffled them over like a pack of cards.

"If they think we movie people are fools, what have they got to say of the public that deluges us with this stuff? Here's one. Let's see what it's like." He read from a welter of passionate script.

> "DEAR MR. HOLBY,—If I could only tell you how much I admire you, you would be the proudest man on earth. There's a picture of you on my bureau now, but it's only a clipping from a Sunday supplement. I take it out only when the door is locked. Mamma would skin me if she knew I had it. I turn it away when I dress, but, oh, I do just admire you so much. If I could only have a real photo of you to kiss good night how proud I'd be. Won't you please send me one? With your own really truly autograph on it? You are my favorite of all actors so manly and virrile and handsome. Oh, I just..."

Tom shook his head and stuffed it back in its envelope.

"Will she get the photograph?" said Mem, with the scorn of one woman for another.

"Oh yes. We can't afford to antagonize a single fan. My secretary will send her a picture and autograph it for me."

"Who is your secretary? A girl?"

Holby slid a glance of eager query under his eyelids. He hoped that there was a tinge of jealousy in her heart. That would be vastly encouraging. But her eyes revealed contempt only, for men and the parasitesses that haunt them.

"No, he's a man," said Tom, dolefully "combination of press agent, valet, dresser, and secretary."

The next letter had a Philippine Islands postmark. It was from a man in Cebu. It said:

> "DEAR FRIEND,—Kindly please send me a copy of your sympahty portrait. Hoping to received it your benevolent reply. Many thanks for my best wishes."

He read a few more. They represented a cosmic clientele. But he saw that they were boring Mem and put them back into his pocket.

"Brave man," she said, "you open your mail in the presence of the woman you... you..."

"I love and expect to marry," he said, gripping her hand. It was a grip of authority. It was Cupid the constable, so different from the pathetic clutch of Ned Ling the clown child.

Just now it was Mem's humor to control somebody. She did not oppose Holby's clutch or resent it. She followed the most loathsome and exasperating of all policies: nonresistance.

You're not going to marry me, Tommy," she said. "I don't want to be one of Solomon's wives."

" Solomon's wives?"

"Yes. You're wedded already to an army of fans. Half the women in the United States seem to claim you as their spiritual bridegroom. I'd as soon marry a telephone booth or a census report. You make Brigham Young look like a confirmed bachelor; he had only forty wives or so. You have a million."

"They make me tired."

"Maybe, but what wouldn't they do to me? I'd get poisoned candy or infernal machines in the mail. I'd never dare marry you. It would be committing suicide."

She was not altogether without seriousness; she felt a primeval jealousy, a primeval sense of monopoly. She writhed at the thought of possessing only a minute fraction of a universal husband, a syndicated consort whose portrait on a thousand bureaus inspired numberless strange women with an ardor they called artistic admiration, as the medieval girls and spinsters set up images of saints and made violent love to them under the name of religion, clothing amorous raptures in pious phrases, and burning with desires that they interpreted as heavenly yearnings.

Mem turned green at the thought of a husband whose real lips she must share with actresses on the scene and whose pictured lips would be kissed good night all around the world.

It was a monstrous, fantastic jealousy, but its foundation was real. She shuddered at the prospect of being embraced by a husband whose virility thrilled a multitude of anonymous maenads. If all these idiots wrote, how many must there be who worshiped in silence?

But she did not express this revulsion to Tom Holby. She did not really feel enough desire for him just now to be jealous, except with a prophetic remoteness. Just now she was curious about another type of soul, about a comic sprite.

She felt sure that no women wrote Ned Ling love letters or set him up as an icon on a bureau. Ned Ling's pictures were not sifting around the globe, setting fool girls aglow, for Ned Ling's published portraits were always grotesque. He was photographed with a caricatured face of white chalk and a charcoal grimace, with a nonsensical hat and collar becoming almost as familiar now as Charlie Chaplin's neat slovenliness, his mustaches, and his splay-foot shoes.

Surely Ned Ling was free from the amorous bombardment of anonymous love letters. A woman might stand a chance of keeping his heart for her very self, and it would be cheerful to have one's own comedian on the hearth.

Thinking these things, Mem said: "I'd be jealous of your public, Tom. It is a big one and you've got to be true to it. I suppose it's because I've got none of my own. I've hardly had a letter yet."

"That's because your first picture is only being released now. Just wait! You'll be snowed under."

"And would you like it if I read you a letter from some man in Oklahoma who had my picture on his bureau and kissed me every night good night?"

"No."

"Would you be jealous?"

"Yes! I'd want to kill him."

"Really?" There was a pleasant thrill in this, a thrill that will be a long time dying out of the female soul, the excitement of stirring up battle ardor in two or more males.

Mem went on, teasing, yet exploringly:

"And would you kill any man who put me on a shrine and worshiped me?"

"No. I'd realize that that was part of the penalty of loving a great artist. There's a penalty about loving a stupid woman that nobody else cares for, too. I'd realize that you have a right to the world's love, and I'd be proud of you, however much it hurt. I shouldn't lift my finger to hamper your glory."

She was just about to kiss him lightly on the nearer ear for the fervor of the first part of his speech. But the last line checked her. There can never fail to be a little something disappointing about a love that is willing to share its prey with anyone else even if it is with everyone else.

Perhaps to punish this sickly saintliness she told him flatly now that she was going to be Ned Ling's leading lady.

This hurt him as much as she hoped.

"It's a comedown for you," he said. "It's a setback. You'd have been the next big star in the emotional field. Now you'll be swallowed up in a comic two-reeler. Ling never gives anybody else any credit in his pictures. All you'll do will be to stand round and feed him."

"Feed him?"

"Yes, do things and say things that will give him a funny comeback."

This was a trifle dampening. If he had held to that line of argument he might have turned her aside. But, as always, he had to say too much.

"Besides, as I told you, Ned Ling always makes love to his leading lady. He quarreled with the last one, Miss Clave, because she wanted more publicity. She wanted to get a laugh or two herself and a line or two in the advertisements."

This stirred in Mem a double emotion: one of curiosity, one of self-confidence. She had had Ned Ling clinging to her fingers like a baby. She could wrap him round one of them, no doubt. Because Miss Clave failed, that did not prove that a wiser woman would.

Holby did not quite persuade her to refuse the opportunity with Ling, but he sent her to it with misgivings. He put a fly in the ointment.

There are always flies in ointment.

A few days later a wasp fell into her ointment. She received one of the first of the numerous letters that were to swarm about her path.

# CHAPTER LI

TIME IN SOUTHERN CALIFORNIA flew on wings that seemed never to change their plumage. At home in Calverly the birds put on their springtime splendor, lost it, and flew away. The trees feathered out in leaves and in a courtship glory of blossoms, then lost all. The flower bushes ran the same scale from shabbiness to brief beauty and back again. The very ground was brown, was green, was bald, was white with snow that went and came again.

But Los Angeles was always green. In December, March always there were great roses glowing, often high up in some tree they had climbed.

Sometimes Mem grew angry at the monotony of beauty. She read of blizzards in the East and North and longed for a frostbite or the nipped cheeks of a Calverly winter. There was music in her memory of the frozen snow that rang like muffled cymbals under her aching little feet as she ran to school pretending she was a locomotive and her breath the steam.

But this was only the fretfulness of the unconquerable human discontent. She had hated winter when it tortured her, and now the California paradise tortured her because it was winterless. Even in heaven the angels grew weary of golden and jasper architecture and harp music and tried to change their government.

Discontent with the weather was only one of Mem's unhappinesses. Her ambition was ruthless and her critical faculty rebuked her. She prayed for opportunities for bigger roles and blushed at her obscurity; yet when she saw her finished scenes she suffered direfully because she had done them so ill. When her colleagues applauded her she said her true thought when she answered: "It could have been done so much better. If only we could retake it!"

She was living the artist's life, goaded to expression, rejoicing in utterance and afterward anguished with regrets that she had not phrased herself a little differently.

As with every other artist in the world's history, her personality, her preferences, her very face and form, offended many people. Nobody ever pleased everybody. She overheard harsh criticisms or they were brought to her one way or another. They hurt her cruelly, and the more cruelly since it was her nature to believe them justified and even a little less than harsh enough.

Some happier natures than hers could always protect themselves by saying that the critic had a personal spite, or was a failure venting the critic's own disappointment, or was too shallow to appreciate, or had been bribed.

But Mem never could wrap her wounded soul in such bandages. She felt that the truth was worse than the worst she heard. She could always find some fault in her achievements that the critics had overlooked.

She could not retake her pictures, however, and when, occasionally, a scene had been shot over again and she could correct some fault, she always found another one, or more, to replace it.

Obscurity was a further anguish. She suffered because so few people had seen her pictures, and the hard times that diminished the audiences looked like a personal injury to her in her artistic cradle.

And then she had a stab of another sort. She learned the curse of success. One of her pictures was shown at the California Theater in Los Angeles, and she sat in a vast throng and saw with pride that people strange to her were leaning forward with interest and devouring her with their eyes. She saw a fat woman sniffle and thought it a beautiful tribute. She saw a bald-headed man sneak a handkerchief out and, pretending to blow his nose, dash his shameful tears away. And that was beautiful to her with a wonderful beauty. She played a minor role, but she heard people speak of her as the mob went out among the inbound mob crowding to the next showing.

The papers the next day in their criticisms gave her special mention. She loved Florence Lawrence, and Guy Price, Grace Lindsey, Edwin Schallert, Monroe Lathrop, all of those who tossed her a word and put her name in print. A marvelous thing to see one's name in print and with a bouquet tied to it.

She had but a little while to revel in this perfect reward, for in a few days a letter came to her, forwarded from the studio.

The writing on the envelope was strange to her. When she opened it there was no signature. There was a savagery about the very writing. Her heart plunged with terror as she read.

> I seen your pictur last nite and it made me sick youre awful innasent and sweet in the pictur and you look like buter wouldnt melt in your mouth but I know beter for Im the guy held you up in Topango cannon wen you was there with that other guy and took your wedin ring off you I dident know who you was then and I dont know who he is yet but Im wise to you and all I got to say is Ive got my ey on you and you beter behave or els quit playin these innasent parts you movie peeple make me sick youre only a gang of hippocrits so bewair.

Mem felt odious to herself, with all the revolting nausea of evil revealed. There is remorse enough for a struggling soul that knows its own defeats and backslidings, but it is nothing to the remorse that follows a published fault.

This letter was more hideous than headlines in a paper. It was more dreadful than such a pilloried public shame as Hester Prynne's. It meant that somewhere there was a man in an invisible cloak of namelessness and facelessness who despised her and jeered at her sublimities of purity. Her highest ambitions were doomed to sneering mockery.

She was thrown back into the dark ages when girls were told that guardian devils floated about them as well as guardian angels, all manner of leering enemies, incubi, succubi, witches, fairies. She could hear such hellish laughter as Faust's Gretchen heard.

She longed to find this man and implore his mercy. But how could she discover him? He was a thief and could only disclose himself by betraying his own crime. Yet he felt himself less wicked than she.

She saw before her a long life of such attacks. She resolved to do two things: lead thenceforth a blameless life, and play thenceforth only such characters as made no pretense of perfection.

She was the more determined to seek a foothold in comedy, in wild farce. She wanted to play a woman of sin, a vampire, anything that would free her of the charge of wearing a virtuous mask.

She burned the letter, but she could never forget it. She could not walk along a street or ride in a car without wondering if the last man who cast a glance her way might not be the thief who had robbed her of something irretrievable. When she sat in a moving-picture theater she wondered if he were not the man at her elbow, and, since few men failed to look at her with a trailing glance that caught a little on her beauty as on a hook, she was incessantly thrown into panics.

In time she grew brazen and said she didn't care. A little later she forgot the terror that walked by, but now and then it would return upon her as often when she was alone as when she was in the range of human eyes.

# CHAPTER LII

THE FIRST THING that struck Mem about the business of selling jokes was the melancholic despondency of it. In the other studios there had been a deadly earnestness at times, but usually a cheerful informality. But Ned Ling was in a state of nerves and dismal with anxieties.

The first scene rehearsed showed Mem being ardently proposed to by a dapper young juvenile whose grace and beauty were to be the foil for Ned Ling's triumphant ugliness. The juvenile was instructed to do a simple bit of business.

Young Mr. McNeal, realizing that the scene was supposed to be mildly funny, tried to play it in a mood of gaiety to "horse" it a little with a slight extravagance of manner and a humorous twinkle in his eye.

Ned Ling checked him at once.

"Cut out the comedy, Mr. McNeal, if you please! It's all right to be funny in an emotional picture, but comedy is a serious business. A joke is dynamite, and if it's handled carelessly it will blow up in your hands and take you with it. I want the audience to blow up, not you. So you carry that scene as seriously as you can."

The criticism hurt young Mr. McNeal, but it warned Mem. She went through her own business with a simple matter-of-factness as if it had no humor in it. This was because she did not know how to make it funny. To her amazement, Ned Ling cried out:

"Great! Perfect! Play it straight! The audience wants to laugh at your expense. Don't let 'em know you know you're funny, or you're gone. But, Mr. McNeal, I must ask you not to crab Miss Steddon's scene."

"Crab the scene, sir? What did I do?"

"You moved."

"Don't you want me to move?"

"Never! Not when somebody else is getting off a point. You can kill half or all the laugh by distracting attention. An audience can only see one thing at a time, get one idea at a time. You've got to ship 'em your jokes like a train of box cars. You can't jumble 'em, or there's a wreck.

"When Miss Steddon's at work, you freeze! And Miss Steddon will do the same when it's your turn. And when I'm with you I'll murder you if you move an eyelid when I'm springing something. And you can murder me if I breathe during anything of yours. And one thing more. Watch out that you don't spoil your own comedy by moving the wrong part of your anatomy. I can kill the best face play in the world by moving my feet or my hands. I can kill the work of my hands by rolling my eye. Remember that! Comedy is the most solemn business there is."

Mem was amazed, dismayed at the anguish of exactitude attending each little bit of silly wit. She had captured her tears and her dramatic climaxes with a rush.

But wit had to be stolen upon, prepared, and exploded just so.

Ned Ling at lunch time told her of a year of meditation spent on one idiotic incident. He had not got it right yet. It might not be ready for this picture or the next. Some day it would come out just right, and then it would appear like an improvisation of the moment.

He was especially delicate about the broad bits. He was a lover of coarse jokes; he loathed the Puritanism that gave them an immoral quality. Yet they would not have been half so funny or perhaps not funny at all if it were not for the forbidding of them, just as nakedness would have no spice, no commercial value, and would suggest no evil thoughts if it were ignored or made compulsory, or if the wrong-headed moralists did not surround it with horror and give it the fascination of rarity.

Mem suffered acutely from Ned Ling's discussions of risky humor. She had never heard such talk.

She was like a trained nurse getting her first glimpse of life through the eyes of a doctor, learning not to swoon at the lifting of the veils.

Ned Ling had a doctor's impatience of prudery, the same contempt for the vicious indecency of what he called the nasty-nice. He jolted Mem horribly, but he shook the furniture of her soul into more solid places.

Like a nurse, like a woman doctor, Mem was far more decent after this course of training than before. But it took all her nerve to keep from wincing, from protesting, from taking up that obsolescent woman's weapon, "How dare you!"

She learned in time to laugh wholeheartedly, like a man, at the coarse verities. She was not educated up to Rabelais. Few women have ever yet gone so high in the upper humanities.

She would never love the great vulgarities, but she was emancipated from the smaller squeamishness, the wide-eyed doll mind, and the Kate Greenaway innocence.

That was why, perhaps, she could revel so wonderfully in *The Beggar's Opera* when she saw it.

It was the first opera she ever did see, grand or comic. Not even a musical comedy had passed her eyes and ears. Her father did not believe in opera, and if he had had his way Mozart, Verdi, and Wagner would have been as dumb as Shakespeare for he abhorred the playhouse, too. The catalogue of his abhorrences was unending. He abhorred almost everything human that he could think of except when it was twisted into a form of prayer. He liked opera when it was disguised as oratorio and the singers wore their own clothes instead of evil costumes. He liked plays about Santa Claus, and he vaguely approved the old miracle plays the Church had fostered, since he never dreamed how indecent many of them were. He was beginning to admit that motion pictures of educational or religious purpose might atone for their sins.

But Mem would as soon have asked permission to go to a dance as to a theater in Calverly.

Los Angeles had, for a city of its size, a minimum of theatrical entertainments. The long haul across the deserts made it prohibitive of late years for most companies to visit the Pacific coast. She had seen a few plays given by the city stock companies and by the Hollywood Community Players. She had even dragged her mother to those devilish amusements and brought her away without a sniff of brimstone.

Her acquaintance with the world was almost exclusively of the movies, movish. Like the people of all other trades, when the cinemators had a free evening they spent it in more of the same. The picture houses were frequented by the picture people of whom there were thousands in Los Angeles.

Her first opera was curiously the last opera one might be expected to see at all in her day.

Somebody in London had been inspired to revive the sensation of 1728. It had run for a solid year in the new London and another season in New York. Its ancient art had glistened like a Toledo blade. It made the epigrams of Oscar Wilde and Bernard Shaw look old-fashioned.

An opera whose hero was a thief and whose scenes were sordid, the gayest of operas, it dumfounded Mem as it had set old London aghast. There where the rival Italian companies had made war in an otherwise undisputed field, it suddenly arose and laughed them off the boards, drove Handel into bankruptcy, drove him to such despair that he went to Ireland and, casting about for something to do beside the operas that were a closed career for him, tossed off in three weeks *The Messiah* (!) and became immortal as a religious force.

Thus much Mem learned before the curtain rose. After it was up she learned to laugh uproariously at the utmost delicacies of indecency. It made an earthquake in Mem's soul to sit alongside Ned Ling and listen to the scene where the heroine horrifies her parents by announcing her marriage to a handsome young man, horrifies them not because she wished to marry a highwayman, but because she wished to marry at all, except possibly some old man for financial reasons.

Mem was aghast when they ridiculed their daughter's talk of love; at length the father protested, "Do you think your mother and I should have lived comfortably together so long if we'd been married?"

This was as terrifying as a scarlet snake, but Mem shook with laughter, then collapsed into dismay. If she could laugh at that, what decency had she left?

Her soul groveled in itself remorsefully until the next epigram jarred it out of its opossumism, and she laughed again.

She had so lost her orientation by the finish of the seductive villainies, that she did not faint when Ned Ling said:

"I've laughed myself hungry. I haven't ordinarily any appetite. Let's go to my house and have a bite."

"To your house?"

"Yes. It's all right. I'm quite alone there. Just a Jap. Very secluded."

She wanted to say: "You tell me not why I should go, but why I should not. And I won't."

But it seemed a silly, little-girlish, old-maidish, prunes-and-prismish thing to say.

Wasn't she an independent woman now, a voter, a free and equal self-supporting citizen of the United States? In her imagination she could hear the wild crew of the *Beggar's Opera* laughing at her for a shy little hypocrite. Lacking the courage to obey her instinct and her training, she said, "Alright," and got into Ling's car.

When he said, "Home," to the driver she almost swooned, but not quite.

The Jap showed no surprise at the late arrival of his master with a lady. Evidently it was the ordinary thing. Mem longed for a mask or a fire escape or a gun. She glanced about for weapons of defense.

But Ned Ling said: "Some scrambled eggs and bacon. Some wine. Would you rather have red or white? Or a little champagne? Let's have some champagne yes? Yes, we'll have some champagne, native California but good."

She felt as Jack of the Beanstalk felt when he found himself among ogres.

But Ling turned out to be an infantile ogre, if ogre at all. He was more like an art-gallery guide at first. He showed her his treasures. He knew something of art, or so she judged him from his talk, for she knew nothing of it herself; but his manner was impressive. He was especially proud of a portrait just painted of him by one of the California artists. Ling spoke of him as of the "California school."

Ling had brought home some jades from a voyage to China. He was addicted to jades, of a certain deep, dark, emerald hue. He hated the sickly pallor of the usual jade. Mem decided to take up jade hunting as a sport when she got rich.

At the table Ling resumed his play with her fingers. She felt only curiosity. She could feel neither alarm nor anger. She was hungry, but he kept one of her hands prisoner and preferred to talk.

Afterward they went into the beautiful living room, a strange room for a clown; more like what she imagined a millionaire's room to be, judging from what millionaires' rooms she had seen in the movies.

He put a Caruso record on the Victrola, that old wail from *Pagliacci*, the heartbreak of the clown who is human in spite of the powder, and feels red blood beneath the grease paint. Caruso was just recently dead and honored with the funeral of a church dignitary, wild minstrel that he was, singing his way around the world on rubber wheels the way the filmers traveled in celluloid spools.

"A few years ago," said Ling, "and a singer's voice died with him. And now Caruso is singing here everywhere. He'll sing as long as Homer, poor old blind Homer, who never saw a picture, never knew that his own songs would live after him in the invention of the alphabet, never dreamed that they would be printed and used as schoolbooks thousands of years after he quit poking about the world singing about the fighters of his day.

"A few years ago and we actors were condemned to oblivion as soon as we left the boards. But we can go on forever now. They're laughing around the world at me this minute. Listen!" He kept an eerie quiet and she could almost hear what he perked his ears to catch. "That's a gang of sweaty coolies in China. They're helped to forget the opium, laughing at me. Hear that! That's starving people in Russia forgetting their hunger because the seat of my breeches caught on fire. Did you hear that yelp? That was one of the exiled kings guffawing when I got shot in the pants by an angry husband. The king has forgotten his own grief."

This cosmic boastfulness did not keep him long in pride. "But I hate my pictures. I'm jealous of them. People don't like me, they just like that thing with the chalky mug. They love him because he's such a fool. I want to be loved because I am Me and not a fool.

"Look at this painting of me. The artist caught the real me. See all the sorrow in the eyes and behind the mouth. See the longing and the unhappiness? That painter got under my skin. He got to me. I love that because it's me."

Suddenly he bent over and kissed his own image on the mouth. It was the mad act of a Yankee Narcissus overcome not by his own loveliness, but by his own loneliness.

Mem was dazed. She had a normal woman's normal interest in her mirror because a mirror is the show window of the goods she has for sale. She had become of necessity self-conscious, self-critical. She had admired extravagantly the reflection of herself in the looking-glass the night she went forth to meet this Ned Ling in her first magnificent gown. But she had never divided herself into such a pair of twins, such a Mutual Consolation Society, Ltd., as Ned Ling had organized.

And, as often happens, seeing that he was so sorry for himself, she felt no draught upon her own sympathy. She simply stared and wondered.

He made her sit down on a long couch and snuggled close to her. She was still rather curious than alarmed. He took up her hand again and studied it, talking in the rather literary manner he sometimes assumed: "Each separate finger has its own soul, don't you think? Hands are families. Your own hands, anybody's hands are a group of people. Hands are different, and fingers — they're wicked capable of such terrible things: holding daggers, gifts; caressing; throttling; playing music; exploring; loving; hating. Queer things, fingers. Your right hand and your left hand aren't the least alike and your face is a third person still."

Before Mem quite realized how solemnly ludicrous a couple of comedians could be if anybody had been looking except God and perhaps that Jap valet, Ned Ling's head was on her breast and his eyes were turned up into hers like a baby's. He was in a newborn prattling humor. That was a secret of his success. He was a baby with all a baby's privileges of impropriety, selfishness, hatefulness, adorableness.

He could revert to infancy and take his audience with him, make old men and women laugh at the simple things that had tickled their childish hearts. And withal there was an amazing sophistication. He was a baby that calculated and measured, triumphed and yet wept and wanted always the next toy. He was thinking of Mem as his next toy and she was thinking of him as her next child.

His warm head and his brown eyes like maple sugar, just as it is liquescent to syrup, and with the same gold flakes glinting, they were quaintly babyish to her in spite of his old talk.

"I want to love and be loved, but not to love too much. I'm afraid of love. It has hurt me too bitterly. Some of them haven't been true to me, and that hurt me horribly. And I haven't been true to some of them and that hurt me still worse. I don't know which is ghastlier, to see a woman laugh at you or cry at you.

Marriage is no solution. I don't see how it can help being the end of love. Love ought to be free like art and speech. Of course art isn't free. There's the censorship. Well, marriage is like censorship. Everything you do and say and feel must be submitted to the censor. They call this a free country and have censorships and marriage!"

She smiled. He was more like a prattling baby the more cynical he grew. His heavy head made her breast ache and yearn for a baby. But he wanted only the froth of life without the body and the dregs.

"Could you love me just enough and not too much?" he pleaded.

If he had said, "Marry me tomorrow!" he might have had her then. But she had not his opinion of marriage. She had played the game without the name, endured the ecstasy and the penalty without the ceremony. She had escaped public shame by a miracle of lucky lies and accidents. The hunger remained for the rewards of marriage, the honesty of a home, the granite foundations of respectable loyalty.

So when he pleaded with her for love that cheated and played for fun and not for all, for a kiss, for caresses, she shook her head mystically as he thought, but very sanely and calmly, in truth.

She was far away, mothering a shadowy child, swaying in a rocking chair throne.

Ned Ling's prayers gained fervor from her aloofness. He called upon a goddess who would not hear. She held his hands and slapped them with a matronly condescension that drove him frantic.

He could not get past the cloudy masonry he had built round her by deriding marriage. It was a good subject for jokes, but contempt for it was more ridiculous than the thing ridiculed.

Finally she yawned in the face of his passion and said, "I'll be going home now, please."

He was so thwarted and rejected that he sent her home alone. She was grateful for that.

# CHAPTER LIII

AGAIN WHEN SHE GOT home her mother was waiting for her. Her father was waiting for her again.

Her mother had fallen asleep with her father's letter in her hand. As Mem slipped in guiltily and stared at her, she leaped up in alarm and cried out in protest, with a sleepy reversion to ancient authority: "Mem, have you proven utterly shameless? Have you gone wrong at last?"

Mem smiled and shook her head. Something in her calm convinced her mother more than any angry disclaimer could have done. She breathed deeply with relief from the nightmare that rides mothers' souls night and day. She smiled as she held out another letter from the old child they were both mothering.

MY BELOVED WIFE, — You will find it hard to believe what I am about to write, for you were never quite convinced that prayers are answered. Well, mine have been and I am more than ever confirmed in my faith.

A miracle has been vouchsafed unto me, even me!

This morning Doctor Bretherick called to see me and stated that he had been entrusted with a mysterious message. A former parishioner of mine, a man whose name he was forbidden to disclose, had embezzled some money years ago and had never been discovered. The still small voice of his conscience, however, was never silenced, and at last it drove him to restitution. But he found that the people whom he had wronged were dead and there were no heirs to receive the funds.

In his distress at being unable to relieve his soul of its remorse, he bethought himself of his old church, and wrote to Doctor Bretherick, who had been his physician in the old days, asking him to convey the money to me for such use as I found best. Doctor Bretherick placed two hundred and fifty dollars in my hands and assured me that more would come from time to time until the principal and the interest had been paid.

I fell on my knees in thankfulness, and even Doctor Bretherick, hopeless old skeptic that he is, was not free from a moisture about the eyes. When I reproached him with his little faith he could not deny that there was something in this beyond his ability to explain by any of his materialistic nonsense.

He would not even give a hint as to the anonymous donor, but I have my suspicions as to who the man is. He left town some years ago and has grown rich in New York. My prayers follow him.

I cannot write more! I am too busy renewing the life of this dear old church. The mortgagees have accepted a part payment and agreed to prolong the loan. The members have taken a new lease on faith and some of the wanderers have been drawn back to the fold. A member on an outlying farm has turned in three fat pigs to sell, and two merchants have endorsed a note which the bank has discounted. The other preachers may be younger, but they cannot point to such a miracle.

As Elijah was fed by the ravens, so some unknown benevolence has rescued this old man of yours from the deeps of helplessness.

If only you could come home now, and if our beloved child could see the light, all would be well. Tell her of my good fortune and say that my cup of joy would overflow indeed if only she might give up her error before the night falleth. I am trying not to ask too much of Heaven, but I am counting on seeing you.

Your loving

HUSBAND.

Never had Mem felt more ancient or more motherly than when she saw this aged child converted again to Santa Claus. His blind confidence in his wrongheadedness filled her heart with tender amusement.

She was thoroughly happy and fully rewarded for the sacrifice of her savings, but she was too freshly come from the home of the farceur to escape a torment of cynicism. She put ice in her mother's heart when she said: "I saw *The Beggar's Opera* tonight, mamma, the wickedest thing I ever did see, too. But if it hadn't been for that, Handel wouldn't have written The Messiah."

This was academic enough to pass her mother without protest. But Mem went on with diabolical logic, "If Eve hadn't eaten the apple, then Christ would never have come to earth."

"Hush, in Heaven's name!"

"Hush is always good advice, mamma, but I can't help realizing that if I hadn't well, sinned is the word with poor Elwood Farnaby, I'd never have run away from home. If I'd never run away from home. I'd never have come out here; I'd never have earned a cent; I'd never have had a cent to send to poor daddy and his church would have gone to smash. So you see..."

"No, I don't!" said Mrs. Steddon, "and you'd better not."

"All right, I won't," said Mem, kissing the frightened face, "but it's a funny world, isn't it, mamma?"

"Not at all," said mamma.

# CHAPTER LIV

MEM DREADED TO GO to the studio the next day for fear of the comedian who had overnight become a rejected lover.

But Ling separated shop from life completely and gave no sign of the self-tormentor, the love puzzle he became of evenings. He was once more the chemist fretting over the minutiae of laugh-getting, pondering the hair's breadth lift of an eyebrow, perfecting the mixtures of action to the least scruple.

The child's lonely heart was forgotten and he was the keen professor in his laboratory. Mem wondered if other scientists became just such babblers when they went back to their homes and their boarding houses.

She also became the woman professor storing up information. She began to wonder if the same accuracy would not be of value in the manufacture and sale of tears and sorrows. She began to revert to her old ambitions and to feel that the business of laughter-making was not her line.

The pathos and the amiable farce of her father's delusion warmed her heart toward the homely sentiments of the everyday people. She wanted to play small-town heroines and enact village tragedies with a sunlight of laughter woven through them. After all, most people were either in or from small towns. The richest bought themselves farms and dwelt in villages, and she had read that Marie Antionette had her Petit Trianon where she dressed as a peasant and fed chickens.

She began to long for a role made to order for herself. She had been putting on other people's ready-made ideas, wearing characteristics that came to her complete, adjusting her own body and spirit to a preconceived creation.

Now, like all growing actor souls, she grew impatient for a mantle cut to her own shoulders, of a tint suited to her own complexion.

One evening when a Thursday night dance at the Hollywood Hotel drew a throng of movie makers of all the branches of the industry, she fell in with a Miss Driscoll, who wrote continuities and was one of the leading spirits of the Screen Writers Guild. She was also one of the chief officers of the new Writers Club, which had just bought a house and opened a clubhouse where men and women mingled in disregard of ancient prejudice.

Miss Driscoll thrilled Mem by saying that she ought to have a picture written especially for her. She said she had been watching Mem's work, had been talking about her a lot to Tom Holby. She paid Mem the marvelous compliment of a personality, an individuality. She wanted to write something "around her."

Four men who begged Mem for a dance were vaguely snubbed. Miss Driscoll's voice was more fascinating, with that theme of her Self, than even the saxophone, with its voice like the call of a goat-legged, shaggy Pan, turning dance floors into leafy forests and putting a nymph or a faun inside each ballgown or dinner coat.

Love of a very fleshly and woodland appeal was of an inferior magic to the spell of a voice that said, "Let me write and publish you as your own self to the world."

Mem was beginning to respond to the same self-splitting introspection that she had pitied or scorned in Ned Ling and in other actors who were always worrying over an infidelity to their Selves.

Tom Holby came up and commanded her to dance. When she begged off, he lifted her from her chair and eloped with her like Jupiter carrying off Europa. But her thoughts remained with Miss Driscoll and this wonderful new world where she was to enact her Self.

Tom Holby soon realized that he had only an empty shell in his arms and he put her back into her chair.

But Miss Driscoll had been carried away by another dancer, and Mem found herself alongside a man whom she recognized as an author of continuities, also one of the chief spirits of the Screen Writers Guild and one of the chief officers of the Writers Club.

And he introduced himself as Mr. Hobbes, saying that he had been watching her work for some time and that she had a distinct personality, a peculiar photographic genius. "I'd love to write something around you," he said.

Mem chuckled with the infantile pride of discovering that she had toes, ten of them! She also had a Me, and an altar was rising to it.

When Miss Driscoll returned, panting and mopping her brow, she said to Mr. Hobbes: "You lay off'n my star! I seen her first."

"Nonsense! " said Mr. Hobbes, "I've been dreaming about her for weeks."

Mem felt divinely foolish as the wishbone of such a rivalry. But when Tom Holby drifted back, as always, and Ned Ling came up to glorify her with attentions, both of them felt that she was cut off from them by some transparent but impassable cloud.

# CHAPTER LV

MEM FOUND IT a marvelous thing to have geniuses begging for the privilege of writing the words to the music of her beauty, librettos for her limber personality.

She had met so few authors, and those few so briefly, that she still thought of them as miracle workers of a peculiar mystery, creators who spun out little universes at their own sweet will.

The hack continuity writers she had encountered had not confirmed this quaint theory, and she soon learned that most of them, somewhat like the dwellers on a certain famous island, earned a precarious existence by stealing one another's plots.

The novelists she had read but not seen were still cloudy beings who dropped tablets from their private Sinais. She felt that if she were even lucky enough to touch the hem of the garment of one of them she would ask him:

"How on earth do you ever think of your plots?"

In good time she would come to know some of the most famous of the men and women who plowed with a pen and were as much hitched to it as it to them. And she would find them also poor, harrowed, plain people, wondering what life is all about and why their sawdust dolls would not behave like humanity. Each of them had his or her favorite critics who made life a burden and every new work a target.

Still, for a time, it was drinking the milk of paradise and feeding on honeydew to find herself inspiring strangers with a desire to build stories as airplanes and chariots for her to ride and drive to glory. It was warming to have strange persons writing in from nowhere and everywhere imploring her to touch their manuscripts with her life-giving radiance, make them walk and lift their authors out of their hells of oblivion.

When the compliment became a commonplace it became a bore, a nuisance, a pest, an outrage. An amazing number of strangers wrote her that their life stories would make her rich and famous, and were far more dramatic than the works of Griffith, Jeanie McPherson, John Emerson, Anita Loos, Marion Fairfax, June Mathis, Thompson Buchanan, J. G. Hawks, Charles Kenyon, Monte Katterjohn, and the other photo-playwrights.

She answered such letters as she could by hand and labored to avoid repetitions of phrase. Then she set her mother to work to copying out forms, and finally made her mother sign them with her best imitation of Mem's name.

"And now I'm a forger!" gasped Mrs. Steddon. "What next?"

By and by both of them were so overworked with the increasing task of answering letters from every kind of person, ranging from little girls of eight to elderly Japanese gentlemen, and offering everything from a prayer for a photograph to an opportunity to pay off a mortgage, that Mem began to hate and revile her annoyers.

Here and there was a letter of gracious charm, a cry from some sore-beset soul, a word of rewarding gratitude from one who felt a debt to her art, a glimpse of some wretch with a cancer of ambition gnawing a hapless soul. Young girls, unluckily married and dwelling on farms far distant from Los Angeles, described the color of their hair and eyes, and the compliments they had had from their neighbors, and begged to be brought to Los Angeles that they might trade their messes of pottage for their birthrights of wealth and renown. They opened their windows to Los Angeles as to the city of deliverance it had been to a multitude.

Sometimes the letter unconsciously conveyed more landscape and character than a laborious author could achieve, and carried with it an air of helpless doom that was heartbreaking. There were many of the following sort:

DEAR MISS STEDDON

May I interduce my self to you?

Im a little Arizona Girl, an I want to know how to be come a Movie Star.

Will you pleace take A few minutes of your time an tell me all about it. Does it take lots of money to be come a Movie Star.

Every since I was 15 years old Ive craved to be a star. My people Objected very much.

When I Was 17 I began Work when 19 I Married.

I An husband seperated, so Now Im on the plains with my fauther an Mather. I have a 2 months Old baby boy.

I ll be 21 in Feb. Im call a disapointed brunette. I weight 117 5 ft. 4 in. I think I11 send you a little Picture of my self so you can see for your self how I look.

I am a prity good dancir. As I was prity buisy my self I must go. Please take a few Minutes An drope me a few lines about this.

Yours truly,

MRS. JACOB LAYTON.

Youth might break through the hasps of fate, though Mem could only answer that thousands of experienced actresses were out of work and there was little chance. There was less hope still for the dowdy middle-agers who wrote from Midwestern villages enclosing photographs that would have ended their chances if they had had any; but they wanted to know how to get famous quick.

Actors without experience, authors who could not spell, people of every imaginable and unimaginable disability, all sent their pleas to this new goddess, and she was as helpless to grant them as the gods above have always been to respond to the petitions that rain toward them from the volcanic fires of the molten hearts of this world.

Mem could not answer even with advice. And she felt that she was making enemies everywhere faster than friends.

Fame, too, has its income tax to pay, and the rate increases by the same doubling and trebling with which the government punishes success in the form of money.

Writhing at the humiliations of obscurity, Mem was coming swiftly up into the humiliations of conspicuity.

The letter from the holdup man was followed by another less terrifying, but no less belittling to her pride. She had just been glowing with the first thrill of the first requests for her photograph and for her autograph, paid for in advance by flattery, if not postage, when her eager eyes met this from Yuma written by a landlady who carried her hash-making propensities into her English:

MISS REMEMBER STEDDON
    *nee* MRS. JOHN WOODVILLE
        Bermond Studios, Los Angeles, Calif.

DEAR MADAME:

Seeing as I seen your pitcure at the theater here last nihgt and recongized you as the lady who left a trunk here saying she would send for it as soon as she and her husband got theirselves located and you never done so and going to the mooving pitcure the other nihgt as I say I saw you or so I believ on the serene as Miss Steddon and very pertty you was to I must admit and so how about your trunk is what I am asking and their is storage charges onto it and Mrs. Drissett who is still with me and seen the pitcure with me says to ask you do you remember her asking you about being a Woodville and your saying you was ashamed of your husbands folks or rather that he didant have no folks at all and she notices as you used another name and hopeing to hear from you soon and do what is rihgt is my motto and I espect other folks to do the same.

                    Yours respecfuly
                    MRS. CLEM SLOAT

Mem's own behavior had been more inelegant than Mrs. Sloat's syntax. Her whole life, indeed, had been ungrammatical to the last degree.

She had slunk away from Yuma with all the ignobility of a coyote, and this sudden searchlight restored her to her craven memories.

She had crept from dark to dark then, but now she was both the priestess and the prisoner of the light, the victim of her fame, the captive rather than the captain of the soul she had for sale, the tremendously advertised soul she had for sale.

Helen of Troy found the face that launched a thousand ships a most embarrassing possession, for the thousand ships went after her and besieged her. And now Mem's past was coming up in all directions like troops of siege.

She wondered now who would be the next to confront her with some half-forgotten distortion of the truth. She wondered if every step she had taken and was to take would leave a petrified footprint like the fossilized traces of a primeval insect for all eternity.

She could not decide what answer to make to either letter, and so made none at all. The writer naturally supposed her guilty of indifference and contempt for her feelings, but her silence was actually due to contempt for herself and her inability to devise a decent excuse.

Now and then she sought escape from brooding in spurts of gaiety. She went about with Tom Holby and Ned Ling, and with other suitors among the various pleasances of Los Angeles. She danced at the Alexandria to the bewitching fiddlery of Max Fischer; and at the Cocoanut Grove in the Ambassador made part of the mucilaginous eddy of humanity that tried to follow Art Hickman's uncanny music.

She missed no Wednesday night at the Sunset Inn, and on one occasion almost won a dancing prize with a wonderful lounge lizard. Thursday nights found her at the Hollywood Hotel. She was dancing fiercely, but was never quite away from her past. At the Turkish Village she drank the thick, sweet glue called coffee and chatted with Lucille. She learned to know the Mexican dishes, the carne con chile and the tamales at the Spanish Kitchen.

She went through the inevitable phase of looking up odd places to eat and enjoying poor food because it was quaint.

She joined the horseback rides that set out from the Beverly Hills Hotel and threaded the canyons till they came upon breakfast spread in a glen. She motored to Santa Barbara and heard the nightingale at El Mirasol, or sat on the terrace of the moonlit Samarkand and dreamed herself in Persia. She motored to San Diego and beyond, tasting the rival delights of the old Spanish Mission at San Juan Capistrano, and the gambling across the Mexican border in Tia Juana.

She took a course of philharmonic concerts, heard the world-famous singers and instrumentalists, and regretted the tongueless career she had adopted.

But she learned to chatter of art and music in little groups of devotees — composers, painters, sculptors, verse makers, story writers — that make up the countless clubs of a city already as big and as busy as half a dozen Athenses.

She was broadening and deepening her mind and her heart, and aerating, volatilizing her spirit.

She toiled all the while at her own technique. When she finished the short comedy with Ned Ling she was drawn back to the Bermond Studio for the principal role in a big picture. She was not yet to be starred, but she was to be "featured" with a young man, Clive Cleland, who was spoken of as Tom Holby's successor.

Young Cleland fell prey to her growing fascinations, but he was so much her business rival and their professional love scenes were such duels for points, that she could not think of him as an amateur in love. Besides, an unsuspected loyalty to Tom Holby was wakened in her heart by the pretense that this raw youth was Tom's "successor."

Tom Holby was out in the Mojave Desert on location, and his absence pleaded for him like a still, small voice that interfered with the murmurs of nearer lovers.

She was full of impatiences of every sort.

She had fallen out of love with herself.

Mannerisms that directors or critics pointed out, or that she discovered for herself, vexed her to distraction. It was a strange thing to recognize in herself a fault that she detested in others and was yet unable to eradicate. Striving to avoid these recurrent tricks, she grew self-conscious, and people said that she was getting a swelled head when she was most in a panic. What they took for conceit was the bluff of a rabbit at bay.

And all the while the longing for a home, a single love, a normal average life, alternated with onsets of cynical defiance for the conventions.

While nature was clamoring in her blood for mating and motherhood, her new freedom drove her to anarchic protests against submission to the functions of the beasts.

Mem was in a chaos morally. She was at her spring, all her senses leaping with youth and desire and a wild joy in breaking through old rules. The moralities were to her the ice that the April brooks sweep away and the torrents melt; the grim white ice of winter that freezes life and puts love and art and beauty to sleep.

She was so horrified by the indecencies of the Puritans and the censors and the critics of her career, that revelry became a duty. The Maypole was a liberty pole.

But the dramatic world had its Puritans as the religious world has its gypsies.

In the picture she was making at this time, the role of her rival for the love of the lover was played by a Miss Bevan, who made such a parade of her undenied virtues that they became vices in the eyes of her colleagues.

By now Mem had departed so far from her early training that she had little left of what she would once have called common decency. She went extremely décolleté to dances; she climbed the mountains in breeches and puttees; and on the stage she wore what she was told to wear, left off what she was told to leave off, without thought of protest.

Miss Bevan, however, was of an opposite mind. She considered her person entirely her own and her future husband's. She refused to wear one gown because it was too low in the neck, and another because it was too high in the skirt. She refused to be photographed actually kissing an actor on the lips. She would let him pretend to press his mouth against her cheek, and she would hide her face behind his but no more.

In one scene she had to run out into a high wind in a frenzy of terror. The airplane propeller twirled her skirts about her and displayed the shapely knees the Lord had wasted on her. She forgot the overwhelming emotion of her role and bent to clutch down her spiraling skirts.

When the director shouted "Cut!" she was distraught with shame and demanded that he retake the scene and temper the wind to her shorn frock. He refused with disgust. She insisted then that the picture be cut before the wind displayed her limbs.

The director answered: "I'll cut the scene just before you began to hide 'em, not because the public is interested in your legs, but because I've got to get you through the door."

Miss Bevan was frantic. She ran to Mem and poured out her woe.

"I think that director is the most indecent person in the world. Don't you?"

"No!" Mem snapped. "But I think you are."

Mem despised prudery and felt that such maniac modesty could only be due to the frenzy of a mind eternally thinking evil. Women like Miss Bevan seemed to her to squander important energies on a battle with dirt, like fanatic house wives who devote so much of their days to keeping their homes clean that they have no time to accomplish anything else.

Mem had devoted her body and her soul to her public in office hours. But there still remained much idle time for mischief, and in these hours, and in the days and weeks between pictures, she found love nagging her insufferably. She was in the humor of the *Florodora* maidens whose motto rang through her mind, "I really must love someone and it might as well be you."

The "you" was almost any attractive man she chanced to be with at the time. And men were frequenting her increasingly, as they have always flocked about actresses, since actresses are the peaches at the top of the basket. The stage and the motion pictures offer opportunity to beauty as the army to bravery, the church to piety, the law to probity, and finance to ingenuity.

Mem's face was her fortune and her mind was its steward. Her perfection of mien drew people to her as a lamp draws a wayfarer or a pilgrim or a moth. Seekers after a night's lodging, a month's flirtation, or a life's companionship saw her from afar and ran towards her.

She was in a marriage mood and her heart and her friends gave her conflicting counsel: Don't marry an actor! Don't marry an author! Don't marry a businessman! Don't marry anybody!

But the *Florodora* tune kept tinkling in her heart. She really must wed someone.

Ned Ling was one of Mem's most abject worshipers. He had taught her the mechanics of comedy, and thereby helped her tragedy. Without being able to laugh at himself, he taught her to laugh at herself and at him.

He grew morbid for her. He cast away his fears of love and his horror of marriage and his sense of humor at the same time.

He clung to her hand and played with her fingers, lolled against her with his head on her breast and implored her to be his mistress, his wife, his rescuer from despondency. But his caresses were like the fumblings of a child at a maternal bosom, and his wildest prayers were mere childish naughtiness to her. The only love she could feel for him was a sense of amused motherhood, and he did not want that.

He flew into tempests of anger at her unresponsiveness and became a tragic clown at whom she could not help smiling.

He made comic exits from her presence, swearing he would never see her again, and comic returns. But Mem would only flirt with him, and with anyone else who amused her.

She came in at four one morning after a party given to celebrate Charles Chaplin's return from his royal progress through Europe, a triumph that seemed to lift the whole motion-picture world in the person of its representative. The film people felt that they were at last a nation finding recognition, as when the emissary of a republic is accepted as an ambassador.

The party was innocent enough, devoted to dances, charades, impromptu speeches, imitations, songs, operatic burlesques, and an almost puerile hilarity, but it lasted almost to the hour when good children are getting out of bed.

While Mem was passing through this phase of moral and romantic skepticism and experiment, enacting pretenses of devout love before the camera and mocking at love outside its range, and her mother was not quite sure that she had not quite gone to the devil, her first pictures were going about the world like missionaries winning proselytes to her shrine.

The whim to be married recurred to her incessantly and grew to a fixed purpose.

It appealed to her various moods in various ways. When she was under the spell of her home training, marriage was a sacramental duty. When she heard it discussed with cynicism or read of the shipwreck of some other marriage, it stirred her sporting blood; she wanted to bet she could make a success of it. When she was in an amorous fever, it recommended itself as an assurance of abundant warmth and safety. When she was lonely, it was companionship. When she was shocked by the recklessness of others or by her own remorse, it was respectability. But it was always something unknown that she wanted to know. No experience of life could be complete without it.

Tom Holby came back from the desert browner than ever, less subtle, more undeniable than ever. He fought hard for her in the spirit of the hero he was playing at the time, a man who acted on the theory that the cave man is woman's ideal and that she prefers above all things to be caressed with a club.

But these highly advertised tactics were not to Mem's liking, at least at the moment. When he grew too fierce, she struck him in the mouth with a fist that had stout muscles for a driving bar, and she brought the blood to his nose with a slash of her elbow.

She railed at his awkward confusion, but thereafter she was out when he called.

# CHAPTER LVI

EVENTUALLY SHE MET Holby at the golden wedding anniversary of an old actor who had been on the stage since boyhood, had married a young and pretty actress at 21, and was still married to her after half a century of pilgrimage along the dramatic highways.

There were other old theatrical couples at the feast, and they made wedlock look like a good investment. The occasion was exceedingly benign, and Mem was so gentled that she accepted Tom Holby's apologies and his company home.

"How wonderful," she said on the palm–gloomed way, "to be loved by one man for fifty years!"

"I could love you for a hundred," Tom groaned. "Let's get married and quit wasting so much time."

Something impelled her to think aloud:

"You're determined to play the simple Septimus, after all, in spite of the censors."

She regretted the mad indiscretion an instant too late. Holby was startled, and startled her by his quick demand.

"You don't mean that you are about to... that you are going to... to..."

"No," she said, "but..."

Like a child or a dog, the simple Holby occasionally had an instinctive understanding of something unspoken. He astounded Mem by saying:

"So that's why you were hiding in Palm Springs, with that phony wedding ring."

"Tom!" she cried, aghast at his astounding guess at the truth.

"Forgive me!" he grumbled.

And that was that. Neither of them ever alluded again to the subject. Deeply as it rankled in both their hearts, they were wise enough to leave buried secrets in their graves.

But in spite of what Holby must have imagined, he doggedly persisted:

"Let's get married."

"In spite of..."

"In spite of everything!" he stormed. "Tomorrow is the nearest day there is."

She loved him for that impetuous determination of his. He swept her past aside as she had seen him conquer other obstacles avalanches, thugs, wild animals, terrors that daunted most men.

She offered a weakening resistance:

"What chance of happiness could we have?"

"As much as anybody."

She had to make an old-fashioned struggle, but her reasons were modern:

"I wouldn't give up my career for all the happiness in the world."

He had evidently been thinking that matter over a long while, for he was positively glib:

"I don't suppose any woman ever gave up her career when she got married."

"How do you mean?"

"Most women have been brought up for a career of housekeeping. A father or mother told them what to do, and scolded them when they did something else. They learned how to make dresses and sew and cook, and that was their business. When they married they just moved their shop over to their husband's home, and expected him to provide the raw stock and tell them what to do and scold 'em if they didn't do it, or spank 'em."

This struck Mem as a new way of putting an old story, but she saw one great difference:

"But that wife lived at home and her husband knew where to find her. And he wouldn't let her do business with any other customer. In our lives, if we lived them together, the husband would be away from home half the time."

"So is the average husband, with his store and his lodge and his club."

"But then there's the travel, when you're on location or when I'd be."

"Travel doesn't keep business men or lecturers or soldiers or sailors from marrying, and half the wives in the world go away for the summer or the winter or on long visits."

"But you'd be hugging other girls before the camera and other men would be hugging me."

"As long as it didn't mean anything."

"But it might come to..."

"Well, for the matter of that, a lot of hugging goes on in a lot of homes and outside of them. I was reading that most of the girls on the street were ruined in domestic service. Chambermaids and cooks are pretty dangerous things around a house for husbands, and husbands for them. And doctors and preachers are dangerous to wives. It's not a nice thing to say, but it's true. Then there are the stenographers in the offices, and the salesladies in the stores, and the cloak models and cashiers and... oh, it's a busy little world and it's always been so. The old patriarchs had their concubines and their slaves and their extra wives. No guarantee ever went with marriage that was good for anything, and there's none now. We've got as good a chance as anybody."

"But what if we should fall out? Divorces are so loathsome."

"They're pretty popular, though. They're more decent than the old way and divorces are as ancient as the world. Moses brought down from heaven the easiest system."

"Yes, but Christ said..."

"Christ said nothing about a woman ever getting a divorce at all. He only allowed a man to get it on one ground. But a good deal less than half of our population even pretends to belong to a church or ever did. I was reading that only a third of the passengers on the Mayflower were Puritans. You can't run this country by the church, especially while the churches don't agree on any one thing. We'd have to have a license even if a clergyman should marry us."

Mem was shocked by the possibility of a civil marriage. It would not be wedlock at all unless a parson sanctified it. Holby broke in upon her musings:

"But here we are arguing. Argument is death to love. Let's love! Let's marry! Let's take a chance! We can't be any worse off than we are now. We'd be happy for a while, anyway."

He took her in his arms, and she did not resist. Neither did she surrender. Her mind was away, and her voice a remote murmur:

"How long could it last?"

"We've just come from a golden wedding, and there were couples there that have had their silver anniversaries."

"But Jimmie Coler and Edith Minot were married on Monday and separated on Tuesday. And Mr. and Mrs. Gaines have lived apart for years, and they would be divorced if she weren't a Catholic. And the Blisses live together, but everybody knows their other affairs."

"The actors are no unhappier than the plumbers or the merchants. We'd have as good a chance as anybody. We'd be happy for a while, anyway. Let's take a chance!"

But Mem was not in a gambling mood. She withdrew herself gently from his relaxing arms. She wanted to ponder a while longer.

Marriage was a subject about which the best people told the most lies. If you are truly respectable you never tell the truth about marriage or religion, and you never permit it to be told in your presence.

Mem cherished the ancient ideal of an innocent bride going shyly into the ward of a husband who will instruct her reverently into awful secrets.

She felt that she had somehow lost the right to be a bride, for there were no secrets to tell her. How could she enter a school when she was already postgraduate in its classes?

She did not know how rare such ignorance has always been. She did not know that many good, wise people had felt it a solemn duty to instruct little boys and girls in all the mysteries long before they came to nubility. She was not yet aware of the new morality that denies the virtue or the safety of ignorance and loathes the ancient hypocrisies, the evil old ideal that a normal man wants to marry a female idiot.

She was pitifully convinced that she was unworthy of Tom Holby's arms. She knew that he had led the average life. She did not expect to find him ignorant of life. But that had never been expected of bridegrooms.

It was from a deep regard for him that she denied his prayer and went sadly to her solitary room as to a cell for a fallen woman. Oh, to have been always good!

There she rebelled against her doom. She grew defiant. The orange tree in the patio had both fruit and blossoms. Her heart was full of knowledge and yet of innocence. She knew the live coals of desire, but she knew also the hearth yearnings of the bride. She had the steadfast eagerness of the wife to bend her neck to the yoke.

She loved her art. She loved her public. She felt at times immortal yearnings, immortal assurances.

The doting author, Mr. Hobbes, waxed lyrical about the future of the movies. He was as much of a scholar as his years permitted, and he mocked the contemptible contempt of the cinemaphobes, the pompous oldsters, and the ridiculous preciosity of the affected youngsters who prated of art and thought it meant a lifting of themselves by their own bootstraps above the heads of the common people.

"They make me sick, the pups!" he said. "Chesterton said it when he said that some of the talk of art for art's sake made him want to shout, 'No art, for God s sake!'

"When the skyscraper was new, the same kind of poseurs howled that it was a monstrosity, rotten commercial blot on the landscape, proof that the Americans were hopeless Philistines. Now everybody that knows says that the skyscraper is the one great addition to architecture that has been made for centuries — the Greek, the Gothic, the American.

"When the drama was new in Athens, that was mocked. Euripides was the popular one and wrote the human thing, the sob stuff of his time. And Aristophanes tore him to pieces worse than anybody ever tore the cheapest movie. He said that Euripides stuff had all gone to hell already. And now we revere it. And Plato spoke of the laugh and the tear just as we do.

"I can stand the contempt of these whelps better than their patronage. I see red when they say that the movies are cheap and trashy stuff now, except a few foreign eccentrics like Doctor Caligari, but that they will someday be great.

"Someday, hell! Pardon my French! Someday is yesterday. Great movies were done from the start. They sprang full armed from the brow of Jove, just as the drama did, and the skyscrapers, and the novels. They're great now. They were great ten years ago. Griffith's *Birth of a Nation* is a gigantic classic. His *Broken Blossoms* converted a lot of highbrows because it was sad and hopeless, but happy endings are harder to contrive than the tragic ones, and no more inartistic. Then there are all the big directors: Rex Ingram, a sculptor and a poet; Reginald Barker, with his Scotch grimness and tenderness; Hopper, with his realism; Al Green's gaiety and grace; Henry King, Hayes Hunter, the two De Milles, all passionate hunters of beauty and emotion.

"It's the critics that are small and always late. The critics always miss the express and come up on the slow freight. They always discover things the way Columbus discovered America, after it had been here a million years.

"Think how marvelous it is for you and me to be pioneers in the greatest art that ever was, the all-in-all art. We are like the Greeks, like the men of Chaucer's time, and Shakespeare's time, and Fielding's. We're presiding at the birth of an immortal art. Some of us don't know it. But posterity will know it. We're among the immortals, Miss Steddon. Isn't it tremendous?"

"It's certainly very nice if it's true!" said Mem, who certainly belonged in the silent drama.

But, as usual, her face was inspired with the emotion, though her words flunked.

Her heart swung toward the author now. Hobbes made love to her in the thin disguise of scenarios and schemes for immortalizing her genius and his own.

The partnership of an author and an actress seemed ideal. But when she was out of Hobbes's range and under Tom Holby's spell, she was easily convinced that the ideal partnership was an actor and an actress. She had been of a mind that actress and director made the perfect combination. Claymore had left his autograph on her soul. Then a rich man wintering at Los Angeles fell into her orbit and began to circle about her in shortening ellipses. He wanted to put big money behind her and organize The Remember Steddon Productions, Inc., and make pictures exclusively for her. But he talked so large and was so large that he frightened off her love, and the wealth of Wall Street, that hell of iniquity and persecution of the toilers, seemed to be sobbing away like the last water in a leaky tub.

This love business was driving Mem frantic. In all the pictures she had played, as in the traditions of her girlhood, love was a thing that came once and never came again. Good women knew their true fate-mates at once and never swerved in their devotion.

Yet here she was, passionately interested in several gentlemen, finding each of them fascinating just so far, and faultful thereafter. Instead of giving herself meekly to the bliss of matrimony she was debating its advisability, practicability, and profit. She must be at heart a bad woman, one of those adventuresses.

Either fiction was very untrue to life, or life very untrue to fiction.


Then came The Pause. Hard times struck the movies so hard that in the studios they became no times at all. The Disarmament Convention met in Washington to prepare a naval holiday and guarantee another end to war, war that is always ending and never ended.

Most of the motion picture factories disarmed entirely, and the rest of them nearly. The Bermond Studios kept one company at work, and it was not Mem's company.

She was stricken with terror as she confronted her problems. The smiling future was a dead past. The garden land of Los Angeles had reverted to the desert.

All that art talk suddenly became bread-and-butter talk.

What could she do now not to perfect her fame, but to make a living? She would be poorer than her father. She would have to discontinue the installments of that "conscience fund" he had learned to expect from Doctor Bretherick. She could not even pay the installments on numerous vanities she had bought for herself from the shops.

Her lovers were as de-futured as herself. Authors, actors, directors all, they talked poverty instead of marriage.

# CHAPTER LVII

NO ONE HAD TALKED hard times longer or louder than Bermond. He had been mocked, hated, accused of greed when he cut salaries ruthlessly, refused to renew contracts, slowed up production. Artists said it was a cheap excuse for grabbing more profits. Having heard him croak of disaster so long, Mem assumed that his studio would be one of the first to crash.

Her contract would be canceled or rendered worthless, or its provisions interrupted by a long vacation. Bermond sent for her and she went prepared for the guillotine. He said:

"I like you, Miss Steddon. You've worked hard. You've made no trouble. You've taken good care of yourself, and in every picture you're a little better than before. I find that the exhibitors are wiring in: 'Give us more Steddon stuff. Our patrons as they go out stop to say how much they like Steddon. Why don't you star her?' What the exhibitors say goes as far as it can.

"I don't want to fight the public, though I try to give them better things all the time.

"We can't star you now. All our stars are going out. We can't put any more money in pictures till we sell what we've got on the shelves.

"But I believe in you. I want people to know you. And when the good times come again you must be ready for them. So I'll go on paying you your salary and send you out on a tour of personal appearances.

"Your last picture looks like a knockout. I'm going to take down Clive Cleland's name and feature yours alone. I want you to go East to New York and Boston, Philly, Chi., all the big cities, and let the people see you when they see the picture.

"We'll pay your traveling expenses, give you a drawing room. That means we have to buy two tickets, anyway, so your mother can go along as our guest. We'll give you big publicity and a nice time in every city. What do you say?"

"Of course!" Mem cried. "And it's ever so kind of you."

This dazed Bermond, who was not used to gratitude. He gasped:

"That's nice! All right. Go home and pack up."

She hastened home, and her heart went clickety-clickety with the lilting thrill of her first railroad voyage. That had taken her from the Midwest to the Southwest. Now she was to triumph back across the Midwest and on and on to the Northeast, the Southeast, the two borders, the two coasts, and all the towns between.

Remember the cinemite was going forth like Peter the Eremite to summon people to her banner of rescue, of sympathy, of ardor.

Her mother was as joyous as she. The crusade was a new youth to her; it brought belatedly all the treasures of experience she had given up hoping for. The best she had ever expected was an occasional change of village, to move as the evicted wife of a poor preacher, from one parsonage whose dullness she had grown used to, to a new boredom. Now she would travel like a dowager empress from capital to capital as the mother, the author of a famous screen queen.

The royal progress was to begin with a transcontinental leap to New York to assist at the opening of the picture on Broadway "On Broadway!" to the actor what "In Heaven!" is to the saint, "In Rome!" to the priest, "In Washington!" to the politician, "In goal!" to the athlete.

The abandoned suitors of Mem made a sorry squad at the Santa Fe station. They stared at her with humiliated devotion.

Bermond sent a bushel of flowers and fruit to her drawing room. He saw to it that there were reporters to give her a good sendoff.

She left Los Angeles another woman from the lorn, lone thing that had crept into the terrifying city, as so many sick lungers, faint hearters, wounded war victims had crept into it and found it a restoring fountain of health and hope and ambition.

She waved goodbye with a homesick sorrow in her eyes. Her consolation was her last shout:

"I'll come back! I'll come back!"

She had a little of the feeling Eve must have had as she made her last walk down the quickset paths of Eden toward the gate that would not open again.

The train stole out of Eden like the serpent that wheedled Eve into the outer world. It glided through opulent Pasadena and Redlands and San Bernardino, a wilderness of olives, palms, and dangling apples of gold in oceans of orange trees.

By and by came Cajón Pass, where the train began to clamber over the mountain walls that were the gate of this paradise; up the deep ravine known as Murder Canyon when this land was unattainable, until a pathway of human and animal bones had been laid down.

Winter was waiting on the other side. There was winter here, too, of a sort, but it was the pretty winter of southern California. The landscape was wistful. White trees were all aflutter with gilded leaves as if butterfly swarms were clinging there, windblown. Soon the orange and fig trees no longer enriched the scene. Junipers and cactus, versatile in ugliness, manzanita and Joshua trees; these were the emblems of nature's poverty.

Yet there was something dear to Mem in the very soil. She could have kissed the ground goodbye, as Ulysses flung himself down and pressed his lips on the good earth of Ithaca.

The snow-sugared crests of the Cucamongas and Old Baldy's bleak majesty were stupendously beautiful, but they seemed to be only monstrous enlargements of the tiny mountains that ants and beetles climbed.

As the train lumbered up the steep, the earth passed before Mem's eyes slowly, slowly. She found the ground more absorbing than the peaks or the sky. She stared inwardly into herself and the common people that she sprang from and spoke to. She found them the same as the giants, not so big in size, but infinitely bigger in number.

The sierras and the foothills were only vast totals of minute mountains. She found the world wrinkles of the canyons, the huge slabs of rock patched with rags of green, repeated in the tiny scratches that raindrops had made in lumps of dirt. The wind of the passing train sent avalanches of pebbly dirt rolling through forests of petty weeds.

Small lizards darted, yet were not so fast as the train that kept on its way out of paradise, winding like a gorged python. On some of the twists of track she could see its double head and the smoke it breathed. The mountains appeared to rise with the train, mocking it as human effort is always mocked, since its every climb discloses new heights; every horizon conquered points with satiric laughter towards farther horizons offered for a prize.

Meek and unimportant as the little pebbles were on the slopes of the mountains, the peaks had also their inequalities, and looked to be forever snubbing one another.

A tunnel killed the picture like a broken film. Instantly Mem imagined Tom Holby at her side, snatching at a kiss. He would have been caught in the theft, for the mountains snapped back into view, only to be blacked out again.

There would have been time for a long, long kiss, for many kisses, in this rich gloom. Once more she found Tom Holby wooing her best in his absence. She wondered if she were not a fool to leave him. He had told her that he had saved money enough to live a long while without working; to travel abroad with her; to give her a gorgeous home. But she had thought of her ambition and followed it.

She reviled herself for her automatic discontent. When she saw the monotony of home as it held most women captive, she was glad she was a free rover in art. When she was free and roving she envied them their luxury of repose.

Now she was by herself. Her mother was nice; but mothers and fathers cannot count in that realm of the heart.

Finally the breathless train paused at the top of its climb. She was stung with an impulse to step down and take the first train back.

Here she was at Summit with a capital "S." Yet there was nothing much to see: a red frame station building with dull green doors and windows, a chicken yard, a red water tank on stilts, a baggage truck, a row of one-room houses crowded together for company in spite of the too abundant space.

Probably the summit of success would be about the same. The fun and the glory were in the scramble up. But it seemed lonely and uncomfortable at best to work so hard for such a cold reward. And she had left orange groves and love and the rich shade of obscurity.

Then the train was on its way again, the helper engine withdrawn aside, panting with exertion. The train would coast down to the levels without help. You don't need help to get down. Only, when you get down, you would find desert instead of a bower.

The other side of the mountains, after all the effort of getting across, would be like crawling behind a tapestry to study the seamy side, the knots and the patternless waste.

Still, her youthful eagerness always served as an antidote for her discontent. The desert had its charms. The dead platitudinous levels made easier going. The flats were labor-saving, and you went faster and safer over them. And you can see farther on the level. Up high, the mountains get in one another's way, as do jealous artists and contradictory creeds.

The next morning found the desert still running by. The ground was as brown and red and shaggy as the hide of an ancient squaw. There were scabs of snow in the wrinkles; in the air an annoyance of stingy little snowflakes.

The mountains along here were cruel and snarling. They would not understand the yearning for warmth because they could not. They were cold as the sierras of critics that Mem must try to conquer. But she could feel sorry for them also. It could not be much fun to be cold and bleak and critical.

The cattle sprinkled about the region were working hard for sparse fodder. Life was like that. In the warm, sweet summer, food and drink were easy to get and luscious. Waking was a dream, and sleeping a beatitude; love was balm in the air. In the winter, though, food and drink were scant and harsh. Waking was misery and sleep shivering; love hardly more than two waifs shivering together to keep warm.

At one station Indian girls ran along the track, offering gaudy little earthenware baskets and bright beadwork they had made to an express train that would not stop long enough even for such passengers as would take the trouble to buy.

The girls wore striped Navajo shawls that were not warm enough. Their other clothes were inappropriate, somehow civilized garb that took away picturesqueness and conferred ugliness instead of comfort: wrinkled black stockings, high shoes, pink plaid dresses.

The poor things! Who had been Indian princesses! A large word for their true estate. Yet it was a comedown from the primeval cliff caves to the trackside, where they offered beads for pennies to the palefaces who had once swapped beads for empires.

Mem saw a resemblance to herself in one copper-colored maid who held up her handiwork. She herself, each of her fellow creatures, white, brown, red, or black, was but a poor, ignorant savage, offering some crude ware to busy strangers drawn past in an express train.

It was self-consideration as much as sympathy that made her hurry to the platform and open the vestibule door. She wanted to buy that girl's merchandise so that people would buy her own soul when she thrust it at them.

But a long, dark train drew into the station, drove the Indian girl back, and cut off all communication. It reminded Mem of a long, hostile criticism, one of those lumbering reviews that ran over her own heart now and then, because her body was in the way, and because the train came from the opposite direction.

Before the westbound train drew out, her own moved on and she never saw the Indian girl again. The next thing she saw on that side was a saw blade of mountains gashing the blue sky with its jagged teeth.

The world was an almighty big place. There was so much desert and then so much farmland, so many large cities.

One night they came to Kansas City, where the train waited an hour. This had been the first big city Mem had ever seen. On this platform she had met Tom Holby and Robina Teele, never dreaming that she would play such havoc in his cosmic heart.

On this platform she had bought her first moving-picture magazines and her soul had been rocked by her first knowledge of the wild things women were making of themselves.

And now when she and her mother went up to the vast waiting room and she bought many moving-picture magazines, there was only one of them that omitted a picture of her own, and that magazine promised for the next month an article about her as the most promising star of the morrow.

The morrow and the next month! What would they do to her? What would she do to the world next month?

The immediate morrow found her on the train again, and staring into the dark in a blissful forward-looking nightmare. The dark was like the inside of her eyelids when they closed, a mystic sky of purple nebulas, widening circles of flame, crawling rainbows, infinitesimal comets rushing through the interstellar deeps of her eyelids.

She had forced her mother to accept the full space of the bed made up on the two seats; she chose the narrow couch and maidenly solitude.

She slept ill that night. Or rather, she lay awake well. Her mind was an eager loom, streaming with bright threads that flowed into tapestries of heroic scope.

She was a personage of importance, a genius with a future, an artist of a new art — the youngest and the best of the arts, the young Pantagruel born about the year that she was born. It had already bestridden the narrow world like a Colossus and had made the universal language a fact. She was speaking this long-sought Esperanto for everybody to understand.

She had already seen clippings from London newspapers referring to her with praise. She had seen in a South American magazine a picture of herself as Señorita Remembera Steddon. She had seen a full-page picture of herself in a French magazine with a caption referring to her as "*une des actrices les plus belles de l'écran.*"

Her art was good to her and she must be good to it. It demanded a kind of celibacy, as some religions did. Perfection in celibacy was not often attained in either field, and the temptations to lawful wedlock and stodgy domesticity were as fierce and burning as to lawless whim.

But here she was on her way to glory. Yet she tossed in loneliness! A pauper of love. Well, she was fulfilling the newly discovered destiny of her sex.

During the night the train crossed the meridian that would have led her to her old home in Calverly and her father. He had advanced a little, but not much from the most ancient patriarchal ways, from the time when a father affianced his daughter, before she left her cradle, to some boy who had hardly fallen out of his, and married her, as soon as nature permitted, to a husband she had perhaps never seen till he lifted her veil and led her away to a prison called home, a locked stable where she would be kept for breeding purposes and supplemented with other mates if she failed of her one great duty.

They had thought it beautiful not so long ago for a fourteen year old child to have a child. Now, in the more decent states, it was called abduction or seduction to marry a girl, even with her parents' consent, before she was sixteen; the husband could be sent to prison for the crime.

Today all the American women were voters; millions of them were independent money makers. And this seemed right to Mem, though preachers had shrieked that it meant the end of all morality. But morality is as indestructible as any other human instinct. The obscene old ideal, that reproduction was the prime obligation of womanhood, revolted Mem. What was the use of devoting one's life merely to passing life along to another generation? The fish, the insects, the beasts of the field, did that much and only achieved progressless procession round and round the same old ring of instincts; each generation handed over like a slave to unborn masters, themselves the slaves of the unborn. Who profited?

To the women of Mem's time and mind the old-fashioned woman was neither wise nor good, but a futile female who deserved the slavery she accepted.

For each generation to climb as high as it could was surely its first duty. Love would take care that successors should be born, and science would protect the young better than all the old mother-murdering systems. It was only in the last few years that science, freed from religious meddling, had checked the death rate that had slaughtered infants by the billion under priestly rule. And now birth control was the crying need.

Marriage had never been the whole duty of man, and Mem was sure that never again would it be the whole duty of woman. A man had always heretofore felt that he should assure his own career before he took on the fetters of matrimony. And a woman would always hereafter feel the same thing.

Terrible euphemisms for slavishness — miscalled as meekness, submissiveness, modesty, piety, propriety — had been held as lashes over women for ages. Now whipping was out of style. A girl could go where she pleased and go alone. She could take care of herself better than men had ever taken care of her. There had always been something wrong about letting the wolves elect themselves as guardians of the ewe lambs.

Her mother was with Mem and that satisfied some people. It made her father happier. But the real reason for her mother's presence was that Mem wanted the poor old soul to get a little fun out of life before it was too late. She and her mother were merely young girl and old girl in a globetrotting adventure.

Mem was still awake, or was wakened from a half-sleep, when the racket of the wheels upon the rails sounded a deeper note. She guessed that the train must be crossing a bridge. She rose and leaned softly across the bed where her mother dreamed of the old home and the exhausting demands of her children.

Mem lifted the edge of the curtain aside a little and peered out. The train was in midair, passing through a channel of rattling girders. The vast water that swept beneath, moonlit and placid, was the Mississippi, going south in the night. It would soon flow past Calverly. She remembered that she had once thought of drowning herself in its flood to hide her shame there and solve her problem. The equation of all the Xs and Ys of her life had seemed to be zero. Now it was infinity. How wonderful it was that she had not yielded to despair! It gave her an idea for a picture.

Nearly everything was taking the scenario form in her meditations nowadays. Wouldn't it make a great film to show a desperate girl flinging herself in a river to hide her shame, and then to have it roll before her the life she might have lived if she had not drowned herself? Scenes of struggle and triumph, usefulness and helpfulness, joy and love could follow and then fade out in the drifting body of the dead girl who had lost her chance.

Mem saw herself in the role, and she shivered with the delight of her inspiration. Then she sighed. The censors would never permit the film. Girls must not go wrong or commit suicide on the screen. They could go on sinning and slaying in real life, as they had always done in drama, but the screen was in slavery now and must remember its cell.

But she at least was eastward-bound, toward the morning that was marching toward her beyond the somber hills of slumber. She breathed deep of the auroral promise in the very stars, whose light was dying in the greater light, even while they lay shuddering, beads of quicksilver scattered along the sky.

# CHAPTER LVIII

THE NEXT THING MEM knew was the shudder of the door-bell. The porter called through the metal panel a warning that Chicago was loping toward them out of the east, and they must make ready to leave the train.

They scurried to get up and pack and get out. Then they went, with their baggage, across the roaring streets to the Lake Shore station and got breakfast there, this on the advice and un-der the guidance of an affable gentleman who met them and said that he represented the Bermond Company's Chicago Exchange and had been ordered by Mr. Bermond to take special care of Miss Steddon. Mem tried to look as if she were used to such distinction, but she failed joyously.

Half a day was all they had for learning Chicago. It was even larger and busier than Los Angeles! Mem felt lost and ignored until she saw in a bulbous glimmer of unlighted electric letters hung in front of a big motion-picture theater the name of her latest film. The theater would not open until 11:00, but her own pictures were scattered about the lobby. And that was something tremendous.

She and her mother drank deep of this cup of fame. They took their luncheons scudding on the Twentieth Century Limited. They had not yet left Chicago when the train stenog-rapher rapped at the door and asked their names against the possibility of a telegram. Mem noted how her mother sat a little higher with proud humility as she answered:

"Miss Remember Steddon and mother!"

There were italics in Mrs. Steddon's voice and exclamation points in the stenographer's eyes. After a moment's hesitation, as his pencil stumbled on the pad, he mumbled:

"That name is very familiar in our home, if you'll excuse me. The wife says you are the biggest comer of them all, and I must say I agree with her, if you don't mind."

Mem didn't mind. She gave him one of her queenliest smiles, and concealed her own agitation until he had closed the door on his. She was encountering strangers who had loved her and were hopeful for her! Wonderful!

Winter was in full sway outside, but the train slid across the white world like a skater, and there was a lilt in its rush. The next morning found the Hudson alongside, moving slowly under its plate mail of ice to New York.

Mrs. Steddon loyally denounced the river as far inferior to her own Mississippi, but Mem found the New York stream better groomed, somehow. It seemed to be used to great cities. It led on to the metropolis of metropolites, the New York that she had come to conquer. She wondered if the city would be nice to her. She had heard that it had a mind of its own and that it never knew who came or went. Yet the Chicago courier had said that New York was "the hickest village in the USA, just a bundle of small towns."

Whatever it was, it was destiny. Yet here again the long arms of Bermond had provided her with a reception committee: a most affable gentleman from the New York office, and two photographers, one with a motion camera, also two or three young reporters whose stories would never be published. But neither they nor Mem knew this, and she underwent the pleasant anguish of being interviewed on the station platform.

Rooms had been reserved for her at the Gotham, and she went thither in a covey of attendants. It was a good deal of high life for a young girl, and when she and her mother were left alone aloft in luxury, she flung herself down on a divan and lay supine, another Danae smothered under the raining favors of the gods on high.

There was more and more to come. Her experience of the city had been experienced by millions of visitors, to whom the high buildings, the Metropolitan Opera, the Metropolitan Art Museum, the Aquarium and other things metropolitan were the realization of old dreams.

She went to a theater or an opera every night, and to a matinee every afternoon when there was one. And she marveled that her father's religion had set the curse of denial upon the whole cloud realm of the drama. On Sundays, the theaters were closed except to "sacred concerts," but the good people who were trying to close the motion picture houses had not yet succeeded.

On her first Sunday night in town she and her mother went to the Capitol, the supreme word in motion-picture exhibition. The new art had already in this building the largest theater in the world. From its vast foyer, illuminated with mural paintings by William Cotton, a marble stairway mounted nobly to a balcony as big as a lake above a lower ocean, both levels peopled with such a multitude that their heads were mere stippling.

The architecture seemed perfection to Mem, perfection with grandeur, yet of an indefinable exquisiteness. Every thing was Roman or Etruscan gold. There was a forest of columns as tall as the sequoias of California, a grove of gilded trees, fluted and capped in splendor.

The sweeping curve of the balcony was like a bay along the Santa Monica coast. Here long divans gave the spectator a Persian luxury. From somewhere back of beyond the projection machines sent their titanic brushes and spread miracles on the immense screen. More than five thousand people were seated there, and a varied feast was served them.

Before the pictures was a Rothapfelian divertissement. A pipe organ roared its harmonious thunders abroad until an orchestra of seventy men sat down before a curtain of futuristic art and played a classic overture. Then the curtains drew back, and a booted girl in white Hussar uniform, with a cloak of scarlet flying from one shoulder and one hip, flung her nimble limbs about the stage to one of Brahms' Hungarian dances. A basso profundo sang, and there was a ballet in gray translucent silhouette against a shimmer of glowing cream.

The first picture was one of the Bible stories, to whose prestige the censors permitted almost complete nudity and horrific crimes denied the secular films. A tenor sang. A news picture unrolled scenes from all the world. Then came a prologue to the film de résistance.

Tonight it was *The Silent Call*, by Laurence Trimble and Jane Murfin. The authoress, as Mem had heard, had bought a police dog abroad at a cost of $5,000 and trained it tirelessly to be the hero in the story by Hal G. Evarts.

The theme was the cross-pull between the wolf and the dog in the poor beast's heart, and the amazing animal enacted all the moods from devotion to man and the gentleness that the dog has mysteriously learned, to the wild raven and man-hate that the wolf has never unlearned. There was no super-canine psychology, only the moods and passions of the animal; but they were deep, passionate, sincere.

With this two-souled, four-footed protagonist the company had gone into the snowy wilderness and brought back a wonderland of white crags, stormy skies, cruel men and brave.

The dog eloped with a white wolfess, and proved a good husband and father until his household was destroyed by relentless man. Then he went back to doghood, fought for the sore-beset heroine, fondled the fearless hero, pursued and tore to pieces the savage villain with fiercer savagery. In all his humors he was irresistible, a brave, sweet soul; and there was incessant felicity in the composition of the pictures he dignified. The highest inspirations of landscape art were manifest.

Fifteen thousand people saw the dog play his role that Sunday in that one room, and a whole herd of him was playing in other theaters throughout the country. He would gallop around the globe, that dog.

The moral of it all to Mem was despair of man. She poured her heart out to her mother in the language of one trained in churchliness; for the rebel cannot escape his past.

"What better things could anybody learn in a church than here, mamma? Aren't God's gifts developed? Isn't he praised in color and music and sermon and sympathy? It's all hymns to me, hymns of light and sound, sacred dances and travel into the noblest scenes God ever made.

"Yet they call it a sin even to go there, and they say there is a bill coming up to close all the theaters as well as the barber shops and delicatessens on Sunday, so as to drive the people to church or force them to stay at home in dullness, poor souls that work all week and don't want to go to a dull church and sleep before a dull preacher. They don't want to be preached at; they want to be entertained.

"What on earth makes good people so bad? And so stupid? They've been trying for 10,000 years to scold and whip people to be good their way, and they've never succeeded yet. That ought to show them that God is not with them or he wouldn't put it in people's hearts to fight the cruelty of the good just as hard as they fight the cruelty of the bad.

"According to them I'm a lost soul on my way to hell. Yet my heart tells me that I'm leading a far, far, far more worshipful life building pictures than I ever could have done back there in Calverly, if I'd stayed there and been good and married a good man and gone nowhere but to church and the kitchen and the nursery all my days.

"And look at that biblical picture tonight! I saw the one before with Adam and Eve both stark naked except for a few bushes. They'd have put the actress in jail if she had played like that in anything but a Bible story. If religion can sanctify a thing, why can't art? And when Adam and Eve clothed themselves, they only put on a few leaves. If that was costume enough then, why should we have to wear long skirts and high bodices now?

"They give prizes to little girls to read the Bible through from cover to cover. Even papa praises that as a soul-saving thing! He made me read it all, and it includes the Songs of Solomon and 100 stories that leave nothing horrible untold."

"Are you talking against the Bible?" her mother bristled.

"No, I think it is all that papa believes. I think it is a good thing for children and grownups to know by heart. But what stumps me is the inconsistency of the professional soul savers who want the law to prevent grownup people from seeing things that children are encouraged to read. In Los Angeles I saw one of William de Mille's pictures where a pious Boer was reading from the Songs of Solomon, and when they quoted what he was reading they had to blot out part of it on the title card. Think of that, mamma! Yet the Book is in every Christian home, or is supposed to be."

"You're not arguing that it oughtn't be?"

"Of course not! The Bible never harmed anybody. But neither did the screen, really. The crime is in robbing the film of all freedom and making it the slave of all the old women of both sexes."

The subject was intensely uncomfortable for her mother. As with most people, morality was a subject that she thought unfit for discussion. Nice people had morals as well as bowels, but believed that their irregularities should remain equally unchronicled.

Mrs. Steddon yawned and said that she was going to bed. It was late, and Mem turned in, too.

In the meanwhile, in the great rhythm of the world the Puritans were on the upswing as so often before. They would gain the barren, artless height of their ideals, and then the billow would break and carry them snarling back to the trough of the sea while the merrymakers swept up to their frothy supremes of license, only to lapse into defeat with equal impermanence of either failure or success.

The world was apparently in for a gray Sabbath and it would satisfy nobody any more than the last or the next Saturnalia. Censorship had already taken the moving pictures almost altogether out of the realm of freedom, and the people of the theaters, the magazines, the books, the paintings, the fashions, the shops, were already murmuring in dread, "We're next!"

But awhile yet there was mirth and beauty, though the shackles rattled when the feet danced too high or ran too far.

Whatever the fate of her art, Mem was flying high. The papers of New York were publishing her engaging eyes, the billboards all about town were announcing her, and in paragraph and advertisement she was celebrated. But so many others were also claiming the public eye! Other newcomers and favorites in impregnable esteem.

People who had come from Calverly were claiming Mem as a fellow citizen and feeling that they gained some mystic authority from mere vicinage. Some of them called upon her in person or by telephone and set her heart agog. She wanted to do them and the town justice.

Somehow she endured until the night her own picture was shown, and then stepped out before what seemed to be the world in convention assembled. She felt as tiny as she looked to the farthest girl in the ultimate seat up under the back rafters.

She parroted the little speech that Bermond's publicity man had written for her, and afterward wondered what she had said. There was a cloudburst of handclapping and a salvo from the orchestra that swept her from the stage into the wings.

And that was that!

She did not know that one of the town's wealthiest men was lolling in a fauteuil down front and that her beauty and her terror smote him.

His motto had been, "Go after what you want, and bring it home!" He prided himself on being a go-getter who had not often come back foiled. He wanted Mem and he went after her. He was willing even to bring her home.

# CHAPTER LIX

THERE WAS NO DIFFICULTY about meeting Mem for a man whose name smelled of millions honestly amassed and gracefully dispersed.

Austin Boas came humbly to Mem to pay his respects, and his enormous name made her tremble as her bisque daintiness set him aquiver. He was shy, ashamed of his own lack of heroic beauty; and Mem was dazed to find herself feeling sorry for him. Pity was a dangerous mood for her.

Boas gazed at her with eyes as hungry and as winning as the eyes of the dog Strongheart. Like the dog, he was earning wealth that he could not spend for his own happiness. And his longing was for caresses and devotion. He would give his life to one who would rub his head.

If Boas had had any lurking thought of dazzling Mem into a mercenary submission to his caprice, he never revealed it.

He was not at all the vicious capitalist she had read about and seen in so much film, bribing poor gels to dishonor.

He sent her flowers, but they were pretty and appealing rather than expensive. He made no proffer of jewelry, never suggested money. Life, she found, rarely ran true to fiction.

Mrs. Steddon was usually in the offing, and Boas may have thought that she was one of those canny mother managers who try to force rich gallants into matrimony. But when Mrs. Steddon was out of sight Mem was a little more elusive than ever.

Boas revealed to her phases of opulence that she had never imagined. The most striking thing about them to her was that they were not so very opulent, after all. His home was somber and dull, his servants cozy old neighbors, his own manner humble. His art gallery, when he led her and her mother into it, was severe, a mere background for paintings; and, after all, not many paintings there. Mem knew nothing about the virtues of what she saw and she cried out equally over the things he had bought by mistake and the happy investments. The Boas automobile, which carried them to and from their hotel, was a good car, but exceedingly quiet. Mem had ridden in a dozen in Los Angeles that were far more gorgeous.

But Boas was lonely. He was pathetic. He reminded her somehow of Ned Ling, who squandered joy and kept none. Boas was drowned in wealth and was poor.

He might have won Mem via pity, if he had not tried to win her from her career. He was a monopolist by inheritance, and he wanted all there was of Mem.

He promised her everything that money could buy or love could propose, with the one proviso that the money should not be her own earning, but his gift, and that the public should see her no more.

Mrs. Steddon was all for him. She pointed out to Mem how good the Lord was in sending her such a catch. She emphasized the good she could do with millions; the poor she could feed and clothe; the churches she could adorn or build; the missions she could endow. But a parent's recommendation is the poorest character a lover can possess.

Contradictory torments wrung Mem's heart. She was human enough to covet ease and the hauteur of money, but she had outgrown the ability to enjoy, or even endure, the old-fashioned parasitism of the woman who takes and takes and takes.

Girls had decided that it was no longer flattery or good wooing to be offered a life of nonentity. Who wanted to be anybody's silly Curlylocks? And accept as a compliment the promise, "Thou shalt not wash dishes nor yet feed the swine, but sit on a cushion and sew a fine seam, and feed upon strawberries, sugar, and cream."

Boas had one terrific rival, the many-headed monster.

It is not hard to seduce an actress from the stage, but it is hard to keep her off. There is a courtship that the public alone can offer, and no one man can give her as much applause as a nightly throng's. That form of polyandry is irresistible to most of the women who have been lucky enough to get on the stage or the screen and to win success there.

One day Bermond summoned her to his New York office and said:

"How about getting to work again? I've got a great story for you and they need you at the studio. On your way back you can make personal appearances at four or five cities, but it's back on the job for you, eh? That's right! That's a good girl!"

Bermond offered Mem neither ease nor devotion — except devotion to her publication. He offered her toil and wages, hardships and discontent, sleepless malaise, and bad press notices.

And she could have flung her arms about him and kissed him.

Austin Boas was at the station to see Mem off. For his last fling he filled her drawing room with flowers, poor things that drooped and died and were flung from the plat form by the porter.

Long after their spell had been forgotten, the sad gaze of Boas as he cried goodbye haunted her.

It was her increasing regret that she could not love everybody and give herself to everybody who wanted her. Being unable to distribute herself to the multitudes by any miracle as of the loaves and fishes, she withheld herself and scattered photographs by the hundred thousand.

She had murmured to Boas, "When I make another picture or two, I may decide to be sensible, and then if you are stil…"

"I shall be waiting," said Boas. And he gave up with a groan: "Marry me anyway and have your career, too. I'll put my money into your company. I'll back you to the limit. I'll…"

That staggered her, but before she could even think up an answer the train started and divorced her from him for the present, at least.

At Buffalo and at Cleveland she paused to come before huge audiences and prattle her little piece. When she reached Chicago she found awaiting her a long letter from the manager of the moving-picture house in Calverly. He implored her to visit her old home town and make an appearance at his theater. He promised that everybody would be there.

This was success indeed! To appear in New York was triumph, but to appear in her native village was almost a divine vengeance.

She had resolved to leave her mother at Calverly, in any case. Mrs. Steddon was wearying of adventure and her heart had endured too long an absence from her husband and the other children. The younger sister, Gladys, had done her best to take her mother's place, but Mrs. Steddon's real career was her family and Mem knew that she was aching to get back to it.

And so one morning they crossed the Mississippi again. At Burlington they must leave the train, wait two hours, and then ride south to Calverly.

As Mem and her mother stepped down from their car in Iowa, both gasped and clutched.

The Reverend Doctor Steddon was a few yards away from them, studying the off-getting passengers.

"Let's see if he knows us," snickered Mrs. Steddon, with a relapse to girlishness.

"Let's!" said Mem.

They knew him instantly, of course. He wore the same suit they had left him in, and the only change they could descry was a little more white in a little less hair.

But he did not know them at all. It amused them to pass him by and note his casual glance at the smart hat and the polite traveling suit of his wife. He had expected a change in his daughter, but he was probably braced for something loud and gaudy. Mem looked really younger than when she left him. She had then been a premature old maid, dowdy and repressed. Now, for all her girlishness, she was a lithe siren, her eyes knowing, her too expressive body carried learnedly in clothes that boasted of what they hid, boasted subtly but all the more effectively. In spite of the emphatic modesty of her clothes, Mem had lived so long among butterflies and orchids, and had striven so desperately for expression, that she did not realize how emphatic she was.

So her father passed her by. When Mrs. Steddon turned and hailed him in a voice that was gladder and more tender than she knew, he whirled with his heart bounding.

Then he paused and stared, befuddled, at the tailor-made model running toward him.

He knew all about the other world and how to get there, but he was lost in the cities of the earth. When his wife rushed into the arms he had flung open to her voice, he was almost afraid to close them about her. He felt a bit like Joseph with the captain's wife clinging to him.

When he stared across her trim shoulders and took in "the sumptuous Delilah floating" toward him with his daughter's countersign, "Poppa!" he was aghast at her beauty. She was ungodly beautiful.

Long ago, when she had sung in the choir, he had noted with alarm an almost indecent fervor in her hymning. Now she had learned to release all the fragrances and allurements of her being like a Pandora's box broken open.

And now he felt that he ought to avert his gaze from her too lovely, too luscious charm. He shut his eyes, instead, and drew her into his bosom with one long arm, and his wife with the other. And they heard his hungry, feasting heart groaning:

"I thank Thee, O God! Now lettest Thou Thy servant depart in peace."

But neither the Lord nor his family granted that prayer. His two children chattered at once. Both seemed children to him. His wife had turned time far back; she looked fairer than he had ever known her; and her traveling hat hid her gray-white hair. Poor thing! She had never known till this year the rapture of being fashionable; had never dared, never understood how, to look her best.

Hiding under his high chin, Mem begged his forgiveness for all the heartaches she had caused him. She wept on his white bow tie, twisting a button on his coat and pouring out her regret for dragging his wife away from him and causing them to quarrel over her.

These tears, these gestures of pathos, were endearing her to the multitudes, who saw her half the time through the radiant dimness of their own tears. Poor Doctor Steddon had never a chance with her. His own tears pattered down on her hat. The blessed damozel "heard" his tears. They would probably spot the crown.

Mem said that it was a crime for her to have taken her mother on East and left him alone, but he protested:

"D'you suppose I wanted my little girl traveling in those wicked cities all by herself?"

This gladdened Mem exquisitely. It showed that, for all her wanton career, she was still in her father's eyes an innocent child who must be protected from the world. Of course, it was, rather, the world that needed to be protected from her. But she would not disturb his sweet delusion.

He said he wished he might have gone along and seen great cities he had never seen. All cities were Carcassonnes to him. He spoke of the anonymous benefactor, the conscience-stricken stranger who had sent him money through Doctor Bretherick. But he could not use that money for travel; it was for the church, and he sighed, "The good man has forgotten to send the last installment as he promised."

Mem gave a start and had almost said: "I forgot all about it in the rush of leaving. I'll give it to you now."

She checked herself so abruptly that she was not quite sure that she had not spoken. She seemed to hear the echo of her words.

Her father was called away for a moment to speak to an old parishioner, and Mem said to her mother:

"This is exactly what we call a situation in the business. The audience knows something the principal actor doesn't know. If poppa had found out that I was the remorseful gentleman he'd have dropped dead."

He came back with the parishioner, who had begged for the honor of an introduction to his famous daughter. The old man had once wished that she had died before she went so wrong, but now he was plainly very glad indeed that she had been spared. He fluttered like a hen whose duckling has swum the pond and come back to the wing.

The parishioner moved on at last, leaving embarrassment.

Doctor Steddon was afraid to ask his daughter the details of her new life, lest she should tell him. She could not think of much to say that would be certain not to shock him. The reunion was too blissful to be risked.

At length — a very long length — the south-bound train drew in and took them aboard. They watched the landscape and indulged in flurries of small talk that rushed and died like flaws of wind on the river. Now it was the Mississippi that streamed south in a burly leisure, while the train flew noisily.

# CHAPTER LX

AND FINALLY CALVERLY CAME up along the track and stopped at the station. The place shocked Mem by its shabbiness and its pettiness. When she left it she had never seen a city and she was afraid of her hometown. Now her eyes were acquainted with the cyclopean architecture of New York, the gardened mansions of Pasadena, and the maelstrom streets of Chicago.

Yet she was as shy before the crowds that waited for her as they of her. The mayor had come down to give her welcome. He was as shabby as the sheriff in a Western movie, but he was the village's best, and he used his largest words in a little speech, as soon as he could push through the mob of Steddon children that devoured Mem and their mother.

The manager of the Calverly Capitol, with its capacity of two hundred, brushed the mayor aside and claimed Mrs. Steddon and his prize. He had a carriage waiting for her, and a room at the hotel in case the parsonage was overcrowded.

Doctor Steddon grew Isaian as he stormed back:

"My daughter stays in her own home!"

This brought Mem snuggling to his elbow, and from that sanctuary she greeted her old Sunday school teacher, several of the public school teachers, an old negro janitor, a number of young men and women who called her by her first name.

Two or three of the girls had been belles of the town and she had looked on them with awe for their beauty, their fine clothes, and their fast reputations. Now they seemed startlingly dubby, gawky, silly; and now the awe was theirs.

Mem noted that her own sisters were dubbier, gawkier, sillier still except Gladys, who had matured amazingly, and in whose eyes and mouth and ill-furbished roundnesses Mem's experience saw a terrifying latent voluptuousness and a capacity for fierce emotions.

The first resolve Mem made was to buy her sisters clothes worthy of them and of her own high rank.

Just as she was stepping into a waiting automobile Doctor Bretherick came along, happened by with a very badly acted pretense of surprise. Mem told him that she wanted to come over and have him look at her throat. She coughed for conviction's sake and he warned her that there was a lot of flu going about.

The car moved off and she felt as if she were passing through a wooden toy town. Her father's church looked about to fall over. It was not half so big as she remembered it, and dismally in need of paint.

And the home! Was it possible that the old fence was so near the porch, and the porch so small? Once it had been a grot of romantic gloom, deep and fatal enough to bring about her damnation.

With a sudden stab she remembered Elwood Farnaby and the far-off girl that he had loved too madly well in that moonlit embrasure. How little and pitiful that Mem had been! There was a toyish unimportance in her very fall, the debacle of a marionette world. But Elwood Farnaby was great by virtue of his absence and his death. He was a hero now with Romeo and Leander and Abelard and the other geniuses of passion whose shadows had grown gigantically long, in the sunset of a tragic punishment for their ardors.

She stumbled as she mounted the steps, and there was a misery in her breast. Then the house opened its door and took her in, into its Lilliputian hall and stairway. She laid off her hat and gloves in the parlor, with the dining room alongside. It was like a caricature of homeliness. Just such a set had been rejected at the studio because it was a burlesque on such a home.

Wonderment at the hallucinations of her youth and gratitude even for the disaster that had hurled her out of the jail filled her heart. She never acted more desperately than in her mimicry of the emotions of rapture at her coming home.

She insisted on helping to get the midday dinner. Gladys protested, but Mem was frantic for something to keep her hands busy, and for little things to talk about, lest her dismay at the humbleness of her beginnings insult the poor wretches who had known no better.

Her mother was having a similar battle, though the return was easier since she had never gone so far afield.

At the dinner table the old preacher's humble grace for the bounty of the Lord saddened Mem again. The poor old dear had suffered every hardship and known nothing of luxury, yet he was grateful for "bounty!"

After the table was cleared and the dishes washed and put away, Mem escaped on the pretext of a visit to the doctor. She was waylaid by old friends on the walks and hailed from all the porches. There was a little condescension in the manner of a few matrons and a few embittered belles, but Mem knew enough to take this as the unwitting tribute of envy.

She found Dr. and Mrs. Bretherick waiting for her. The doctor got rid of his wife and closed the door on Mem. Then he flung up his hands and cried:

"Well!"

He shook his shaggy poll and mumbled a wide grin, and repeated half a dozen "Well's" of varied meaning, before he exclaimed:

"Well, if I'm not a success as an author, manager, and per-doocer of A-1 talent, show me one. Our little continuity has certainly worked out beyond the fondest dreams of author and star."

His star took less pride in it than he. Somehow Mem drew humiliation from the lowliness of her origin, instead of pride. This room had seen her first confession of guilt. In this room Elwood Farnaby had made his last battle for life.

A horrifying thought came to Mem: if he had not died, she would have become his wife and the mother of his premature child. She would have been a laughingstock, material for ugly whispers about the village. And she would have been the shabbiest of wives even here. She would never have known fame or ease or wealth.

"What a scenario it would make!" she thought, in spite of her wrath against herself for harboring such an infamous thought. But she could not deny her mind to it. Suppose a story were written around her life: a girl in her plight has a choice of two careers; in one her lover lives, makes her the partner of his humble obscurity and poverty, and she becomes a shabby, life-broken dowd; in the other her lover dies and she goes on alone to wealth, beauty, and the heights of splendor. Which would she choose? The very hesitation was murderous. Yet how would she choose? Would she kill her lover or let him live, a vampire to destroy her soul?

She felt a compulsion to penance and a humbling of herself at the grave of her thwarted husband. She was afraid to walk through the streets to the cemetery, and she asked the doctor to drive her thither in the little car he now affected.

He consented and rose to lead the way. She checked him and took out her purse.

"I want to give you the installment I forgot, of the conscience money. Please get it to papa as soon as you can. And here's a little extra."

The doctor took the bills with a curious smile. She seemed to feel his sardonic perplexity as she mused aloud along a well-thought path.

"If I hadn't been a fallen woman I couldn't have saved papa's church from ruin. How do you explain it? What's the right and wrong of it all?"

The old doctor shook his head:

"I'm no longer fool enough, honey, to try to explain anything that happens to us here. I don't even wonder about what's going to happen to us hereafter, if anything. As for right and wrong, humph! I can't tell 'em apart. When some terrible calamity comes, your father says, 'It is God's will; he moves in a mysterious way!' Well, I let it go at that for good luck, too. I neither thank nor blame Anybody for anything, and I don't pray to Anybody to make it come out the way I want it. According to one line of thinking, your misstep was the divine plan. According to another, good can never come out of evil. Of course we know it does, every day; and evil out of good. The only folks who know things know 'em because they think that being pigheaded is being knowing. It's too much for the wise ones. So let's let it alone and make the best of what comes. We're only human, after all, so let's be as human as we can, and I guess that's about as divine as we'll ever get Down Here."

He led her out to his woeful little tin wagon and they went larruping through the streets, out into the cemetery. That at least had increased in population and some new monuments brightened it, set like paper weights to hold down poor bodies that the wind might else blow away.

A few mourners were moving about planting flowers, clipping grass, lifting away old scraps of paper, or just brooding over what the earth had gathered back unto itself. They looked up startled and offended at the profaning clatter of Doctor Bretherick's car.

Some of them Mem recognized. One or two women, whose grief was so old that it was almost comfortable, waved to her. She had a sudden fear that if she paused to kneel at Elwood's mound and worship, there she would start a wonder that intuition would change to ugly surmise. The scandal had died before its birth, like the stillborn child. It would do Mem little harm, for she had been the victim of much harsh talk and was always under that cloud of suspicion that envelops all stage people in the eyes of the conventional.

But Elwood in his grave ought to be spared from such a resurrection. The tongues of the busybodies must not dig him up and play the ghoul with him.

In a panic of indecision as to her true duty, she recognized old Mrs. Farnaby mourning by a little hillock. Swaying near her was her husband, old Fall-down Farnaby, still somehow capable of intoxication.

The doctor knew better than to pause at all, and Mem's only rite of atonement was a glance of remorseful agony cast toward Elwood's resting place. It showed her that the founder of her fortunes was honored only by a wooden headboard already warped and sidelong.

One last favor, she mumbled to Doctor Bretherick, "Get a decent tombstone for the poor boy and let me pay for it."

"All right, honey," said the doctor. And the car jangled out of the gates again into the secular road.

And that was that.

# CHAPTER LXI

WHEN SHE REACHED HOME, Mem was so beaten down and frustrated that she begged permission to rest awhile in bed for the night's ordeal. At the supper table the younger children beset her with questions. Gladys was particularly curious and searching in her inquiries.

Then came the hour of the theatergoing. Nobody had dared to ask Doctor Steddon if he would accompany his family. He had not made up his own mind. He dared not.

The family tacitly assumed that his conscience or his pride forbade him to appear in the sink of iniquity he had so often denounced.

The family bade him goodbye and left him, but had hardly reached the gate when he came pounding after. He flung his arms about Mem's shoulders and cast off all his offices except that of a father, chuckling:

"Where my daughter goes is good enough for me!"

He made almost more of a sensation in the theater than Mem. There was applause and cheering and even a slow and awkward rising to the feet until the whole packed auditorium was erect and clamorous.

Seats of honor were reserved for the great star and the family that reflected her effulgence. As soon as they were seated the young woman who flailed the piano began to batter the keys, and Mem's latest picture began to flow down the screen.

She could feel at her elbow the rigid arm of her father undergoing martyrdom. She felt it wince as her first closeup began to glow, her huge eyes pleading to him in a glisten of superhuman tears. The arm relaxed as he surrendered to the wonder of her beauty. It tightened again when danger threatened her, and she could hear his sigh of relief when she escaped one peril, his gasp as she encountered another.

He was like a child playing with his first toy, hearing his first fairy story. He was entranced. She heard him laugh with a boyishness she had never associated with him. She heard him blow his nose with a blast that might have shaken a wall in Jericho. A sneaking side glance showed her that his eyes were dripping. And when the applause broke out at the finish of the picture, she heard his great hands making the loudest thwacks of all. This was heartbreaking bliss for her.

Then the manager appeared on the narrow stage and spoke of the honor of having with them the great star of whom Calverly was so proud, and he took great pleasure in interdoocing Miss Remember Steddon, "America's sweetheart."

This stolen attribute embarrassed Mem only a moment in the sea of embarrassments that swallowed her. She hardly knew how she reached the stage or what happened there. Whatever she said, she said to her father, staring down at him as so often from the choir gallery. His eyes were bright with a layman's ecstasy in a child's glory.

She came down and made her way slowly through a phalanx of friends with outthrust fingers, snatching at the hem of her fame, eager to be able to say, "I shook hands with Remember Steddon once."

The family rode home in state, the children and the mother loud in comment, the father silent. The old parson had to think it all out. Once at home, he sent the children up to bed and held Mem and her mother with his glittering eye for a long while before he delivered his sermon. It was his nature to be forever praying for forgiveness for something, and now his very pride took the form of contrition:

"My beloved wife and daughter, I ahem, ahum! I want to plead for the forgiveness of you both. I have been wrongheaded and stiff-necked as so often, but now I am humbled before you in spite of all my pride. It has just come over me that when God said, 'Let there be light,' and there was light, he must have had in mind this glorious instrument for portraying the wonders of his handiwork. Our dear Redeemer used the parable for his divine lessons, and it has come to me that if he should walk the earth again today he would use the motion pictures.

"You have builded better than you knew, perhaps, my child, and now I ask you to pardon me for being ashamed of you when I should have been proud. You were using the gifts that Heaven sent you as Heaven meant you to use them. Your eloquence is far greater than mine has ever been. Never have I seen the beauty of purity amid temptation so vividly brought home.

"I would not presume to seem to criticize you, my darling, but I implore you to keep your heart and your art clean, not only for your own precious sake, but for the sake of the people whom you are helping in their own struggles with temptation. Your art is sacred and you can't, you won't, sully it in your life. God forgive me for my unbelief and send you happiness and goodness and a long, long usefulness in the path you have elected."

He rose and bent down to kiss Mem on the brow. Then he escaped into his study, leaving the two women to weep in each other's arms with a joyous abandon.

None of her father's thundering against wantonness, none of his chanting about the divine delights of self-denial, ever had such influence upon Mem's soul as his meek surrender before her power as an artist.

Nothing has ever made anybody want to be good so much as the rewards, the praise for having been good.

That night Mem knelt again by her old bed and, on knees unaccustomed to prayer, implored strength to keep her gift like a chalice, a grail of holiness. She woke with an early-morning resolve to be the purest woman and the most devout artist who ever lived.

Other hours and other influences brought other moods, but consecration was her spirit now.

The next day she left the town with all its blessings, no longer a scapegoat, sin-laden, limping into the wilderness, but a missionary God-sped into the farthest lands of the earth.

It seemed that all Calverly was there to wring her hand and waft her salutations. The family was woebegone at losing her — all but Gladys, who wore a mysterious smile that puzzled them.

The conductor called, "All aboard!" and hasty farewells were taken in clench of hand and awkward kiss.

Mem ran to the rear platform and waved and waved lengthening signals of love to her dwindling family. She noted the absence of Gladys and wondered at it as she went to her drawing room. There she found the girl ensconced in fairy triumph, smiling like a pretty witch.

"What on earth are you doing here?" Mem cried.

"Going to Los Angeles with you. I may never be great like you, but I'm going to have a mighty good time trying. Can you blame me for running away from that graveyard when I see what came to you?"

How could Mem blame her? How could she fail to understand her and to promise her help? All the world was filled with runaway girls striking out for freedom and for wealth and renown. Mem's little sister was only another in the multitude, and she was so pretty, so desirable, delectable, magnetic, that her future looked all roses.

"I'm jealous of you," Mem said. "You'll ruin my chances, you're so much better looking, and... and..."

"Oh, you!" Gladys laughed in disclaimer.

There were many questions to exchange and Mem soon learned that her sister had flung off the chains that one or two ardent lovers had tried to fasten about her. She had substituted for the old saws the modern instances. She had changed the old ditty to run, "The boy I left behind me." Gladys was not beginning her future with the dark groping fearsomeness of Mem's. Mem had been like a pioneer who fights old Wilderness and makes the path easy for the followers.

When Mem, with a last faltering reproach, asked her sister if she were wise to toss aside the devotion of a good man, Gladys laughed.

"Let love wait! The men have kept us waiting for thousands of years, till they were ready. Now let them wait for us."

There was no gainsaying this. It had been Mem's own feeling when she left Los Angeles and her lovers there.

Consternation must be rife at home in Calverly, where Gladys's elopement was doubtless realized by now, but there would be more consternation in the hearts of countless men when the fascinations of the Steddon sisters should shine upon them from the silver sheet.

Mem resolved to save her sister from the anguishes she had known in her own pilgrimage. She felt already a veteran and a guide with a diploma from the college of life. Her first thought had been a remorseful feeling that she had not only gone wrong, but had led her own sister astray, as well. Now she felt that she had led her sister out of the dark into the light.

She had been somehow rescued from oblivion into the higher opportunities. She would make her name famous and keep it. If she ever got a husband she would still keep her name and not use his, except for the sweet purposes of domesticity.

Life had not plucked her to fling away or merely to adorn the buttonhole of some lover. Life had transplanted her into a garden where the choicest flowers bloomed. She would make herself the rosiest rose that she could. She would yearn upward toward the sun and spread the incense of her soul as far as the winds of the world would carry it. And when she died she would leave her name and her face in immortal pictures of deathless motion.

She had sinned indeed, her life had been redeemed from nullity through her sin at home. She would sin again, but then everybody sinned again and again. But she would make atonement by entertainment, purging her soul, not by hiding in the wilderness, but by shining like a little sun around the world, blessing the world with sympathy and the nobility of tears shed for another's sorrows.

Let love wait, then, till she had made the best of herself. And then let love not demand that she bow her head and shrivel in his shadow; but let him bloom his best alongside.

She wondered who that fellow of her destiny would be. Tom Holby, maybe Austin Boas, or still another perhaps. Or others, perhaps, including him! Or them! In any case, he (or they) had better behave and play fair! As for being a mother, let that wait, too. She was going to mother the multitudes and tell them stories to soothe them.

There was far more in this dream than vanity, far more than selfishness. The hope of the world lay therein, for the world can never advance farther than its women.

She had a soul to sell and it was all her own, and she was going to market.

The dawn was hers for conquest. Mankind was her lover and her beloved. That one-man passion called love could tarry until at least the late forenoon.

THE END